The Judas Kiss

THE JUDAS KISS

David Butler

NEW ISLAND

THE JUDAS KISS
First published 2012 by
New Island
2 Brookside
Dundrum Road
Dublin 14

www.newisland.ie

P/B	ISBN	978-1-84840-168-6
ePub	ISBN	978-1-84840-169-3
mobi	ISBN	978-1-84840-170-9

British Library Cataloguing Data. A CIP catalogue record for this book is available from the British Library.

Cover design by Nina Lyons
Typeset by Mariel Deegan.
Printed by ScandBook AB, Sweden 2012

New Island received financial assistance from
The Arts Council (An Comhairle Ealaíon), Dublin, Ireland

10 9 8 7 6 5 4 3 2 1

Contents

Part I

I	Bluebottle	2
II	Malcolm	37
III	Fergal	53

Part II

IV	Gwendolyn	88
V	Bluebottle	115
VI	Fergal	140

Part III

VII	Br Martin	158
VIII	Doyler	181
IX	Br Martin	214

Part IV

X	Gwendolyn	240
XI	Fergal	256
XII	Bluebottle	286

PART I

I | Bluebottle

I see you're looking at this scar. Every scar tells a story, right?

It's one ugly mother, and be warned, this is no pretty story. It leads to murder. And I don't mean the Rev Green in the study with the lead piping. No. This murder is messy - a stone inside a stocking sticky with blood.

So there's no use looking here for Sherlock Holmes or Colonel Mustard. The characters in my story are a vagabond; an old queer and his nephew; a sculptress; a dealer; and the Bro, the only decent skin in the whole damn bunch.

And I include myself in that.

In those days I was still in Luke's. I was fourteen. That surprises you. Guess I always looked old for my age. My voice broke when I was eleven. I'm serious, eleven.

So this day, I'm sitting across from Sr Veronica. She wasn't the worst of the born-agains, not by a long chalk. It was a day exactly like any other day. But this day everything changed. I could no longer stomach it, that was all.

Guess what I couldn't stomach was her monumental patience. She used to sit cow heavy in front of me, her face as ruddy as a lit oven and her breath smelling of baking soda. Used to sit so close sometimes her entire face'd be out of focus.

So this one day she has on her maternity dress like wallpaper and her wire-framed bifocals, and her fat born-again smile, and all at once I can't stand it for even a second longer. I let go. I snap. You know what I do?

Without even having thought it, I reach her face one god-almighty slap. Like that, with the open palm. Except I don't quite connect. Still, I can see the whole fat cheek of hers flame up red and indignant like a slapped arse, and her mouth hanging open. And her glasses are skewed up halfway across her forehead. It's like something out of a film, it is.

I can tell you one thing, I don't wait around for the reaction. The hysterics. I glance once back from the door and I can see how her eyes are scalded with what must be hot tears. And how she's drawing in sharp gulps as ugly as a fish that's drowning in air. So I run for it. And I can tell you another thing. I keep running, so I do. That was last April twelve months.

I knew of course there was no way I could go back to Luke's. Not after that little episode. Now the thing is, I'm just as surprised as anyone else by what's happened. I swear to you, the thought of hitting Sr Veronica never once went through my head. It was more as if all of a sudden I was a witness to the fact. Do you get me? Her fat cheek has just been slapped crimson, I can see the marks, and my fingers are tingling with the slap. So it must've been me that done it.

Another funny thing, I bet the born-agains would've let me right back in. I bet you anything you like, even after what I just done. I couldn't do it, but. Know what stopped me? Their silences. I guess you'd've had to have known the bastards. You'd have to have felt the superior, hurt edge that was on all their silences, whenever any one of us in Luke's done something mean or vicious. There was never any question of punishments. Nothing quite so crude as punishments. No, it was the hurt look.

Not exactly hurt. More, how can I put it? More disappointment. It was intended you be left in no doubt but that you'd let yourself down. *You'd* abused *them*, like. You'd abused their unshakeable trust in human nature. But even still you hadn't exhausted their stores of born-again patience. Oh God no! To do that, you'd've had to have killed one of them. And even then, I bet you they'd have swallowed hard and prayed for the grace of forgiveness. They got off on that kind of thing.

You ask me, they crave one thing above all, the Bros. And that's to show you and everyone in your vicinity how their faith has placed them above all thoughts of revenge. In the meantime of course, you're immersed up to your throat in their disappointed silences till they have you all but drowned.

I swear, it works too. As God is my witness I've seen some of the hardest kids in Luke's break down and snivel, just because they weren't being obviously punished for acting the maggot.

So there was simply no way I was going back there. Back into their fold! It wasn't the first time I'd had to sleep rough, and anyhow by now it was well into April. No more frosty nights, you follow? Those clear nights that savage you into fit after fit of shivering, your whole entire body clenched up tight as a vice-grip with the cold. Go through one of those cloudless November nights, you'd know all about it. I swear to you, it's as if the stars themselves bare their teeth, and the whole universe is a giant set of jaws.

One thing I'd always had was presence of mind, even when I was small. It might've been April, but still there was no way I was going on the streets again with only the one set of clothes, with no blanket and no sleeping-bag and with nothing to read. This all flashed through my head even before I'd gone out the main door. But at the same time, I knew it was too risky to try to get back to my locker. It was all too likely I'd've bumped into one of the Bros if I tried sneaking back through the compound. My dorm was in the new wing out behind, with only the one narrow corridor connecting it to the main halls of residence.

So later that day I dropped in on the supermarket where they'd placed Gobber Molloy. Of course he was out the back having a smoke. I swear to you, if it wasn't that the store manager was the brother-in-law of one of the directors they'd have got rid of Gobber weeks before. But anyhow he was only there to stack shelves and push dirt around the floors, earning pennies.

I touched Gobber for a few quid and a smoke, and I arranged he'd leave a sports-bag with a blanket and change of clothes under the hedge by the main gate. That and maybe a couple of books. That surprise you? Jesus, it's not as if we can't read. Just cause we've no parents? Maybe that makes us better at reading, ever think of that? Anyway, out on the streets there's fuck all else to do.

Don't think there's anything remotely poetic about being on the streets. You sit out under a blanket with the crowds milling past you, you might just as well be invisible. Or worse than invisible, seeing how they go out of their way to avoid looking at you. When they're not giving you a dig that is. And solitude can literally drive you mad. You end up talking to yourself. I've seen it a thousand times.

But those same books were the part of the plan that was the riskiest. Too risky by half, except for it was Br Martin was in charge of the library. The Bro, I do call him. Not to be confused with the Bros. That's the rest of the bastards. But the Bro is this old man, half deaf and glasses as thick as jam jars. From day one we'd always got on. One thing I keep meaning to do is to drop him a note. A postcard or something. Tell him that he was the one solitary person in that whole saccharine cesspool that ever made a difference.

It was their policy in Luke's that everyone was encouraged to read. I think that's meant to be Protestant or something. Of course naturally it had to be some spiritually edifying book out of their born-again library. But then, the library was also one way of getting out of an extra work detail. Myself, I'd've gone to the library anyway. Even if all they had was their fundamentalist bullshit I'd still've gone. I'd always loved to read, ever since I was that high. One of the only memories I have of home, I mean before the refuge and everything, is lying reading Rumpelstiltskin out loud on the playroom floor. At least, I think it's a memory. Home. Christ! There's a word!

Naturally, as I say, their library consisted almost entirely of their born-again bollocks. Texts and commentaries, miracles of faith. The favourite was these predictable stories written by some one-time prostitute or publican about how I found Jesus and how He showed me the light. There was precious few novels of any description. But still, over the years, Br Martin had helped me to find the few gems scattered among all the dross. It was him introduced me to Rilke. The poet? That shook you! You never thought a lad like me'd be reading poetry.

The problem was, of course, that Gobber Molloy could barely read his own name, let alone a book. I doubt he'd been to see the inside of the library but a half dozen times in all the years he'd been there. Or if he did go, like I say it was patently so he wouldn't have to do maintenance or gardening in the wet. But now he was supposed to ask Br Martin for the library's one and only copy of Rilke, and this on the self same afternoon yours truly'd run away?

What I was counting on of course was that the Bro would realise what the ploy was all about, but then he'd decide to let it go without kicking up any kind of a fuss. Knowing the way he looked at things behind those thick glasses of his, I figured he might even decide that it'd be all for the best. All for the best in the best of all possible worlds. So to cut a long story short, I picked up the bag just after curfew, and not only did it have the Rilke I asked for, there was even a volume of John of the Cross squeezed in there too. I can tell you one thing for free, there was no way in this wide world that Gobber Molloy put John of the Cross in there off his own bat! Are you mad?

•••

I was on the streets the best part of two months before I met Malcolm. That's probably not even his real name, the bastard. It wouldn't surprise me if he lied about it, seeing how he lied about everything else. But there again I never told him my name, so there you have it.

Let's just say he looked like a Malcolm.

It wasn't exactly the first time I'd gone home with anyone. A couple of nights, if funds were very low or if everything had got drenched and it looked like the rain was never going to fucking stop, well, what would you've done in my place? Some of the tired old fags are so nervous they let you walk all over them. You learn quickly enough how to recognise those ones. And with their sort, you have to do precious little, but still you can ask more or less what you want.

Though Malcolm wasn't exactly like that either.

He was sort of laid back and ironic, right from the start. So this particular day he was sitting out on a café terrace with this newspaper held up in front of his face, but I could see all the same he was watching me from behind it. It became so it was like a game between us. From time to time he'd lift up the cup from the saucer and let the tiniest drop of espresso sweeten his lip, and if he caught me looking at him he'd let on to frown. He had on this Panama hat, what they call a cravat, and a crumpled old suit that might once have been cream coloured but looked pretty soiled from the doorway where I was squatting.

He says he's only a few years over forty. Forty my arse! I can guarantee you he's a damn sight more. He's such a fucking liar. Anyway, queers always lie about their age. But old Mal looks like everything about him's become swollen over the years. Bloated. Life or appetite or debauchery, blame what you like. I've seen it a hundred times.

So it turns out Malcolm lives in this huge big semi-detached out in Sandymount, the last one in a big old-fashioned terrace. He says to me, sort of off-hand and everything, that it's two-hundred years old, like I'm meant to be impressed. The place is just a five-minute walk down to the bay, too, he says. So I guess immediately he must be loaded.

Course it goes without saying the garden is overgrown, everything gone to seed and growing into everything else, just like himself. And of course the house itself is cluttered up with all sorts of junk. Antiques, as he likes to call them. Old globes and maps and candlesticks and china plates and ashtrays. And there was figurines, and beer-mats, pottery, and bottles, hundreds of bottles, and old sticks of furniture everywhere about the place. You name it, it was in there.

And of course half of the statues and paintings was of the male nude. Some pictures that he said he done himself were scattered on the floor of one of the back rooms he called a studio. Studies was his word for them. I always told him to his face they were nothing other than child's porn, the dirty fucker.

So to begin with, he uses the charcoals as a pretext. To have me pose for him. Undressed, it goes without saying. He used to give me a good few quid for it, I'm no fool. Then the next thing is of course one day he asks me can he take photos. Course I told him to fuck right off. You let your photo be taken, you wouldn't know what sick faggot website you might wind up on, especially with a character like Malcolm! No, he swears, he doesn't even have a digital, only this banged up old Polaroid he's had knocking about the place for years. So to cut a long story short, he begged and he blubbered so much that in the end I got two hundred out of him for a half dozen shots, and the solemn promise I could have them back the minute I quit the house.

Once or twice, too, there was this ancient battle-axe friend of his used to come around, blue-rinse brigade and about a hundred years old. But a real old lech! Jesus! She was meant to be a sculptress or something, even more wrinkled than he was and just as able to knock back the sauce. She had her voice destroyed with the fags and the John Jameson. I don't know what happened exactly, but this one day the way she looked right at me brought on some sort of, you know… A reaction, we'll say. She croaked something I didn't quite catch into Malcolm's ear and they laughed their heads off and so I let on to be real angry and to cut a long story short I never posed for them again. So that was that.

He also had this coven of cats. If there's one animal I've never been able to abide it's a fucking cat. He must've had a dozen. I swear to you, you'd trip over them if you weren't watching! And so the whole interior of the house was always reeking of cat-hairs and cat-shit and dried up saucers of cat-food. The few languorous plants he kept about the place had long since been poisoned by one of the toms always fouling the flowerpots with its mess. I can remember that particular cat's name. Caligula. I fucking hated that cat with a vengeance. They were all of them either named after Roman Emperors or else their mistresses. You know, Agrippina, or Cleopatra. But this particular tom was the pampered favourite, despite the fact he had a vicious temper on him and was forever fouling the place. Fucking Caligula!

The house had one hell of a good library, though, I'll say that for ole Mal. It even had a selected Rainer Maria Rilke. Dog-ears and pencil marks all over the 'Torso of Apollo', you know the one? Well if you did, you'd know what I was talking about.

It was bilingual, with the German to one side. Not that I can speak a word of German. Volkswagen and Heil Hitler, that's about the size of my German. But this book was translated by I can't remember who. But it must have been by another poet. Put the Bro's version in the ha'penny place so it did. I've this one page I've managed to keep all this time right here in my pocket, right next to my heart. "A bat zigzags through the air as a crack runs through a teacup." Understand what I'm saying to you?

Goes without saying I'd long since lost the Bro's copy. You try keeping things together when you're camping in doorways. One night I'd come back to the particular porch I was stopping in to find the bag and blanket gone, my clothes dumped out everywhere and a scatter of torn pages, like feathers about a bird that's been ambushed. I swear I nearly broke down and cried when I seen that.

Philistine fuckers, just tore it up out of spite so they did.

Malcolm was away most of the time, and when he wasn't he was always half tight. So I pretty much had the run of the place. To be honest I knew I had a damn good deal of it. Don't expect me to be graphic about my end of the deal. Picture postcards like? If I was going in for that sort of shite I'd've sold the story to one of the tabloids, made a few thousand quid out of it. Sex. Murder. Disfigurement! This story has it all, man!

To understand any of it, you have to understand Malcolm. It was him first called me Bluebottle. Not on account of the leathers. The leathers came later on. Fact it was Malcolm bought me them. One of his 'little presents', the euphemistic cunt. I could see his hands was trembling. He said he figured the leathers sort of went with the name he'd so cleverly hit upon. I never told him my real name. Fact I never told him any name at all. After all, the boy can't be named for legal reasons, right? Ha fucking ha!

It came out of one of those nights when old Malcolm was being philosophical. He had this scratchy, vintage opera music he used to put on loud as anything but which always made him either weepy or a drama-queen. He was half-tight as per fucking usual, on one of his vintage burgundies. Did you know a single case of that stuff costs more than an entire sound system? I swear to God. But he could knock back the sauce all right. It was as if he couldn't bear to look at the world sober. Or maybe what he couldn't bear was to have the world look at him, not until he was half screwed.

I think I must've thrown a bit of a tantrum earlier on. Let me explain something about our arrangement. About Malcolm. You see, Malcolm wasn't a bit like the other fags. Everything about him was… what's the word I'm looking for?

One way or another, everything was pretence. He had a way of using words like they were meant to be disguises. I was a 'street urchin', that was the part he really got off on. A rough diamond. Everything, but everything he was looking for had to be couched in other terms. There was my 'pocket-money'. There were 'treats'. There was the whole bit about 'life-drawing'. Even his accent, for Jaysus' sake. You'd think he'd never been away from Oxford a day in his life, though I'd swear it was more like D4 he'd never left.

So anyway, this particular morning I'd thrown some sort of a tantrum. It's a funny thing, you live for a while with someone like that, you begin to take on their ways. I guess I was beginning to act like some kind of a Prima Donna too. I don't know. I couldn't even tell you what the whole thing was about. Probably money. You see, ole Mal wasn't quite as plush as his Sandymount address would've had you believe. All I can tell you for sure is, I'd thrown a few of his plates and bits of antique crystal again a wall or floor before he'd swanned out.

So that night, when he was waxing all teary-eyed and trying to make up, he came out with one of what he called his epigrams. He told me I was "prone to periodic rage". Which was fair enough. I always had been, even in the refuge. Then he raises one hand up like some philosopher-king, or queen more like. 'The rage of a bluebottle racing its single syllable against a windowpane', he said. I've always remembered that.

Looking back, I think I liked old Malcolm.

One night, though, it all got too much. The whole Jaysus set-up must've got on top of me. Malcolm had been getting more and more sarcastic, but with him, I sort of knew that was a defence thing. He was pathetically in love. I'd look sometimes at his shabby dandy's clothes, his debauched old face, and I'd feel like vomiting. It's not the right word. I suppose it must've been some class of that rage he was talking about. Rage at him. Rage for him.

So this one evening he's playing his sad faggot music and I'm staring hard at a book trying to ignore him. Before I know what's happening, he rolls his dirty eyes at me and pronounces one too many of his "epigrams" into his wineglass. Next thing, before he can even react, I've pulled one of his silver handled walking sticks out of this holder he keeps by the drinks cabinet and I'm all of a sudden belabouring him about the head and body with the handle of it. The first blow is there, to the temple, and it sets the hat crooked on his crown, like he's some king of the fair about to be toppled. The second sends the wineglass shattering over the tiles.

After that, all I remember for certain is a blinding whiteness. That and the ache in my biceps. And the hot stickiness of the silver handle when I'd finished with him.

•••

Maybe you don't believe me. You probably think I don't have it in me. But you have to make allowances. In here, they keep you sedated up to the eyeballs. Did you know we're not even allowed down to the canteen unsupervised? Maybe they think we'd try to overdose on coffee or something.

So like I say, this night, for no obvious reason, I set about the old fag. Beat him to within an inch of his life I did. I still couldn't tell you why I done it. I mean, theft can hardly have been the motive. I'd every opportunity any day of the week to rob the place. Still, will I tell you something? I made it a point to rob him of everything I could take before I left. Don't ask me to try to explain it.

Anyway, it amounted to fuck all. A few bottles of his famous *Nuits St. Georges*, maybe two-hundred euro in cash. The selected Rilke.

The irony, of course, is that when I seen him on Grafton Street in broad daylight not a fortnight later it was him that had to look away. His face was still discoloured and all trussed up in bandages like a faggot mummy, the left arm in a sling and only the one eye uncovered. I stared straight at it, all leer and insolence. The eye rolled stiffly towards me and then had to flit away like, and I'd swear I seen him flinch under the bandages so I did. But there was absolutely nothing old Malcolm could do about it. I was still fourteen in them days, so he'd a lot more to fear from the guards than I had.

After I departed Malcolm's palace of decadence I went on a bit of a wild spree. Bad idea, when you're out on the streets. Too many eyes watching you. So then on the third night I was jumped by a couple of drug fiends I was pretty fucking sure had been shadowing me. Robbed me of every penny that was left, they did.

That's one scene that I could never abide. Addicts fucking sicken me. Filling their veins with all sorts of garbage until they've trashed what's left of their minds, and speaking at about one mile an hour. What's it Rilke says in the drunkard's song? Filthiest card in the deck? Well, you ask me that's just exactly what junkies are, man. Not a single screed of will-power or aspiration, as the Bro would've said.

Let me tell you something else the Bro used to say. Used to say we're every one of us more ape than angel. But addicts've let go of the ladder entirely. All dignity, gone. Teeth rotten and muscles wasted away to bone. All this pair of scabby fuckers could manage was to hold a knife to me, a street kid, and empty out his pockets. The one thing they didn't bother with was the book.

So I hang around the city centre just long enough to get a bit of cash together, and then I strike back out for the coast. I guess the time I spent out in Malcolm's must've given me an appetite for the coast.

So I struck out for Irishtown as soon as I'd the guts of another two hundred stashed in my shoe. It's one thing begging for coppers in the city centre full of tourists and shoppers. 'Can you spare some change for the homeless?' For "the homeless", you know, as if you're a registered fucking charity! But it's another game entirely when you move away from the central shopping planes. You can't just sit idle and look downcast. A whole day might drag to an end with no more than a dozen passers by. The days were getting shorter, too. Shorter and wetter.

I probably would've stayed on in town a bit longer, got a bit more cash together, only those two drug fiends were all the time sniffing around, like fucking Adam and Paul gone wrong. So I push out past Ringsend one damp morning, might have been early October judging by the leaves. By midday I'm sitting with my back to the sea wall underneath what they call a Martello Tower out in Sandymount. I'm watching the mudflats stretch out half way to Howth Head. Tide is on the turn. There's a chill blowing in off the bay, but I'm feeling on top of the world. I've bought a stick of French bread and a hank of salami for the journey, I tell you, there's nothing like a sea breeze to strop an edge onto your hunger for you. And I'm sort of toying with my hunger, the teeth drooling and the guts growling like a bear. And then my eye lights on the spires of Dun Laoghaire. Now nothing will do me but to get there! I figure it looks not much more than an hour away and so I put the salami and the French stick back into the bag untouched. They're what you might call an incentive to get a move on.

Of course Dun Laoghaire isn't going to be any different from anywhere else. I already know that. I'm not fucking stupid. Still, it feels good when I get there, so I stay on a couple of days. Make a few more pounds, or at least I break even. Would've done a damn sight better if there hadn't been a scrap over territory with the local down and outs. One of the cunts made a lunge with a broken bottle that could've cost me my eyes if he'd connected. Big roundy face on him the colour of a beefsteak.

So then of course the soles of the feet start getting itchy and it's next stop Dalkey. I can tell you one thing, it's always in the richest, snobbiest neighbourhoods that you get fuck all charity. Not that I care. It's not their money I'm after.

One morning, one beautiful clear October morning… how can I explain it to you?

I'm sleeping rough in behind the park. Brambles, thick rust coloured ferns, everything always wet with sea mist. But it's cosy enough, the way I've it arranged. Cardboard boxes, a bit of canvas. But you can never stay long without someone watching you. Some busybody must've put in a complaint because this particular morning I'm woken up by the business end of a boot. A couple of Garda Síochána, jackets luminous yellow like they're traffic signals or something. I give them the same old rigmarole, first-name, age, no fixed abode and haven't eaten since Tuesday, but there's not the tiniest spark of sympathy in e'er a one of them. So I'm bundled roughly out onto the road, my bedding is kicked apart and binned, and I'm warned in no uncertain terms to be history before midday.

Two big fuckers from Kerry they were.

So next thing I'm mooning up along Vico Road but truth is, after the nerves have calmed down, I'm feeling great. One hundred percent pure fucking wonderful. I've always been a lousy sleeper, but when I do get a night's kip, it's as if the whole world has just had a makeover. The previous night had been dry and overcast. In sleeping-rough lingo, that means warm. And until them two fascist wankers had booted me out of my den, I'd slept like a log. I even dreamed, which I never do. Seriously. Dreamed I was on a huge big ship on the ocean so I did.

D'you know those clear days in late October when there's not a single cloud anywhere, just a big blue vault of ozone, and the sun so low it's like the light is carving everything out of sugar or something? So I'm about a half mile above Dalkey and the air is liquid cold but Christ, the view! Sorrento, I think they call it, like it's somewhere in the Middle East, but I can guarantee they don't have this shade of blue over there. As much granite as blue, like cigarette smoke. Or the shade you do sometimes get in an eye. Nothing gaudy about it. To my left is Dalkey Island, with its bucket and spade tower, to the right the whole sweep of the bay down as far as the Wicklow mountains, and I'm a hundred feet up above it all. Fucking magic.

That's the moment. That's when the whole vision seizes me. What the Bro would've called my epiphany. It comes in one go, not bit by bit. It's like one of the temptations the born-agains harp on about was set before Christ by Satan himself. But what I've always wanted to know is, if Christ was really the Son of God and all-powerful and everything and the Devil knew he was, which he obviously did, what was he doing wasting his time trying to tempt him? Unless he's fucking thick.

Now here's the thing. This is supposed to be my country, right? And I know nothing about it. A handful of daytrips from Luke's is all. Anything I knew about Ireland beyond that was from the telly.

Don't talk to me about education. In Luke's, geography was the formation of ox-bow lakes and the three types of rock: igneous and whatever you're having yourself. And as for history, there was Christian monks on one side writing their manuscripts and the Vikings on the other with their axes and helmets like something out of the Viking Splash and that was about as far as it went. They were scared stiff to even whisper the name of the likes of Pádraig Pearse or Collins. I don't know how the government let them get away with it.

Want to know what Rilke says about education? I don't have the exact words. But it's something the Bro used to always say to me ever since I was a kid so I still remember it. Rilke says that, with our words and everything, we surround the child with traps. The words turn his eyes backwards, away from the world. D'you get me? That's what Rilke says anyhow. And that's how we come to carry death inside us. Not like the animals, who of course don't have any words. A word for death, like. And so they see only the world. But like it really is.

That's in one of the elegies so it is. I wish to fuck I had them written down.

So I'm looking out over the bay and I can see the hulk of Bray Head like Moby Dick come up to breathe and suddenly I'm walking. Not just walking, pacing. Striding. It comes to me in that very instant that I'm not going to stop. Not until I've seen the whole Jaysus island. Another thing Br Martin used to say to me was we pass like shadows across the world, Book of Job, I think he said it was. Well, I was about ready to let my shadow do a little passing of its own.

From where we're both sitting now, of course, the whole thing might seem half-baked. But sure fuck it, what had I to lose? Might just as well sleep rough in one county as another. So I figure I won't stop the first day until I'm somewhere a good way beyond Bray Head. Then the next day or two, who knows? Arklow, or Wicklow town. Brittas Bay maybe. All these are just names to me you understand. I've no clear idea how far away they are, or even what order they're supposed to come in. I'm heading south, that's good enough for me. My head is light and I'm soaring like a bird. I'm like a swallow that flies away for the winter.

I see this small little newsagents some way off the road, and I have that queer idea you do get sometimes that Fate has set it there just because. But I'm too cagey to take any of the banknotes out of my sock. Who knows when I might need to dip into that reserve, am I right? I'm not stupid. I know that winter's just around the corner, I can already feel it breathing down the back of my neck. But in loose change I count out the price of a hot polystyrene coffee. It's the first one I've had in a week. Probably longer. The old boot behind the counter looks at me and the pile of coins I give her as if I'm soiling her precious establishment. Good riddance to you too, lady.

What I hadn't counted on of course was the way life always deals cards off the shitty end of its deck. Like some cheap con artist. I wasn't a half-mile down the road when one of my boot-laces went. Snapped, just like that. I suppose the pace I was marching at had put it under a strain it wasn't used to.

The boots was a couple of sizes too big as it was. I'd dug them out of some skip or other, but they were in pretty good nick considering. But now all of a sudden I'm tramping about like a circus clown trying to keep the left foot somehow in the inside of this gaping canoe. What's worse, when I get back up to the newsagents it turns out she doesn't stock laces. Then she shakes her blue-rinsed head when I ask her, all politeness, if she'd have a spare piece of string. With the look she gives me you'd think I was asking after her virtue, the stupid dried up old bitch. Picture of the Sacred Heart over the counter and another of the Pope's mass in the Phoenix Park.

The caffeine I've taken has my heart skipping about like a bird in a cage. I'm not used to coffee, and the dose on the empty stomach goes straight into the nervous system. My fingers are fidgety, and I'm considering with my eyes whether to give this withered up old cunt a dig in her sanctimonious mouth for her. But then her son appears in the doorway, a right tub of guts with wheezy asthmatic breathing and a fat red face on him the size of a woman's buttocks. I shuffle past him with a glance like I'm giving the finger, only he's too sly or too stupid to notice.

I swear, I could've gone back that night when they were asleep and set fire to them, I'm feeling so agitated. The coffee has me paranoid and full of the jitters, and the lousy boot is falling off at every step like the whole world's bent on making a mockery out of me and my big plans.

I lose the entire morning scrimmaging about trying to find a length of twine or wire that'll hold that boot on, and all the time my left foot is clenched up like a fist until it's cramping. I might as well be a cripple the way I have to hobble along the footpaths. By the time I do find something that'll act as a stopgap, it's clouded over and there's rain on the wind. It's crazy, it's infuriating, the tiny little tricks that put paid to our finest ideas. You think you're in charge of your life? Yeah right! Fate just mocks you, you and your plans. A snapped lace, for Jaysus' sake.

In the afternoon the rain comes down, and I haven't even got as far as half way along to Bray. It's a pitiless, freezing rain. Almost sleet. Just as soon as I can, I duck into the shelter where the next DART station is but I'm already soaked through. The whole chest, clenched up rigid with shivering.

The rain is obviously down for the day. It never stops, just turns to a drizzle every so often. What an acquaintance used to call the pelt of the rain mongrel.

'She's down from the mountains, brushing the city with her wet fur.' Don't worry, you'll hear all about Raymo soon enough. Raymond Fowler. Meanwhile as per usual I'm attracting all sorts of funny stares from the guy at the ticket counter, and when I see him on the phone and still watching me as he speaks, I figure it's time to push on. Always some fucker watching you. So I exit before there's any trouble and I push on down onto the strand.

The weather has turned ugly since the morning and by now huge waves, brown with sand, are jostling one another to crash onto the length of the shoreline. I can no longer see Bray Head with the cloud so low and swollen. Then by chance I turn around to see how far along the bay I've come. For the second time, I get the distinct feeling Fate has set up this exact scene with me in mind. There, not two hundred yards back up along the beach, set right into a shoulder of rock, is a cluster of what might've once been old fishing huts, all corrugated iron roofs and missing windows. But it's just exactly the sort of gaff which'll let yours truly bed down for the night and dry out the leathers.

•••

The night, I said. Turns out I stay on in that dilapidated cluster of rooms for closer on two months.

At first I'm cagey about the place. There's every brand of bottle and beer can and used condoms strewn about the floors. It's disgusting. And on top of the smell of the sea there's this musty-cabbage stink of piss. In a couple of rooms there's circles of ashes and embers, black and grey and oily like they were lit with diesel or something. The walls are made of this damp concrete that's crumbling away like it has a disease. And of course any window has long since been smashed, so depending on what way the wind is blowing, some of the rooms are as cold and dank as caverns. But what has me on edge for the first couple of days is those bottles and beer cans. The thought that someone might come back and stumble across me stops me from being able to settle. I can tell you one thing, there's fuckers out there would kick you senseless for sleeping rough, just for the hell of it. I even know of one street kid was set on fire by them. I swear to God. Name of Ger.

By the third or fourth day I'm beginning to feel more at home. It's cold, it's damp, but there hasn't been a single visitor while I've been camped there. I'm beginning to think that maybe the lovebirds only use the venue in summer. The low, dirty clouds haven't once shifted since I've arrived, and I'm beginning to toy with the idea of wintering out in the gaff. Being woken up every morning by the crash of waves. A body might go farther and fare a lot worse.

The more I think about it the more I like the idea. I've no clear idea as to what the date or even the day of the week is. Say it's the first day of November. Good. Say I want to start on my wanderings by the last day of February. Four months, say eighteen weeks. So I start to do a few calculations. I count through my bundle of euros. I have them stowed in three different hideaways by now because my feet get so wet through the boots that the outer fivers are already frayed and torn. So I'm jotting out my sums on the floor with some charcoal from one of the fires. Cans of beans, bread, teabags. Nothing at all fancy. But however I do my sums it always seems to come to the one answer. I'm going to have to pay Malcolm another visit.

So the very next morning I count out fifty from one of my bundles. I'm going to need to get something besides the filthy set of clothes I'm standing and sleeping every day in, that's for sure. And I'm going to need soap and a razor and a towel, maybe even a haircut. The thing is, I don't want to call on Malcolm smelling like some sort of a tramp. Don't think there's anything remotely faggot about that either, right? Maybe I just don't want him to see how dirty my life's become.

I'm in the habit at this stage of trekking the mile or two down along the strand to Shankill whenever I need to stock up. The way I have it figured, that sanctimonious old bitch up in the other shop would be just the sort of busybody would figure out where I might be staying. Say if I was ever to go back sniffing around her premises, I'll lay you ten to one she'd be suspicious as hell about where I was sleeping. So I give her and her obese offspring as wide a berth as possible.

I've been staying put about two weeks now, and the longer I stay, the more sense it all makes. Wintering out. Then it strikes me that I might as well hit Malcolm for some of his books while I'm about it, some real classics. Maybe even touch him for a case of that expensive vino he keeps down in the cellar.

The scenario just gets better and sweeter as the DART caterpillars its way round the great curve along Dublin Bay. I could've never imagined a sight more beautiful, and in the end I miss my stop and have to walk back out from Lansdowne fucking Road. But I go on talking to myself all the way up to Malcolm's front door, right until the very moment I'm tugging at the bell-pull and grinning broadly, all dry clothes and freshly shaven and even a comb dragged through my locks, first time in more than a month.

I'm only newly turned fifteen, but I had to shave. I swear to God, ever since I hit the teens. I must have developed early, as they say.

So I'm waiting a while, and the waiting pisses me all the way off, and so I begin to pull the rope a lot harder. I've seen something move behind one of the lace curtains, something more solid than a breeze or a shadow, or one of his infestation of cats. Come on Malcolm, I shout. Come on and open the door, damn you. When the shadow backs off, I give the rope one god-almighty pull and take a step backwards to where I might be scrutinised.

There's this tiniest of disturbances. But it's enough to tell me he's hiding behind his lace curtain. I try to square the outline of the image with the last time I seen Malcolm, when he was all swaddled up in bandages and stiff with the worry, but something between the two images won't square.

I march the few steps of gravel back to the door, I yank the bell-pull so hard that the hall is set ringing long after I let go of the rope. Nothing. So then I pummel the reinforced glass with the side of my fist like I'm determined to break it. A few moments after that, the frame of the bathroom window inches open and a thin, girly voice, foreign sounding, says please, he is not here. Where is he then, I shout. He has gone to Cannes. Cannes!

You have your shite. Tell him I'll be back for him later on. Tell him it's Bluebottle. He is not here, please, he has gone to Cannes.

The flap of the window pulls shut, as tight as pursed lips. I literally stomp away, feeling this white anger inside me. All the time I'm walking away I'm chewing over the high-pitched, wheedling words croaked out of the bathroom window over my head. Cannes! He was no more in Cannes than I was.

I sat out with my back to the sea wall under the tower, and in the blackest of moods I began to reconsider my options. The tide is so far out, the wrinkled sand is like a desert going on for miles. It looks like you could walk all the way to Howth so it does.

But at least I'm calmer by now. In fact I'm listless. I was told by the Bros, when I was first taken into Luke's at the age of three, I was prone to mood swings so violent that they had to bring in experts. Psychological advice was sought. That's some admission from a community of born-agains, let me tell you. A wonder they didn't think I was possessed by our friend down below. The rages would come on me suddenly, so Br Martin told me, and when I was in their grip I'd scream and kick and hurl objects so deliberately and violently it was clear I was intent on causing harm. Actual bodily harm. This at the age of three, mind. Three years old.

But this time, my mood's subdued and dark. Like I could do something in cold blood. Truth is, I think I'd been looking forward to the encounter with old Malcolm. Just like when that shoelace snapped and I'd lost the entire morning, now it seemed as if Fate was intent on dealing me another filthy card, right off the arse end of the deck.

Cannes? No. Try as I might, I couldn't see Malcolm having the, what's the word, the initiative to get as far as Cannes. I've been told since he did get over to France, but that was a good few months later, and anyhow, he was literally dragged there by what's her name, the artist woman.

But that's neither here nor there.

It seemed to me now, staring at the mud-flats, that that girly, foreign sounding voice rang hollow, like it was some sort of a ruse. I began to think that maybe Malcolm was in there after all. I even had one ridiculous vision of old Mal, kneeling down to look small and with a tea-towel pulled around his head, crouched up at the jacks window and wheedling out to me like he was an old woman or something to please go away. I don't say I believed it, the vision just came to me, that's all.

By this time it was getting dark. Dark and chill, with only the barest cloud clinging to the horizon like sea wrack at low tide. I could see what they do call the evening star twinkling up beyond Dun Laoghaire pier. Br Martin told me it was no such thing, it was the planet Venus, but that when it appeared in the mornings they used to call it Lucifer. The tide was in far enough by now that its reflection winked back up at it from the silver water. Gives you an idea of how long I must've been sitting there, my arse so cold by this time it was like it was made of concrete. I stood up and stretched my legs, which hurt like fuck cos I'd let them go to sleep on me. I still had no clear idea on what I was going to do, but I can tell you one thing, the thought of the DART journey back out to the shack with my tail between my legs did not appeal. Not in the slightest.

Here's the curious thing. The next thing I remember, I'm forcing the window around by the conservatory at the back of the house. Mal's place. I swear to you, it's not that I've forgotten what happened in between. It's more like the hours didn't exist. I mean, it's now one or two in the morning. As God is my witness, I have no idea what I did in between times. The next thing I'm aware of after stretching the cramp out of my legs, I've forced the bottom sash of the window up away from the sill, and I'm chilled to the marrow of my bones.

I damn near upset a saucer on my way through the window, damn near set it crashing onto the tiles. I only held onto it because my palm was pressed down so hard into a wet sponge of cat food that the plate was pinned to the sill. Sure enough, I seen one of the toms flit through the moonbeams tigering the far wall. Then it sort of limbos under the drape into what Malcolm used to call the arras. Talking out his arras, I used to say. Another cat is sitting upright on the arm of the sofa like it's made out of porcelain, only for the fact that it blinks as it watches me. So I sneak past under its gaze.

What time was it? There's this grandfather clock by the main stairs that Malcolm is too hit and miss to keep regularly wound. But then I remembered having once changed the battery of an electric clock up at the main hallway. The clock is over the shoulder of this kitsch plasterwork that's supposed to be Orpheus or someone, naked of course but for his harp, and that's how I seen it was already well past two. The hour would explain how still the house was. All the same, there's this oblong of yellow stretching out like a mat over the hall floor, so the light must be on in the pantry. Now if there's one obsession that Malcolm does have no matter how wankered he gets, it's that he never, ever leaves a light on anywhere in the house when he goes to bed. Too mean by half.

So I take a couple of paces in the direction of the oblong of yellow and the next thing it's turned out. At the same moment I hear the soft pad of bare feet climbing the three steps that lead to the pantry and beginning to cross the hallway. I freeze just a split second before the figure comes into view. What makes it stop, and then turn around to face me, I couldn't tell you. Some instinct for preservation, maybe.

The sight of me petrifies him.

The inside of the house is lit by a sort of light like it's underwater or something. Everything is dyed in blues and silvers. But still I can see this frozen youth that's staring at me is coloured. Not black, but not white either. He's bare-chested, bare-foot, only a striped pyjama bottoms hanging loosely from his hips. His eyes are white marbles, too shocked to blink. In his hand there's this tilted glass of milk which has begun to piddle over Malcolm's afghan rug. I'd put his age at no more than twelve. I mean, there's not so much as a single hair anywhere on his skinny body that I can see.

Boo, says I.

His mistake is to cower away from me. Until he does, I've no thought of advancing. But his height shrinks several inches as he retreats. Then the milk glass slips from his hand and thumps once on the rug before squirming across against the foot of Orpheus. His eyes are too entranced by mine to follow it. I step towards him real careful like he's a deer out in the Phoenix

Park, and then all at once we're chasing around the hallway. He bolts for the pantry, but a feint of mine blocks him.

Please, he shrieks, I say you he is not here. The foreign note again. Arabic. Or Hindu, I don't fucking know. So I give chase along the rear wall and follow hard as he dives into the study and backs in behind the sofa. We circle it, first clockwise, then anti-clockwise. As Raymond Fowler would've put it, the choreography is faultless. What do you want please? It's the voice of a boy scarcely into puberty. Terror makes it teeter over the edge of breaking. Please! he cries. It's fucking hilarious.

To end the stalemate I lunge at him over the top and when I tumble wide of his bony waist he slips back out through the main door, shrieking like a terrified girl. I'm enjoying myself immensely. You get so crazy with loneliness sometimes that any kind of human interaction is a breath of fresh air. I get to my feet and hurl myself out after him with such a yowl he must've taken me for a psychopath bent on murder. Sure that must've been how it looked.

I slide and stumble as the afghan glides away beneath me, but somehow I keep my balance. By this juncture he's scrambling on all fours up the first flight of stairs. I lunge after him, and as his forearms are about to reach the mezzanine my hands lock fast about his left ankle. He kicks back like a doe in a snare and at one point the ball of his heel catches my cheekbone. But inch by inch the manacle grip I have on him drags his body downwards.

He kicks out again when his fingers finally let go of the landing banister, and his heel this time grazes my nose awkwardly enough to cause it to spurt hot blood. I grab higher with my right hand and, whether terrified by this advancing grip or by the sudden spatter of blood, he lurches forwards. This final lurch I easily put paid to. But the energy of it leaves the pyjama bottoms at half-mast about his hairless calves.

In all the chase, I've not the slightest notion of what I'm going to do once I've trapped him. Now, feeling his terror, seeing the strangely pale buttocks so pathetically bared, this wave of cruelty that's almost smutty sweeps up through me. All resistance seems to have left his body by this stage, and I can see the bony shoulders vibrating where he must be whimpering.

'Get up!' His baby convulsions continue. 'I said, get up.' When he turns limply over to rise I grab both his wrists in a ferocious grip and I yank him after me, down the stairs, across the hallway, and over to the main door. The whole manoeuvre is comical on account of he keeps tripping on his pyjama bottoms, and has to shuffle after me like a hobbled pony, all his belongings on show. It proves one thing, though, as if there was any doubt. Malcolm has a taste for unripe fruit.

When we get to the front door I fling it open, and the draft of frosty air is like a bucket of iced water thrown into the house. I feel his body clench up beside me, with terror or with the cold, I don't know. Now do you see this belt? Do you see it? Well by Christ you'll feel it if I find you anywhere around this house again. Do you hear me now? Saying this I give him one god-almighty shove out into the frost that was sparkling on the lawn like granite. He stumbles and trips, but instantly scrambles to his feet and away, one hand trying to hold the pyjamas up around the bony hips. I suppose they must've been irreparably torn, coz the last I see of him is the pale arse bobbing in the moonlight like a rabbit's as he teeters over the garden wall and out onto the street.

I don't know why I'm after telling you that episode in such detail. It's not as if I ever saw that Arab kid again. And as for Malcolm, it didn't need the evidence of that night to tell me what a sick fuck Malcolm is. I swear to you, ten or eleven years old. Twelve max. They could have locked that bastard up and thrown away the key for that so they could.

No. What amazes me looking back, it's the first time I ever done something mean just for the sheer pleasure of it. Any of my rages before that were sort of blind. They were more like fits that came on me, and I'd no strong memory of them bar the scabby knuckles I used to get. But this time I'd enjoyed every minute of it, scaring the wits out of that kid, then firing him out into the cold with his pants down around his ankles. I suppose it's what the experts in here with their white coats would call sadistic pleasure. If he'd've come back, even to beg for his clothes on that freezing night, I'd've enjoyed thrashing him so I would.

Course, it wasn't too long before I got paid back for it, twenty times over. Twenty times over man! What goes around comes around, the Bro used to say. Anyone tries to tell you different, they're lying.

So I stretched out on Malcolm's bed with one of his vintage bottles and I suppose I must've dozed off because when I was woken up by the pounce of one of the fucking felines onto the duvet, the bedside clock said it was almost five. I sent it screeching, I needn't tell you. The cat, I mean. Still, I figured I'd better leave before the neighbourhood began to wake up. But in my drowsy state I found precious little I could take with me. A pair of gold cufflinks that might have been worth something if I hadn't almost immediately lost them, a silver hip flask, a fancy bottle of after-shave that smelled so good you could have drunk it.

Turns out it's a Sunday. I found out because it meant I'd to wait for fucking hours before the first DART back out in the direction of Bray. So to kill time and to keep my mind off the cold I began to list in my head all the items I *should've* taken. A can-opener for starters, cutlery, towels. For God's sake, the portable radio he keeps beside the upstairs bath! That radio should've been the first thing I went for. But in my dozy state I hadn't even thought of taking a solitary book with me.

I got so furious with myself that I all but marched straight back up to Malcolm's house. Even though it was already bright and I could hear occasional traffic, I had literally to sit on my hands to keep myself from that folly. In my agitated state I must've left those bleedin' cufflinks on the bench behind me, the one bastardin' thing that might've been worth a few bob.

I got out at Killiney and walked down as far as the strand with that light-headed feeling you do sometimes get when you don't sleep. I felt agitated, a bit paranoid maybe. But you know what they say? Just because you're paranoid…

Looking back, I'd be tempted to say it was what they call a premonition. Except I'm often prone to a sort of a nervousness which I swear makes my entire body feel like it has pins and needles. Just like after too much coffee, when you get the jitters and anxiety starts fiddling with the heartstrings. Gobber Molloy once told me he got the same thing an odd time he sniffed solvent. The fear, he called it. I had the fear that morning all right, and it was enough to make me cagey.

I circled the hut a couple of times before I went in. There was nobody about. I was whistling, very deliberately. I'd no intention of startling some tramp or other into pulling a blade or a bottle on me. But the place was empty.

There, in dirty charcoal, was the fragment out of Rilke I'd scratched on the plaster over my mattress the very first night I'd camped there: *night, when a wind full of infinite space gnaws at our faces.*

Jesus Christ, man! It was like Fate was putting down its thumb-print for what it had in mind for me, if only I could've read it properly.

The fear didn't go away. Not all afternoon. I'd heated up a tin of beans just as the light was beginning to go, and I remember I was thumbing through some old magazines when this little scrap in the corner by the bed caught my eye. Like a sweet-paper, greeny blue, and a silver glitter on the inside. I went over and, already filled with loathing, I moved it with my toe. There underneath, like some class of excrement or a creature that lives under stones, was the discarded balloon.

So I no longer had the place to myself.

Even with the beach raw with winter the fuckers wouldn't keep away. I looked with disgust at the mattress I'd dragged out of a skip all the way to the hut not two weeks before. As I examined it, the nervous edge I'd been feeling turned to sick. I hadn't noticed before this how stained that old mattress was, and now the great yellow stains seemed like the accumulated sweat of year upon year of lust. I flung the can of beans from me and I ran outside into the dusk. And I heaved my ring up.

•••

Want to know something funny? I'd never been with a girl. I mean, I'd scarcely had anything to do with them. In Luke's the lasses were kept pretty much apart. We slept in separate wings and everything. But anyhow I was too young when I ran away from there to have known much. Gobber Molloy told me he'd got the wear off of one of them a couple of times. She'd put her hand down his trousers and all. But even if I was to believe him that's as much of girls as I knew.

Just to get things straight, I'm not going to give anything bar the girl's first name. No way. I don't want her involved. That time was the one period in my whole bastardin' life when things weren't, what's the word? Dirty. Soiled. You think I'm going to spoil all that now by going into the nuts and bolts of it you can think again.

All I'm going to say is, her name's Judith.

She'd been going with this scumbag from Shankill from the age of fourteen. This wanker who thought he was some sort of a big shot. Name of Anto. But there was no way this Anto was letting her go. She had real class, and he must've got off on being seen with her. An ugly fucker with a shaven head and studs through the lip. But Judith had class. I don't just mean the way that she looked, either. Everything about her was pure class, man. She'd eyes you wouldn't believe. But it wasn't that either. Let me put it this way. Her hair was a white blonde when I saw her first, but the roots showed dark. You know what? It suited her that way. On anyone else it would've looked trashy. She sort of made it look special. Ach, I can't explain it!

Anyway to cut a long story short, one night when I got back to the hut I found her in there. This was about a week after the episode with the condom. I'd become a lot more cagey about returning to the place, and this night I'd seen the flickering red of a campfire inside, so I waited in the rocks until I saw the party leave. Then waited another half-hour with the windows gaping darkly at the sea as the fire died. Three of them had left, two guys and a girl. I wasn't expecting to find anyone else, but you can never be too careful.

Her back was turned to me as I stood in the doorway. I can't explain what held me there. Why I didn't back away, and return only after she'd left too. She was hunched down on the floor, staring into the embers of the fire and pushing them about in circles. She had on a large parka jacket, with grey fur around the hood. One lock of hair had escaped a hair-band.

For about a minute I don't think I moved so much as a muscle, but then I seen her tense up as though she'd sensed me. She grabbed the largest ember out of the fire and spun around.

'Don't you come fucking near me!' She was on her feet, though crouched down low, and the orange light of the faggot was circling through the air like the tip of a sword. I could see two pupils glinting, an animal's eyes. 'You stay away from me, do you hear!'

I did exactly that. I didn't take a single step inside the hut, and I held both of my arms away from my body so she could see they were empty.

'This is my home,' I said. I think from my voice she must have guessed how young I was.

Doesn't sound a promising start, does it? But she trusted me. Don't ask me to explain it, but I think it was my using the word home. From the moment I said that bit about that kip being my home, she made up her mind she was going to trust me. It was as if, in that exact instant, I could see the decision being made.

Nothing happened between us, then or afterwards. We met a few times over the next week or two. Always at night. Always in the hut. But nothing physical happened, you know what I'm trying to say? She told me all about the fix she was in. The possessive rages that this low-life she was with was prone to. All about his gang, the Pitbulls, and how they'd carved out their territory and how they made their money. She told me how for months she'd wanted out. Once, she kissed me. It wasn't, like, erotic exactly. But that kiss had me wide-awake all night after she left.

I'm not saying nothing *would've* happened. That's a different story. Of course now we'll never know. Not with the scar and everything. But I can tell you one thing. She said she'd never felt so comfortable with anyone. Sometimes, we'd just sit and I'd have my arm around her shoulder and I'd watch her brow as she poked the flames, losing herself entirely in them. Or maybe she'd talk. But it was like she didn't have to. I'd sit there beside her and I was totally content. D'you know what I'm saying? Maybe our hands would touch, but she said she was scared to get involved. To get me involved. There's no way I want you getting mixed up with any of Anto's crowd. And nothing I could say would budge her on that. But it seemed to be enough, at that time. Just knowing I mattered to her. The future would look after itself, right?

So this one day we decide to climb up Killiney Hill. Up as far as the obelisk they call the Famine Folly. Judith tells me there's this pyramid near the folly where, if you walk up anti-clockwise or something, you're supposed to get a wish. All the while we're climbing the hill she's saying how she had this dream about running away, leaving the country, so you can guess what my wish is going to be.

We stopped at a bench just short of the folly, where you get this spectacular view of the sea. It was cold, but I don't think I ever felt happier. Our fingers were touching. Not exactly holding hands, but touching. It felt like pure electricity, man. And our heads was that close.

There was the sea, wrinkled like tinfoil, and a breeze that would skin you alive rushing up through the gorse. But it was as if we were in a bubble of charged air. I bet you anything we would've kissed. But of course Fate had other ideas.

Judith! That you? We spin around. This guy in a parka has appeared behind us not a stone's throw away. The real corporation accent. Jack! cries Judith, eyes big as saucers. Listen Jack…

Who's that fucking wanker with you, huh? And she's already on her feet, stumbling over towards him just as fast as she can. Listen Jack, he's nobody. I was just up here for a walk…

Now, I knew all about this Jack. He was what you might call Anto's right hand man. But the thing of it is, one night when Anto wasn't around he'd made a play for Judith. So she told me. Came on real heavy. But she wanted nothing to do with him. And ever since that night I reckon he'd had it in for her.

I knew well as I watched her chasing after him that she'd have her work cut out making him stay quiet. Not that there was anything much he could report. Not without lying. But even as I sat there, hours later, shivering and watching the sea still bright against the darkness, I was sort of hoping that the whole thing would come to a head. Fuck it! What had I to lose?

But if it was to blow up, then what? I didn't want to think about running away with Judith, maybe jumping on the boat with her. The thought made me way too giddy.

Like I say, now we'll never know.

So the following night at about two in the morning I suddenly start awake. There's three or four figures making rapidly for the hut across the shale, maybe it's the sound of the steps has me woken. I've only just time to pull on my pants when they're already inside, and as I get to my feet the four of them surround me. Eight arms, eight knees. One of them pushes me from behind. I collide with the one on front of me and he gives me a shove backwards. A knee is driven into my left thigh, a blow lands on my ear and I stumble about like I'm drunk.

They spend maybe a minute at this game. Two arms aren't enough to ward off the blows and digs, and a fist into the solar plexus has left me suffocating in air and unable to cry out. The one to the front of me has allowed his hood to fall back and I know from his shaven head and the ugly half dozen rings in his ear and lips that this must be Anto. He also has this one huge ring that Judith mentioned, here, through the right eyebrow, for all the world like the pin of a hand-grenade. Pretty boy, says he.

Then I'm thrust backwards over a stooped figure and I crash over his back into the ground. I'm about as helpless as an upturned beetle. Kicks rain in, and I protect my head with my elbows as best I can until I'm grabbed by the eight-armed beast and forced over onto my stomach. My hair is dragged and my face pressed on one cheekbone. It's pushed so deep into the mattress it's as if every spring is bared. Two of them are kneeling on me, pinning my limbs. On the wall I can just make out the charcoaled line out of Rilke: *night, when a wind full of infinite space gnaws at our faces.*

Nearer to the tear-duct I see something glint. The huge shaven head enters my field of vision, and the blade of a Stanley knife so close to my eye that I can't bring it into focus. At the same time, I hear the sound of liquid being doused over the mattress and over the walls of the hut, and a sweet nose-full of petrol makes me gag.

Her name is whispered into my ear, Judith, so obscene it sounds like a curse. If you so much as talk to her again, pretty boy, I'll slice open your eye for you. I'll cut it out of your fucking head.

A second pair of hands, thick with the fumes of petrol, is pressed to my cheek and jaw. I swear to you, if I ever see you with her, I'll cut the bollocks off of you. Then there's a shock in my gum, so intense I jolt like you would from an electric socket. The two hands press down on my face with the weight of an entire body. It's like my head's in a vice-grip. The blade carves through cheek and into gum with a pain so fucking extreme the entire universe is white agony.

By the time the pain subsides enough for my senses to come together, the entire hut is a whirlpool of flames. Somehow, I've crawled outside, out into the infinite spaces.

•••

There you have it. The story of my branding. And you could argue, if it wasn't for the scar, there might never have been a murder. Raymond Fowler said it must've been done with a double blade. He said they do do that deliberately, to make it impossible for the doctors to run stitches across the gash. Jaysus, they needn't have worried. Where was I supposed to go to get my face stitched back together?

For the next few days I must've looked like your man the elephant man. My whole cheek was that swollen, my jaw was clamped shut, and I could only manage liquid through a straw. My lips had ballooned out, and the entire right side of my head looked like it'd been used as a football. I hid in the rocks, shy as a monster. From what I could feel with my tongue I thought for a while an entire piece of cheek was missing, and I was worried too that if the gums got infected where the blade had sliced them I might lose half the teeth out of my head. So, despite the pain, I used to regularly souse out that entire side of my face in salt water. Always at night, when there was no-one around like. I made a sort of a pack out of some old tee-shirts, and this I tied around my head. If anyone had've seen me, I swear, they couldn't've hollered louder if I was a giant cockroach.

The next night, or maybe the one after, I salvaged a few charred items from what was left of the hut, and I scuttled down along the shore before it was bright. All I had in the world was that half-filled refuse sack of cans and old clothes. I figured I'd push on well past Bray and hide out amidst the rocks, caves and wild grasses of the Wicklow coast. But the gash must've got infected because there was a yellow slime on the inside of the cloth whenever I pulled it away from my face. Besides which I was increasingly light-headed and feverish.

It was by now about the third day or night since the scarring. The disfigurement. One side of my face was still swollen out, grotesque as a Halloween pumpkin. I'd find myself muttering continuously between clenched teeth like a fucking wino or something. In fact, my entire body was clenched up with the cold the whole time. I only put up with the spasms because all senses were concentrated in the bone-deep ache the right-hand side of my face had become. I knew I was conscious only at those moments. The rest of the time I slipped into delirium. I used to let myself go. It came as a relief. And it was in a deep delirium that Raymo found me.

Raymond Fowler.

I think, if it hadn't've been for him, there's every chance I'd've died. If not of exposure, then of the infection. It already had my temperature way over a hundred and the edges of the gash discoloured and soft with puss. I was too delirious to be able to tell you exactly what Raymo done to me.

I do know he was anything but gentle. I don't mean he was deliberately rough, far from it. But he wasn't squeamish either. There was moments, when he prised the gash open between thumb and fingers, that I snapped and hit out at him. The pain was too frightful. But he was strong as a wrestler and just as determined. With moss and spittle and white spirits and anything else to hand he made sure the gash was properly cleaned. Then he run a needle and thread through it that he'd just that minute disinfected over the spout of a kettle. The pain was that intense that I literally wept. Only he must've thought I was weeping for my disfigurement, cos he tried to comfort and reassure me. But the pain of disfigurement didn't kick in for several days.

Raymo was a vagabond. He'd been in the army. The British army. He still had the tattoo there on his arm from his soldiering days with a regimental motto and everything. Brave man to keep it on show down here. I think he told me he'd made lance-corporal or something. But years ago, when their unit had been stationed up North, he'd deserted. Don't ask me exactly what had happened. It wasn't a time he liked to talk about.

I suppose he was in his early forties. Maybe he was less, the weather has a way of ageing you. I'd be hard put to say from his accent where he was from originally. Liverpool, maybe, he had that way of spitting his 'c's and 'k's when he talked like you get in Brookside. But he'd been living as an outcast for years and his speech was gone peculiar.

For a man that kept on the move, he'd assembled one hell of an amount of possessions. Pots, pans, jerry-cans, all sorts of knives, a griddle, a sewing kit, a canvas tent. There was rolls of wire which he used to make snares, there was field glasses, there was a wooden box full of tools of every description, and every condition, and another box with literally dozens of books. Practical stuff mainly, like teach yourself how to, you know the crack. There was a large enamelled basin for washing and another for peeling vegetables, a mirror, a plastic coated rope that he put up for a clothes-line and a fine, nylon line that he used for fishing.

I don't want to give the impression that Raymond Fowler was some kind of wild man of the woods. He had a flute and a penny whistle that he used to take with him into the nearest town to squeeze some coppers out of a few old tunes, and there was a mongrel he called Keaton that was three parts sheepdog and one part fuck knows what and had eyes of different colours.

I swear to you, one eye normal like a regular dog's, and one eye light blue like you might see on a wolf or something. Whenever he went into a town to busk, he'd tie a colourful scarf around Keaton's neck and have him lie down and listen to the old tunes. He swore to me that that dog used to add the same again to his takings.

I found out later, when I got to know him, that whenever he was ready to move on, Raymo would always have some refuge nearby where he could hide the bigger half of this inventory of his, all wrapped up in thick plastic bags and then buried under gravel and rocks and branches. There was maybe a half dozen such caches, as he called them, spread over an area the size of several counties. You see, he made it a point never to stay more than six or seven weeks in the same area. Settled folk could be funny. And he'd had a run in once or twice with gangs. Over the years, or so he said anyway, he'd staked out territories as far afield as Wexford, Carlow, Kildare, even parts of Waterford and Kilkenny. All the same the chief caches were all within County Wicklow, which made me kind of suspicious.

All of this he told me many weeks later, after we'd begun to trust each other.

From living so long outside of society, he'd got out of the habit of speech. But in any case I was hardly more of a companion than was the bloody mongrel, Keaton. After several days in his care the swelling and the stiffness had gone down enough for me to manage solid foods, and I could've managed talk if I'd had a mind to. But as the pain receded, it was replaced by a black fluid of bitterness and depression. I swear to you, I was so flooded with its cold that I was unable even to muster up anger at what they done to me. Instead, it was as if the whole world had lost every trace of warmth or purpose. I sat or lay for hours, gloomy, hardly moving more than thirty yards from the tent in an entire day. And I took all that Raymond prepared for me in sullen silence. Routinely he'd ask after the gash in my cheek, but I'd say as little as possible in reply. The Judas kiss, he'd christened it. How's the Judas kiss today, he used to ask.

One morning he began to uproot the camp. I've never figured out what exactly drove these migrations of his. One day all seemed comfortable and settled, the next he'd be packing items into boxes and pulling out tent pegs so fast it might've been in the face of an enemy advance. It was pointless trying to question him at these times. The line of his mouth was shut rigid as a clam, and every gesture was manic. I wonder what they'd make of him in here, huh?

Once, I tried to intercept his arm. It was the only time I ever tried that game, that's for sure. But as soon as ever the dog seen him starting to uproot and to pull down and to dig a big pit for the rubbish, he'd bound about and yap with excitement as if he was still a puppy and not the ten-year-old mongrel he really was.

But on this morning that I woke up, I wasn't used to it. I didn't know what to expect. There I was, right in the eye of his migratory cyclone. And I was filled with this deadening dread that I was about to be left alone. Honest to God I was that scared they were about to disappear without me that I didn't know what to do. To make things worse, whatever little bits I did to try to help with the packing only seemed to double Raymo's impatience to be gone. The bloody old mongrel was pawing and yapping with excitement at every item that disappeared into the bundles, and there was me cold stiff with the horror.

He himself disappeared at about midday under a load it was hard to believe that two men could have carried. Appalled, I sank onto the square of flat white grass where the tent had been, and I stared at the rubbish pit for what might've been one hour and might just as easy have been three. I was only alerted as to his return by the sudden intrusion of Keaton.

'Come on,' he goes, flicking his cap roughly away from me.

That moment was the exact end of my convalescence.

II | Malcolm

Gwen warned me, you know. Right from the very first. Told me the whole affair was bound to turn out badly. Of course, the thing with old Gwen is, I always have the suspicion that she's jealous when it comes to my boys. There was one whose name was, never mind his name, but my name for him was 7UP. Oh, a foul-mouthed, thieving little beast, can't have been more than…

But then, the thing of it is, Gwen never understood what precisely I see in them. Never wanted to understand. My rough diamonds, I call them.

Perhaps you've heard of her? She was quite well known in her day you know. Quite a reputation. She even had a solo exhibition in the, where was it? Damn it, where was it? The Serpentine? The Hayward? One of those fashionable London galleries in any case. Wouldn't have believed a word of it if she hadn't shown me the catalogue. Dreadful liar, Gwen.

Of course in those days she was still Gwendolyn Liebknecht. No? Perhaps you're too young. In the late seventies she had the first in a series of disastrous marriages. Absolutely disastrous. Trust Gwen to always seek out the worst possible male and then to tie the conjugal knot.

Moved back over here after she got hitched to Justin Furlong, the media mogul. Dreadful, hulking beast of a man. Dreadful. There's more culture in that wilted orchid over there. All he could manage by way of conversation was the latest mergers and share options. That and rugby. Went to one of the rugby schools, played inter-provincial, by all accounts. But art? Literature? Of course she was on the rebound at the time, been abandoned by that actor fellow, the Corsican. Claude…? Damn it, you know the chap I mean. Swarthy, eyes like the devil himself. Claude something.

That was in 1981. The reason I remember with such certainty is that the last piece that Gwen did before she left England was entitled Royal Wedding. Raised one hell of a stink, too. Ha ha! Good for you, Gwen!

1981. Christ, where do the years go?

The boy, yes. The boy.

Picked him up off the street, you know. Begging on the streets of the capital, that's what he was reduced to. Just like so many of them. This progressive society *soi disant*, with all its pieties and crocodile tears and its love for those abstract nouns, equality, and social justice, what does it care? All so much claptrap. It sickens me to hear them.

Of course in the eyes of society I'm the monster. Will I tell you what I really am? I'm the creature that society is afraid to see if it chances to peek into the mirror. Hypocrites and phrasemongers! I've given these boys something beyond a price. Beyond their programmes of social hygiene. Out there, the best, the very best that any of my boys can hope for is a hostel, an institution. Four walls. But never a home, you see. Never a home.

I'd seen him several times on the street corners, oh yes. I have a remarkable eye for detail you know. Gwen always jokes that I should have been a detective inspector. That would have kept you on the straight and narrow, she says. But all the same it's true, I've always had the most remarkable eye for detail.

Mother…

Now this one day, I saw that the boy was watching me. This surprised me. I'm very discreet when I examine people, you know. I make it a point of principle that they shouldn't realise they're being observed. But he had a brazen look, and on this particular day, from the very moment that I glanced in his direction out of the corner of my eye, he stared straight at me. Unblinking. I daresay it was a form of challenge. I daresay he was absolutely sick and tired of being the object of scrutiny from whoever happened to pass by. And what's more, he was brazen enough to challenge the right of anyone to look at him, for all that he was dressed in rags and begging with a McDonald's carton.

I have to say I admired him tremendously for it.

It must have been about a week before I saw him again. I'd had things to do that took me away from the city. Financial. Bit messy. The older brother, Godfrey. Lives in Cork you know. There's nothing like a squabble over money to inject bad blood into a family. But I've always been hopelessly impractical when it comes to money, Gwen will tell you.

Mother used to…

In any event I was glad to get it behind me. Put things on an even keel.

But the moment I left the train and the taxi pulled over Kingsbridge and down Ormond Quay, I had an inkling I'd see him. More than an inkling. It was a certainty, as if Providence herself was about to take a hand in the plot.

So I told the driver to forget about home and to leave me off on the corner of Kildare Street. I made for a café I know on South Anne Street, outdoors, you know the genre, the continental style. It was the most glorious day!

And sure enough there he was. My boy. I could swear to you, it's as if I knew that there was nowhere else in the entire capital city that he could possibly be, on this most glorious of days.

Did you know it was I who gave him his name? Bluebottle?

The eyes, you see.

The fact is, those brazen blue eyes had followed me all the way to Cork. Even when things became quite acrimonious between myself and Elisa, Godfrey's god-awful wife, still I couldn't quite take everything seriously. I knew full well that she wanted Godfrey to pay me off. To see the back of me with a single lump sum and to stop baling me out every time mother's house got me deeper into debt. Elisa had a positive weasel of a lawyer with her, slick with hair-oil. And those horrendous round glasses that flashed every time he'd a point to make. That was when I would have dearly loved to have old Gwen beside me. Gwen will take nonsense from no one.

I'm wandering. Sorry. Or perhaps I'm not. Perhaps it's to the point.

Gwen looks after my cats whenever I'm away, you know. Now the last time that I'd been away was during the period when 7UP was staying over. There was another little tike too, never cared much for him personally. But to 7UP, ah! They were inseparable. Thick as a pair of artful dodgers. Freckles and protruding ears, this side-kick. TK, I christened him, after the shock of ginger on his head. Ha ha!

Now the fact is that old Gwen couldn't abide either one of them. Two cheeky monkeys. Scarcely housetrained, if the truth be known. But I had commitments that took me away every year. Christmas, you see. So there was nothing for it. I asked Gwen to look in on the cats, and the boys.

One couldn't be too careful where the boys were concerned. I have a snooping busybody of a neighbour, Ms Ramsey, a rancid old spinster. Looked after her invalid father until he died. Made his last years a misery, I have no doubt. Just across the way there, the house with the blackthorn.

She spies upon me from behind her lace curtain. Caught her at it too, and doffed my hat at her. A pious mouth and a face you could use to chop firewood.

Now the point of all this is that when I got back, early in the New Year, my two fledglings had flown the nest. Fouled up the place, took whatever they could lay their dirty little hands upon, and then left without having the grace even to shut the hall door after them.

Of course Gwen was furious with me. I could tell how livid she was by the fact that she refused to speak. That's Gwen, you see. When she's truly furious, not so much as a squeak out of her.

Some people from Social Services came snooping around a short time after that. Tip-off from across the road, apparently. I can tell you it was most fortuitous timing. I was permitted to act the bumbling old toff, cravat and fedora, head up in the clouds. Absolutely insisted that they look around the place. Wouldn't hear of them refusing. Led them into every single corner. Every nook and cranny. Honestly, it was days before Nero would forgive me. And as for Caligula!

Of course the nudes raised a few eyebrows. Nothing against the law there, though. Bugger-my-neighbour is quite the pastime around Sandymount.

Gwen called around later that evening. She was in a mood to forgive me. But then I made the unforgivable indiscretion of describing the visit I'd had from the young couple from Social Services. Thought it would entertain her. Nothing doing! This time her fury found a ready tongue.

Well, in the heel of the hunt, had to promise her that there would be no more street Arabs staying over. No more rough diamonds. Of course I knew she was absolutely right. That game had got far too dangerous, and I understood perfectly that our interfering Queen Bitch across the way would never rest easy until she had the old pederast behind bars.

And I did behave myself, too.

But do you know what happened? Providence again, you see. Can you guess?

Just on the very eve of my departure for Cork to negotiate with my dear brother the precise terms of my ruin, Ms. Ramsey had a stroke. Gorgeous, isn't it? I actually watched the ambulance call at her door from the upstairs bathroom. Then I saw the stretcher being taken outside. In a trice I'd towelled the foam from my chin and I positively tripped down the stairs, terrified I might miss something. I promise you, the paramedics must have been either bemused or appalled at the unconcealed glee with which I asked after our dear neighbour's health!

A stroke! Priceless, isn't it? I returned from Cork like the prisoner whose chains have been removed.

So there I was. The sun beamed down on the cafe, people were smiling in the streets as they passed by, and my boy was watching me whenever I peeped at him from behind the newspaper. Don't think I'd formulated a plan. No. I was much too excited to have done anything of the sort. But somewhere in my heart there lurked the knowledge that the coast was clear for me to bring him home. Besides, it had been more than five months since that episode with 7UP, and until now I'd kept my word to Gwendolyn.

How can you understand what I was going through, if you haven't ever teetered on the very brink of a weakness? You haven't… no, I daresay you haven't. Form of vertigo, you see. The giddy urge to let oneself fall over the edge. There's an intoxicating moment, just a half second before the downward plunge. All the restraint that one has so painstakingly built up, that one has been so proud of, all willpower, all self-respect is just on the point of collapse, and you realise with a gorgeous panic that the moment is already passed when all could have been saved.

•••

Has an absolutely vile temper you know. Dangerous. I noticed almost at once that his knuckles were raw from it. Chafed skin. Scabbed. More than one of them was swollen. Do you know what was the cause? Sometimes he'd fall victim to what I call his white rage. Truly seismic, in its suddenness, its intensity. But you could see the signs a few minutes in advance. Oh yes. The jaw would tense, you see, and the skin would have an unusual pallor. The eyes, too. They'd widen, seized with an almost religious fervour. And then you know what he'd do? He'd stand within inches of a fridge or a wall, I mean a bare concrete wall, and then he'd shut his eyes tight and begin to pummel the living hell out of it. He'd open his mouth and there'd be an appalling, repressed scream, something like gas escaping under pressure. Dreadful!

The whole business might go on for fully five minutes, until his poor fists were ragged and streaked scarlet with his own blood.

Tried to interfere with him the first time I saw him at it. Laid a hand on his shoulder; the muscle was tensed up as hard as rock. I shook him lightly, attempted to speak, but fist after fist slammed into the door of the fridge with such violence that it was rocking back and forth as if it might topple forwards at any minute. Then like a bloody fool I tried to physically restrain him. What a perfectly stupid thing to do! Pure stupidity! I can tell you, I never again tried to interfere with him when the white rage was on him.

But I'm maligning him. Bluebottle! His elegance, you see. His poise. Everything about the boy was so… not feminine. Feline. Do you see the difference?

Viens, mon beau chat, sur mon coeur amoureux
Retiens les griffes de ta patte,
Et laisse-moi plonger dans tes beaux yeux,
Mêlés de métal et d'agate.

Baudelaire. Exquisite, don't you think? 'Eyes of metal and agate' !

And his wordless intensity! He loved to read you know. Sometimes he'd curl up for hours at a time, lost in some book or other. Lost. The way he'd curl over a text on the sofa or on the floor, it was as simple and divine as a study by Matisse.

Gwen saw it at once, what's more. I could tell by the manner in which she observed him. Eye of an artist. The first occasion that she saw him, I noticed it. Her eye, fixed, screwed up, taking in the proportions. Marvellous eye for proportions, Gwen. After that I knew that her objections would be no more than a matter of form.

Ha ha! Then there was one night, wait… Yes, it must have been perhaps a month after he'd agreed to stay. I'd convinced him to pose for me by this time, you see. He was quite blasé about the whole business. He'd sit indifferently, or with an ironic look, or he'd become absorbed in some book. It didn't seem to bother him so long as I didn't make any comments. I don't mean instructions, suggestions. All that was par for the course. But if I tried to say anything to him, ah! Then the mood would change. Then he'd turn sarcastic, or scornful, or openly hostile. I learned very soon just how far I could venture in our little games.

But this one evening, I'd asked him if he minded if Gwen sat in. He'd seen her about the place of course. I explained that she'd been a sculptress, explained that in her day… all about the exhibition, you know? He shrugged, bored, magnificently indifferent.

But then, do you know what happened? Shall I tell you?

It was quite delicious. Entirely unexpected. All of a sudden, about ten minutes into the sitting, he inexplicably became aware, as only an adolescent can, of the fact that he was absolutely stark naked. Suddenly he was awkward. Suddenly there was a flush to his cheek. Oh come on! You can guess what it was all about.

Gwen made some droll observation in the third person about the event, perfectly inappropriate. She's an absolute terror, Gwen. Can cut anyone down to size with the most innocuous comment, just with an inflection of tone or a precise arch of an eyebrow. It's an extraordinary, malicious talent. But I had to laugh! We both of us laughed! In any event, this new humiliation only poured petrol on the flames, and my dear boy positively withered out of the room, his hands over his waking modesty and a most delightful fire under his cheekbones.

Of course he pretended to be furious with us. Refused absolutely to pose for either one of us after that episode. But from that time he avoided Gwen like a child who's been caught doing something wrong. I think, you know, what he was afraid of most of all was the ironic twitch at the corner of her mouth every time they ran into one another.

To think of it, old Gwen! Sixty, if she's a day!

•••

Have I shown you my collection of 78s? No? It's quite the passion with me. Quite the vice. Can scarcely afford it of course. Have you any idea how much you have to pay for an original recording of an artist such as Gigli?

Taken me years to build up the collection. All the great operas. Donizetti, Bellini. Verdi, of course. Thank God he left those intact!

It's extraordinary, do you know, Gwen has no time at all for Verdi? Joe Green, she calls him. Too much Italian melodrama, she says. I could never understand that. As if all opera were not melodrama. '*Tu che a dio spiegasti l'ali*'. That's Donizetti. Edgardo's aria, from 'Lucia de Lammermoor'. If that were put into English prose, well, the whole effect would be lost, wouldn't it?

Used to get on his nerves, he said. Honestly! There were times that he used to act just like a petulant little boy. But he could be clever, too. He had a very fine mind, far older than his years. What was it he told me, once? Wait now! That I… what was it, damn it! That I was trying to construct, no, that I tried to erect a false notion of a past so that I could be nostalgic for it. Oh, something like that, at any rate. God, this memory of mine! Head like a sieve.

For a rough diamond, he was immensely clever with words, my Bluebottle. Always reading, you see. Perpetually curled around one book or another, absorbed in his own world, just like Trajan used to curl up around his tail. Over there, by the urn. Trajan! Caligula, dear God.

Do you know what I was playing, on the night he left me? Providence again, you see. I often think about it. I have a 1932 Mozart, 'Don Giovanni', the complete set. '*Vorrei e non vorrei*', ha ha! It could have been penned for the passion that I felt for him. The contradictory emotion that the mere thought of him aroused in me, and that made me wretched. It was hopeless of course. He would always be entirely indifferent to the passion that had me in thrall to him. What is it Wilde says? 'The comedy of life is that our soul is born old and gets younger; its tragedy is that the body does the opposite.' What was I to him but a pathetic, ageing figure, and one with monstrous appetites? He neither saw, nor wanted to see, that this was something beautiful. Something sublime. And that I was absolutely wretched because of him.

You know what it did? It brought out the bitch in my nature. It was something I simply could not control. Every day, we'd row. Every blessed day. It had me close to tears, more miserable than you can possibly imagine. It was intolerable. So strong was the feeling that I'd begun to feel for Bluebottle, for the merest memory of Bluebottle, that it was like a tide whose dangerous undertow drags you out past your depth to where you must struggle simply to stay afloat. This surge was strongest when we had recently parted or when, like a Peeping Tom, I could watch him unobserved. But no sooner would I try to speak to him, or he to me, than the bitch would wake up in me and begin to growl and I'd find something to find fault with. Some bone to fight over. It was pure perversity of course. Or defensiveness. I daresay that this constant needling that went on between us was a vain attempt to draw a cover over my absolute, my naked misery. But he remained indifferent. Perversely, criminally indifferent. It was a situation that could not go on but that, for the life of me, I could not disentangle myself from. Life without Bluebottle could quite simply have neither colour nor meaning for me.

I can state it more plainly still. He was life itself, no more and no less.

We moved inexorably, but inexorably, towards disaster, just as the tectonic plate is impelled towards the fault upon which it must fracture. I could sense it coming, and every day I was more miserable. And every day he was more contemptuous.

It was as if I were utterly helpless. Every day, every morning, I'd needle him. I'd begin at dawn with the resolution that this time it would be different. But I was a wreck, you know. Physically, I mean, not just emotionally. It had been weeks since I'd slept. It always has such an effect on my mood when I haven't slept. When one can't sleep one looks, you know, so much older, so much more ravaged. And of course I'd been drinking more heavily of late, and you must be aware of the effect that that has on one's appearance. On one's morale.

But each day I'd begin with the resolution that this time it would be different. I'd always be showered, newly shaved, just a merest hint of cologne. I'd be composed, studying the paper or, if it had arrived, the post. There would be fresh coffee on the hob. His place would be already set for him, with a freshly cut grapefruit, a French baguette or croissant still hot from the bakers. I knew that there was nothing he liked better than to drip honey over a fresh crust.

But every day he chose to get up later. Don't think this was laziness, oh no! You see he'd be awake, almost from the time that I'd left my room. I'd always put my ear to his door, and sometimes I'd hear him, moving over the floor or turning over in the bed. On occasion he would even be humming to himself. No, if he got up later every day, it was purely in order to rile me. He knew that I'd made an extra effort to obtain fresh bread, to have the coffee freshly brewed for him, and so he'd wait upstairs until it had begun to spoil.

When his lordship did deign to rise – it was increasingly closer to twelve than to nine – then he would stroll leisurely up to the table, resolutely ignoring me. Never, never once, would he say good morning first. Now that was all very well, that behaviour I could forgive, but there are two things that I'd taken him to task over, again and again. One was drinking milk out of the carton. If there is one thing that I cannot abide, it's when people flout table manners. It's a form of carelessness that I find offensive in the extreme. But with Bluebottle it was never carelessness. Oh no! It was open effrontery. He did it simply because he knew how it would upset me. Upset my equilibrium. And the second thing he would do would be to pick the baguette from the table and walk all about the house, dropping crumbs over the tiles and into the carpet. Really, it was too much.

I knew we were heading for a crisis. I knew it couldn't go on. Whenever he was around me, he did his level best to be offensive, and to upset me. It seemed to make not the blindest bit of difference to him whether I was being nice to him, all forgiving and complaisant, or whether the bitch in me would snap at his heels. He remained divinely indifferent to my moods, acting for the most part as if I wasn't there. But the moment we were apart, and every day there came the moment that I left the house, I knew in advance that I would be even more utterly miserable away from him. I was obsessed with him you see. And so I was wretched when I was with him, and wretched when I was apart from him. '*Vorrei e non vorrei*', you see? Ha ha!

But the precise form that the inevitable crisis took I could not have anticipated. Every day, I was terrified by the thought that upon my return I would find the house empty. From the moment I turned the corner into our cul-de-sac, my stomach would sink as low as my shoes and my heart would flutter about in the desolate certainty that this time, he had flown. And so, every evening, when I'd turn the key and hear the music playing out too loud from the stereo, always some vulgar pop station, and every evening when he'd greet my enquiries with a grunt or a choice phrase that a corner-boy might use, I'd almost weep with relief. Of course I couldn't show any of this to Blucbottle. To have shown him this weakness would have been simply to pour petrol on his scorn. Worse still, and this thought terrified me, it might suggest to him that the cruellest way he could punish me would simply be to one day vanish.

I'd made up my mind to be jocular, to treat his provocations as if I was a party to them. After all, it's in the nature of every adolescent to act petulant. A matter of hormones you see. The mistake I made was to continually rise to the bait. But then, as I shooed flies away from the bread with a tea-towel, and as I watched the coffee pot slowly begin to stew on the hob, I could already feel the bitch begin to stir inside me.

A quarter of an hour went by. Another. At half past eleven I called up the stairs, still calm, still trying to temper my reproaches with a frivolous melody. But no, he would not answer. I heard the creak of floorboards as he made his way from desk back to bed, but not a solitary word. There was no point in attempting to bring up a tray with breakfast on it; he always kept his door locked. It was a condition he had laid down very early on that he would only stay if he had a door that could be locked from the inside.

Finally, at a quarter past twelve, he mooned down the stairs and into the living room. I'm not hungry, he all but spat, not even deigning to glance in my direction.

You left all of the downstairs lights on last night, you know, I remarked over my shoulder, after he had passed. I was still struggling to remain composed. It was something that we'd rowed about many times, he simply would not learn to turn the lights out when he was finished in a room.

Probably I shouldn't have said anything. Perhaps, if I'd left the house, then, without having said anything…

There was no answer, you see. I moved to where I could see him. He was slouched across an armchair, his feet up against one of the bookshelves. Just like a spoiled adolescent. I said, you left every downstairs light on when you went to bed last night. Why don't you change the record, he intoned. He was picking at his nails, a habit I despise. I knew that if I stayed looking at him a moment longer, I'd say something cutting.

I began to clear away the breakfast things. I clattered and banged, I wanted him to be aware that I was upset with him. Besides, I genuinely was angry, so much so that my hands were trembling. Then he appeared in the doorway.

Hey, you're not my mother, you know?

And that's the moment when the bitch in me slipped her leash. Before I could restrain her, she had done the damage. Yes, I said, well maybe if you'd had a mother you'd have better manners now. I was horrified by what I heard myself say. I reached out my hands towards him, my eyes wide, already damp, but before I could apologise, he laughed. It was an ugly laugh. A dark, ugly, perverse laugh. If he'd answered me like a corner-boy, if he'd struck me, if he'd used a vulgar expression… but that laugh, and his eyes so cold! It set shivers up and down my spine. It distorted every feature in his face.

Then, when the laugh had finished, *if I'd a fucking mother like yours, Jesus*! Just like that. Emotionless, pronouncing every syllable.

Dear God, that day was a living hell for me. Will I ever forget it? A living hell. Of course, I shouldn't have said that about his not having a mother, but he knew perfectly well that the subject of Mother was out of bounds. Even then, if it had at least been in the height of an emotion… but no, he'd said it, slowly, cruelly, to calculated effect.

I left at once. I slammed the door with such force that the chimes fell down. I've never had the heart to put them back up. Of course, once I was away from the house, once I'd calmed down, my own sin became magnified in my eyes a hundred fold.

Thank God that Gwen was back in the country. She'd been away. France. But I knew she'd been back for two days.

I was so agitated that even after I got there it took me a good hour to calm down. Gwen could see immediately that something had happened. Normally, she's quite merciless you know. If you eat green fruit, she used to say, there's no use complaining when you get stomach cramp. But today she was disposed to be understanding. She was working on a piece in her back garden that was, as she put it, *proceeding*. Perhaps that's what made her less dismissive of the agonies of my illicit passion. Without actually condoning anything, I could tell she understood there was something special about Bluebottle. Finally, she convinced me that I was making a mountain out of a molehill. She convinced me, too, that he would still be there when I returned, and the whole business forgotten. I finally did return at about six o'clock, tender, on absolute tenterhooks, but with a mind to forgive everything.

He was reading, humming to himself as blithely as if nothing had happened. He was lying on the floor, eating crackers, and with crumbs all about him. He made a sort of grunt when I came in, but I had decided to forgive everything, and I stuck to my resolution. Instead of a reproach, I cooked up a chicken chasseur, it's a dish I know he is particularly fond of, and I'd even brought home a couple of bottles of *Faustino VII*. Affects to prefer Spanish to Burgundy. Silly boy.

At table he was animated. I should have picked up the warning signals. But the truth is, I was so happy we were simply not fighting that I misinterpreted the brightness in his eye, the agitation in his movements. He began talking twenty to the dozen about some book or other he was reading. He asked me again and again what I knew about Lou Andreas-Salomé, you know, Nietzsche's mistress? He said something about Rodin, and I told him that he should talk to Gwen about Rodin. I daresay I had a rather self-serving agenda here, because I desired above all that my two dearest companions should at least get on. For once, he didn't redden when I mentioned Gwen.

He has the most amazing appetite for knowledge you know. A hunger to learn, and always at the rate of twenty to the dozen. Entirely endearing, when he has a mind to be.

I opened a third bottle of wine. I wasn't drunk, but the whole evening was going so splendidly I daresay it went to my head. When supper was ended, ha ha! When supper was ended, I took out Mozart's 'Don Giovanni', the 1932 set. I'd located a book about Rodin's studios, and Bluebottle was leafing through the plates. But what I didn't take in, what perhaps I refused to take in, was the brightness in the eye, the tension about the face. About the mouth.

And the pallor!

Know what was playing when the white rage descended on him? Can you guess? '*A cenar teco m'invitasti*'. A cenar teco m'invitasti! It was the first thing that I remarked upon to Gwen, when finally my jaw had loosened up sufficiently to let me speak. The sinister stranger that arrives. And, oh God, that scream when Don Giovanni is dragged downwards to hell.

As I lay in intensive care and then in traction over the weeks that followed, I came to understand, you see. The hour of reckoning. The Faustian pact. But do you know what else? Every blessed bruise on my body, every discolouration, every dislocation and every fracture was infinitely preferable to me than if I had arrived home on that evening to find that Bluebottle had abandoned me.

It was a form of intimacy you see. Perhaps the only form of intimacy of which the lad was capable. After all, he'd injured his own body so many times, in that rage that makes him pound brick walls.

Of course he left. I knew he would. But somehow the pain of it was numbed by the physical pain. Does that make any sense to you?

And Gwen was marvellous. Truly marvellous. She handled the police as though it were second nature to her. That's a woman for you. She gave out that it had been a break in. Had me play the amnesiac, ha ha! Can you imagine it? I began to recall, eventually, that it had been a gang of at least three, all wearing balaclavas.

I'd lost over two pints of blood, you know, and eleven fractures. Eleven! It was the mercy of God that that prying spinster, Ms Ramsey, was still recovering from her stroke, staying with some relatives down in Greystones of all places. Who knows how difficult a busybody like that might have made things.

I saw him once more you know. I mean before the… before they...

It was on Grafton Street. Sinuous Grafton, Gwen calls it. Curved like a saxophone! I could sense his presence, even before I pivoted around. Eyes of metal and agate. Pale, brazen fire. I was still trussed up, bandages, plaster of Paris, closer to death than to life if the truth be known.

And then those insolent, magnificent, mocking eyes, like Divine retribution.

III | Fergal

I drag the pillow low over my ears, a buffer, a brood hen. But the knock-*fuckedy*-knock doesn't stop for more than a half-minute. Christ!

Rat-at-at, insistent as bad news. It's the third interruption into the bedroom. The third eruption.

I could ignore it. But… just *suppose* Mahood's men have found out where I hole up?

Not at all! Go back to sleep, Mr Bateman.

Rat-at-at.

Surely not the guards?

Surely not the guards.

Rat!

Fuck! As delicately as is at all possible, I attempt to raise my corpse to the vertical. As someone wrote once, there's a pail of distilled pain teetering inside its skull, and the slightest wrong move will swill it over the lip. Rat-at-at.

Rat-at-at-at, driving once again in under the temples. The meniscus of pain shudders with each syllabic (well put, that!). Eyelids pressed tight, a blind man, mouth a dried sewer-bed, nerves ragged and stomach uncertain, the corpse levitates. I edge it over to the net curtain. Gingerly, I inch the hem to one side.

Cue bassoon music.

He is standing in wan sunlight, backed away from the door and out onto the flags of the pavement. He is measuring the door's reticence. Creased suit and fedora, the punch-line of an off-colour joke.

Uncle Mal.

Once he's safely ensconced in the inner sanctum, *viz.* kitchenette, and the jug-kettle is rattling towards its premature boil, he assumes his perennial mask. The grand tragedian. A vaudeville expression, all the weight of the world's suffering behind his bloodhound eyes. A squabble with one of his comic-opera lovers, I've little doubt, squats behind it. I never see Uncle at other times. But that he's quite capable of sitting for an hour in this tragic pose, sighing, fondling the bridge of his nose, making a show of making small talk without a single word pertaining to the main plot, of that I'm only too aware. Today, I'm not in the mood.

Uncle? Ha! He was the only friend, the only *male* friend, of my father's. The late, lamented Manus Bates. During my tender years I'd been farmed out to Uncle, who'd been entrusted to look after my moral upbringing while daddy was otherwise preoccupied. What larks!

All the while as the water gurgles he casts loud sighs across the kitchen table, an angler casting line and hook. I am indifferent, a cold fish. But when the kettle clicks off just short of the boil I suddenly want to be shot of him, and at liberty to wallow alone in my hangover.

'What is it this time, Uncle? The Vice Squad found you out?'

'Fergal! Fergal!' His face blossoms open into *how-could-you-possibly?* 'Dear me, no!'

For a second I'm almost amused. Almost. A bare flicker of amusement. But I move my head carelessly and the pail teeters and slips so that a drench of pain slops over its sides. I'm forced to shut my eyes until it has run out off the bare floorboards.

'Tea?'

'I don't suppose you have Earl Grey?'

Uncle. Uncle Mal. Like the bad penny that only crops up once you've forgotten about its existence. Malacoda. *Qui mal y pense.*

When my father passed on and his stern pettifogger wrote me that I'd come into this flat – I expect it must have been his little love nest, a city refuge where he'd entertain his mistresses – I actually believed that Fate…

no. No. What I believed was that at last, perhaps, he had forgiven me, my father. From beyond the grave. I wouldn't have put that gesture past him, the old hypocrite.

Nelson Street. I'm sure there's an irony in that, if you can be moved to look for it. Life delights in ironies. At least, the life of Fergal Bates, Esq. appears to.

Naturally I jacked in my job on the very day the inheritance came through. Tuppenny journalism, if you could call that a job. My dear daddy certainly never did. Three days a week pinning down the editor of some regional to take on an article that wasn't of the least interest to either one of us. Tabloids pushed through the letterboxes of the indifferent middle-classes. At one time I tried to kid myself that I was 'building up a portfolio'. More latterly, that it was all 'raw material'; 'slices of life'. I'd picked up those particular euphemisms from one or another night course, once I'd dropped out of a perfectly respectable Law degree. Trinity College, no less. Father, forgive thy son, for he knows not what he does.

Mal was sitting across the table from me, sighing like the aggrieved mother in a Boucicault melodrama.

'Out with it man. What's his name this time?'

'Oh Fergal! If you saw what they've done to him!'

'Done to whom? Is it to Spider?'

Spider was a sullen, downy-lipped teenager with black dreadlocks. Half-cast, on balance of probabilities. At one time he'd tried to blackmail Uncle. He was his first great, illicit love, by all accounts. He'd long since disappeared, but I could imagine the sort of people that Spider might have fallen in with. That might indeed have done anything to him. Nigerians. Russians. Or would they be Bosnians? You mess around with that sort of folk, you end up navigating the canal from the inside of a suitcase.

'Spider!' A gesture of high drama. A wave of the hand. Not Spider, then.

'Uncle. You're being obtuse.'

He sobbed. I think he sobbed.

Let's agree he sobbed.

I decided to make tea. Earl Grey it wasn't. The bags dribbled a tepid red fluid not unlike terracotta into the not-quite-boiled water. In the absence of milk, the liquid would leave a slick on the mugs' inner porcelain (fine image, that). I tossed the bags into the corner of the sink, where they collapsed like a pair of punctured lungs. Kitchen sink drama. The headache was getting no worse in any event.

'My boy! My dear boy! What have they done?'

Uncle was filling up the whole tawdry stage with his aside, his tragic apostrophe, cradling the mug as though it were the only source of warmth on a dying planet.

'But which boy? Which one is it?'

'Oh Fergal, how can you have forgotten already! I told you everything about him.'

'But which? You see, I lose track…'

'Last summer. I christened him. I called him… oh God!'

'Yes? You called him what?'

He sipped at the tea, winced. 'I called him Bluebottle.'

Somewhere in the murk and sediment a bauble briefly glistered. A memory. A half memory.

'Last summer?'

'Last summer.'

'Then he was the one…?' I shifted in my seat. My one open eye trawled the orange film ebbing away from the interior of my mug, combing it for the *mot juste*. It refused to surface.

'Wasn't he the psychopath? Uncle? Wasn't he the young gentleman who put you into intensive care?'

All the martyrdom and religious masochism of this trifling world was contained in the magnificent cliché that defined Uncle Mal's gaze at that moment. Cut to close-up on face. He speaks not. Any mere word would be *de trop*.

•••

An hour later, or was it three, we had repaired to one of those dives named after one or another O'Casey character that populate the north inner city. A dim, musty, carpeted, foul-smelling den with badly stuffed upholstery and an inextinguishable racing channel over the toilet door. Here it bothered me not a whit to be seen in the company of so ludicrous a figure as Uncle. That he was ostentatiously queer, and with appetites which transgressed upon the criminal, was, here, neither here nor there. There was, too, the small matter of Mahood's crowd and their bottomless hunger for repayments, two inconveniences to be avoided at all costs. Here, I was hardly likely to be spotted. And the fact was, today Uncle had hard cash. Besides, in a curious way, his tawdry tale was beginning to interest me. Who knows? It might even do for 'raw material'; a 'slice of life' for one of Bateman's great film-scripts.

I was by this time beginning to become tolerably acquainted with the bones of his present lust. I was, in proportion, being slowly resuscitated by double shots of whiskey, and could feel red blood slowly tincturing my cheeks. Despite the evidence of the kilos, ever since a boy I've been prone to anaemia. My hangover was by now little more than an occasional belch; a sensation of dryness behind the eyes.

'You know I've been away,' he continued.

Now that he said it, there was a sort of ruddy brown flush over his skin that was inconsistent with our present climate.

'Antibes.' He tapped his nose, as though Antibes might have been the latest STD.

'Where's that? The Caribbean?'

'Oh my dear boy! Cannes. The Côte d'Azur.'

'You don't know anyone French!'

'Gwendolyn! Gwendolyn! You've met her, of course. Gwen has a part-share in an apartment in Antibes.'

Gwendolyn something-or-other-foreign, I forget. An ancient piece of stone and dust. In point of fact, a sculptress, gin and horses, the real D4. Uncle several times introduced me to the crone. But we never hit it off, if that's the expression.

You have to give him credit, though. Uncle always had a real nose for the quality. Cannes, no less.

'I needed to get away. A change of scenery. A change, how can I put it, a change of ecosystem.'

'Ecosystem?' I knew well that I was walking onto prepared ground. But I was beginning to feel altogether better. Reanimated. Hair of the dog, and now a whiff of carrion.

'You've no idea how claustrophobic the society of Sandymount can be. Prying eyes! Prying eyes! Everywhere I looked, there was a sort of malicious glee at my broken body. My discoloured face. My crutch. Fergal Bates, you can have no idea! Not until you've lived there, in one of their cul-de-sacs, treacherous as any lobster pot. Lived among them as an outsider, I mean.'

Here it comes, I thought. One who has dared to be different.

'One who has dared to be different! Oh, the snubs I've put up with. The daily slights. You grow used to them, you know. Over the years.'

We'd had tragic Mal. Now we were to have long-suffering Mal. But I knew him of old, and wondered what five of trumps he was holding back, judging the precise deal to play it on. The game and the whiskey were beginning to beguile.

Have I mentioned that Uncle can drink? Boy, can he put them away!

'But Fergal, this time it was different. I was broken, you see. A broken man. A broken, clockwork clown. The mainspring, quite gone! I don't mean in the body. My dear boy, one is broken in the body, and in time, the body repairs its wounds. Its transgressions. But the soul! The soul!'

This Bluebottle character, doesn't it make a blind bit of difference to you that he came within a trice of killing you? I held my tongue. He would have anticipated the play. It was too obvious.

'Do you know, it positively did me good to be away? Gwen couldn't stay much more than a fortnight, but she introduced me to a set who were, how shall I say? That saw fit not to judge.'

'That was your new ecosystem?'

'That. And the sun. And the glamour. The French, you see? I grant you that Gwen's circle are almost entirely ex-pat, but something of the French has rubbed off on them. A sense of acceptance. A sense of, how shall I say… *élan*.'

Elegance and debauchery, I thought. A circle of ageing lechers sipping claret by a swimming-pool. Ecosystem my Jap's eye! A change of lobster-pot was the extent of his achievement. Mal, old man, you should have been a pair of ragged claws, scuttling across the floors etc., etc.

'How long did you stay, old man?'

'How long? Three months. Four. Long enough to begin… to begin to put the pieces of my life back into some semblance of order.'

'Come on, Mal. You don't strike me as much of a Humpty Dumpty figure.'

He inhaled, half closing his eyes. He would forgive this.

'I was perfectly resigned to the fact that I'd never see him again, you see. Never again. It would be a quiet existence. A postscript. A coda, nothing more. It would be enough for me to know… to know that…'

He lumbered up from the couch, all but upset the table. He shuffled out across the floor. He made directly for the men's room, his head at all times angled away from me. A pair of ragged claws.

While he was away I examined the hat, picking it up, turning it, placing it on my crown. It slipped down easily so that my eyes were half in shade. I toyed with the idea of making my escape, but I knew the flat would be cold and accusing, and I'd scarcely the price of a pint to my name.

Suddenly he was standing before me. I angled the hat back and touched its brim, as though I was an extra in a Western. Gunfight in a Ringsend saloon.

'Last week he came back.'

'Who?'

'Bluebottle! Bluebottle!'

This was a surprise. So too was the genuine distress in his eye. I sat up, and might even have offered to buy the next round if it had been within my means.

'He came back? Where?'

He ignored the question. *Infra dignitatem.*

'Oh God, when I saw what they'd done to him!'

Uncle had evidently decided that the coming monologue should be delivered from a standing pose. He inhaled. There was something wonderfully ludicrous in the tableau, something of the carnival, an old queen in a crumpled beige jacket preparing to deliver a maudlin speech in an inner city dive to an audience of one with whiskey tumbler empty and oversized fedora angled back on the scalp.

'Do you know,' he began, addressing the question some three feet above the crown of the hat, 'from the moment I heard the bell-pull, I had the feeling that it was he? If the truth be known, I'd had a foreboding. All week, a foreboding. A general unease. I'd achieved a sort of an equilibrium you see. Over the previous months. Oh God, it was hard won, a form of denial, but there it is. I was no longer in thrall to a tempest. But something was abroad that told me that this hard won equilibrium was about to come crashing down. That he was, how to put it, that he was in the vicinity. Some quality in the air, an electric charge. A darkening hue. Do you know, the kind of imperceptible change that tells you when a storm is about to break?'

This was a rhetorical question. In fact, the weather had been unseasonably mild. I was gazing at the thick, distorting glass at the bottom of my tumbler, my tongue thick for the want of another drink, while Uncle's thespian gaze remained fixed on the wallpaper some three inches above the hat.

'And then the trill of the bell-pull upset that equilibrium. I felt my heart skip a beat. My stomach, tense up. I made on tippy-toe for the door and watched the dark figure stretch and distort under the glass as though under water. I couldn't have been more nervous if I were a teenage virgin on the night of her debs dance.'

Mal, a teenage virgin? Please!

'He had a hood pulled up over his head, as though he were a corner-boy. I saw this in my mind's eye just at the very moment that I undid the chain. You know how careful I've been since the… I was about to say since the break-in! Ha ha! But I saw him in my mind's eye you see, and that image, that vision, was precisely how he now stood on the threshold of my door. Taller, perhaps thinner, undoubtedly thinner, a hood pulled up over his head in the manner of a monk's cowl and his face angled away from me.'

'Angled away from me,' he repeated. 'Just like this.'

He held the pose. Turning the other cheek. I could see the barman was watching us out of the horn-rimmed corner of his spectacles. He was going through one of those indefatigable barman's routines, I disremember which one. Pushing a rag in circles over the Formica, at a guess. There were only two other customers in the entire bar, both down at the heel, extras out of the Thrupenny Opera.

'Oh God, when I saw what they had done to his face!'

After a minute, he sat. What is the sound of two hands clapping? But I'm being unfair. He was hamming it up. But the distress, the despair, the fright, these were genuine enough. I went out to relieve a twitching bladder, and to postpone the moment when my voice would intrude its dry sardonic.

I must have taken my eye off the ball, because some time later, some hours or rounds or perhaps even bars later, Uncle played the trump that he'd been so carefully concealing. By this time I'd had the whole lurid story.

Cupiditas pecuniae radix malorum. The want of lucre. My own want was acute. Temporarily, I could see no other way of getting through with legs unbroken until the following Thursday's rendezvous at the Post Office.

I imagine I should feel more grateful I've no actual rent to pay. I have daddy Bates to thank for that small mercy. Incidentally, I've often wondered what Freudians would make of it, the son sleeping between the sheets where the father made erstwhile love to his clutch of mistresses.

I looked at him, at Uncle, and rallied once more to the ramparts the ragged mercenaries of my resistance.

'No, Mal. It's out of the question.'

'But it would only be for a few weeks. A matter of his finding his feet.'

'I said no.'

'But I, *we*, have no-one else to turn to.'

'No Uncle. No. No! The place is too small for myself for God's sake.'

'I promise you. On my solemn oath. He'll only be there at night. He won't interfere with your writing.'

My writing! We maintain the myth that F.D. Bateman writes film-scripts, Uncle and I (Idea for a film-script: A precocious child takes pornographic images of himself. Some years later, to put himself through college, he flogs them. Interesting point for debate: whom, precisely, is he exploiting?).

'It's simply not practicable. In any case, there's only the one bed.'

'But *I* have stayed on the sofa, Fergal.' This was almost true. Briefly, in the days of Spider, a very nervous Uncle Malcolm had holed up in the flat while at every newsflash he expected to hear how thugs from the Vice Squad were ransacking his Sandymount house. In point of fact it had been I who'd tossed about under a blanket on the sofa while the bedsprings groaned under Uncle's bulk.

'I can stretch it to a hundred,' he sighed, doubling his ante. 'Thirty, right here and now.'

'Fifty now,' I squinted. I swear I could hear the piano playing barrelhouse as the camera zoomed in on my calculating eyes.

'Thirty is all that I have.'

'Really?'

'I swear to you,' he swore. 'You'll get the balance on Monday.'

'But a hundred a week, I have your word on that? I'll throw him out the second you renege, you old bastard. Oh, and in cash, none of your damn cheques either.'

Can we speak of money in iambics? I could already count the mercenaries who were deserting my ramparts. Turning coat.

'You'd be doing me a very great favour,' he winked. Uncle was not nearly so drunk as I was.

'And it's only for a very small number of days, I have your word on that too?'

'Fergal, I swear it.'

• • •

I banged about in the kitchenette the next day, putting some sort of an order on things. My humour was variable, but eased by the fact that my surrender was now irrevocable. The thirty quid he'd slipped me was already well spent. Stubborn witnesses to Uncle's visit, a pair of teabags had welded to the corner of the sink. They left angles of rusted tannin when I prised them away.

He'd spoken of premonitions. One rust mark was an exact prelude to the angular scar they'd carved into the boy Bluebottle's cheek. With twin blades of a Stanley-knife, apparently. What he called, with the poetry of the streets, his Judas kiss.

I grew increasingly nervous as that first evening dragged on and still he failed to show. I suppose I'd grown used to solitude. You live in the confinement of your indolence, and days slip by, hidden like good intentions from the scrutiny of welling distaste. By God, perhaps F.D. Bateman should be a writer of novels!

The longer he didn't show, the more fidgety I became. At one level the whole business was as laughable as a farce. The penniless son of the late Manus Bates, finally sunk to this pass, that he agrees to take in an adolescent rent-boy as a favour for the erstwhile friend of his erstwhile father. As he awaits the arrival of the boy he is as nervous as, how had Uncle put it? Nervous as a teenage virgin on the eve of her debs dance. Laughable. Pitiable. Pathetic.

On the next day, a Sunday as it so happened, I left the flat almost immediately upon waking. I could no longer face its sardonic silences. But in any event it was a fine day, and on fine days nothing pleases F.D. Bateman better than to pace out the thousand acres of his meagre kingdom. The Pale of the Dublin tenements.

I was still agitated, too agitated to sit for long on my customary bench in the City Basin. In any case, there was a Romany gipsy with glistering teeth of doubtful gold, and a cloth bundle, a doubtful child, who had taken to pestering me for my still-more doubtful money, and who would not be bought off with a handful of meagre coppers. Her curses in pursuit, I made my way through the maze of dwarves' houses behind the Basin and pushed on down past the Black Church, counter-clockwise from an old superstition. Dominick Street. Bolton Street. I wandered next up the hill of Henrietta Street with its gaunt, spectral houses, as some hack once wrote. But passing through the arch of the King's Inns, I caught a glimpse of one of Mahood's men.

Now, this specimen was a low-life by the name of Anto, one of the most feared predators of my ecosystem. I turned abruptly back towards the river. I had no wish to have my legs broken. Mahood: usurer, loan-shark, peddler of violence and hard pornography, top-feeder apparent, I have never seen in person. Indeed, I have a suspicion he might not exist. But his heavies both exist and persist. So, too, my obscene indebtedness.

It was not lost on me, on my Dublin odyssey, that I was harbouring a dread at the idea of returning to the flat. Scared to go home. Bates, you pitiable bastard! The fact is, from the moment I'd accepted Uncle's lucre, from the moment I'd stuffed the grubby red notes into my pocket and groaned that yes I *supposed* the boy could stay, it was as if the objects of the house had turned inquisitor. The books were observing me; the speakers, whispering about me. The naked light bulb was the eye of a resentful muse. And the laptop under the window was ready to accuse me from inside its silent coffin.

I found myself abruptly at the foot of Parnell Square, directly opposite the Gate Theatre, peering into a dusty laneway I hadn't before this noticed. It might have been a cul-de-sac, or a set of warehouse entrances. Rutland Place, declared a blue sign. Rutland, bedad! I'm constantly delighted by these anachronisms. This strumpet city abounds in oddities of history that cry out for a camera. I once even stumbled into a Britain Place, imagine that! In his splendid new docudrama, F.D. Bateman zooms in on the royal insignia lurking under every green-glossed post-box: VR, ER, GR. Dynastic graffiti! Vestiges, claims inscribed into the organism of the city.

'Post-colonial', he calls it, with that characteristic wit as dry as the Cork Dry Gin he elegantly swills…

Cut to the street. Cue bassoon music.

'So this is where you've got to!'

It was Uncle. He was advancing avuncularly, dust-coated, soft-hatted, walking-caned, from the direction of the Rotunda hospital. A lanky figure in a hooded coat hesitated some several steps behind him. 'We called around to your flat this morning but of course you'd already gone out! Turned into the early bird and flown the nest, ha ha! You never cease to surprise, you know.'

He was animated, bluff, beaming, but I could tell immediately it was all pretence. He was excruciatingly ill at ease. The figure in the parka remained at twenty paces, face in shadow. There was a small sports-bag at his feet. I noticed that Uncle's eyes flicked periodically towards him as he strained to sustain the banter.

'Did I tell you? Elisa has been put into hospital. The sister-in-law, Godfrey's wife? Some young thug tried to snatch her handbag, and like the bloody virago she is she put up a fight. Can you imagine? She got one hell of a shiner for her troubles. Swollen up the size of an egg!'

He leaned forward and touched my forearm, the humorous conspirator, but his eye remained tethered in the direction of the other.

'Be one hell of a brave man would risk giving Elisa a belt in the eye!'

I nodded towards the Rotunda. 'You were in for a visit?'

'Good God, no. Cork! My dear boy, I could never permit my in-laws to reside in the capital.'

Who exactly Uncle believes he's trying to impersonate I've never quite fathomed. MacLiammór, up to his Hilton Edwards. Ha ha! But I'd never seen the act come across quite so forced as it now was. The presence of that boy had him terrified.

I began to realise, with fond malice, that Mal was hopelessly, but hopelessly, in love.

I've never got to know the boy's real name. He insists it can have no importance. I've no parents, he says.

Bluebottle, then.

Zoom in to scar. The famous scar, translucent, lurid, eloquent. It's a semaphore of his humour, angry red, or livid as a squid. I learned in time that the white display is more to be feared. It has the rough form of the letter C, with just a hint of G. This harsh guttural depresses his smile, on the rare occasion he attempts a smile. It may or may not contribute to the endearing impediment in his speech. What it undoubtedly does is it causes his head to list so as to angle that cheek away from whoever is addressing him. He himself isn't greatly given to words. You might even think at such times that he's being coy.

He made no great fuss about making his bed on the sofa. He had scarcely a possession to his name, that single sports-bag with a few changes of clothes; a tin whistle which I never heard him play; an odd item of rather choice Italian toiletry. I detected Uncle's trembling hand behind the latter selection.

He looked far older than his years. Undernourished, of course. Thin as a rake. But still he would have passed for eighteen, twenty at a pinch. Very different from the run of prepubescent ephebes that habitually set Uncle Mal salivating. I have on occasion considered it would be a civic duty, a credit to me in fact, to put that pederast behind bars. But we all have our weaknesses. Everyone his speciality, as someone said. *Book of Fergal, chapter two, verse four.*

Once you got past the scar, the striking feature was the eyes. *Were* the eyes? Luminous, even with the brow in shadow. I would've thought twice about leaving a girlfriend alone in his company, if I'd had one to bring back to the flat. Besides, you can never tell how a girl will glamorise a scar.

We'd little to say to one another after Uncle Mal had left us alone. After I'd shown him the door. Mal had been fussing around the flat like a mother hen from the moment we got back there. I pretended to get annoyed with him. Bluebottle watched me chase his benefactor off the premises with perfect equanimity.

The point is, I'd no intention of making this newcomer feel that his stay would be anything more than a temporary arrangement. To begin with, at least. We were both momentarily in a fix, that was the extent of our common ground. But I wanted him to be aware that everything about the flat had become estranged, even hostile, from the moment I'd taken Uncle's thirty quid. But it was an inconvenience! An intrusion! At this rate I'd never begin to finalise my film script, ha ha! Bates, you're hilarious!

He should sense all this, for I was in no humour to explain. It was implicit in the coagulating bowl of soup that cooled on the table well before he finished a shower. It was implicit in my early departure to my room.

I had no wish to apologise for my life. I mean, of course, to myself. There was in addition the very real fear that the longer this adolescent moped about the place, the more likely it was that I'd have to deal with the fallout from middle-aged, lovesick, ludicrous Mal. Even now I sensed that he was hovering no more than a street away.

Two days later, money again. *Plus ça change*… I found myself dragging the reluctant soles of my boots across the thin gravel of Martello Mews. He had not made good on his promise to pay the balance.

A caricature opened the door to me, a parody in dressing-gown or smoking-jacket, the hair unkempt and eyes red-rimmed with insomnia. His face looked even more debauched and pitiful than in the fairground hall of mirrors custom has us call memory.

'You know what I'm here for, you old bastard.'

'Come in! Come in!'

The house was dim, and silent as a grotto. Unheated. Perhaps he could no longer afford the diesel to heat it. I'd forgotten about the infestation of cats, and vague feline shadows moved about the sidings as we stepped across the tiles of the back room. The dead air was asthmatic with cat-smell.

'Tea?'

'I don't suppose you've Earl Grey?'

'You're mocking me. It's unkind of you to mock me.'

The scarlet tail of his dressing-gown-cum-smoking-jacket billowed out behind him as he disappeared into the scullery, a cat following fervently after him.

'Perhaps you'd care for something a little stronger?'

'Perhaps I would, then.'

'Whiskey?'

'Whiskey would be adequate.'

He returned with two Waterford crystal tumblers of undiluted volatile amber. I noticed that the glass he retained was filled beyond the halfway mark. He sat on a divan so close that our knees all but touched.

'Well, Uncle. Bottoms up!' I had a whim to be jocose.

'How is… ,' he sipped at the drink, lowered his eyes, tongue-flicked his chapped lips. 'How is our guest behaving himself?'

I looked at the bloated face, the pink eyes, the silver hoar of stubble. Two ribs of hair, unoiled, stood up like antennae.

'It's just like you said it would be. I barely see him. He's gone before ever I get up in the morning.'

'Ah!'

A cat, a white snowdrift, had been slinking across the tiles. With a lithe ripple it was on his lap.

'Go on, Cleopatra. Shoo!'

The pard pattered past on silent pads.

'I scarcely see him in the evenings, either.'

'Oh?'

How to describe the chasm that separated this 'oh' from the previous 'ah'? In its feigned casualness lay a depth of anguish impossible to sound.

'No,' I repeated, twisting the knife, 'I scarcely see him at all in the evenings.'

A silence descended like dew through the gloom. I did nothing but watch as the precipitation fell, as relentless as failure. He was staring uneasily, now at the pussies, now at his drink, now toward the ceiling, now at the sleeve of his dressing gown, now at my face, now at the chessboard tiles. He couldn't bring himself to frame the question.

'You promised to bring me the balance by close of business yesterday.'

'I beg your… oh yes, the balance. Sixty, wasn't it?'

'Seventy.'

The mention of any debt would normally have been distasteful to him. Now he seized upon it, leapt up from the divan. Crystal glass still in hand, he made for a writing desk in the hallway, the dressing-gown sustained on the dead air behind him. I saw him set down the glass and run a few fingers through the ivory tusks of hair. He began a routine with several of the drawers and then I saw him pull out a chequebook.

'Cash!' I called after him.

His hands spread to either side of the table for support. He looked like a petty felon who was about to be castigated. 'Fergal, please!' The vowels sounded viscous, as though thickened with phlegm.

'I haven't…,' but then he stopped, considered, and went on excitedly, 'I'll drop the cash around to you! Later. Tonight, in fact!'

He turned to face me. Was it a trick of the dim light, or did I catch a spark of hope in his visage? There was a coven of feline acolytes, Persian, Tabby, ranged about the hem of his dressing gown. It gave him the aspect of a sorcerer in a pantomime.

'Otherwise a cheque will have to do,' he smiled.

'Oh, a cheque will be just fine!'

•••

The ploy was never likely to keep the codger from the door for long. Needless to say, my cruelty had been quite gratuitous. The boy was absent from the flat during the hours of daylight, it is true. I have an idea he begged. Or busked. But once the sun went down he had nowhere else to go. If I saw little of him after it got dark, it was because I'd taken to the habit of retiring early to my room.

On the Wednesday night, *quelle surprise*, there was an intrusive, importunate, inquisitive, imploring rat-at-at-at at the door. As I crossed the front room to answer it I looked at the boy who was lying on the sofa, head propped on forearm. Eyes, inscrutable, looked back at me.

'Why it's Uncle Mal!'

He hovered at the threshold like a gnat at the mouth of a flytrap. Several parcels wrapped in parti-coloured paper were dangling from the crook of his arm like old posters after the carnival has left town. But as he tried, unsuccessfully, to peep around my bulk into the interior, he was entirely at a loss for words.

'Was there something you wanted, Uncle?'

A damp, malignant smile depressed his mouth. 'Is…?'

Two contrary impulses were nudging at me. To one side there hovered a cherub, all harp and soprano-voiced, urging me to put the old roué out of his torment. On the other, a pitch-forking devil, who longed to sink the prongs of incertitude deeper into Uncle's anxiety. A subtle beast, he whispered into the portal of mine ear how, if I was not on my guard, the flat might presently be turned into the stage-set for the final act of a third-rate romantic farce.

Uncle was scrutinising my face to see which familiar would get the better of the argument. At length I half-closed the door, and my words to him were spoken with excessive volume.

'I thought we agreed that you weren't to come around here?'

'I wanted… then he *is* in?'

I shrugged.

'Look. I brought a few things.'

'You're not coming in.'

'But just for a minute,' he pleaded. 'Look, Fergal, I brought some gifts with me. Some provisions. A blanket.'

'Maybe,' I said, 'he's not alone.' This devil was some piece of work! I watched as the green-eyed monster tormented Uncle with its howling.

'Not...?' His mouth was unable to form the next word. I stared at its trout's gape.

'Oh for God's sake!' In a sudden fit I swung open the door and all but hauled the bugger into the room. Was it pity impelled me? Disgust?

Bluebottle had not moved so much as a muscle during this exchange, and when, with palpable relief at finding him unaccompanied, Uncle began to set out his magi's gifts on the floor before him and then to tease out their strings with mutinous fingernails, he looked on as if he did not know the man.

One of these offerings became the occasion for my getting to know something of the lad's past. Indeed, it marked the beginning of our rapprochement. This Trojan gift was a sandalwood crate containing two bottles of Spanish wine.

Naturally, Uncle's cheque had still to clear, but as the tribute he'd brought included a number of delicacies – slices of cured ham, stuffed olives, a jar of pickled herring – I decided to prepare a banquet for two for the following night. We'd been living on meagre fare up until now, although to give my lodger his due, every morning I'd find a stack of coins on the table, the grubby harvest of a his previous day's begging. I admired the lack of commentary which accompanied these offerings. With what was left after a couple of libations, I daily restocked the communal breadbin.

Uncle's capacity to put away the gargle I've already had occasion to admire. Whether from lightness of stomach or lightness of experience, Bluebottle was his opposite. After two glasses of red, his complexion was already suffused with that colour, the scar was a crimson sickle, and the slight lisp that I'd noted above had begun to drag its paws. The combined effect was to shave a couple of years from his mien, and to suggest an ingenuous youth who was hard to square with what I thought I knew about him.

Now, I had not the least appetite to press him for details pertaining to his personal life. Whether, how often, or with whom he made the beast with two backsides I had no wish to know. During the course of an occasional, meandering binge, Uncle had tried to qualify, for my benefit and edification, the desires he feels for young boys. I've never felt anything beyond an intestinal revulsion at the urges he styles Athenian. An aside: I once asked Uncle, *en passant*, if he downloaded images from the net. Child porn, that sort of thing. I daresay I had in mind the possibility of palming off some of the hard-core tapes that I'd found nestling among the latest consignment of Mahood's snuff movies. Mahood, purveyor of fine porn and snuff to the discerning. If I didn't shift the merchandise soon, I'd be even further behind in my repayments.

'Good God! What do you take me for?' Uncle had been genuinely offended.

There was one detail in the present affair that intrigued me, however, and which I felt I would have to approach with caution. What suggestion was it, precisely, which had propelled Bluebottle to set upon the old pervert with his own silver handled walking-stick? That tickled my curiosity.

Whether it was as a result of the rich food or merely the fact of conversation, I was suffused with well-being. I had been increasingly solitary of late, my body weary of its poverty of diet, my mind equally so. Food for thought.

As the evening progressed and the second bottle of wine was uncorked, he began to grow loquacious. This was unexpected. In the several days that he'd been staying in the flat, we'd scarcely exchanged more than a hatful of words that hadn't pertained directly to the mechanics of cohabitation. As I drew the stubborn cork from the bottle, he began to declaim very animatedly about the Wicklow coast. We'd already had one or two lines misquoted from a poet, German I'd hazard, and a brief and scarcely coherent treatise on born-again Christians. But now he was trying to describe some bucolic idyll spent with a vagabond down on the rugged headlands of Wicklow.

The tone had altered. I looked up from the neck of the bottle and saw that his brow was troubled, his scar, pallid. There was a detail that involved a dog. But it was if he couldn't quite recall it. The gaze of a dog. It had persisted in following him. He'd thrown a stone at it. He was staring at me as if I could help, as if I should know how to interpret his story and fill in its lacunae, whereas I could do little more than fill the wineglasses. Each according to his abilities.

Rat-at-at-at. Unmistakable.

'Stay perfectly still,' I told him. I commanded him.

He flushed. For the briefest second I thought he was in pain. But he was choking on a snigger, trying desperately to stifle it.

'Shush,' I warned.

The lights were out in the front room, but if Uncle had pressed his nose to the pane, as I'd stake my life he would, then the glow from the kitchenette would be apparent. I motioned not to allow our shadows to move. I tried to contain all movement and sound with gestures. But the contortion on his peony face made the comedy infectious, and I too had to bite sharply into my lip. The laughter in my abdomen began to give muscular leaps, birth-pangs of jollity, during a minute's silent interrogation. Then: Rat-at, tat-*taaa*-tat? Helpless, I watched Bluebottle's fork touch off the wineglass to complete the phrase. Tink! Tink! Musical. Ludicrously effeminate. We both spluttered into stifled spasms of laughter, clutching the table, agonising to keep them mute.

Rat-aaa, TAT!

Peremptory, this one. The final syllable, abrupt as a magistrate's gavel. It was not so much a demand as a reproach. It punctured all possibility of restraint, and we fell helplessly about the floor. I've never discovered if he overheard our howling before the bassoon notes faded him into the distant night.

Some time later, still weak as children, I suggested a toast. The second bottle of Spanish was now well drained, but I'd dug out the dregs of a cheap sherry heavy with precipitate. 'What should we drink to?' he lisped.

'I don't know. Our girlfriends?'

'I don't have one!'

We began to shriek with laughter again, convulsively. Breathlessly. It was painful. 'Neither do I,' I gasped. And we were once more drowning in hysterics.

At length the spasms subsided.

'To all girls!'

The sherry, black with powder, was rough and sweetly volatile, but potent. I looked at him. A rent-boy need not be queer, I considered. Perhaps the same thought struck him, and at much the same moment. He propped himself up on one elbow and looked at me with intent. 'What?' I asked.

'I did have a girl.'

I rolled over and looked at the shadows moving across the ceiling, marvelling at the bizarre turns of events that life deals out. How had we arrived at this conjunction? 'I don't doubt it!'

'You think I'm lying to you?' It wasn't that there was menace in his voice. Far from it. It may even have been an appeal of kinds. Whatever it was, it had the effect of finally stifling my laughter. 'Why on God's earth would I think you were lying?'

'Forget it!' he said. I rolled over. Now it was my turn to affect solicitude. 'Tell me. Really, I'd like to know.'

'Just forget it.'

But he did tell me. In the course of the next half hour, in a broken and excruciatingly repetitive narrative, he told me the story of his scarring.

The girl's name was Judith, Julie, something of that ilk. He made much of his refusal to impart to me her surname. He need not have been concerned, I've no head for such trivia. The picture he gave of this Judith, or Julie, is itself confused. Judy, perhaps? She was older than him, but not by much, and yet he didn't know her age. He'd never asked. Her hair was blonde streaked with bay, or else it was bay streaked with blonde. I imagine her eyebrows would have suggested the latter. She was well spoken, though her talk was marked by endearing verbal tics such as *I done* and *I seen*. I believe he said she hailed from Bray. I can't entirely lay the blame on my memory for the irresolution of this portrait. His story was tangled, and he seemed to be himself trying to tease the truth from it as he went on (by God, I think I will begin to write!).

On one thing he was inordinately clear. There had been no sexual commerce between them. I can't imagine why he insisted with such vigour on this point. It seems to me that the orthodox position for the adolescent male is to declare carnal knowledge on the flimsiest of pretexts. Besides, hadn't his point of departure been to convince me of his heterosexuality?

No sex, then, between himself and Judith. Or Judy. Perhaps we can settle on Judy. After all, the story won't lack long for a Mister Punch.

He was holing up at the time in some abandoned shack, down around Killiney I think he said. In any case, by the sea. He'd come up with a madcap scheme to walk the perimeter of Ireland. The foreshore, in its entirety. I imagine, at his age, that my highest ambition had extended as far as trying to cajole Aisling O'Rourke to come around the back of the bicycle shed. She never did consent.

Judy, on the other hand, would have consented. This at least is the impression the boy had formed. It was to have occurred, if the gods had seen fit, on a day that he took her up to visit the Famine Folly. All love is folly, I sighed into my wineglass. It was a poor quip. I should have said all love is famine. It would have had more bite.

He introduced another character into the narrative at this point, the Punch that every Judy cries out for. *Cue strings, sinister pizzicato.* I can state for a fact that this villain's name was Anto. I have remembered, because one of Mahood's menagerie goes by that name. There was a detail about facial rings that added a touch of colour. Whether or not this Anto, his Anto, believed Bluebottle's story about the celibate admiration for his girlfriend, it was not an attention that he welcomed. Lest there was any doubt on the point, he carved a notice of territorial claim into the boy's cheek. The famous Judas kiss.

A quip came to me as the boy spoke. This, Mr Bateman, is what they call a slice of life. I did not share the quip.

Now if I were to risk an opinion, I'd say there's something not altogether above-board in the proceedings. This assault takes place by night in a shack on Killiney beach. Hold on! Wasn't it during the excursion up to the heights of folly that the young lovers had been spotted by Anto's lieutenant, whose name escapes me? I am troubled by the change of scenery. How did Mr Punch know where to find the boy?

A delicious thought. Can he have been betrayed by his paramour?

I didn't share the suspicion any more than I shared the quip. That night, it seems, I was in no mood for sharing anything beyond Uncle's horn of plenty.

Here, the chronology gets even more confused. A man rescues him from a high fever. A vagabond. Ex-army. They live out in the wilds, up hill, down dale. They wander far, over three counties, at the least. They survive on watercress, on molluscs and seaweed, on fowl, rabbits, earthworms, vegetables, roots, berries and I know not what. I'm embellishing. In fact, I believe he said they busked. No. His friend busked. The scarring was still too raw for him to endure the stares of crowds. How long this idyll lasted he couldn't say, but what was remarkable was that all this time he guarded the face of his beloved in his memory as one guards a strand of hair in a locket.

Then one day, inevitably, they find themselves back in Bray and environs. Time has folded back upon itself, the catch on the locket has been forced, and the emotion is as naked as it has ever been. He is in a state of high anxiety all the time they're camped behind the Head. He is terrified of meeting his loved-one. She has never seen his disfigurement.

And yet he's drawn inexorably to the town. Curiosity does battle with modesty and each day curiosity grows more bold. He begins to chance the strand of pebbles and driftwood that runs between the promenade and the sea. At first only when there is a drizzle, or before the sun has properly risen, or after it is quenched. But gradually, gradually…

One morning he finds himself in the vicinity of the DART station. He thinks to buy a newspaper. He glances carelessly up the street, and his gut is jerked out through his gullet with astonishing violence a split second before his eye has had time to register the figures. He shrinks behind a tree trunk, but needs to hazard a second glance in order to be sure.

The second glance lengthens into a stare. It's as if he is looking, from his hideaway, upon the ashes of all hope. He confirms that it is his beloved, Judith, or Julie, and that she is not alone. But neither is she in the company of Anto, his ear-ringed nemesis. The man whose arm is around her shoulder is taller, and in a flash he thinks he recognises him. He has seen him once before, at the Famine Folly. *If thou remember'st not folly, thou hast not loved.*

Her head is tilted back, and she is laughing.

I've gotten carried away. His romance was delivered in fits and starts. He was struggling with it, like Jacob with the Angel. And his eyes riveted me as if I was in some way to blame.

•••

We return to kitchen-sink reality. The next day was a wet, blustery squib the punch-line of which was delivered by an unbearably smug cashier who informed me with shaking head and superior smirk that, no, Uncle's cheque had still not cleared. This left Fergal Bates in some difficulty. I had promised Mahood, through an intermediary, that he would get his three weeks' interest without fail. These last two words carried a degree of weight out of all proportion to the ease with which I now report them. When the first batch of snuff-movies arrived in the flat, I'd sneaked a look. Apparently, the reason for the mutilations, the irrefutable slices of life, is to prove that the whole thing can't have been staged with actors. Now, whether or not Mahood existed beyond a *nom de guerre*, Bates had no wish to star in one of his movies.

Without the cushion of Malcolm's cash, I'd have to spend another day ducking like a shadow through a city full of eyes. Worse, I could think of not a companion, not a client, not a solitary acquaintance, but who had fought shy of my approaches in recent months. In short, my credit was shot.

I could see little point in a return trip to Sandymount. It was blindingly obvious that Uncle would not only be in a high dudgeon on account of our carry-on of the previous evening, but that he'd once again give me the run around without parting with so much as a cent in hard currency. I suspected his finances were little better than my own at this juncture. This was a minor tragedy. I estimated that a matter of a hundred might fob off Mahood until the end of the month. I was forced instead to lay low.

On Sunday morning, an abject Bates was surprised by a call to the mobile. It was Uncle. He pertains to that stubborn generation which hasn't quite come to terms with the fact that, in spite of the absence of any connecting cord, one need not holler to be heard. Conversely, his apparatus appears to suffer from perpetually bad coverage. When his voice is not braying it is breaking up.

Holding my phone at a scarcely adequate distance from my ear, I patched together a lunch invitation to the Royal St. George Yacht Club in Dun Laoghaire. This was doubly surprising. Firstly, to the best of my knowledge, Uncle has never once set foot on so much as a paddleboat. Ever since baptism, the thought of any immersion in water terrifies him. Secondly, I was convinced that he'd been avoiding me, having fobbed me off with that pup of a cheque until it became obvious that it would never be honoured. Estimating the extent of his infatuation with the boy, I suspected a ruse.

He met me at a monument that, to judge from its stone crown, must have been testament to the passage of some King or Queen through the port during a more regal age. F.D. Bateman, take note! Uncle carried doubled over his arm a Mackintosh the colour of a mushroom, while a black beret hunkered nervously on his crown. The beret made his head look twenty to thirty percent larger, and as round as a Montgolfier balloon. In fine, he cut an even more ridiculous figure than was his custom. He could have been some private detective out of a French farce, squinting into the watery sunlight. He seemed genuinely pleased to see me, though, and I couldn't help but return his broad banana-boat smile.

'Well, you old pederast,' I enthused, nodding toward the forest of masts, 'I never would have put you down for a sea dog.'

'Far from it,' he shuddered. 'I get nervous every time I have occasion to cross O'Connell Bridge!'

Oh, he was in a good mood all right. But I determined not to let my guard down quite so soon. One can never be up to the tricks of the older queer.

'So why the invitation? Did the cow calve?'

He tapped a pocket of the Mackintosh and winked, and I all but looked behind me to make sure that we weren't on Candid Camera. He was evidently relieved to have occasion to play the comic. Still, he looked like he hadn't been sleeping. There was something haggard about his performance, something of the Rouault clown. The beret made his eyes small and piggy and calculating.

'At last,' he pronounced at last, 'some good news. Something truly providential.'

'Let's go inside,' I said. 'I haven't eaten in two days.' It was the whitest of lies. He manoeuvred us past the Yacht Club, the Royal St George, and in through a doorway yet more discreet, yet more exclusive, and three times yet more swanky.

On the very rare occasion I've been seen with Uncle in what one might term society, he has that odious habit, while ostensibly sustaining a conversation, of revolving the head like a radar to see what literati and glitterati are in the vicinity. Normally this would irritate me enormously. But today I felt unaccountably sorry for him. I'd have been secretly pleased if just one person had retuned his solicitous gaze, or nodded to him in vague recognition. But every month he was looking older, more out of fashion, more faintly disreputable, more like some seventies car that has miraculously evaded the scrap-heap.

It was quite a food-emporium he was introducing me into. There were lilies, mirrors, and rich crimson wainscoting straight out of a *fin-de-siècle* brothel. Good God, I thought, what sort of windfall has this man come into? We had a table reserved, just as well as it happens, since from a nuance of his eyebrows I understood that the bald *maître-d'hôtel* was less than enamoured of my shoes and trousers. Then, there were at least a half-dozen terms on the menu – copperplate and garnished with nothing so vulgar as a price – which might have required a phrasebook if it weren't for Uncle's felicitous insistence on ordering for us both. His French accent was every bit as preposterous as his beret. The chilled white, a Chardonnay, could not be likewise faulted.

Somewhere between a starter of raw molluscs and a bait-sized main that gazed morosely from where it lay marooned beside a leaf in the centre of a colossal white plate, Uncle inquired, casually, after my guest. I say casually. He chose a moment when he was too busy detaching a morsel from the sprat to dignify the inquiry with a glance, and his voice rose in loose imitation of matter-of-factness.

'To tell you the God's honest Uncle, there's something not quite right about that boy.'

The morsel of sprat was suspended in mid air and he squinted at me, mouth ajar. I shut one eye and nodded.

'What do you mean?'

'What I mean is, well, last night at about three or four in the morning… I'd been out drinking, you see… a friend was down from Newry…'

'Yes. Go on.'

I watched the flake of white fish hover inches in front of his dangling nether lip.

'The fact is, I'd rather a lot to drink.' I nodded meaningfully. His expression was immobile and blank, as though fixed by a flashbulb. I kept my own eye fixed on the white flesh trembling before the dragnet of his lip. 'And?'

'Well, you know how it is.'

He shook his head, almost imperceptibly. 'How what is?'

'The bladder. Come on, Mal! You know, you go to bed half tanked, and then, at about four in the morning… tink!'

'Tink?'

'Tink! Tink!'

His bottom lip still hung open giving his head the appearance of a prehistoric rockfish. I paused, to try yet more his prehistoric patience. 'The bladder?'

'Precisely!'

'And so, you got up?'

'Precisely. You know Mal, it's a true pleasure talking to you.'

In a trice the fork was empty, the morsel dispatched by a bob of the Adam's apple. He lifted his wineglass and drained it, trying to feign indifference, or to hide impatience, probably both.

'So I rose and made for the toilet, without turning on the light, out of consideration, I suppose. He's a very light sleeper, your boyfriend.'

He was still trying to feign indifference, picking at his canine with thumbnail and examining what he found as though it were a scientific curiosity.

'But something made me pause.'

I had him. The old rockfish was entranced again by the lure.

'I bent over to look. He was unconscious, I could tell by the streetlight. But there was something peculiar about him. Something… what's the word?'

Uncle was gazing at me, hungry, wary.

'Something out of the ordinary. He was so perfectly rigid it was as though he was carved out of stone. The light was yellow from the neon outside, but still he seemed pale. Pale, and preternaturally tense.'

He drained the remainder of the Chardonnay bottle into my glass as though my story depended on it. He was transfixed.

'The scar, you know the scar? Well, it was bone-white. No. I'm wrong. It was drained of all colour, like a question mark made of cellophane. And every limb was tense and rigid. It was almost as though the lad were in pain. You know, Uncle, if it wasn't for the fact that he was as still as a statue, I'd have assumed he was in the throes of a nightmare.' I lifted up my glass, allowed my tongue to dip like a cat's into the dribble of wine remaining, sixty notes a bottle. My tongue came up with scarce fifty cents worth. He wasn't taking the hint. 'But do you know the most curious thing?'

He shook his head. Then he nodded it, by way of encouragement.

'The hands.'

'The hands?'

I winked, drained the glass. His own hand made the subtlest gesture. The message its solitary erect digit conveyed was remarkable. In a trice the ice bucket was swept away and a single glass of chilled house white replaced the previous.

'The hands,' I went on, shaking my head in baffled admiration. 'Under the streetlight, it looked like it might be ink. But I knew at once. I knew it was blood. Congealed blood, blackening every knuckle and dribbling in runnels down as far as the sleeves of his shirt.'

'Dear God!'

'He must have been in some sort of scrape while he was begging. It's a tough city out there.'

'And that was last night?'

'That was last night.'

We said no more about the boy. Over coffee, a blend of Java and Colombian supremo if memory serves, and a couple of heavy-sweet Amaretti, his talk wandered over items of trivia and society gossip, his tongue at odds with the frown on his forehead. When I assumed that we were about to go, I made to rise, but two fingers on my forearm detained me.

He reached into his breast pocket, and I sat back as I watched him peel off four yellow fifties from a thick cylinder of notes.

'Will you do something for me?'

I looked at him, a leer of distrust on my mouth.

'A message, that's all.'

With this he slid the two hundred across the table to me, as though it was the most common thing in the world in this establishment to pay out a cash bribe over lunch.

'Tell him…,' he squinted, gazed at the empty coffee cup. 'Tell him that I'll expect him, tomorrow, whenever he's finished in town. Will you pass on that message for me?'

I nodded, too surprised at the lucre to remember to ask him how he came to be so suddenly plush. So surprised was I that I almost forgot to ask for the balance on the cheque. Almost.

I'd taken a few small liberties with the story that I'd told Uncle. There was, for instance, no friend from Newry, and I'd been far too broke to afford more than a couple of cans of pissy export lager, but the fact remains that Bluebottle had been acting peculiar all Saturday morning. He had never been one to hang about the house during the day, but all that morning he'd shuffled agitatedly about the rooms, death pale and sullen, and then abruptly he was gone, without having shut the door behind him.

When he returned after a number of hours he was even more quiet, and he had in fact torn the skin on a number of his knuckles. A fight, some trouble with other street entertainers, how should I know? He wasn't disposed to talk about it. As for his sleep, I'd been woken by his shouting, and found him in the grip of a nightmare, his arms flailing and his teeth clamped like an epileptic. I made no attempt to wake him.

After leaving the Yacht Club I took a stroll around Dun Laoghaire and then made leisurely into town; brazen, swaggering. Put but some money in thy purse. For once I was ready for Mahood's men, so that of course they were nowhere to be seen. More eyes than Argos at other times, but today they were as if blinded by my newfound wealth. It was still early when I got back to Nelson Street, but Bluebottle was home. The air in the flat had that stale smell from having been inhabited continuously all day. His demeanour was quite the opposite of the previous morning, for now he was lethargic to the point of depressive. I began to suspect that there was something profoundly amiss with the wiring inside that boy's head.

By the following morning he seemed to have recovered his equilibrium, however, and over breakfast I passed on Uncle's message. He spluttered his milk and Rice Crispies.

'He said I could *what*?'

'Call round. This evening.'

'And what else did he say?'

'That's it. That's the whole extent of his message.'

'Malcolm asked you to tell me that I *could call round*?'

'This evening. Whenever you're finished your busking.'

'I don't busk.'

He picked up his bowl and finished the Rice Crispies by the sink, staring out the back window. He shook his head.

'That's it? I can call round? This evening?'

'That's what the man said.'

'I don't get it.'

I shrugged. Bluebottle threw back his head and laughed. Then he put the bowl to his mouth, drained his breakfast, and left.

I didn't see him for all the rest of that day. I had my own business to conduct with Mahood, but his heavies never seem to exist except at the margins of undesirability. Whenever an encounter is desired they are nowhere to be seen. I finally ran into one of them towards evening when I was passing along in front of St. Michan's – by a curious twist, it was the character in my own circle of hell that shared the name of Anto. Don't they say that Providence delights in symmetries? My particular Anto is said to have nailed a man to a door by his ears in Dolphin's Barn without batting so much as an eyelid. So street lore has it. But today he was agitated. He scarcely counted the bills I pressed into his hand, and all the time he looked over his shoulder. The watcher watched, I smiled, without quite smiling.

Having bought another month's grace from him at a less exorbitant rate of interest than custom would have suggested, I knew exactly in which dive I'd find a couple of deadbeat acquaintances at that early hour. For I had a whim to cut loose. Unfortunately, predictably, inevitably, by ten o'clock funds were low, and our hero neither drunk nor sober, neither eager nor satisfied, as he gravitated back to the flat.

It was empty. I didn't give this circumstance more than a passing thought. If Uncle had come into cash, it seemed a reasonable conjecture that our little rent-boy would not be returning that evening. Quite possibly, not for several days. Several nights. With a dissatisfied, yeasty taste in my mouth, I lay down on the sofa where he was accustomed to sleep.

I must have dozed. When I woke up it was after one. Beside mine ear my mobile phone was flashing and bickering. It seemed to me that it had just been ringing in another context at the other side of wakefulness.

Mal's number showed on the LCD. One in the morning, for fuck's sake.

'What do you want?'

'Did… has he come back? Is he there?' A woman's voice, urgent and emotional, fragmented by something more sinister than the customary poor reception.

'Back where? Who? Look, who is this?'

'For God's sake, this is Gwen. Gwendolyn Furlong! Look, I'm a friend of... but it's awful! Simply… I can't…'

'Sorry, you're breaking up on me.'

'Awful! But tell me can't you! Has he come back? Answer me! Has he… is he there with you? Now? As we speak?'

'Who? You know I was asleep when you…'

'Oh Jesus! Look if…'

And then the phone went dead. It was cut off, or hung up, or Mal's battery expired, or it was out of credit, or perhaps the coverage collapsed. In any event, I was left staring at my own apparatus and wondering if Mal's would come to life again to throw some light on what had preceded.

After a while I stretched back out on the couch and stared at the ceiling. The shadows extending from the arms of the light gave it the appearance of a spider, infinitely patient. With fingers interlocking to make a cradle for my head, I'd just begun to doze, but then I sat bolt upright. My God, I laughed. Suppose he's killed the old bugger and made off with his money!

But I was no longer laughing when I saw the state of him as he stood in the doorway, the streetlight falling like gilt over his bloody figure.

PART II

IV | Gwendolyn

Mal would never be told by me. That was the problem. Really, he's just a big child. Far too caught up in his own fantasy world to take advice from any one of us, any of us stupid enough to look out for him.

Really, it was too much. If you attempted to reason with him, he'd go off and sulk. Or he'd seem to be agreeing with you. Although, of course, he was never any good at pretending. Putting up any kind of deceit. As transparent as that glass of water. He'd smile, or he'd nod, and behind the effusiveness you could see that he'd remained aloof. Nothing had changed.

Oh, of course, later there would be renunciations. Tears. Penances.

That was his essence, you see. A big child, with a child's appetites, a child's whims. A child's pig-headedness, too. And the temper! Christ, the temper! Ha ha! The tantrums! He was simply unable to hide it from anyone when he was out of sorts. He'd huff and he'd puff. He'd stamp his foot. He'd sulk. Course, the mood wouldn't last. A child's fury, it would blow over at the merest caprice of good fortune and there, that was an end of it.

I could never stay furious with Mal for long.

Do you know what the first thing was that we fell out over? That we almost fell out over? Seems so trivial now.

But I'll have to set the scene for you. This was ten, no, my God, twenty years ago. Twenty years. More! Christ, where do they go?

I'd been living in England, you see. From a very young age. Eleven. When I was eleven, when I was *not quite* eleven, I left the stud farm in

Kildare for an English boarding school. Do you know, I've never returned to Kildare for more than a couple of weeks at a time. Never. Not since father remarried.

Course, it goes without saying that he stood against absolutely everything that was ever of the slightest interest to me. Ha! Nearly had an apoplectic fit when I told him I was going into Art College, told him in no uncertain terms too. I didn't care a tuppenny damn if he wrote me out of the will on account of it. Fact is, he did just that. But that was when he heard that I'd become engaged to Horst Liebknecht. Two weeks before I turned nineteen. Course, he had to change his tune later on, after Jamie died. Couldn't bear to let the stud farm fall out of the family's hands you see.

England, yes. London! London! You simply can't operate in a vacuum. In any case, can you imagine me married to some horse-trainer in Kildare or County Meath?

So I'd finally begun to establish myself. I won't say get a name, no, not as yet. But at least I was no longer left standing like a wallflower at the champagne launches and gala nights. Is there anything more excruciating than to know no-one and so to fall prey to the attentions of some bore no-one knows? Through Horst, I was on first name terms with a handful of the people who really mattered. Once you were seen conversing with one of these, well, suddenly you were somebody one could no longer afford to ignore.

It was at one of these interminable openings that I first rubbed shoulders with Mal. Can't imagine what he thought he was doing there, he hasn't the slightest judgement when it comes to art. Perhaps he was there for the canapés, ha ha! I have no doubt they were first class; with Horst you could always count on the detail. Course, one thing Mal was always uncannily good at was sniffing out a social event. Inveigling himself onto the invitation list, particularly in those days. Nobody has ever adequately explained how he used to do it, but time and again he'd pull it off. Over the years, I expect he became something of an inevitability. Every sort of social occasion, too. You know, I've an idea he told me he was at the Royal wedding? I expect that was a fib. But he'd a knack of showing up, just like the grand-aunty who gets quietly soused in the corner at every family re-union, but whom no-one can quite remember having invited.

He was something or other in the diplomatic corps in those days, but very, very small fry. Somebody or other's secretary. Now, my memory is wont to play tricks on me, particularly as I've grown older. Still, I'd bet you anything you like that the immediate cause of the tiff we had was a piece by Louise Bourgeois. Horst insisted much later on that it couldn't have been Louise, that it must have been one by that chap that takes after Bellmar, his name escapes me. But I'm not convinced. As for Mal, well, Mal's memory is less to be trusted than my own. Mal has it that it was a sculpture by Giacometti, can you imagine anything so stupid?

He was in the company of Aaron Madding, the dealer, when I saw him enter the gallery. Do you know, I took an instant dislike to the man? In those days he was very… not quite handsome, it's the wrong word. Very elegant. Exquisite about his appearance, and always so immaculately turned out. Immaculate! And he always wore such a disdainful look on his face. I knew he must have a very dry wit, because he had poor Aaron puce with laughter.

At first I determined *not* to meet him. I was very arrogant, you know. Fully expected that like all the younger men, sooner or later he would make his gambit, pay his respects, flirt a little. They all did, you know. Even the married ones. Especially the married ones! It mattered not a jot if they were queer, what's more. My dear, we are talking about the arts! The gay glitterati are always twenty times more shameless with a young girl, for goodness sake!

But from over our shoulders Aaron Madding's guffaws kept intruding on my conversation. Spoiling it. Course, I had to let on it was all terribly amusing. But really I was getting quite resentful at this newcomer. Seemed that every time one of our circle was just at the critical moment in their anecdote, heads would be turned away by a… by a sputtering whinny. All through the gallery, eyes were being thrown up to heaven and meaningful glances exchanged. But still, one could see that every ear was straining to catch some witticism from this impeccably dressed Irish… *parvenu* with the haughty drollness in his expression.

He'd just passed behind our group and was approaching the Louise Bourgeois – Horst is simply wrong, I remember distinctly it was a Louise Bourgeois – when I overheard him mutter into Aaron's ear something to the effect that he'd seen the very piece the previous week lying in a skip outside Bernice McEvitt's. You know, the dressmaker? Bond Street. Very gaudy, all the rage at one time.

Well, I simply couldn't let that go! Excused myself from my circle and took my place at his side.

'Do you mean to say,' I challenged him, 'that you really can't tell the difference?'

'I'm sorry, the difference between what?' He was supercilious, but really rather too aware that we were the centre of attention.

'The difference between the cast-offs of a second rate fashion designer and a disturbing, erotically ambiguous statement in fabric?'

'Oh I see,' he said, nodding, playing to the gallery. 'I'm sorry, which is it you're wearing, dear?'

There were sniggers, or perhaps I imagined them. There were several in the present company who would have delighted to see me brought down a peg. We'd exchanged barely two sentences, and already I was far too deeply in to allow him get away so flippantly. Aaron was watching me as if I was a suffragette about to leap under the legs of a racehorse. For this reason, perhaps, he failed to introduce us as one would have wished. Instead he limited himself to the crass observation: 'Gwendolyn is Irish'.

I examined the newcomer. 'You're Irish, I think?'

'Oh dear,' he said. 'Is it so *veerry* obvious?'

'It explains your lack of discrimination.'

'Oh, I discriminate, I assure you.'

'In what?'

He was fiddling at his cuff, though there was no thread that I could see. I hadn't noticed until then that his fingers were altogether blunt. He'd begun well. There was a lazy condescension in his tone. We were both aware that the ears of the whole gallery were imperceptibly inclined towards our duel. But then, he did the absolutely unforgivable. Do you know what it was he did?

The washroom! He simply ran to the washroom. Really, you've never seen a rabbit beat such a hasty retreat. I don't know quite what came over him, but he didn't so much as make his excuses, to Aaron or to myself. All at once he was scurrying to the safety of the washroom, and I would swear to this day that I saw him blush like a virgin.

Mal all over you see. Failure of courage, just when everything is set for a small triumph. It breaks my heart.

Justin Furlong, the media mogul. Daresay you've heard of him? He's the reason I wound up back on this island. Fell for him hook, line and sinker, I may as well tell you.

That surprises you. No doubt you think of me as an old dyke. Marriages of convenience, sleeping with the enemy, that sort of thing. Oh, I'm well used to it by now. You have to grow a thick skin to survive long in this business. Old Gwen's become a regular pachyderm. Daresay I've turned into an old rhino, shortsighted and territorial. Blundered against a few people in my time, too, and they're hardly the types that are likely to forgive or forget.

Of course, there have been lovers. Claire. Sabine du Frei. But men, too. I've idealised men, after my own manner. That's the story they've no wish to tell. Course, years ago they read my *Tapettes d'Avignon* purely as an affront. 'An aggressive disarticulation of the male body' – that's what Toby Anders wrote about it. I was their man-hater, you see, their *vagin-denté*. Aaron Madding never tired of repeating that there's nothing quite so efficacious in establishing a reputation as a *succès de scandale*. Always suspected, the old kike, that the timing of Lucille Rowan's boarding school revelations was just too convenient. The tabloids ran it the very day that *Tapettes* took the gold medal in Antwerp. I can assure you, I had no part whatsoever in her decision, hadn't seen Lucille in years in point of fact. But there's no denying that story of high jinks in the locker room gave the gutter press quite a trough to dip their snouts into.

But I fell for Justin, almost from the moment I laid eyes upon him. He was a magnificent creature. Tall, athletic build. Though it wasn't simply a question of muscle tone. Do you know what it was? He walked like a cat. A great cat. A woman can fall for a detail like that, you know.

Marriage with Horst was long since dead by this juncture. Pains me to say that Father was right: one had married far too young. And he was such a cold fish, particularly after the, well… best not wash too much dirty linen in public. And in any event, I think I was quite ready for a change. It was such an incestuous aquarium that we swam in. Justin Furlong had to travel as part of his job, but his base was Dublin, so that was that.

You know, I've more than a sneaking suspicion that Mal was green with jealousy over my new conquest. In public, behind the cold smiles, it was patently obvious that he and Justin quite simply couldn't stand one another. But I've always had the suspicion that secretly this was because Mal fancied the boxers off him.

Wasn't too long after the divorce with Horst Leibknecht that Mal had his own little *succès de scandale*. Diplomatic corps had to drop him like a hot potato. Even succeeded in having the whole thing hushed up, which was quite a feat for the Irish. A juvenile. I understand through a pal of Justin's that it was somebody's son out of one of the Arab delegations. He was bloody lucky there were no criminal charges pressed. But one way or another, he was suddenly off all the invitation lists. He moped around London for a few more months. That's when he began to acquire that hangdog look that so infuriates me. Course, his career was over. Not that the career was ever anything more than a means to open social doors and live the high life. But the constant snubs were destroying him. You could see it. He even began to neglect his appearance. To droop his shoulders and clutch people too earnestly by the arm, fatal that. And to make a general nuisance of himself on the phone. Really, he was already halfway to becoming a laughing-stock.

And then news came that his mother was dying. That very evening he packed up, lock stock and barrel, and left London for good by the Euston boat-train. She took six months to die and I believe it was quite hideous. He became a recluse after that. Took to brooding. Drank alone.

•••

Only really got to know Mal several years after the marriage with Justin wound up on the rocks. Inevitable, I suppose. The simple fact is that you grow bored with the body, and we had precious little in common once you took away the physical. In any event he ran off with a trollop from Guernsey, so that was that. Can't say I was terribly disappointed. In point of fact it was rather convenient, since after the settlement I was left with half the Foxrock address. Eventually sold for over a million, quite a sum of money in those days.

And also the studio. Set of dirty brick warehouses that his company used at one time for something or other, but absolutely ideal for a studio. Justin didn't even put up a fight. Daresay he knew that once I'd made up my mind, there was precious little he could do that would induce me to change it. Can't imagine what I'd have done for studio space if it wasn't for those warehouses.

Course, ever since Jamie died I'd been quite independent, financially I mean. I daresay Justin resented that. The men in my life have always been deeply uneasy around a woman of independent means. Say what you will, human nature doesn't change.

Do you know, I actually failed to recognise Mal when at last I bumped into him? Almost had to be introduced! It was at the time of the exhibition with Orla Keefe. Brian Hammond of the Ormond gallery got that show up. Orla was very vocal in the gay rights movement, an ugly thing with dreadlocks, terrible skin. Had been arrested more than once, apparently. So it made perfect sense to wheel out an old dyke like myself who still had a whiff of the bad girl about her. Course, I refused point blank to let Brian dust off any of the London pieces, that would have been too much. After all, one doesn't want to be thought of as a living fossil. Caused no end of arguments between us, he said he simply couldn't understand my conceptual work. But in the end I prevailed. Always do, you see.

All the in-crowd was there on the opening night. The big fish in the little pond. Quite a number of the press, too. Was there some sort of national debate going on about abortion? I imagine there was. In any event, they were all there, the bottom feeders, ready to squabble over the merest scraps. Remember vividly how stuffy the gallery was. Do you know the Ormond? It's such a small affair, quite airless at the best of times. But with such a crowd, all jostling elbows and open mouths cackling and chattering and devouring crackers, it was quite simply unbearable. Small wonder I didn't recognise him at first when he laid hands on my shoulder.

How he'd insinuated himself into the Ormond gallery on this of all nights is quite beyond me. He'd lost all touch with anyone who might have had any pull, and as for art appreciation, for God's sake he's never admired anything so far as I can see beyond the nineteenth century. Infallible eye for kitsch!

You know, it was a shock when I realised who he was. He'd aged, you see. The features were all there, but somehow botched. Where was the elegance? But the worst of it was, it was like looking into a distorting glass. Here was a living caricature of all the years that separated us from the first time we'd encountered one another. There's an expression, the face of a friend being a true mirror? Well that's exactly how it seemed to me, looking into the face of this ruined man. And of course the next day there it was, staring out from the society pages of *The Irish Times*. Mal, the old codger, all smiles with his rosy cheeks and butterfly collar and flute of champagne, and myself – as aged and ugly as the wicked step-mother out of one of Grimm's tales.

Seemed I simply could not avoid him after that. At every turn, there he'd be. Like some message sent by a malicious demiurge. Really, it became something of a bad joke. If I'd go to the Yacht Club for supper with an acquaintance or a dealer, there he'd be at a table directly across the room. Even ran into him at a flower show! In the RDS, for God's sake! Looking at irises!

Daresay there was something inevitable about the fact that it would be *I* who would call on *him*. Isn't it always the way? The people you most look down upon and yet you already know that somehow their life is inevitably wound up with yours? Daresay I decided to take him under my wing. Didn't pity him, that's too strong a term. Perhaps I simply decided to take him on as a project. To amuse myself with him. I don't mean to be unkind, but he was quite the laughing-stock you know. Among the queer community, I mean.

But I must say, the boys came as something of a surprise. Oh, I don't mean to suggest that I was surprised he should like boys. There was nothing more natural than that his penchant should incline towards the younger male. No. What I mean to say is, I'd known Mal for in excess of a year before I became aware that he had *live-in* boys. I mean, I must have been to his house dozens, what am I saying, perhaps a hundred times. Quite late at night too. And yet there was never so much as a solitary piece of evidence left lying about the place that there was anyone actually staying there, on that I'd take an oath.

He really is an old sly-boots. You know, I often think he'd have been quite capable of killing a member of his family, his brother in the country, say, and then dicing up the body and feeding it piece by piece to his cats, so that not one shred of evidence of the crime was ever found. Ha ha!

Where he concealed his live-in boys I've never fathomed. Course it's a large place, built in the old style, all alcoves and mezzanines. But you can never count on boys to be discrete at the best of times. And these were gurriers, taken in straight off the street if you don't mind. For an intelligent man he has precious little common sense.

Might never have found out his secret, you know, if one day he hadn't shown up at the studio in a state of absolute panic. Oh, he really was in a bad way, agitated to the point of hysteria! It was all I could do to make him calm down and take a sherry so that he might give me some clue.

So that's when the whole thing began to come out. Piece-meal, what else would you expect? At first it took me quite a while to understand what the problem was. Seemed that someone named 'Spider' was trying to blackmail him. Threatening explicit revelations. Letters to the press, letters to the police, that sort of thing. Course, what he conspicuously failed to tell me until he was well onto his third sherry and I was losing all patience with him was that this Spider character was only thirteen years of age! Can you imagine?

We never found out what happened to Spider. Something unsavoury, I've no doubt. None of his threats was ever carried out, and to the best of my knowledge, no money ever passed between them. But Mal, ha ha! Mal was very slow to learn. Not three months after this episode, I found he had actually a pair of street-Arabs staying in his place. A pair of them! Can you imagine what he was thinking? Ill-mannered, dirty brats, particularly the foxy looking one. And that neighbour of his always snooping on him. Had them there in broad daylight, what's more! At least, I came across them during the day, climbing the old crab-apple tree in the back garden.

We had our run-ins over the years. This kind of indiscretion was madness, pure and simple. I sometimes wonder if there wasn't a small part of Mal that secretly longed to be caught. *In flagrante delicto.* To be exposed as a danger to public morals. Reviled by the gutter press. What a horrible thrill that would be! One way or another, he continually flirted with indiscretion. Constant source of friction between us, I needn't tell you.

But one could see immediately that the infatuation with the boy he called Bluebottle was far more dangerous. The boy they disfigured. There was, how shall I say?

This time there was genuine misery in him.

You see, I knew Mal of old. Everything had to be high drama with Mal. Everything. Really, he was just like the lead tenor out of one of those interminable operas that he listens to. All tragedy and gesture. Of course, one didn't believe a word of it.

This time was different. You knew from the very first there'd been a sea-change in Mal's life. He was absolutely miserable, there's no other word can describe his state. Absolute, abject misery! Even when he smiled, even when he laughed, there was a deep... *wistfulness* behind it. As if he was making an appeal to you, directly. With his eyes, you see.

I think I've come to understand what had him so miserable. Don't laugh, but for the first time in his life, Mal was actually in love! And this new state of affairs made him realise once and for all just how much of a human wreck he'd allowed himself to become.

With the others, the pretence was enough, you see. Deep down he must have seen what a grotesque figure he was to them. One hand providing them with shelter and food while he was lavishing caresses on them with the other. To them, and of course he knew this and I daresay couldn't have cared less, he was an old lecher, soft and gone to seed. They were scarcely more than gingerbread children, and he an ancient troll out of Peer Gynt. There was gratification, perhaps. But with these others, it simply didn't seem to matter what role he had to play to earn it.

Not so with the one he called Bluebottle. There's a phrase, isn't there, the love that feeds upon itself? Or is it appetite? Grows more acute with every bite. *Othello*, probably. Oh, I began to fear for him, from very early on. And when I met the boy it confirmed the worst of my fears. Course, it's easy to say all this now, when one knows full well how things will turn out. But I can assure you, the very first time I set eyes upon that boy, I feared for Mal. Could already see the bloody end of it. Told him so, what's more.

He looked older than the others. Gaunt. Almost wolverine. Eyes of a wolf, too. But desperately graceful. The others, those that I'd seen, had been mere pubescent boys. Barely out of short pants. But here was a man-child.

One day, quite innocently, by which of course I mean not innocently at all, Mal asked me if I thought he'd make a suitable subject for one of my sculptures. Never been sure quite what he had in mind. Laughed and dismissed him out of hand. But his casual suggestion troubled me. Course, it had been years since I'd done any figurative work. Certainly nothing of any consequence. Not since the late seventies. But what I found so deeply disturbing was… Mal, in his own ludicrous and self-centred way, had actually managed to put words to a thought that had remained to this time subliminal. Fact is, from the very first introduction – he was lying out in the yard curled around some book or other – I'd examined this boy with the eye of an artist. Tried to decipher him. What an Austrian tutor back in the Academy liked to term 'ze *noumenon* of ze subject'. Came as quite a shock to realise I was doing it, I can tell you.

I knew how to play old Mal. We were just like an angler and an ancient pike. I resisted and mocked his idea. But I always tantalised him just that little bit more with an image, a morsel, a suggestive word. Unbeknownst to him, I'd already begun to fill a notebook with first thoughts. Line and shadow, great blue silhouettes and aching curves. The boy had a way of becoming absorbed that made it easy to watch him without his realising it. Or perhaps he did realise.

So I played with Mal and laughed him off until at last one evening I relented. Agreed that the boy would sit for a few preparatory sketches. Course, that whole episode turned into a complete fiasco, you can imagine, a boy of fourteen! I'm relieved it did, because it broke the spell once for all. He was just a boy after all. From that day on he was mortified whenever he saw me! Ha ha!

It would take a lot more than a little embarrassment to break the spell where Mal was concerned, let me tell you. Oh yes.

It happened that I won a commission for a large outdoor sculpture from, of all places, Carlow County Council. Road scheme. Much of the work was *in situ*. So the upshot of that was I began to see a lot less of either one of them. If I'm honest, it made very little difference whether I was in Dublin or Athy. Hate seeing people when I'm working on a project. Become quite the recluse. On the other hand, the fact that so much of the work was in Athy meant that when I did come back to Dublin, to all intents and purposes I'd left the project behind me. Able to come up for air. Ironic, isn't it?

I don't know if you've ever been jealous. It really is the most wretched state of affairs. At such times one becomes terrified to be still. One simply cannot be left alone with one's imagination. One tries to rationalise everything, of course. In particular one is disgusted to be hostage to so clumsy an emotion. One tries to argue the utter worthlessness of whomever one happens to be obsessed with. But of course it makes not the blindest bit of difference! The heart really is a traitor. A traitor, pure and simple.

And it's such a maudlin organ, the heart. A bloody music-hall sentimentalist.

Old Mal was displaying every one of the symptoms. There was the inordinate interest in my work. Ha! Can you imagine? He was desperate to throw himself into any activity that might give him an hour's respite from the rats gnawing away inside him. But he had all the symptoms. There was the joviality, the forced nonchalance, the sickly smile. There were the abrupt swings between open accusation and a most effusive defensiveness. No-one could say a word against the boy but Mal himself, you see. When he was not lamenting his own sorry decline, he was outraged by his beau's behaviour! His lack of appreciation! Every Sunday he'd come around to the studio, not so much for advice. No. It was for the opportunity to lance the boil of his frustrations. But just let me say one solitary word against the boy!

If that was all there was to it he might have been an object of pity, but I scarcely would have feared for him. After all, one can cause any infatuation to swell into an obsession simply by dwelling for long enough upon it. But I'd seen with my own eyes the change that was wrought in him whenever the boy was present. Oh yes. And then, I'd witnessed a *sang-froid* in the boy that was so far ahead of his years as to be chilling. To make matters worse, he was dreadfully unstable. Prone to mood swings. To the most appalling violence. It really was a disaster waiting to happen.

•••

I was very leery of introducing him to life in Provence. Knew of old how intolerably dependent he can be. And moody too, like all dependent people. But after what that blaggard had done to him, I felt that he needed an entire change of air.

He'd already been in intensive care for four days before I found out, you know. Can you believe it, the old fool was too embarrassed to give them my details at the hospital? Ha ha! Probably thought there was more to fear from my tongue than from the young psychopath who'd just thrashed him to within an inch of his life! But of course there's many a word in jest… there really was a great deal to fear from the spying of the neighbours. Mal never really fitted in you see. For that matter, neither have I. I'd warned him, time and again until I was quite blue in the face, of the risks he was running!

I don't know precisely who knew whom, or who had pull in what circles, but from the very first there was an unusual degree of police interest in the present assault. We had to be constantly on our guard. With no exaggeration, he could literally have been looking at a custodial sentence. I can assure you he'd never have survived the scandal, let alone everything that would have gone with it.

The attack had been of the utmost severity. Left him in dreadful shape for several months. There were fractures, bruised ribs, and more. There was even the suggestion of a cerebral clot. Thankfully nothing more came of that! But the curious thing is, you might have thought the turn events had taken would be absolutely disastrous for his morale. Not a bit of it! On the contrary! Brought out a side in him that was, for want of a better word, really rather admirable. For years he'd been doing very little but become a parody of himself, you see. Equally adept at denial and self-pity. Then, precisely when he'd let himself decline far too deeply into the mire to expect anything else out of life, along comes a creature whose poise drags the very guts out of him. Not only are all advances disdainfully refuted, but the object of unrequited desire comes within a trice of killing him, for God's sake! Then disappears into the black night that undoubtedly gave birth to him!

Even at the level of appearance, and I can vouch for the fact that Mal has always been as vain as a debutante, he became gloriously indifferent. And he really looked dreadful. Discoloured, swollen, awkward in his movements and with one eye from which for weeks the blood refused to drain. It was almost a badge of honour with him!

But he tried to be equally disdainful in regard to the neighbours and this really wouldn't do. There's a thin line between defiance and stupidity, and Mal seemed to have lost all sense of it. But it was November before my commission in Athy was finally finished, and it's the grace of God that he managed to stay out of trouble before I had the chance to take him in hand. Oh, if you could have seen the malicious opportunism with which the locals asked after his health.

By this time he'd graduated from the crutches. Was able to rest, if not actually sleep, without recourse to a heavy dose of painkillers. At last, too, he seemed to be able to talk about the boy without the violent oscillations of mood. Gone, too, the obvious dissimilation that forced the effigy of a smile to paper over his despair. I've thought about it, and I put it down to this: Jealousy only operates in the present tense. It operates by conjuring spectres of the betrayals that are happening at this minute. At this minute, but always with an eye to the future, intimating that these betrayals will persist. Now, once jealousy is shorn of the uncertainties of the present, well! It loses its power, you see. Faced with a past betrayal one can be disappointed, or angry. But where is the anxiety?

Mal was at last in a position to categorise what had happened. He'd been visited by a monstrous passion from a being who would, in his eye, be eternally more fallen angel than man. He was hurt by the loss, he was devastated by it. But also he was honoured, you see. He was honoured that such intensity had ever entered his degraded life.

I'm not putting words in his mouth. I'm actually quoting what he said to me that New Year's Eve.

An anonymous letter made it all the more imperative that I get him away. This note was pushed through the letterbox one morning in January while he was shaving. Ever since the accident (the accident!) the task of shaving had become quite laborious. Lower jaw had been fractured and a couple of teeth knocked loose. The result was that, mercifully, the note fell directly into my hands. Now, from his reaction it became immediately clear to me that this was by no means the first anonymous letter he'd received. But it really was quite appalling. It was not merely filled with innuendo and disgust, there were actual physical threats! Criminal threats. And of course the worst of it was, whoever had written this was entirely aware that Mal was in no position to go to the police. In fact, this was the very crux that these cowards were counting on.

But the incident made up my mind for me, once for all. I'd always been leery about the idea of bringing Mal over to meet the Provence set. If the truth be known, I'd dismissed the notion years before. For me it was a form of refuge, you see, from everything that was Dublin. And besides, I could just imagine him, Malcolm Little, playing to the gallery for all he was worth, and being entirely oblivious that behind the smiles there resided a malicious disdain for everything he was. It was a reflex he couldn't fail to arouse in several whom I could already name. But that letter quite made up my mind for me. Against my better judgment, perhaps, I set about convincing Mal of the necessity to spend some time away from the country.

He proved a tougher nut to crack than I'd expected. Perhaps he secretly harboured the hope that one day his Bluebottle would come back for him. Christ, I realise what that must sound like now! But in any event he threw up one excuse after another to postpone the trip to Antibes until the day I sat him down on his bed, placed the ticket in his hand and packed his suitcase for him! That's what it actually came to in the end.

I wasn't altogether wrong about the French set. Of course, one never knows quite how one's acquaintances will act when faced with a new set of circumstances. For Mal, how shall I put it? For Mal it was almost like a new beginning. For one thing, it was his first extended sojourn away from the morass of Martello Mews, so it was bound to recall his London years. But as he hesitated between the roles of sardonic observer, of exiled victim and of impartial ear for anyone who wished to vent their spleen, there were several who surprised me in their response to him. None more so than Valerie.

How can I begin to do justice to Valerie Yates? I think that if Valerie were to die, I should lose all interest in this world. We've been dear friends for longer than I care to remember, yet you know, she never fails to surprise me. When I'm not exasperated by her, which is most of the time, I'm hopelessly mad about Valerie.

Do you know Provence? Provence has a peculiar effect on everyone who's drawn into it. I daresay if Mal had been likely to stay for any length of time, I should have warned him. He would simply be exchanging one morass for another, and the new every bit as insidious as the one he was fleeing. But the difference is this. In Sandymount you might lose the shine off your ideals, but you're always driven on by something. Envy, snobbery, ostentation. So far as Provence is concerned, what the swamp drags down with insatiable appetite is years. Entire years. You see the difference?

In other places it's quite possible to drink seven days out of seven if one has a mind to. In Provence, it's impossible not to. Days lose their edge. They go out of resolution. Days become weeks become years. What am I saying, several of the set I knew had been hanging around the south of France for decades! Literally. Others were more recent arrivals, but all of them had this in common. They'd been there long enough for the rot to have set in.

Don't misunderstand me. I'm very fond of Provence. The sudden verticals, the erupting poplars, the cypresses like dark flames. Those small squares of pollarded plane trees. Thick trunks with exquisite, impressionist barks. The leaves throwing leopard patterns onto the tabletops. Try to get there at least once every year, and sometimes as many as three times. But there's quite a deal of difference between the migratory bird and those expatriate geese who've allowed their flight feathers to be pulled.

There was to be a party up in Fayence. But I simply have to tell you who was to throw it. Girl named Sasha. When Sasha had first come to Provence she was a timid, mousy thing. Entirely in thrall to her husband. And that suited him down to the ground. Wanted nothing better than a cage-bird, and might well have succeeded, too. But that would be to reckon without the lunar influence of Valerie Yates.

Fast forward ten years. They have two children, two boys. I say they, though only a complete fool would risk a bet as to who the father is. I have a suspicion that there was a Pole named Zbigniew something or other in the picture. It would help explain the blond hair. Now the point of all this is that the husband, Jeremy is his name, has of course developed a pathological dislike of Val. Up to a point you can sympathise with him. After all, he'd gone to extravagant lengths when he first arrived to make his cage-bird happy. Fabulous place in Fayence. The curious thing is, over the years he'd even become reconciled to her occasional affairs, once they remained strictly on the right side of the tracks. Oh I won't say he was happy with them, I wouldn't go that far. His type is ostentatiously possessive. But what he can never forgive Val for was having opened up that completely other can of worms. The forbidden fruit. That gave the cage-bird Sasha her power, you see. Moved her entirely out of his gravitational pull. Couldn't stand to see her even talking to this older virago. Been like a hornet, ever since he first recognised his wife's body in some of Val's more explicit pieces.

Have you a better picture of the precise circle of hell into which I was about to introduce poor Mal? Compared to one or two I could mention, he was a holy innocent! Really, I mean it. The worst vipers among them were the faded idealists. Those who'd stagnated the most, and were now bilious with sarcasm. Scared stiff of seeing anyone escape the swamp, much less succeed.

But as I said, Martello Mews was teeming with such righteous loathing, I simply had to get him out at all costs. And so to Provence.

•••

To begin with, Mal played the jaded expatriate. The victim card would come later. I'll give him his due, he was better at it than I'd feared. In Ireland he's always so hopeless. But now I was surprised to find that I almost resented his success. To me it was so patently an act, you see. In any event, every one of us is appalled at the successes of those whom we're closest to. Nothing you can say will ever convince me otherwise.

What did interest me was how Val would respond to him. You probably have the wrong impression of her. She's no Mephistopheles, far from it. There's very little of the scandalous in her conduct, and as for her art, well! The public has grown so accustomed to being shocked that perhaps the truly shocking thing is to return to more conservative form and subject. Besides, love between woman and woman is at least as old as Sappho. A great deal of the time Val keeps very much to herself, particularly when she's working on a new piece. Perhaps that's why her few words, always mordant, hold such tremendous sway. A single phrase from Val at the launch of an exhibition can be enough to sink a reputation.

As you can imagine, she's never wanted for enemies.

I wondered if she would tolerate Mal. If there's one trait she could never abide, it's self-pity, and let's face it, Mal can be pretty bloody maudlin. It had been his theme for nigh on twenty years! But he had this advantage. At the time he arrived in Antibes – it was late February – Val was involved in mounting an exhibition in a university in Montpelier. She'd returned to a more traditional form, and I for one was delighted. I'd always felt that the work using her own hair as primary material had been a little too precious. The *Printemps* exhibition meant it would be almost a month before the two were introduced. By this time he'd already played the worst and most blatant cards in his hand.

Do you know what happened? One evening about a week after arriving, he stepped out of the shower to overhear Céline Gaspar taking him off for the benefit of Paul and Stephanie Cartwright. You see, she'd been so entirely sympathetic when he'd opened his heart to her two nights before. So understanding of his weaknesses. His desperate, illicit passions. But Mal took it on the chin. Rose to the occasion. Where he drew it from to this day I do not know. Walked straight out to the balcony and joined in the fun from above, playing first himself and then the boy. Ha! Good for you!

After that episode, this became his act. One day he'd set himself up as an object of pity and pillory, but the next day he'd be the most devastating and irreverent at firing cabbage stalks at the figure he'd earlier presented. I'd rarely seen him so amusing as when he was playing himself. Like an overblown Ustinov wallowing in the pompous misery of obsession.

Course, it wasn't an act that could last. Sooner or later, and of course sooner, the Antibes set would tire of his antics and find newer ways to get at him. It wouldn't be long before they'd knock this newcomer squarely off his comic plinth. But the wave lasted just long enough for him to meet Valerie Yates before the crest had broken and dissipated.

Sasha was having a small soirée up in Fayence. You do remember Sasha? Hors d'oeuvres around the pool, nothing too elaborate. There would be about a dozen of us in all. Val was invited, but she wasn't sure if she'd be back from Montpelier in time. Of course it goes without saying that Jeremy was away. Some conference for middle-aged cuckolds down in the port of Marseille, ha ha!

Now, the previous evening, Mal had had rather a torrid time of it. He'd finally had a run in with Jules Mayberry, you see. Jules Mayberry, the former cultural attaché? No? Well, I say former. Jules was attaché some time back in the early eighties. One of the Thatcher generation. Made a fortune, property I think, then lost it just as promptly. Paul Cartwright says at one time he'd been tipped as one of the young Turks. Ruthless. Nothing but disdain for the weak and penniless. Patriotic to the extent that he was the only one who was ever allowed disparage the Empire. But had been going steadily down the toilet ever since the Falklands! Alcoholic, of course. And absolutely merciless. His type always are. One couldn't trust him, not as far as one might spit.

Somehow, I expect he'd got wind of the fact that Mal had been something or other in the Irish diplomatic corps over in London. In any event, it was obvious he'd decided not to give him the tiniest opening in what he considered his own social back yard. Besides, there's nothing easier than cutting the feet from under the new kid in town. Ignored all Mal's pleasantries. Kept up a look of ennui, if not open disdain, all through his performances. Misled him with occasional feigned interest and then trumped or interrupted any anecdote that might have elicited a smile from elsewhere in the crowd.

Really, an altogether unpleasant character. Took the wind quite out of Mal's sails. He was entirely taken aback by the experience. So you see, I thought it might do him good to get away from Antibes for the afternoon.

Val finally showed up at about six or seven. By this stage most of the party had been drinking for most of the afternoon, and there'd been at least one ugly incident between Jacob Haffner and Stephanie Cartwright. This sort of thing is *de rigueur* out in Provence. Absolutely par for the course. It resulted in Stephanie throwing her drink in his face, and not for the first time, I can assure you. Jacob has an unfortunate effect on most women.

Now, the two boys had been running around freely all afternoon. Sasha's boys. Rupert would have been seven and Maurice, maybe five. Sasha has a dog that Val arranged to get for her, had to let on it was someone else or Jeremy would never have allowed it. Doberman. Named Marcel Duchamp, ha ha! Very placid thing really, but huge. It gave me the shivers to see Maurice, naked as the day he was born except for two floats on his arms, with his little penis like the spout of a teapot, and that great black beast every bit as tall as him.

But I was far more furious with Mal. Almost upon arrival he'd taken up position on a deckchair just offset from the pool, and all through the afternoon he'd observed the various goings on from a distance, like some benign Buddhist idol. Handkerchief on the head on account of the sun and a Martini glass perched just so on the arm of the deckchair. I suppose he was already half tight by the time Val arrived.

I could understand Mal holding himself aloof from the group, not wanting to get involved. Particularly after what had happened the previous evening. But what I could not forgive was the attention that he was lavishing on young Rupert. I kept flashing dagger looks in his direction, but he contrived not to see them. Or else he didn't see them, being so taken with the young swimmer and his dives, though I don't believe that for a single moment.

Oh, I don't mean to suggest that there was anything actually improper about his behaviour. I think I'm in a position to know the sort of youth that held a fascination for Mal. And Rupert was only seven, for God's sake. But to spend half the afternoon encouraging and applauding Sasha's little boy! Throwing coins for him to dive after. Acting the buffoon and threatening him with a wet towel. Sending him like a good boy for grapes and olives. And all this when for two weeks his great performance had been the wounded paedophile! Can you imagine a stupidity more crass? This, at the house of a dear friend? Sasha didn't know him from Adam, of course. But you can imagine the malicious glee with which the likes of Céline Gaspar would fill her in at the first opportunity?

Oh, I was absolutely furious with Mal, I can assure you!

It only increased my anxiety when I heard Val's car pull up outside. She continues to drive a *deux chevaux*. Scarcely practicable, but then that's Val all over for you. I was anxious because sooner or later word was bound to get back to Jeremy, you see. It mattered not a jot that Val had not even been there until quite late in the evening. The fact that Sasha hung around with such a disreputable set in the first place was laid squarely at her door. But stupidly I hadn't expected the two boys to be at the party, and so it never entered my head to warn Mal in advance. Not of course that he isn't old and ugly enough to realise for himself what he's doing! But you could never know with the likes of Jeremy just how he might manipulate any pretext that involved the boys.

Now, whether or not Val realised any of this, her instinct was absolutely impeccable. Course, over the years I'd told her all about Malcolm Little. But she can have had no idea of the extent to which he'd been playing to the gallery ever since he arrived in Antibes. One way or another, she had no sooner arrived at the party than she set out towards the pool, and her first act was to dismiss the boy.

'Rupert. Help Mummy to find some more plates, would you?'

The fact is it was already beginning to get quite cool, and I think poor little Rupert was worn out from so much attention to his antics.

There's a small alcove at some remove from the house, overlooks the next tier of the grounds. The place used to be a small farm, terraced. The two of them repaired to the alcove with their drinks and do you know, they spent the entire evening out there. Every so often, a few words of conversation would drift over to the house, or a peel of laughter. But there they sat, undisturbed, until long after they'd become silhouettes. There was a beautiful, diaphanous twilight. Very Provence. Cerulean, with just a rind of moon over the mountains. And, like a shadow between cardboard cutout trees, the taut figure of Marcel Duchamp. Everyone in the house took turns looking out at the scene. Céline Gaspar even suggested that perhaps they were lovers, meeting again after twenty years. And really, at times I did feel quite envious.

I've never quite got to the bottom of what precisely they can have talked about for so long. When she's not being a society bitch, Val is famously reticent. As for the other character, any time I'd ask him, he'd become infuriatingly vague. Oh this, that, nothing in particular. I can tell you one thing for free, Valerie Yates is not in the habit of sitting out for hours talking to a stranger about 'this, that, nothing in particular!' She does not suffer fools gladly. But there you have it.

•••

I realise you're impatient for me to get back to Sandymount. To the scene of the crime. But the interlude was crucial, you see. In all, he was away from that quagmire for thirteen weeks. Prior to this I doubt he'd left the country once in twenty years. Soon after the party at Sasha's I had to come back to Dublin, and only saw him when I flew out again six weeks later.

He managed just fine without me. So you see, taking into consideration how he comported himself in Provence, for all his foolishness, I had every reason to hope that he was finally over his infatuation.

Three months. Thirteen weeks. That's how long he was away. It was not inconceivable that in this time even that witch Ms Ramsey would have tired of keeping watch from her bath-chair at the top window of number twenty-six, Martello Mews.

But of course, the boy came back. Mal tried to keep it from me at first. But it was immediately apparent from his poorly concealed excitement. One day there was a light in his eye and that unmistakeable illusiveness in his manner. At every turn his voice betrayed him. And his hands. Most of all, the forced inconsequentiality of his conversation. Without realising it, he was constantly tripping over himself, just like a schoolboy whose laces are untied.

He'd learned nothing, after all. Oh, he was as sly as ever. This time he tried to conceal the fact of the boy's return from me by farming him out to Manus Bates's young fellow. Manus was a very old friend of Mal's who'd died some years before. But there's something distinctly unpleasant about the son. Something vaguely sinister. One could imagine him making obscene phone-calls, torturing animals, that sort of thing.

But I was far too old a hand to be taken in by any such ruse. Within a matter of days I had sniffed out where Mal was keeping his great love. I haven't become such a recluse that I don't still have a network of social spies I can call upon! Besides, Mal is so bloody conspicuous. He simply *could not* stay away from that flat, not for more than a couple of evenings at a time.

All the same I was entirely at a loss as to what to do. I knew it could only end badly. But what to do about it? What to do?

It would clearly have been pointless to try to reason with Mal, to try to point out the absurdity of his infatuation. You see, the boy had come back to him of his own accord. He hadn't looked for it, that was the point. And so it mattered not a jot that this Bluebottle only wanted to use him, to touch him for money. It didn't make an iota of difference that he couldn't have cared less whether Mal had lived or died from the beating he'd given him.

I knew it could only end badly. But what I didn't foresee was just how rapidly things would come to a bloody climax.

I met Mal on the Saturday for brunch, in a café in Ranelagh. Lattes, paninis, quite the place with the beautiful set. We'd do this maybe once a month. But I realised at once something new was afoot. Mal was being evasive, you see. Eventually, he let slip just enough for me to know that he'd come to some sort of an accommodation with his brother. House. Money.

Now, it so happens that the manager of the bank where Mal has his main account is a very dear friend of mine. It goes without saying that I'd never once abused his trust, never even inquired as to the state of Mal's affairs. But now I was terrified. Terrified that he might do something absolutely crazy. He was in such a giddy state. There was simply no way of knowing what sort of a scheme he might be hatching.

So some time later I called around on the Maguires. Without going into any of the particulars, I simply told Dan that I was very concerned for my good friend Malcolm Little. He'd been acting very eccentrically of late. He might do something of the utmost stupidity now, and then later of course regret it. You might compare him, I explained, to a manic-depressive. And so I pleaded with him simply to keep me informed, if Mal were to do anything out of the ordinary with his account over the next few weeks.

I'd expected resistance. I'd assumed I'd have to plead a little, to offer all sorts of assurances. The Maguires are very upstanding, even old-fashioned. I knew that what I was asking would fly in the face of the banker's ethical code. But Dan really was marvellous about things. He could see I was genuinely upset. Took my hand and pressed it warmly. I consider myself very fortunate to have friends like Dan Maguire.

And sure enough, on the Monday afternoon, the dreaded phone-call came. It seems that Mal, the fool, had gone into the bank in person and withdrawn the entire nine thousand from the account! In cash! Can you believe it! Nine thousand, in fifties and twenties. I can only assume it was on the strength of the settlement he'd made with his brother.

Course, the news only made me all the more desperate. On the one hand I had the horrible certainty that the fool was likely to just hand the lot over to this juvenile in a great, grandiose, lovesick gesture. But even that wasn't the worst of my worries. You must remember this young man was a psychopath. Now, suppose that Mal decided he was only going to give away a smaller amount. It was an absolute certainty that he could not do so without letting slip the full amount, whether because he was too much of a showman, or simply because he's absolutely hopeless at keeping anything of any consequence secret for long. I had a vision of Mal, counting out several hundred from a brown paper bag stuffed tight with the full amount. Now, can you just imagine what the sight of all those multicoloured bricks of money must have on a homeless and altogether violent delinquent?

That night I could not sleep.

I'd tried to ring a couple of times. But infuriatingly, Mal had his phone switched off. I tossed and turned, very cross with him. But do you know, I simply could not get that image out of my head? Mal, grinning like a prize fool and counting out a little bundle of twenties for this scar-faced ruffian who reaches silently for the walking-stick with the silver handle.

By half eleven or twelve, I could be still no longer. Threw the blankets from me and hastily dressed. I felt that there was not a moment to lose. I would simply have to take matters in hand before that idiot did something that could no longer be revoked.

It takes about twenty or thirty minutes on foot to reach the cul-de-sac where Mal has buried himself. I've never been afraid to walk the streets, no matter how late. Besides, I felt I needed the time and the fresh air to organise my thoughts. How I'd explain my arrival. What precisely I'd say to him. I mean, I couldn't very well come straight out and admit that the manager of his branch had breached confidence and informed me about the withdrawal. Perhaps I might invent a friend who had overseen the transaction. But this recourse did not satisfy me. It sounded too… And then, there was the absolute necessity to have him see how grotesque and misplaced this present infatuation really was.

I must've worked myself into quite a state of agitation because before I knew it I'd left the main road and was entering the Mews. I still hadn't determined how best to broach the subject. But then something caught my eye. Something straight out of a disturbing dream. There, skulking by the wall and evidently in some distress, was Trajan. That can't be right, I thought. He was licking furiously at his side. Trajan, I called, moving nearer. But the tom hissed loudly, and then dragged himself in through a gateway, one leg trailing behind.

I looked straight at the house. The light was on in the hall. From the manner it lit the driveway and front lawn it was clear that the door was ajar. I felt an awful certainty clutch at my heart. Another of the cats disappeared into the hedge as I stepped through the gateway, and there was an inhuman yowling. It was like an augury.

I'm not sure if I saw blood or only had the intimation of it. But as I stepped into the hallway I felt as if I was entering the dreadful certainty of a nightmare. And, my God, when I finally found poor Mal! You can only imagine the state he was in.

V | Bluebottle

There's this line out of Rilke that goes, whoever has no house now will never have one. Whoever's alone will stay alone. I swear, that line could've been written about Raymond Fowler.

Now it suited me down to the ground not to have to talk all the time. Not to be pestered. But he never once asked me about my background or my family, or how I was brought up or anything. Or what my plans were now I'd run away, which seemed kind of funny. But like I say, that suited me just fine. I thought it was a bit weird, but then I'd had my fill in Luke's of the Bros always prying into what was none of their fucking business in the first place. As if they could understand the human personality, just by asking a few born-again questions about your early childhood.

Raymond Fowler was what you might call a loner. His dog Keaton, that was company enough for him. But he did talk. In fact he never fucking stopped. He'd sort of talk to himself, when he was setting a fire or when he was shaving or pitching a tent. His words at these times were aimed nowhere. Or else they were aimed equally at the dog, at myself, or if it was getting late, at the blackbirds which, as he used to put it, were busy chipping away at the twilight.

That's how I learned there was so many deserters from the British army down here in the Republic. Did you know that? Ok, I say so many. He only ever mentioned three by name. That in itself speaks volumes, but. Whatever they thought they were signing up to in their teenage years, the Troubles sure as hell wasn't it. He never told me directly, but I've a good idea from scraps and hints of what it was that finally snapped this one night he swam south across Carlingford Lough. Turning wood-kerne, as he put it. It was on account of a couple of teenage lovebirds that was shot thirty or forty times by the patrol he was meant to be in charge of. They'd been joy-riding somewheres outside of Newry and never slowed down when they seen the barricade. Can't have been much more than school kids, he said. So that was that. He'd had enough.

The other thing about Raymo you couldn't miss was his expression. His skin was so tanned or weathered that even in February it was a kind of a ruddy-brown. But that set off his eyes. The whole expression of his eyes was intelligence. It wasn't book-learning, either. It was more than intelligence, but. It was as if he was just on the point of bursting into laughter. Perpetually, just on the point of it. Made him look younger than he was, too. Specially when the tweed cap covered the long, straggly ribs that he'd drag back over his scalp and tie into a braid like a rat's tail.

And it was like, whatever you said to him, no matter how far-fetched, those eyes had heard it all before. That's why they were constantly laughing at you. And what's more, they knew exactly what it was you were going to say before ever you thought of saying it. It was weird so it was, the suntan and farmer's cap and baby blue eyes. It took me weeks to see through it all. In fact he was no more intelligent than I was. But in all honesty, I'd bet anything you like it was on account of that expression in his eyes that made him so successful whenever he went busking. That and the dog.

Oh, he talked all right. I don't just mean to himself, which was non-stop. An odd time, when the mood was on him, he could talk for Ireland. Just so long as it wasn't personal, that was the only rule. Nothing personal. He said once that the whole trouble with people is that all they ever jabber about is who'd said or done what, and then what they themselves had said or done that was in some way more clever. People are self-obsessed he used to say. Which is why the best thing to do is to give them as wide a berth as possible. Only for he needed to eat, I swear to you, I don't think he'd've had any use for people at all. He was what I guess you'd call a simple man, Raymo.

Naïve, maybe. Surprisingly ignorant when it came to some of the most basic facts about the world. But I swear to you, he had a turn of phrase an odd time that made an impression on me. Maybe it was from his store of books that he picked them up.

The Judas kiss. He didn't get that from out of a book. Oh he was quick witted, Raymond Fowler, make no mistake about that.

For all his living rough it was rare enough he snared an animal. A rabbit say, or a pheasant. Or that either one of us managed to trap a fish that was anything much more than a wet piece of paper. Still, it was on these great occasions, when we'd left nothing but a cage of bones or a fish head for the dog, and the two of us lying back and watching the first constellations, that he'd feel the urge to philosophise. If that's the word. He'd stretch out, both arms propped behind his balding head, and it was as if the whole of creation was gearing itself up for the chill and the darkness.

Then, without ever once looking at me, he'd begin: 'Did you never think…'; or 'Did you ever wonder…'. And then off he'd go.

At these times he could talk all right. When the mood was on him. Once or twice I made the mistake of trying to start a talk with him, when he was setting a snare, say. Or when he was trying to figure out with his binoculars and compass and charts just where exactly we were supposed to be. Then he could be one gruff, anti-social fucker. But I learned soon enough to tell his moods apart.

One night in particular stands out, though it's as much for what was to happen later on. I can't say for definite where we were. We were within easy earshot of the sea, that much I do know because I can still hear the sound of the rollers, and I remember the tickling of the tubes of scutch-grass to either side. Porcupine spines, he called them. Porcupine spines, rising with the cold out of the damp sands. It must've been February or March, because I remember Raymo pointed out Leo as it set. The question mark, and then the great rectangle. One thing about living out in the countryside, you get to know your stars. Fowler had a book on the subject, part one only, and missing the front cover. But what was left dealt with the winter constellations, which is what you see most of the time anyhow.

There was this thin shaving of a moon, barely the width of a thumbnail. It set almost immediately after the sun went down, and that set Raymo to talking, or to thinking, which came to pretty much the same thing with him.

'Some philosopher once wrote,' says he, in his Ringo Starr accent gone wrong, 'that none of this would exist if we weren't here to see it. The stars, and the moon. All of space, like. And the Earth too. It exists, so this guy said, as nothing more than a figment. He didn't mean a figment of the imagination either. It seems it all comes out of our heads. Or put it this way. We project it all, just like the projector inside a cinema throws a film onto the screen.'

Suddenly he rolled over. 'You don't believe in God?'

'In God?' I hadn't given the question much thought. One result of growing up in the midst of born-agains, you don't bother. That experience poisons the fundamental questions for you.

'In God,' he insists. 'Do you believe in God?', like he's asking me if I believe in the existence of Africa, or of Liberty Hall.

'You mean Jesus Christ? Redemption? Heaven and Hell and that whole divine comedy?'

'No,' he all but shouts. 'I mean, look! There! Look at the sky!' Here he made such a huge gesture with his hand that the bloody dog sat up and rushed over to where he was pointing. I'll always remember that.

'The entire universe, up above you, stretching on for maybe millions of miles, like. Like it's a colossal ocean. You see, we're only at the shore of the universe. That's where we are. If you listen,' says he, quiet now, 'you can almost hear it.'

I listened, but I could hear nothing beyond the breakers rolling thunderously onto the dark shore. It was March and my clothes felt damp on the stone-cold sands. I shivered. 'But what has any of that got to do with God?'

'You don't imagine all this is accidental?'

Now it was my turn to roll towards him. 'There was this one of the brothers where I was… at school, a Br Martin. An old guy, with thick glasses on him from reading. He used to say that where you see a watch, there must be a watchmaker. It's an old argument apparently. But I remember this one time he showed me this book on astronomy. He turned over the plates, one by one, like they were made of gold leaf or something. Wouldn't let my grubby hands next or near them. The thing about the Bro is, he had this incredible love of books. Didn't matter a flying damn to the Bro if they were sacred or profane.

'So then I'm looking at these plates over his shoulder. Nebulae and clusters and galaxies and what have you. And so he begins to tell me about this old theory. He says it's a heresy, but sure that's Br Martin for you. A heresy! Man is a miniature of the cosmos. You know? The cosmos and the individual are reflections of each other. Look at the galaxies, says the Bro. You see their spirals and whorls? They're the thumbprints of the creator.'

Fowler only grunted. I think he was impressed, all the same.

Months later, the night I'm stood there looking at the pattern of bloody thumbprints I'd pressed onto Fergal Bates's bathroom mirror, that night lying under the stars came back to me.

But I don't want to give the impression that it was always like that with Raymond Fowler. Far from it. Most of the time I was cold and achy and short of sleep, and never knowing what sort of form he'd be in. Every night I'd struggle to get comfortable, and then wake up at five or six in the morning, chilled to the marrow and with the uneven ground pressing into the bones. The lack of sleep had me groggy and irritable. I smelt perpetually of sweat and smoke and damp clothes, and there never seemed to be enough food to go around. Or else it was dismal fare, the cheapest tins and soggy teabags and perpetually mildewed bread, enough to make you gag. I can nearly taste it thinking about it.

Things came to a head in early April. It must've been April. The gorse had the entire coastline an egg-yellow. Fledgling Spring, Raymo used to call it.

It's a real pity he never got to meet the Bro. I think he'd have liked the Bro.

This particular day, Fowler was in one of his gruff moods. No use trying to coax a word out of him at such times. Even the dog kept its distance. He was scraping out forkfuls of tuna flakes in brine into a pot of spaghetti, this for about the fourth fucking time in so many days. Here's a line of poetry I wrote. *Is there any sound more grating than fork tines scratching out the entrails of a tin?* What d'you think of that?

We'd had a moody silence the night before on account of I gave half of my portion to the dog. Now it was exactly like his military fucking mindset to make a point of having more of the same the next day, though we could just as easy have had corned beef or baked beans. D'you know, to this day I still can't so much as smell tinned tuna without my stomach getting giddy?

For about ten minutes I'd been watching his back. Every single move slow and deliberate, the fire just so, the salted water, the old style can-opener you have to push through the lid, the colander, the wooden stirring spoon. I could feel the resentment swilling about inside me. And I knew that he knew all about the surly eyes that were watching him. When the muck was just about ready for serving up, he turns his head ever so slightly, and growls as if to the dog – 'plates weren't properly washed.'

'So wash them!'

I hadn't particularly planned to say this. In fact I hadn't planned to say anything. I'd given the plates, pots and cutlery a resentful dip in the vice-cold stream the night before. And even that much I'd only done on account of that was "the arrangement". When it came to cooking, I was never allowed to do anything beyond peeling the potatoes and gutting the occasional fish.

'What did you say?'

'I said wash your own fucking plates.'

He stopped moving. The pot was suspended about six inches above the coals.

I was already on my feet. I hadn't expected everything to come to a head quite so sudden or over something so stupid as tuna fucking pasta. I was shaking. But not with fear or loathing. With adrenalin. Everything that'd happened me, the disfigurement, the soakings, the lack of sleep, the tuna in fucking brine, had come to a focus in the plaited rat's tail that hung down the back of his limey neck.

'You wash the plates, or else you get the hell out of here.'

'Fuck you!' I shouted. I was staring at his rigid shoulders. I made no move to leave. He knew I was there, stock still, staring. But he refused to look around. Instead, after maybe ten seconds, his shoulders relaxed and he began again to churn the pasta and tuna. 'D'you hear me?' I shouted, even louder. 'I said fuck you!'

I heard him guffaw, or hiccup, or cough, or clear his throat, and I could see the grey stubble on the jowl that was turned in the direction of the dog. Keaton began to skulk over to him, low, wary, but with the tail moving in circles. I know what you're going to do, you bastard. You're going to give my portion to the dog. The dog, too, seemed to know he was involved in what the Bros called "a transgression". And he kept a servile eye turned towards yours truly.

I doubt I could've thought of any act of vandalism more serious than to attack the stay of the tent. One time, in fact it was soon enough after this, we came across a couple of gurriers kicking the place apart. I even recognised one of them, from the night of my scarring. A little, weedy fucker that had held back. How he got into the Pitbulls I don't know. And now here he was kicking our camp apart? By Christ, Fowler didn't half let go on that occasion I can tell you! Knocked seven colours of shite out of the two of them.

No, you simply didn't trespass onto either of the two tents. Not if you wanted to live.

So that's precisely what I found myself doing. I was thrown violently to the ground in a split second, even before the wall of the tent had a chance to sag. With amazing agility for his age and bulk, Fowler was pressing his knees hard into my biceps and holding my jaw fast in one hand, the other raised like a mallet over me and his Liverpool accent so angry it was all spits.

'You touch the tents again you fuchhin' die, you hea' me?'

'Big man!'

His entire weight was on my ribcage. It was impossible for me to breathe. All the same I can remember the sour smell of cloth and smoke and plug tobacco that permeated his bulk. He was breathing fast. I stared up at the silver grey stubble and tried to muster a spit. Then I seen his fist open into a palm. He all but strikes me with it. Instead he shakes my shoulders with restrained violence till I swallowed my spit. Just as well I did.

'What the hell fuchhin' devil has got into you, huh?'

'Fuck you!' I could feel myself teetering on the brink. On the edge of a great abyss of emotion and pity and self-loathing.

'Fuck you,' I screamed, no longer at him, at Fowler, no longer at the plight we were in and the daily grind, no longer at Luke's and the smug sons of bitches on the outside with their cars and suits, no longer at the knife that they'd dug into my face but fuck you, fuck you God and fuck every bit of your lousy fucking creation!

I'd had fits before. The white anger, they called it in Luke's. But nothing like this. This ended, quite literally, in tears. I was struggling to breathe with Fowler squatting heavily on my chest and nearly parting the muscles from my arms with the pressure of his kneecaps. But inside me there was more like this great tsunami of emotion. Some mixture of pity and horror and sick that rose up and blinded my eyes. Then it was spent. And then I was convulsing with tears of pure brine. They scalded my eyes when I felt the weight lift off my chest and I drew in the first great gasp of air. Oh, suffering God, the sweet air of the evening, how dear it seemed to me at that moment.

My eyes were still shut fast and the sweet air was filling my lungs and do you know what happened next? I swear to you, it nearly made me choke, the… poignancy of it. My cheekbone was nuzzled and the next thing, I felt Keaton's tongue like rough fabric dabbing the salt track of my tears.

I swear, that broke my heart so it did.

But Raymond Fowler wasn't through with me yet. Not by a long shot.

All I'll say is, it had the desired effect. After that episode, I was what the Bros called a chastened character. Oh, he read me the entire riot act that night.

From that time on there was no way I was going to be allowed mope around at the campsite while himself and the dog went into a town to beg a few coins with the flute. No way.

'You think you're the only one that was ever scarred?' he hissed at me. 'You feel sorry for yourself? You want to see some of the fuchhin' injuries that's part and parcel of soldiering – just kids, with shrapnel wounds, amputations, faces left like a friggin' jigsaw, or melted with third degree burns. I've seen it all, so don't you come crying to me with your scar.'

So he said, anyhow. I didn't exactly see when or where that was all supposed to have happened. The only place that he'd served was South Armagh for fuck's sake. Not exactly the Mekong Delta. But it had the desired effect just the same. It got so I even began to go into the towns with him.

•••

A few weeks later it all came to an end.

I'm still damned if I know what happened. Images, snatches, that's all I have. Like trying to piece together a crime-scene out of some bad dream you've woken from. Or maybe you haven't woken from it, that's the point.

So this one morning, I'm scurrying along a country lane and about fifty yards behind, skulking after me, is Keaton. Every so often I stop to throw a stone at him and he cowers down into the bank of the ditch. But then once I set off again and turn around after a couple of minutes he's there, shadowing me. It's like he's some incarnation of shame or guilt out of a ghost story.

I must've been running for more than a couple of hours already because it feels like my legs are made of rubber and my shirt is clinging to me with the sweat. But it's like I woke up running. My head is banging, like I've eaten rat poison or something. One thing I do know is that I started running before first light. That much I do remember. That, and himself left for dead, the scalp black and congealed and my fingers sticky with it. And I've already covered more than a mile before I notice the dog shadowing me. Get away, Keaton! Fuck off! Get away! Shoo!

At one point I stop and I double over with my hands on my abdomen and while I'm drawing breath I keep half an eye on him to see if he'll come up to me. But it's like there's an invisible circle drawn around me at about twenty yards that he's too smart to enter. Instead of which he hunkers down low at the edge of it and keeps watching me. One eye brown and the other such a light blue that it's almost white. It's just exactly that line in the elegies I showed you, the bit about the animals. The animals know we're not at home in the world. So then I hit him on the hip with half a brick and he lets a yelp out of him and when I make a feint at him he scampers away backwards like a crab. But still I can't get rid of him.

Christ, is that pale eye going to follow me all the way to Dublin?

It was Mal's idea I go and stay with the fat guy. I didn't tell him what had happened. The truth is, I couldn't have, even if I'd've wanted to. But in any case, he was all in a flap and started swallowing mouthfuls of bitter tears about the state of my face. He hadn't seen me since. I swear, by the way he was whimpering you'd think it was his own face had been carved up.

But by the time I got to his place I didn't know if I was coming or going. By this stage I'd slept under a half dozen hedges, too confused and too careful to try to bum a ride. I got the impression every car was looking out for me. Every window I passed had a pair of prying eyes behind it.

It was getting late, not quite dark. He opened the door after a couple of minutes in that oriental dressing gown of his, looking puffy and already half pissed. I'll tell you something, you want to have seen his expression when I stepped out into the light and pulled back the hood. Pure comical, man! He couldn't've been more surprised if I'd been the ghost of his mother.

'Oh my poor boy,' he exclaims, hands to either cheek just like a drama queen, 'what have they done to you?'

He sort of mooched around for the next couple of hours, hovering, all sniffs and sobs. I watched him from the sofa as impassive as any one of his cats. Oh my dear boy, he kept sighing to no-one in particular, as if it was some kind of a mantra. As if maybe by saying it he could turn the clock back to some night before they gave me my Judas kiss. But there was fuck all chance of that. And besides, there was some spark in his weepy eye which said he was over the moon that I'd returned to him. The old faggot.

But I wasn't to be allowed to stay there. He fussed and bumbled about all the next morning, to-ing and fro-ing, making excuses, debating with himself, explaining, begging forgiveness. It simply wasn't an option. He was under surveillance, around the clock, even now, even as we speak, oh my dear boy, my dear Bluebottle, you can't begin to imagine how they persecute me!

So the long and the short of that is, he offloads me onto this fat nephew of his. Nephew, so-called. Nephew, my hairy hole! It was some ex-lover, I've no doubt, from years ago when he was maybe a bit thinner. Used to call him Uncle. Like, *Uncle*? On the other hand, there was some well-thumbed porn-mags I'd found in the bathroom so maybe he was straight after all. A closet heterosexual, ha ha! But a sorry case one way or another.

I wasn't about to put up any major resistance. A great will paralysed. That was me. I had too much going on in my head to be bothered by where I was to find a bed for the next few weeks. The less we knew about one another, the better it suited me.

My first thought was to try to find Gobber. I knew I needed to talk to someone who'd known me from before. I'd never really made any close friends at Luke's, what you might call confidents, but I suppose there'd been a few times I'd talked through the small hours to Gobber Molloy. At one time we shared a bunk.

Eventually, what I planned to do was to go back to find Br Martin. If there was anyone who could explain to me what was going on, who could put some sort of shape or sense to any of it, it would be the Bro. But for all I knew, he could be dead, or gone away. Maybe Gobber could tell me that, too. But then, before I ever attempted to find the Bro I needed to get straight in my head just what exactly had happened down in Wicklow.

So I hung out for an entire morning at the bus-shelter across the road from the supermarket where Gobber used to work, the hood of the parka pulled up over my head. He didn't show, and when I saw the first of the staff cross over the road on their lunch-break, I decided to chance asking after him. If they were curious, I was an old friend up from the country.

He hadn't worked there in months, the fucker.

This set me right back. I had to be wary. I mean I had to be on my guard against everyone. This was the capital city, and anyone could be a plain-clothes cop. But you know what they say about losing yourself in a crowd? And I remembered once, too, having read this story about a guy who hides a letter by leaving it out in the open, in full view of everyone, while the cops go through his apartment. So you know what I do? I take to sitting on one of the Liffey bridges with a cardboard box set out in front of me, the parka drawn up around my face on account of the breeze that comes up off the river. Homeless. You can't be any more invisible than that.

You have to understand. What I needed above all was time. I needed to think. I needed the mental space to set out the bits I recalled and to try to piece the jigsaw together. I could probably have hung about by day in the flat up off of Eccles St, but the truth is I didn't entirely trust this guy, the one who referred to Malcolm as Uncle. There was something devious about the cunt. Besides, he had a habit of making the atmosphere unpleasant, as if my staying there was this big burden to him.

Let me try to give you an idea of what I knew. What I thought I knew. I remembered only fragments, feelings, images. What made it worse was it was next to impossible to be sure these weren't imaginary. The first continuous memory I had, the first that I didn't doubt, was of that morning in the hills, weary from running and with Keaton shadowing me at a safe distance. I knew well I'd done something bad. But this is where it becomes confused.

What I couldn't shake from me was that sense of guilt. I was nervous, the way you are when you've done something real mean or dirty. Something to be ashamed of, if it ever came to light. But then, that's how paranoia is always meant to feel, right? The rage of a bluebottle, Malcolm had said about yours truly. But paranoia is more like the rage of butterflies. I tell you one thing, you get to know all about it in here in this place, that and everything else that's fucked up.

But it's like sometimes you wake from a bad dream, and the emotion is just as real and as heavy as if you'd actually committed a crime. D'you get me? That emotion can hang about your neck for the entire day and drag you down with it. Even though you've done nothing.

So that's how I felt. That, and a splitting headache. And my mouth was like a rat was after dying in it. Pure dry, and a rotten, bitter taste. Like I say, it was like I was after eating rat poison. And guilt, like a tonne weight. And then as well, just like out of a dream, there was this vision I kept on seeing that set my heart clambering up the walls of my ribs every time I seen it. It was of Raymo. Stretched out, he was. Bloody, like I'd left him for dead. Only it didn't seem real. D'you want to know what was really weird? The image of him stretched out was like it was in black and white. Even the blood was black. I know it sounds mad, but it was like something out of an old picture.

It wasn't real, maybe. Only for the fact, there was a second kind of evidence. This was even more mad, so it was. My hands, and my fingers. These were ragged, like as if I'd been handling rough boulders. They were still shaking whenever I stopped for breath. Now, I'd often made mincedmeat of my hands in the past. My knuckles and everything. Nothing new there, says you! But this time, when I went to examine them, there was no cuts or gashes that could've explained the sticky streaks that were caked across them and that had both shirt cuffs stiff and blackened. I was a right mess. And the heart was skipping inside of me like a trapped bird.

I sat on a milestone and I stared at the dried blood, with the dog hovering just out of range like a guilty shadow. But the only memory I could drag up was of staring at Raymond Fowler's broad scalp with the thin hair pulled into a rat's tail behind. Hour after hour, my mind kept running in circles, like a hamster caught on a treadmill.

•••

One day, while I was sitting on Capel Street Bridge trying, like I say, to give myself the space to think, I became aware that this woman had stopped across the way and was staring straight at me. Struck me like a kick in the solar plexus it did. I tried to shield my face as best I could, and I stopped looking over at her. But after a few minutes, when the traffic stopped for the third or fourth time, I could sense her shuffle over and stand in front of me. So when she wouldn't budge I met her stare. Full on, like.

It took me a while to recognise her. D'you know who it was? That ancient sculpture woman that used to come to Malcolm's place an odd time. An old tweed coat, open, a head-scarf, a face that was as tanned and wrinkled as the wicked witch of the west. Everything about her gave the impression she was sizing me up. The way she might look at a piece of sculpture, say. So I stared back, unflinching.

The comedy continued until she unclipped a purse, pulled out a bundle of twenties, maybe ten of them, and poked them towards me like the barrel of a gun. My hand remained by my side. Like I was going to take her money without knowing what her game was?

'Take it.'

'Why?'

'Take it!'

'What's this about, lady?'

'Take it, damn you.' There was no way I was going to, not without some sort of an explanation. Just cause I was down and out? She seemed to cop.

'I want you to stay away from him.' It probably sounds mad, but I stared at her like a fucking eejit, not understanding. She might as well've been speaking a foreign language. The tightly rolled bills were so close to my face they were of focus, and above the blue blur I watched the aged mouth move and repeat the request. She must've thought I was being deliberately thick-headed because she began to poke my shoulder with her roll of money.

'Do you hear? I want you to promise that you'll leave him alone.'

'Malcolm?' I asked. The penny had dropped.

'He has nothing for you!'

I think I must've laughed at this. At the novelty of it! Seriously, I think I must've laughed, or guffawed, because a glower darkened the face. The face had approached so close that I could see the powder on it like dust on a moth.

'I will not have you destroy him again,' it hissed.

I levered myself up, awkwardly on account of she was standing so close, and painfully on account of I'd hardly moved all morning and my legs were dead. To anyone watching, the whole thing must've looked like a caper out of the silent movies. Staring menacingly at my eyes, she tried to force her pistol of money under my palm, which was pressed downwards onto the bridge's iron lattice.

'You can keep your money, love,' I whispered at her ear. 'I don't want it.'

I don't know who'd written that particular piece of script for me! It must've been just exactly the right thing to say, all the same. Because I'd less trouble than I feared easing the old bat away from me and then walking stiffly in the direction of Parliament Street.

I was getting very uneasy our little scene might begin to attract attention. Some cop was bound to get curious. And cops I did not need!

So later that night, the comedy continues with a scene even more bizarre. Up among the hierarchy of angels they must've been having a good laugh for themselves. Some time after dark, Mal, pathetic, love-sick Mal shows up at Bates's place with an expression on him like one of the Magi before the manger, and with this entire camel-train of gifts.

Bates of course makes short shrift of him. He seems to derive a queer pleasure out of goading a codger even less upright than himself. You ask me, his being such a loser has brought out a right vindictive streak in him. My stock, on the other hand, would appear to have risen considerably. Once Malcolm has been dismissed, Bates jokes openly with me for the first time. Then he has this whim to set out a banquet from the gifts that had been left, the real posh food like I couldn't even dream about when I was in Wicklow. There's even some vino.

I suppose, what with the disappointment after having waited for Gobber and then the unpleasantness of being recognised on the bridge, it's sort of inevitable the first show of camaraderie loosens my tongue. That and the vino, for if the truth be told, I've never in my life got used to wine. Raymond Fowler had nothing but disdain for anything alcoholic. So in the end, unlikely as it sounds, Fergal Bates became the first living being to hear my partial confessions.

Looking back, I'm not sure what good the episode done me. It broke the silence, if nothing else. But as to putting some order on the tangles of my memory? That was too much to ask. We got drunk, and I babbled about Judith and the better times with Raymo. In spite of the vino, some trace of suspicion held me from telling fatboy the detail of the dried blood. It ended, I says to him, just like that. One day. Abruptly. One morning, I was simply running away.

But it was no good. Talking was all very well, but it done nothing to remove the guilt. The next morning I was still paralysed with the feeling of having done something wrong and shameful. The rage of butterflies. Just because it couldn't be brought into focus didn't stop it messing with my head.

The hierarchy of angels had another great laugh a weekend soon after that when Bates informs me that Uncle, as he insists on calling him, would be expecting me on the following night. *Expecting* me! Can you imagine? What sort of a role did the old faggot imagine he was playing? Or how exactly did he see my end of the bargain? *Expecting* me, I ask you! Still, it never really entered my head not to go to him. If nothing else, taking part in his sideshow might help calm down the rage of butterflies that for weeks now would give my stomach no let up.

I spent the day mooching around at one remove from Luke's. It would've been a lack of courtesy not to. Besides, I still had the vague hope of catching a glimpse of the Bro. Br Martin. I knew which was his dormitory. But all day, the tiny window remained stubbornly blank. Blank as a false eye. Of course, it was possible he was away. But for some time now I'd a darker premonition. Maybe my flight from the place had somehow caused all possible bridges back to be burned. D'you get me? Maybe the Bro had died. How would I have found out, on the streets or out in the sticks? And I hadn't even managed to get to his goddamned funeral.

Being so close to the building had a peculiar effect on me. The institution. You could imagine it being a hospital. Or a mental home, say. Some relic of the Victorian era, where any kind of sickness was to be hidden away. It was the sight of the grey, pebble-dashed, dismal walls, with their outside drainpipes like metal entrails and the rows of doll's house windows, that kind of short-circuited the long months I'd been away from Luke's. All of a shot, I could feel a series of emotions rise up in me that I would've sworn were dead.

But at the same time, this same building was a betrayal of the past. Like it was a poor copy, not quite right in its dimensions. Even the hoarding by the main gate, with its weekly advertising jingle taken out of John's Gospel, seemed in some way a replica. I was gripped by the bizarre idea that the same would've held true if I'd chanced upon any of the Bros.

Towards evening, I took my leave of Luke's for the last time.

I still had several hours to kill before I was 'expected' at Mal's place. *Expected*, for Jaysus' sake! I hovered in the vicinity of a major road junction, and when the lights were red, I watched the immigrants weaving through the cars with bundles of evening papers. Watching them, it slowly began to dawn on me how immensely fucking dumb I'd been. Never once over the past week had it entered my head to scan the papers for the news story that'd throw light on what precisely had happened. I mean for fuck sake! If he was dead, if a body had been discovered, there'd surely to God be news of a man-hunt!

I called one of them over and took a late edition from the top of his bundle. Fingering through it as I walked, but always with one eye to the street in case there was a guard, I made my way down along Pearse Street in the direction of Ringsend. The possibility of stumbling upon an article raised the butterflies inside me, and before I realised where I was going I'd pushed on blindly towards the Pigeon House. Here I sat on a stack of breezeblocks that was overgrown with burdocks and hidden from the public view. Finally I got to leaf through the paper from the front page to the back. But there was not a solitary word in it to accuse me of any crime.

So far so good. But there again, a lot of time had passed since I'd run away from Wicklow with dried blood on my hands.

So now I began to consider how I might gain access to old newspapers. Public libraries must keep back-numbers. It stands to reason. But the problem here was, in order to register in a library you have to have proof of a permanent address. Someone would have to vouch for me, and I had no desire at all to ask fatboy. Not after the hints I might've given him the night the vino had loosened up my tongue. Anyway, he always let on he couldn't wait to be shot of me out of his flat. I doubted old Mal could be relied upon to co-operate either. He may have been sick with desire, but with his type, fear of a legal compromise would always win out. In the eyes of the Law I was still a minor, and it wouldn't do at all to have a minor registered at Mal's address.

Still, as I walked out along the coast road I thought I'd give him a try, if only to see how pale he'd turn, how he'd wriggle and squirm in order to get out of the bind.

This thought put me in a good mood. Maybe I have that same cat's impulse to cruelty I'd noticed in fatboy Bates. Or maybe Malcolm was simply one of those individuals who invites cruelty from anyone that finds themselves in a position to mete it out to him. But I was also light-headed.

I hadn't eaten since I'd left the flat about twelve hours before, and I'd scarcely a crust of bread then. One habit I'd picked up from sleeping rough was to stash my pockets with sachets of sugar whenever the opportunity arose, and I now opened six or seven in a row and swallowed down their contents. Bad idea mate! I was instantly dizzy, and might've killed without remorse for a glass of water. But of course naturally, between where I stood and Mal's place, there was neither shop nor pub. I arrived with tongue and lips swollen with sticky residue, and with tiny white sparks exploding like fireworks at the edge of my vision.

Malcolm was dressed up for the occasion. I swear, he was dressed up with such formal casualness that, if it hadn't been for the raging drought in my mouth, I would've laughed in his face so I would. His clothes was elegant but not entirely buttoned, or not correctly buttoned. His coiffure was delicately disordered. All part of the game, of course.

'I hope you're hungry!' he announced, rather too grandly.

From behind his back there floated a delicious waft of something roasting. You must remember I was famished. But my tongue was by now literally cleaving to the roof of my mouth.

'I need a drink,' I mumbled.

He seemed delighted with this riposte, because his mouth gaped open and his eyebrows arched. I began to wonder if I'd been the author of a great witticism. But Mal was already leading the way into the flagged interior. He lost no time at all in conjuring two glasses of a chilled, sweet white wine that he must've had ready in the fridge. More sugar! But mine was drained almost before he had time to propose a toast.

'Happier times!' He looked at me meaningfully as he said it. To my left, I noticed there was a number of feline shapes ranged like china ornaments on the outside sill of the window. Mal followed my eyes even as he was topping up my glass.

'The cats,' he exclaimed. 'I banished them!' He leaned a little closer to me and lowered his voice, as if he feared they might overhear. 'I've banished them for the night. A lesson in humility. Cats take everything so much for granted.'

Oh God, I was thinking, will I have the patience to endure this for a full hour? It never even struck me that he'd said 'for the night'.

Soon after this I was seated at the table and Mal, who'd put on an apron, was fussing over a game-bird of some description. The air behind him was nostalgic with one of his wheedling operas. The sweet wine of his was if anything making my thirst more cloying, and the sparks were now swarming like midges about my vision. It was while waiting for mother-hen to bring over the main course that I experienced a weird fucking turn. Seriously spooky, man.

There's this huge liver-spotted mirror that used to hang towards the top of the stairs. The frame must've been damaged, or else the reverse needed to be re-silvered, because it was now leaning against a card table somewhere behind my left shoulder. A shadow crept across it. I was instantly certain of what the reflection, half-glimpsed, had been. And this horrible shudder ran through me as I looked quickly away. A violent, icy shiver. I knew, if I turned back, the uneven eyes of Fowler's dog, the one brown and the other like ice, would accuse me from the depths of that mirror.

I was perfectly aware I was hallucinating. I'm not fucking stupid. It wasn't as if it was the first time I'd had visions. Or that I'd been in the grip of the fear. You might think being aware of that would help to calm the jitters. It doesn't.

Mal had by now taken his place at the head of the table, and must've set a plate with a steaming breast of game-bird before me. He was watching me, wondering what held me from moving. So in order to stop him asking I cut a piece off the bird and placed it in my mouth. All the while, my heart was skipping about, and I was having serious trouble with the spirals of fireflies orbiting my eyes. The only small relief was, I found a different wine before me. It was a red which tasted vaguely of grass, but which at least gave me some chance of slaking my thirst. Of course, I was guzzling it.

'Well?'

'Very good!'

He kept watching me.

'Tender,' I tried.

Mal was trying very hard not to be on edge. Not to let his concern show. He always becomes so obviously forced at these times. But it was all I could do to stop my hands trembling, and to ignore the shadows that were beginning to creep about the corners of the room. My glass was empty.

'You're really putting it away!'

'Thirsty.'

I began to eat conscientiously. Methodically. It struck me I needed something solid in my gut. Some soakage. At times I was vaguely aware that, from the far end of the table, Mal was engaging in some sort of banter. I saw that his mouth was moving. His teeth. But the words and guffaws remained unintelligible. So I smiled or nodded at each pause or guffaw.

The shadows moving about the corners of the room are becoming more solid. I'm getting seriously spooked. The silver pool of the mirror is lurking over my shoulder and I'm scared to look at it.

My glass is more often empty than full.

'I'll fetch another bottle.'

What's happening? What's going on? I'm nervous, like when I know a fit is coming on. Over my shoulder, I feel the eyes of Fowler's dog. A shadow darts across the floor and I stand up, overturning the wine glass. A dark trickle on the white cloth. Crimson.

'I'll come with you, Mal.' But the words don't come out.

Another shadow. It disturbs the foot of the curtain. Cat.

Malcolm is at the entrance to the cellar. He's moving something in his hands. Keys, a ring of gaoler's keys. Cellar. So now he locks it up? Perhaps since I robbed him?

I watch him sort through the keys, an old man. He's unaware that I'm there behind him. He's an inch or two smaller than my memory of him. When he opens the door to go down the stairway his movements are arthritic.

I listen to him shuffling about below. The cellar is tiny, not much larger than one of those medieval chambers the Bro once told me about. What they used to call a 'little ease'. The door has angled until it's almost closed. It leaves a wedge of thin light like a frame around it. Now a cat. A familiar. It appears and nudges the door with its ear. I step forward as if I'm going to help. But instead I pull the door shut. Then turn the key in it. I wait, listening for the steps of the old man on the cellar stair.

Come on, he will say. Very funny. Later, open the door, you've had your joke. And then, this is getting quite tiresome, you know.

•••

To seize a cat is about as crazy as to do battle with brambles. Or rose bushes that've been enchanted so they thrash about. I'd no conscious intention of doing it. But then, I'd no conscious intention of locking the old man in the cellar either. When I returned into the dining room I found the place was already infested with the fuckers. Malcolm must've left a window open somewhere to the rear of the house. As inevitable as rising water, they'd found a way to enter. There were even a pair of them tugging over the carcass of the bird. Jesus, I hate fucking cats. They make my flesh crawl they do.

I'm not sure what happened next. All I can say for sure is, my actions of that evening had the effect of calming the panic inside me. The butterflies. And of banishing Fowler's dog. With what a court would no doubt describe as foresight, I shut both the doors to the room. The windows, too. Then, ever so softly, I set several plates on the floor, bated with bones and shreds of meat. I think I might've even been humming, to allay their suspicion.

Then I set upon them like a man possessed.

I was in a state of exhilaration when I arrived back at Bates' place some hours later that night. My hands were trembling, but now it wasn't only adrenalin. It was from the literally hundreds of gashes and scrapes that the cats' flaying claws had torn, from my elbows down to my fingers. Sharp as needles they were. In my ears there still echoed the horrendous, human clamour of that menagerie as it tried to escape. Also, the frantic slapping of Mal's palms against the locked cellar door. I can't say for certain if he screamed. In my dreams, he does.

I found myself standing on the threshold of the flat, with no memory of how I got back there. My forearms felt as if they'd been immersed in scalding water, or as if someone had poured paraffin over them and set them alight. But here's the mad bit. Loads of people must've seen me. It would've taken about an hour to walk in from Sandymount to Nelson St, and it wasn't so late that the streets was empty. I wonder what these people must've thought, watching the very figure of homeless youth emerge from the night like a strange fish, to flash past before sinking once more into the murk. This hooded figure, hunched over arms that were black and raw with blood? Obviously no-one thought to call the police, much less an ambulance.

I stood by the railings for some time, my fingers trembling as if they'd been flayed. I was unsure if I'd ever enter that flat again. The wisest course would be simply to walk, and to keep on walking. After all, it seemed as though at present I was in some way invisible. I fancied I could pass right through this heartless city, unchecked and unnoticed. As though I'd no more substance than a shadow.

But instead, of course, I beat at the door and then stood back, so the streetlight would fall on me. After about a minute he opened the door. Fatboy. To this day I remember the slowly widening eyes, and the gradually listing grimace on his lips that was not quite a smile.

He removed his bulk and allowed me to pass inside. The face, and this I remember like it was yesterday, was still contorted into an expression of half disbelief and half complicity. It was like I was in some way fulfilling this mad expectation of me he'd long held. But one he hardly dared to go on hoping for. That look of his threw me. This was some bad fucker I'd been thrown together with! And so all at once I was all efficiency and bustle.

'Dettol,' I ordered. He shook his head blandly.

'Dettol,' I repeated, pushing my bloodied forearms literally under his nose. 'Disinfectant!'

He shook his head again, his face as rigid as a mask.

'I have none,' he squeaked. His voice was reverent and ridiculously high. 'But you will need to wash those.'

'I fucking know!'

'I think there's some soap in the shower.'

I stared at him, then swung about and paced into the airless cubicle that contained toilet, sink and shower. A noisy, naked bulb hung from the ceiling. I drew the bolt noisily and noisily turned on the shower.

It was while I was in the bathroom that I began to press the ball of my thumb against the mirror, dipping it into what scratches were still open whenever I ran out of colour. To this day I don't know why I done it. Leaving those bizarre hieroglyphics, those sticky thumbprints all across its surface, tracing out the word "Fowler", only the cuts had dried before it was finished. Each thumbprint was like a wax seal. A miniature red galaxy, as the Bro would've said.

I returned after quite an interval. The pain of the hot water on my arms had almost made me pass out. I'd had to sit on the toilet, the seat down, while I passed the shower nozzle over each arm in turn. My head was swimming, screaming, and both hands trembled wildly, making it difficult to pick away the torn bits of skin. Through the door Bates asked after me several times, but I ignored him.

When at last I re-emerged, my forearms wrapped in towel and tee-shirt, he'd taken up position opposite the sofa. The way the lamplight fell across his waxy face made it appear more like a Halloween mask than ever. Or like one of those gargoyles you do sometimes see in churches. And the crooked grin more lop-sided than before. He was staring at me in absolute amazement. I swear, he could've been a second-rate medium whose spells have finally conjured up the impossible demon, years after all faith or hope has died.

Suddenly it hit me. Christ, he thinks I've done in the old codger!

I began to laugh. Who wouldn't have? It was too comical.

I lay down across the sofa, threw back my head, and began to shake and howl with laughter. This fat fuck, with his leer of a malicious disciple, actually thinks I've done old Mal in! I laughed, choked, heard Bates try to echo a single note of my laughter. His was more like a hiccup. I glanced at him, extended my arms upwards and waved them, like trophies. The tee-shirts began to unwind, like unfurling bloody flags.

My Christ, I thought. He thinks the blood that's dried through the cloth is Malcolm's blood! And he's fucking delighted!

I looked at him again. He was nodding, like one of those toys you do see on the rear window of a car. Dear God, I thought, what a world. What a world!

At some point that night or in the small hours of the morning I began to grow feverish. My mouth became dry, and though I had Fergal Bates bring me glass after glass from the kitchen tap, I may as well have been pouring the water onto sand. Images and even voices began to swim about me, but I couldn't bring them into focus. By this time all consciousness had moved down to my forearms, which felt like they'd been wrapped in razor wire. At times I became aware that I was talking to the ceiling, to the lamp, to the wine glass, and I could feel my forehead burning.

I slipped into oblivion by slow degrees.

I don't know how long I was out of it. Days, probably. And I don't know what sort of tranquillisers they'd put me on when they'd done my arms. They were cleaned up, and in clean bandages. They were now ten times more itchy than sore.

But what I do know is, when I did come round, and long before they brought me out here to this nuthouse, the eyes of the dog had stopped following me. And the rage of butterflies was still.

VI | Fergal

The place is being watched. Fuckedy fuck. *Not* a film-script I want to be in.

This time I'm sure of it. The stakeout, if that's the word for it, has been going on for more than a fortnight. Ever since the night of the massacre round at Uncle's, so far as I'm aware. Or the morning after.

At first I thought it must be Mahood's men, trying to ratchet up the pressure. But for once I'm ahead of payments. Besides, it's not their style. A brick through the window or lighter fuel through the letterbox, that's more the style of Anto and cronies. They'd hardly have the patience to stake a place.

These watchers have no shortage of patience. They squat alternately on the Eccles or Berkeley end of the street, drinking interminable black coffees in what is termed, with no irony intended, an unmarked car.

But I don't want to get ahead of my story.

Two cats were killed outright. Another three had to be destroyed. Nominally, an entire Roman dynasty. But I was in no position to realise at the time that the tally consisted solely of tabbies. Bateman had been sound asleep when that mobile-phone sounded its tattoo on his eardrum. The screech of a hysterical banshee, foretelling murder and mayhem. Of course, I should have known it would have taken a lot more than a psychotic adolescent to put paid to the likes of Uncle. But when, soon after this, the boy stood on the threshold, bloody-armed and reticent as a character out of Millington Synge, I actually believed for a moment the old reprobate was dead.

All for some grubby bundles of money. It'd be the price of him!

The young assassin's mind began to ramble, even before it got light. Some of the scars on his arms were really quite horrendous. Scarcely surprising that the cerebral cortex should take refuge in delirium. Before he'd taken to the couch, he'd rinsed the scratches and wrapped them in old tee-shirts, hardly the last word in hygiene. When finally I got Dr Jacqueline Moneygrubber to call out, she had quite literally to peel the tee-shirts from the wounds, pulling lines of soft scabbing away from them. My testicles were so appalled at this operation that they squirmed up tight into my bowels, the darlings. But that was later on. By that time, the boy had already been mumbling into the air for the best part of two days.

But the author really must endeavour not to get ahead of his story. On that first morning, Fergal Bates was entirely at a loss as to what to do. He hadn't slept a wink, as the idiom has it. First the vatic phone-call, then the bloody apparition. For hours after that, the visitor's slow slide into a delirium, venting itself in intimations of violence and assault. I was mentally exhausted at the riddle these snatches set me, and all night as I kept vigil my eyes filled with sandy insomnia.

The crux, of course, was that I still didn't know if it was Uncle who'd been set upon. Everything appeared to point to it. It's not as if it would've been the first time. But the longer the night wore on, the more convinced I was that eternal, interminable, indestructible Mal hadn't had so much as a hair of his oversized head touched.

Neither had a cursory search of my Samaritan's pockets produced any evidence whatsoever of stolen cash. I admit to the search. After all, we're among friends. This absence, I have to say, came as a surprise, even a disappointment. I don't mean I had any designs on the money. Far from it. It was simply that filthy lucre featured prominently in the film-script I'd been mentally preparing. But if money had not been the motivation, what could possibly have impelled impulsive youth to batter old age? My mind ran in tedious circles. Around dawn I may even have dozed. I started awake, cold and stiff, prodded by the nagging inconvenience of what to do.

What to do?

Even supposing I'd forensically determined the felinity of the flayed forearms, my experience of feverish adolescents whose limbs had been lacerated by cats' claws was hardly extensive. Instinct did insist that the old bugger was alive and well, but conscience (or something) wanted to be certain of it. Still, I was most reluctant to redial Uncle's number for fear that the Old Bill might later trace the call. Might indeed be already awaiting the contact. Counting on it, in fact. To postpone my indecision, I decided to boil up a mug of rust-coloured tea. Earl Grey, as it so happened. Now, while the kettle was struggling asymptotically towards the elusive boil, I chanced to turn on the radio. I'd missed the main story, but none of the remainder of the news mentioned an aggravated assault. Could it be that the death had been so violent and gruesome that it had stolen the top spot? It was hardly likely, but doubt continued to niggle.

I abandoned the teabag to its desolate mug and took this doubt with me down to the local greasy spoon. Nothing quite like rashers and sausages while the mind is chewing the cud of possibilities. But I can't have been thinking clearly that day. Our hero actually spent a good twenty minutes poring over the morning papers before it came to him that these went to press before midnight, and justified their ink by rehashing for breakfast the undigested scraps of the previous day. Nor was there much point trying to squeeze any small-talk out of the staff. The present company consisted of a couple of visa workers, Hong Kong or China, no more knowledge of city gossip than they spoke Irish.

I was still pondering how best to get the pertinent information, the breakfast no more than a memory of rind and yolk streaked across the plate, when I noticed a tweed coat pushing determinedly past the window in a direction consistent with Nelson St. I had been about to pay, but now I waited. Let her go up, I thought. Let her find the door locked. The house, silent.

But I was sitting on an ants' nest, the native hue quite sicklied over. Not two minutes later, Bates had not only overtaken the woman, but had let her into his abode, muttering explications in the manner of a truant schoolboy. I remember only the severity of the old girl's mouth. What annoys me is that I can't say for certain if the silver Capri was already parked at the top of the lane. In my mind's eye I see it.

But of one thing I am certain, and that's of the precise moment when I went into the bathroom. I'd left the sculptress attending the invalid's couch while I entered the necessarium, as much to give myself a chance to think as to relieve the pangs of a neglected bladder. It was a relief that would have to wait. No sooner had I switched on the light-bulb than I was aghast to find my reflected face submerged beneath a pox of bloody thumbprints. Worse, in my confusion I was not only unable to decipher the letters they were intended to spell out, I actually dreamed that I was in some way implicated in the crime they celebrated. There was an 'f'. There was an 'l'. An 'o'. Murder most foul. It's astonishing the tricks that fatigue will play on the mind, when abetted by a *soupçon* of residual guilt.

Before returning to the main room I cleaned the marks off with a damp towel. This wasn't easy. They continually smeared, leaving dirty brown trails across the maculate surface. But I persisted at the task until I'd removed any significant trace. It was as if I were removing evidence of complicity.

But complicity in what? There was the rub.

To give her her due, from the very first the old woman took charge of everything. She actually seemed to thrive on it. I don't mean I saw her smile, or give any intimation that she was enjoying herself. Nothing so crude. But it was evident that she was in her element.

One of the first things she did, having glowered at me when I inquired as to Uncle Mal's health, was to open her purse and pull out a roll of yellow fifties. I knew by the look of them where they'd come from. She unfurled three hundred worth and passed them to me as if they'd been so many fivers. My God, I thought, just how much money did the old bugger come into?

'His arms will have to be seen to. He'll need a tetanus jab. Antibiotics.'

She was pursing her lips, as if sucking on the sourest of lemons. She scraped around the floor of her purse with a prehensile fingernail and pulled out a piece of notepaper on which was scrawled the name, address and phone-number of a GP. The infamous Dr Jacqueline Pennypincher.

'Have Jackie come out. This afternoon, if she can. Use my name.'

'Mal…?' I began, curling the syllable into an interrogative. I was at a loss as to how to continue the phrase. I mean, I couldn't very well ask is the bugger dead.

'Mal must never know that I've been here.'

'But is he…?' I began to giggle. 'Then he hasn't been killed?'

'Killed? Don't be ridiculous!'

'But all the blood?'

'The blood,' she shook her wig, 'is from the cats.'

'*Cats?*'

Her eyes squinnied at my lips, disdainful of the feeble echoes that were rebounding from thereabouts.

'He attacked the cats.' She poked at a makeshift bandage. 'I daresay they defended themselves.'

'Good God!'

'Now listen to me, if the boy tries to leave, you are to dissuade him. If he persists, you are to ring me at once. At once! It doesn't matter what time it is, day or night. Do you understand?'

'But how long do you think…?'

'I am making arrangements. That boy is not well.'

There was something so mean in her mien as she said this that it made me shiver. I tried for a flippant tone.

'What do you mean, arrangements?'

'Arrangements! He is not right. I don't mean his arms. But they have places for people like him.' The mouth was pursed up with such distaste when she said the word 'people', it hit me she'd have been as happy if her Dr were to administer a dose of strychnine.

'In the meantime, I want you to look after him. Do everything that Jackie tells you. If she gives a prescription, see to it that the boy follows it. If he is to have soup, you must bring soup to him. That,' she pronounced, magnificently, 'is what you are being paid for.' She pressed the back of her withered hand to his forehead. 'He's been running quite a temperature,' I supplied, smiling helpfully. 'He's been feverish ever since he got here. Been talking to the four walls. About a dog.'

She looked at me with intense distaste.

'You are to make contact,' she specified, 'with nobody but me. Is that quite understood?' She clipped her purse shut and pursed her clipped lips. 'As far as Mal is concerned, or anyone else for that matter, this individual has returned to whatever black gutter it was he crawled out of.'

My God, I thought, looking at the boy after the woman had left, you really have had some party out there with the cats. But how was it you left all that lovely loot behind you?

The tube of six fifties I fondled in my trouser pocket gave me the opportunity to renew, without delay, my old acquaintance with John Jameson, a much neglected friend, and it was while returning from the off-licence I became aware of the unmarked silver Capri. I sat, poured myself a stiff whiskey. Mahood, I thought. Yesterday or the day before, I see to it he gets a hundred up front. Suspicious that. When was I so wont to be so forward? So he has me followed. Finds out where I live. Then today he puts on the frighteners. See how much more the fat guy's got. See how much can be squeezed out of him. *Ite* of him. Nordy bastard. If he exists.

But two goons in a silver Capri simply didn't square with Mahood's *modus operandi*.

A second shot of whiskey. The next proposition was that the car's presence was on account of this Bluebottle character. I knew well it couldn't just be the business with the cats. If that was all there was to it, why not send around some bleeding heart from the ISPCA? At the most, some uniformed Garda Síochána freshly up from the country, leafing through the notebook and licking the stub of a pencil. To escertain de fects.

No. Forget the incident at Mal's place. People drown bags of kittens every day of the week. *Ergo*, if the delinquent was the object of the surveillance, it must pertain to the earlier incident. The subject of his nightmares.

But was I making too sudden a leap? On the third shot a third conjecture began to take shape. This one appealed. This one *seduced*. The jokers in the car – I wasn't as yet in a position to say that one of them sported a moustache and tinted glasses, the other a lazy eye – had been hired by the old witch, Gwendolyn. She had to be quite sure that neither one of us was stirring up any mischief.

This solution, I say, appealed. Yet it never quite satisfied. Would she really go to such elaborate lengths? And why two gumshoes? In the film scripts I'd begun to dream up, private eyes are famously loners with monosyllabic names who work out of seedy offices. Who ever heard of them prowling in pairs? My mind, its gear teeth worn quite smooth, failed to engage with any answering hypothesis and so returned by default to the first conjecture. Mahood's men. But that made no sense, and the aesthetics were all wrong. And so, the Garda Síochána. It's funny, with all the advantages of what they call hindsight, that the obvious solution didn't immediately suggest itself.

Caught in this eddy of doubt and speculation, I decided the best bet would be to tease out the possibilities with paper and pen. But first, the ongoing reunion with John Jameson, Esq.

Several handshakes into it, I was startled out of a beautiful reverie by the sharpest of screams. My invalid had at some point fallen to the floor, where he was now writhing about in the throes of a nightmare. Before attending to his ranting, I edged aside the net curtain. It was almost dark. But I made out what the Americans call the hood of what was almost certainly a silver Capri, this time to the Berkeley Rd end of the street. I'm sure it was a Ford. A Capri, on balance. But silver? It was tinted by the streetlight, but might well have been silver. Damn their eyes, they existed!

Whether to take my mind off the surveillance, or whether because a stratagem was already beginning to lay its surreptitious egg, I knelt and, over the next few hours, attended closely to the boy's ravings. Nothing too coherent came out. That would have been asking too much. But what he did say he said repetitively. Compulsively, in medical parlance.

His mind was circling, closing in on some primal image. A housedog circles down the ancestral wild grass before it lies down to sleep, and in REM its limbs twitch the rhythm of an imagined hunt. His body was intent on twitching out the truth like so much Morse. And its message, if my imagination wasn't being a little too liberal, involved nothing less than the collision between a brick and a cranium. The words he mumbled appeared to revolve around stark monosyllables: blood, brick, black, back, broke. Brick onto the back of a broken head then, and blood dripping blackly. Immediately, my spirits pricked up. This currency was sterling. You never know in what tight corner you might have occasion to use a shard of information the like of that!

From the twitching that accompanied his mutterings I elaborated a crime scene that involved at least two blows, one to the side of the head, oblique, glancing, perhaps a little tenuous, and then another, vertically, most decisively, this one requiring both hands. What the graceless abattoir worker calls the *coup de grâce*.

Murder most foul! I kissed my fingers.

It wasn't lost on me that all these theatrics might well have been some wish-fulfilment fantasy. After all, which one of us does not dream about bludgeoning to death our nearest and dearest? But what swung it for me was the detail of the dog. In mime, the boy kept trying to shoo away the dog. Connecting the gesture with what the wine had previously revealed, I was less disposed to confine this canine to the realms of pure fantasy. I looked at the prostrate figure, and in my mind's eye I saw him shooing away the dogs of guilt.

So have you really battered in a skull, my friend? I stood, stiffly, and edged back over to the curtain. It was now well after midnight. No sign now of the car on Berkeley Rd. It might never have been there.

•••

On the next day the witchdoctor called. There's hardly a need to dwell on the details of her ministry. In fact, she did precious little, it seemed to my supercilious eye, other than take a cursory reading of the pulse and scrawl out a prescription, the extravagant tab for which yours truly was left to pick up. She insisted, too, the dried-up crone, that I surrender my bedroom to the patient. Luckily he was able to get there under his own steam. I was in no humour to play Mother Teresa. Oh, and she changed the pus-lined bandages.

For this ten-minute interlude, she charged sixty euro. That works out, and I think my schoolboys' maths cannot be faulted here, to one shining euro every ten seconds. Manus, I howled at my father's ghost, how was it you never directed me towards such a profession?

I watched her gold-plated Mercedes convertible pull tersely away and then, in astonishment, watched the gap it had left being plugged with a Ford Capri, silver. This time there could be no doubt, either as to the make or the colour or the duo of goons inside. Lord God, was there to be no end to this farce?

The duty of collecting Bluebottle's prescription from a Dorset Street pharmacy at least gave a pretext for passing close by the car, with its pair of extras out of the kind of B-movie disdained by F.D. Bateman. It was thus that I became familiar with their demeanours, *viz.*, a lazy eye; a moustache with tinted glasses. The one in a leather coat, the other in denim. Or vice versa. I swear I could smell the coffee and doughnuts and Old Spice as I passed, sweetening the undercover waft of stale air and armpits.

They conspicuously failed to register my passing. So that sealed it. This was a stakeout.

But which of us were the tinted shades and lazy eye here to watch?

Besides the antibiotics, I invested in paper and pen. For a would-be author of film-scripts, I really had become quite remiss of late. By evening, the boy, who had been awake prior to and during the doctor's visit, was back in a wordless land of nod, and I, exiled from my bedroom, sat by the darkling window, uncorked the dwindling Jameson, and began to set out the various hypotheses, temporarily suspending judgment. Later, I would consider how these conjectures might be tested.

So then: (a) Mahood; (b) the filth; (c) private eyes. If (a), there was nothing to be done. I could meet the next repayment, but to clear the debt entirely was quite beyond my resources. It's true that at one time I'd hidden a snuff-movie, the real horror-show, in case it ever became necessary to barter or blackmail my way out of a tight corner. This was pure bluff, aimed chiefly at my own cynicism. Deep down I knew I'd never really have the balls for that sort of play. But there we are.

If (b), then a refinement was required. In the first case, whom were the filth here to case? Or, as a corollary, did the stakeout involve Special Branch, or merely the Vice Squad? If the former, what was the crime? If the latter, what were they waiting for? As I fondled this conundrum, a further refinement to my schema became necessary. It wasn't entirely clear who they might be after, if it was the Vice of the old Moralities. Were they watching the minor, who can't be named for legal reasons, with a view to hauling in that corrupter of youth who dwelled in Martello Mews? If not the minor, had they somehow traced one of the videos, snuff or hard-core, to the author of these present musings?

I shivered at this thought. It was entirely repulsive. My pen was on the point of hastening to the third conjecture when I had a premonition that someone was about to arrive, and I turned to the window just in time to see the tweed coat push past in the direction of the door. More money, was my first thought, which cast down the biro. I shall have to touch her for more money.

She knocked. Rrrat-at-tat! No nonsense.

I swung open the door and, in a brilliant and spontaneous gesture, I waved amiably in the direction of Starsky and Hutch. They did not return the salutation, but that was not the point. The point, as I came to realise almost immediately, was that the old woman's face was carved from mahogany. Would it have remained so, if the gentlemen were in her employ? Bates, you bloody marvel! In my astonishment at my own genius I was slow to stand aside, and she pushed past me as though she were my landlady, even closing the door after her.

'How is he today?'

'Itchy,' I said. 'He complains constantly of the itch.'

'But is he quite lucid?'

'Oh yes! He asks constantly for tea. Tea with lemon, if you don't mind. For food too. It would seem his appetite has returned with a vengeance.'

She wasn't interested in my embellishments. She made for the door of the bedroom, knocked the same peremptory tattoo, and before entering turned a Gorgon's stare in my direction. I remained as still as a statue.

She re-emerged after the briefest of interludes, the antibiotic bottle in her talon. She grimaced at the label, but broke off the pantomime to hand it to me.

'I haven't my glasses. What does it say?'

'It says take two, three times a day, before meals.' She nodded, grimly. 'They cost me seventy-two euro,' I added, smiling sweetly. But the witch was in no mood to take up the hint.

My story is beginning to be freighted with excessive detail. That's fatal in a film-script. The old woman left, but called in, twice daily before meals, for the next several days. She parted with no more fifties, which aggrieved me. Although it did seem that Mahood's men, Anto et al, had disappeared from the face of the earth. Conversely, Dr Jackie Skinflint dropped by promptly each noon to collect her tribute, and to administer a peremptory injection to a patient every day more placid.

All the while, the silver Capri lurked at the periphery of awareness, now to the Berkeley end of Nelson St, now to the Eccles. Once I saw Starsky, hovering beside a skip and talking into a mobile phone, once Hutch, propping up a streetlamp and cupping a fag under his palm like a truant schoolboy. Or vice versa. Farce delights in repetition with slight variation.

And in the refuge of the flat, there were repetitions with slight variations aplenty. By the time that they came to take the boy to the funny farm, I was no longer in any doubt but that some mischief had been perpetrated in the Wicklow Hills. During one of her rare loquacious moments, Gwendolyn had described the carnage wrought on Uncle's coven of cats. Very well, I thought, failing once again to precisely locate the Capri through the net curtain, but sensing its presence. If the gutter press had got hold of that massacre, they would undoubtedly have had their field day. But it's hardly likely to interest the Special Branch. Conclusion? If it is the boy they're after, it has something to do with that Forty-coats character in Wicklow. The one with the mutt. So that, assuming these unlikely clowns actually are plainclothes detectives, it can only mean that the body of an itinerant has been found in the corner of some Wicklow field. *Habeas corpus.*

Good! I began to consider how this piece of deductive reasoning might be of use to me. And yet…

And yet… what I could not fathom was, why the stakeout? To what possible end? Why not have the suspect assist them with their inquiries from the comfort of a Store Street cell? Why not at least talk to the boy? Were there no items of clothing recovered? No fingerprints to be matched?

The Vice Squad, too, would surely have made their move. And as for Mahood, no. It simply didn't fit. So that perhaps, after all, they were the old woman's stooges? I wrought my hands in despair, knowing my circling was as futile as any banged-up Capri. So I decided to let events take their course. When there is nothing to be done, do nothing, *the Gospel according to Fergal, chapter five, verse two*.

There was neither struggle nor drama when they took the boy away. Jackie was on hand, and a young medic whom I did not recognise but whom I could well imagine in a psychiatric white coat. But Bluebottle himself seemed quite content to go. Complicit, even. A diluted smile was turned vaguely in all our directions. The eyes refused to focus, and it was unclear whether they were directed towards the future or the past. Who knew what poison that vile witchdoctor had been administering.

After the party had gone, the flat felt as though it had been abandoned.

And now for the unpleasant twist. The sting in the scorpion's tale. The whole menagerie had moved on from the flat, written it out of the script as it were. But the next day, as I made to leave the flat, there was a Ford Capri stationed across the road. Off silver. At first I thought this must be a simple matter of inertia. A mix up in signals. I'd developed the impression, not unreasonably, that the pair were not the sharpest tools in the box. Nevertheless I stayed inside the flat, half-concealed by the net curtain, and fixed the car's bonnet in the corner of my eye. But an hour passed, two. If the old sculptress had hired them, and had dissimulated that time when she saw me wave to them, she was being uncharacteristically remiss about letting them go. A considerable outlay, and an unnecessary one.

But if they were Special Branch, why had they not followed the suspect?

I began to grow itchy, or defiant, whichever applies. I suddenly had a vision of Fergal Bates pacing energetically to the door of the Capri, tapping at the window, and challenging the two goons inside to declare their hand. By God, I'll do it! Pulling on this new garment of resoluteness, I strode to the door of the flat. I swung it open, and stepped out onto the street just in time to see the brake-lights disappearing around the corner.

Ha! Good riddance!

•••

This all happened over a week ago. The problem is that, if the silver Capri has disappeared from Nelson St and environs, the same cannot be said of the state of being watched. What is apparent is that the surveillance has taken a more subtle turn.

On occasion I've actually caught sight of their old car, but never parked, and never so close to the flat. Several times, it has crossed a street in front of me. Or I've seen the rear end disappear down a side-road. But they've become clever. More often, I've caught sight of one or other of my tormentors prowling insouciantly behind the wheel of a different make and model. And several nights ago, I had the nasty surprise of seeing Hutch, he of the tinted glasses, emerging from a basement flat off Berkeley Rd.

An even nastier surprise lay in wait for me on the day I went to Sandymount for the last time. When they removed the boy from the flat, they'd taken with him my only ostensible source of income. Needless to say the three hundred euro was by this time little more than a single trouser pocket weighed down with the meanest coppers for ballast. The problem of Mahood and his repayments was not so easily reduced.

Three hundred. It is a tidy sum. Sufficient for an entire month's grace. The old woman thought she'd paid me off with a single instalment, whereas in my mind's long vista, I'd fondled the prospects of a future quite free from Mahood. Now, with the boy gone, the cash-cow had dried up. It was quite natural that my thoughts should turn, should return, to Uncle Mal.

My calculation had the beauty of symmetry. Gwendolyn had counted on buying my silences at three hundred euro a pop. Good. It was not unreasonable to conjecture that three hundred could be winkled out of Mal for breaking this same silence. Now, beyond introducing the theme, I knew that the sculptress had had the boy committed. St. Pat's? John of Gods? Grangegorman, perhaps. Ascertaining that detail would surely earn a further three hundred. It would simply be a case of my narrowing the field to the precise institution and ward.

Mal's place was dark and cold. In eclipse, so to speak. Through sightless windows shadow had seeped in until every corner and threshold lay submerged in it. When there was no reply to my banging at the door, I edged around to the back of the house. I did this quite brazenly. A flicker from the curtain of a window in the house opposite intimated I was under observation.

The rear garden was even more neglected than was its habit. I pressed my nose to the lichen-stained windows, and saw only abandon inside. It seemed the bird had flown the nest, no doubt at the old woman's instigation. Cannes, in all likelihood, or perhaps the brother's place down the country.

But it took a full five minutes before I realised why precisely Martello Mews was such a mausoleum. No feline eyes peeped out from the overgrown jungle. All about, there reigned a deafening absence of cats.

I paced angrily out of the cul-de-sac, cursing the old hag who had cheated me out of my revenue. In my black mood I even gave the finger to the snooping curtain that eternally o'erlooks Uncle Mal's. Now how, I muttered, can Bateman be expected to meet his thrice-damned repayments?

It was a question I had thought rhetorical, but Fate decided to reply with a consummate trump. As I made to cross Tritonville Rd I noticed a 4x4, in the livery of the Garda Síochána, cruising slowly from a townward direction. I'm unsure what precisely drew my attention to it. I squinted at the windscreen, and through the reflected sun, I made out the shape of a woman, uniformed, behind the wheel. There was also a man, plain-clothes, to the passengers' side. I jolted. Starsky? The present outline and the silhouette of memory were certainly congruent. But it was quite impossible to be sure.

The white 4x4 was approaching at an unreasonably slow pace. A surreally slow pace. With neither lamppost nor tree-trunk to duck behind, I awaited its passage in perfect vulnerability. Naked, as you might say. It cruised by, whispering over the asphalt, and as it passed a head to the rear turned to take me in. A hooded figure.

Christ, I thought, Anto!

Certainty, of course, gave me the two fingers.

Hooded, and moving, I had no chance to make out the tattoos that decorate Anto like the frames of an adult comic-strip. But the incident has played havoc with all my initial conjectures. It's difficult now to see how any of the discretely continuing surveillance can have a connection with the Bluebottle affair. The Judas kiss, and the cats' holocaust. At the same time, even if I'm mistaken in the hooded figure, every last one of Mahood's men has disappeared. I've asked around for them. Not a squeak. Not one of the blaggards has been seen this last fortnight.

Now. Let us put two and two together.

Mr Fergal Bates of Nelson St is being watched at a time when Mahood's men are off the streets. It is entirely possible, nay, probable, that his name should appear in one of their little black books. Perhaps the entrée is garnished with an outline of transactions balanced against his debts. Perhaps, too, an inventory of the tapes he has sold on. Not exactly Walt Disney, these. Now, it would be entirely reasonable to assume that any official interest in such a bill of fare would involve the Vice Squad.

Starsky and Hutch, I could well imagine working for the Old Vice.

And now the rub. They have not arrested nor questioned me. So then they consider me to be small fry. This does not alarm or bother me. In Mahood's murky aquarium I would consider myself to be small fry. But, and in this 'but' lies the very crux of the situation, the hope that I might lead them to bigger fish is sadly misplaced. I know nothing. Should there come a time that they have sufficient evidence or impatience to draw me in, with the best will in the world I will have nothing to communicate to them in regard to Mahood. I have never seen the man.

This unpalatable state of ignorance explains why, earlier this week, the same Fergal Bates began to frequent the reading room of the National Library, Kildare St. What a thrill! Right next to the seat of government, and under the very noses of the Garda Síochána! In all it took me three visits to find what I was looking for. I had to pan through a lot of silt before I unearthed the first trace of glister. But then, I'd no dates to work with.

I obtained photocopies of all the relevant articles from a fastidious spinster, flat-chested and parsimonious. How often do we observe these two traits to be linked! She hugged her withered dugs tightly to her ribcage as though they were purses from which the contents had been pilfered, and eyed me as though *I* were the thief! I furnished her with innocent request slips. So as to allay any suspicions, I had her photocopy a number of red herrings, too.

Once safely back in the flat I set out my treasure across the kitchen table.

'Vagrant in critical condition after violent assault.' All of the headlines tended towards a consensus on the key terms. 'Police baffled by assault on vagrant.' 'Still no clues as to violent assault on Wicklow vagrant' and in a later edition of the same broad-sheet 'Still no clues as to identity of Wicklow vagrant'. Mention was made, sensationally, of a distinctive tattoo.

On the following day there was a conjecture that he was ex-army, in the briefest of articles tucked beneath a blurred photo of a British paratrooper. Then I struck a particularly rich seam, the pay-dirt for which I had been so eagerly prospecting. 'Wicklow vagrant dies three days after violent assault.'

This fine piece of journalism mentioned several blows to the head with a blunt instrument, possibly a rock. Murder most foul, I cried! After another half-dozen diminishing mentions, the story sank from view in all but the *Wicklow Times*, north edition.

The story sank to indifference's murky bottom, but in my breast pocket I carry its essentials. I carry a plea-bargain. State's evidence. On the day that these goons decide to take me down town and to sit on me, I'll stir the mud of that half-forgotten pool. And then I will a tale relate that will open their pig eyes wide for them. A tale of cruelty and desire. A tale of blackmail, lust, and disfigurement. A tale of compulsive paedophilia, and a violent assault that led to the death, after three days, of an unnamed Wicklow vagrant.

Oh, they'll have their story all right. And if I have to hang half the country to give it to them, so help me God I'm the man to do it.

PART III

VII | Br Martin

Can it really be thirty years? As many as thirty? Dear God!

Days drift by, become months by degrees, and before you know where you are, entire years have stacked up behind you. A lifetime, in point of fact.

When I first came to St. Luke's, I had no thought to stay on here. It was a temporary refuge, nothing more. But there you are. The Lord works in inscrutable ways. He makes of the most intractable wretch an instrument of the divine will.

A wretch, I use the term advisedly. On the incomparable advice of Messieurs Webster and Roget. Wordy chaps. At that time I'd given way to despair, utter despair. The loss of hope. There is surely no more wretched state than that.

But you've no wish to be troubled about Thomas Ffrench, the tiresome old wretch who was born again through the grace of God as Br Martin. Or only insofar as this old wretch pertains to the case for the prosecution. Or the case for the defence. The world is everything that is the case. Now who said that, I wonder?

I'd been extraordinarily fond of the boy from the very first. Scout's honour! Even when he'd seemed quite impossible. Quite impossible. He used to throw fits, violent, temperamental fits that put the fear of God into poor Sr Thérèse! This from the time when you'd think he'd be scarcely old enough to walk, let alone upend the furniture! Oh, I don't mean tantrums. Every child is prone to tantrums to a greater or lesser extent.

No. These were full-blown, violent rages. The poltergeist in Pampers, I used to call him. How's our poltergeist in Pampers today?

Dear me, at such times it really was as if he were possessed. There's a term that has quite gone out of fashion! To be possessed. It's an inspired choice of verb, if you think about it. Did you know that *possessio* in Latin means an occupation? Forgive me, I'm beginning to wander. One mustn't allow an old wretch to wander into vagaries! Be warned, I've been librarian here at St Luke's for almost three decades, and we librarians are quite lethal. Give us the least excuse, and we'll have you meandering through miasmas of quotation and digression until you've quite forgotten what it was you came to find out in the first place, ha ha!

But the boy really was prone to violent, psychotic seizures. Poor, beleaguered Sr Thérèse! She'd never encountered anything quite like it. And do you know, for the best part of a year he absolutely refused to speak? What am I saying? It was closer to two years. Two years. All through infants and first class, I'm quite sure of that. Not so much as a word. In point of fact, they thought for a long time that the boy was retarded. Or autistic, if you prefer. I really should be careful about using terms that have gone out of fashion. But there's no disrespect intended. Please forgive an old dinosaur for persevering with the fossils picked up in youth.

The boy was considered to be autistic. Br Malachi said so. Sr Bernadette was sure of it. Even the *cigire* from the Department was of the same opinion. We do have occasional visitations from Marlborough St, you know. Perhaps you thought they only concerned themselves with card-carrying Roman Catholics?

Give me the boy and I'll give you the man, that's what the Jesuits like to say, isn't it? Well, I like to turn it on its head. If you want to understand the man, you must look at the boy. With your permission, I'll give one vivid picture of the boy when he first came to us. One little anecdote, that's all. But bear with me. All this nonsense about a murderer, well, you can make up your own mind…

Despite his refusal to talk, or to pay the least screed of attention in class, behind his stubborn silences, I sensed a most lively intelligence. God forgive me, perhaps it's been his insatiable curiosity over the years that's made me value him above all the others. There's none of us above favouritism. Not even Christ himself, if you put any faith in the Gospel according to John! And what of the lost sheep, ha ha, and the poor ninety-nine righteous! But I sensed there was something *behind* his silence, that's the point.

On the other hand, Br Giraldus had dismissed him as a retard, so that was that. Case dismissed! Our fraternal order may have its spiritual homeland in Lincoln, Nebraska, but I've always suspected a Communist spectre lurks behind the nomenclature. Br Giraldus is chief secretary of our communist party, ha ha! At the risk of Siberia, I tendered the opinion that the boy was far from stupid. Of course, the view of the politburo prevailed. The boy would not proceed to second class. In first class he would remain! And he would be put in the charge of Sr Dolores, who for her sins looks after the remedials.

And then one day, *dies mirabilis*, one marvellous day, just as term was drawing to an end… are you by any chance familiar with the Ladybird series of books? Peter. Jane. Peter and Jane. Oh, they've long since fallen out of fashion, I expect. But in a fiefdom like St Luke's, one has a certain latitude to chose one's own materials. Always provided that they are broadly consistent with the national curriculum, of course. Our venerable Sr Agnes has selected the raw materials for the junior primary ever since the founding of the Free State, and she has never to my knowledge been accused of espousing change for its own sake! Ladybirds it was in the beginning, Ladybirds it is now and Ladybirds it ever shall be, world without end. Thou art Peter, and upon this rock… Occasionally, I regret to say, her steadfast faith has been the source of friction between us.

Dear Sr Agnes. She's so consistently… consistent!

Now, this particular term, the first class had been reading one or other volume in the Ladybird series, I forget which. Let's say to avoid any dispute between us that it was 6B or 6C. Years ago, before my reign began in the kingdom of the books, my predecessor Br Jacob had invested in two dozen complete sets at fifteen percent discount, so the least one could say was that every child had his or her own copy to take to bed for as long as was deemed appropriate. I suppose to that extent Sr Agnes has a point. Certainly, when I was in boarding school, a most miserable time, my only solace was to be able to sneak a book into the dorm bunk and read it under the covers by the light of a pocket torch. It quite ruined my eyesight, I needn't tell you.

In any event, on this day, this marvellous day, Br Giraldus was showing Br Nathan around the facilities. Br Nathan had flown all the way here to be with us from Lincoln, Nebraska. This was only the second such visit since Luke's was founded. It was quite an honour, quite a big deal. Now to cut a long story short, our visiting dignitary had been to the senior house and around the dormitories and the canteen. They'd even been to inspect the darker recesses of the library. All present and correct there! It only remained, before the commandant left, for Br Nathan to have a look at one of the junior years, and Sr Agnes had the notion to bring the honoured guest into the first class. A Miss Dewey, Eileen Dewey, had been taking the first class for a number of years. Wholly lay. A large, Offaly woman. Heart in the right place I'm sure, but dreadfully dull. Offaly dull, I used to say!

It seems that the class was arranged into two rows, with the underachievers to the rear. The dunces, to use the old word. Sr Dolores's wards. God forgive me, I'd give my eyeteeth to have been there and to have witnessed what happened next at first hand. It's entered into the institutional folklore ever since, I can tell you. Eileen Dewey asked one of the girls to do a little prepared reading, out of 6B or 6C. Good. And all went along well enough, if you allow for the poor thing's nervousness! Here was a complete stranger, one before whom even Br Giraldus was deferent! And then there was the American accent, so entirely unfamiliar twelve and odd years ago! The children have no television here that isn't under the strictest supervision. We live in a world without soap, ha ha!

Now, putting on a little demonstration of acquired learning was all very well, but Br Nathan, to his eternal credit, was far more interested to see how the young students might cope with a problem a little out of the ordinary. It so happened that on his first evening, as the plane landed in Dublin airport, there'd been a thunderstorm. I've an idea this must've been towards the end of the Christmas term, but let that rest.

'Can anyone tell me,' he began, in his unfamiliar American drawl, 'have you ever noticed that you see the flash of the lightning, but it's only after a delay of a few seconds that you hear the crash of the thunder. Can anyone tell me, now, why that might be, hmmm?'

The classroom is in total silence. We have to imagine the scene. Br Giraldus is frowning, doing everything in his power to sustain a faltering smile. Eileen Dewey is altogether more horrified and is fidgeting with the corner of her shawl. And as for the poor prize pupil! Dreadful embarrassment. So the silence goes on for the best part of a minute, agitation all around, and then, against all expectation, a hand goes up towards the very back of the dunces' row. Of course you've guessed! It's our autistic boy himself, the one they'd said was retarded! You have to remember, he hasn't spoken a solitary word in over a year.

'Well?' beams our American friend.

'Is it because,' begins the little man, thinking at the same time as he's speaking, 'is it because, Brother, your eyes is to the front of your head, and your ears is all the way back there?'

Ha ha! How's that for stout reasoning? From a five year old! Dear God, when I think of it! Soon, of course, it emerges that not only can the child speak, but he can read. And not only can he read, he's already up as far as 8A or 8B. Sr Dolores is in the dark. It's news to her. And you could've knocked Eileen Dewey with a feather. On further investigation, it seems he's been borrowing the books from Garret Molloy, one of the dimmer boys, in second or third class at the time, and has been helping *him* to read!

'But why is it,' puts in Br Giraldus, back in the classroom and not knowing whether to grin or to glower, 'that you've never said anything before now in Miss Dewey's class?'

Do you know what he answers?

Says he, with a shrug, 'I was waiting for her to get onto something I didn't know!' Ha ha! Priceless! Can you imagine? A five-year-old. Dear God!

I'll move on. The years pass so quickly. In an institution where there are always children, they positively race! From about that time until the day he ran away for the second time, the boy seemed drawn to the library as though it was an Aladdin's cave. Drawn to all those infinite possibilities its treasures hold out to the childish imagination. It is my conceit to imagine, in this respect at least, that I, dusty old Br Martin, must have retained the soul and imagination of a child. Ruined my eyes at it over the years. But that's neither here nor there. I have no way, and therefore want no eyes. Ha ha!

God knows there's little enough in St Luke's for a child's imagination to latch on to, and so the library was a universe of wonders for him. He continually plied me with questions, from the time that the books he held open were as wide as his little arms. I had the fancy then that they were like the gates of a fantastic world to him.

It's not often given to us to be entrusted with one who's in any degree responsive. It's a true gift, if and when it happens, every bit as rewarding to the teacher as to the pupil. More so, I'd venture to say. Would it be too much to suggest that from the first it was as though he'd been marked out from the others? The fancy of an old man, perhaps. One always wants to feel one has made a difference. One wants to feel that one has been useful in some degree. Chosen, if you like. There's another word that's not much in fashion nowadays.

And then he ran away.

Let me be precise about this. He ran away twice, in point of fact. The first time, he would have been around thirteen. It's impossible to be entirely accurate. All the children at St Luke's have either been orphaned or abandoned, and it's not always possible to be precise about their dates of birth. I've an idea that in his case we've a birth certificate and all the other particulars. The police have been most concerned to put his calendar age beyond all reasonable doubt. I've never had occasion, though, to ask Br

Giraldus for permission to consult the records. But in any case, he must've been around thirteen.

That particular episode didn't last long. A couple of nights out in the cold, at the mercy of tramps and the weather, soon made him see sense. A number of our boys run away every year once the hormones begin their insurrections. Some of the girls, too, but the majority come back soon enough.

Perhaps it was for that very reason that I took the second occasion far more seriously. He'd grown up a lot in the months in between. Perhaps, if you'll allow me to express it in this way... On the first flight he was Huckleberry Finn, but now the runaway was more the brother to Holden Caulfield.

The first intimation I got that he was absconding was when Garret Molloy, of all people, asked me for our volume of Rainer Maria Rilke. I couldn't have been more surprised if a passing crow had asked for Jerome's commentary on the Bible. God forgive me, but Garret Molloy is scarcely able to spell his own name. But there was something in this particular request that was more like a secret code. You see, the boy had asked me on numerous occasions who was the greatest poet of all time. The second years had begun to do a bit of Milton with Br Andrew, a man in thrall to the language of Tyndall and *Paradise Lost*. Yet faithful how they stood, their glory withered! I don't know what nonsense Br Andrew had been filling their heads with, but the boy asked me in all seriousness if it were true that English was the only modern language in which you could write truly epic poetry!

I've more than an idea he was trying to pen a few lines of his own at the time. Once adolescence hits and the hormones begin to rebel, the male body starts to sprout downy hairs and bad verse in equal quantities!

The library has so little poetry. It's been a source of constant friction between myself and the politburo. Unless I can visibly demonstrate that a spiritual message lies behind a given text, it's absolutely hopeless. Eliot, yes, but our political commissars wouldn't hear of Pablo Neruda, much less Philip Larkin. At least with the *Duino Elegies* one had the advantage that Rilke is perpetually on about the angels. *Der Engel Ordnungen*! How many evenings did we read through Rilke together, the boy and I? Even the very evening before Molloy's untimely apparition! I'm quite sure of that. So I handed over the text without raising so much as an eyebrow, knowing full well for whom it was really intended.

Perhaps if I'd known then that it was to be the last time I'd see him, I would have been a little more circumspect. But there we are. With hindsight, even a blind old bookworm is allowed twenty-twenty vision.

A year went by, or the bones of it. I heard nothing. Not a solitary word. Perhaps he had taken the boat to England, or who knows, perhaps he'd gone even farther afield? He was always a restless soul. As days became weeks and weeks months, I expect I became accustomed to hearing nothing. He certainly wouldn't have been the first to have high-tailed it out of Luke's, and not a single one of our young fugitives has ever seen fit to provide us with the details of their extramural careers! Occasionally you might hear something, but always at second hand, and almost inevitably when they'd run into trouble.

Of course, I remembered him in my prayers. Religiously, as they say. Ha ha! Every night and morning, I prayed for his safety and enlightenment. But if I'm completely honest about it, I think I was more than a little piqued at this particular boy's ingratitude. Or his thoughtlessness. He must have known how anxious the old Jedi would be on his account. Then one night, just over a month ago, as I was making my way across the yard after vespers, the most peculiar apparition stood out from behind the bicycle shed, and made down on me as I stood stock still. The collar of the anorak was zipped up as far as the eyes, and a shawl was pulled over the head in the most bizarre disguise. It was hardly a necessary precaution. No-one had thought to replace the light bulb under Br Giraldus's office. Besides, with my glasses like two milk-bottles, it would've been next to impossible for me to make out his features at the best of times. Behind the muffler, two bushy eyebrows quivered like antennae over alert, nervous eyes.

'You're Brother Martin?' growled a peculiarly theatrical voice through the zipper of the anorak. I was quite taken aback, as you can well imagine, but I nodded with as much severity as I could muster. The figure advanced a half-pace and touched me on the forearm.

'I need to speak with you.'

'Look here,' I said, feeling the situation to be more ludicrous than threatening, 'who the devil are you? How did you get in here?' At that moment a light came on in the canteen, throwing an orange lozenge out over the courtyard cobbles to where we stood. Our shadows stretched instantly as far as the toilets; a geometry strangely appropriate, as it turned out!

He ducked around like a man guilty of some crime, just as there sounded the rattle of bolts and chains behind one of the canteen doors. At this hour Br Malachi is accustomed to put out the rubbish from the evening meal. But the eruption of so many, how can I say, so many dungeon-like sounds was enough to disturb the equilibrium of the night.

'Who are you?' I repeated after him, as the figure scurried out of my ever-murkier field of vision and was lost into the dusk, for all the world like a beggar out of a Gaiety pantomime.

I don't know what it was about the incident that made me think of the boy. I suppose in my mind's eye I'd often seen him homeless on the streets, wrapped in a blanket and begging for coppers with a McDonald's carton. There's the great image of globalisation for you! But this unlikely character who'd called me by my name had been fifty if he was a day, and moreover, was only as tall perhaps as the base of my glasses. It was hard to be certain, as he was stooped.

I did my best to put the incident out of my mind, and for a few days I was indeed caught up in other, more trivial affairs. Pecuniary details, the bane of many a life of contemplation! Then one day, early, I found a note in a rather childish hand, letters unjoined, thrust under the door of the library. There was a crudely drawn map of a nearby park, a time, and the following message:

'Really must speak to you. Come alone (this underlined, twice). Matter of life and death.' Curiouser and curiouser! I had not the slightest doubt as to whom it was from, but could he mean tonight? And how the devil had he got into St Luke's for the second time, and worse, had got into the corridors, to push the note under the door? This development really was most worrying.

I determined to go and meet the man. I simply couldn't have him breaking into the place at all hours. In an institution like St Luke's, the safety of the children must be paramount. But I decided against telling Br Giraldus of this strange affair. Not until I had something more substantial to go on. I simply couldn't risk having the politburo believe the old chap had finally lost his marbles.

It turned by degrees into a most dreadful evening. Very wild, and with one of those penetrating Dublin drizzles that seem to make an absolute mockery of umbrellas and overcoats. I thought twice about heading out into it I can tell you, and I looked several times at the note to make sure there was no date indicated. But date there was none.

The park was deserted, as you can well imagine on such an unsavoury night. It's scarcely a park at all, more a public square with the distinction of a few low shrubs. In any event, they gave precious little shelter. I waited for perhaps ten minutes past the allotted time and then, with a rather bad-natured toss of the head, I made my way back towards the gate. Just as I arrived, the figure stood out from behind a lavender bush. He was dressed just as ludicrously as on the previous visitation, though on this occasion in what looked to my eyes at first like a fur coat, and with a damp newspaper suspended an inch over his head, no doubt for added comic effect.

'Now see here,' I growled, not amused in the slightest, 'I've had quite enough of your antics. I've a good mind to go and report this carry-on to the police.'

At the sound of the word 'police' it was as though I'd thrown scalding water at him. He visibly shrank away from me, though his hands came together and advanced.

'For God's sake,' he beseeched, 'no police!'

'Then perhaps you'd like to tell me what all this nonsense is about?'

'What?' he said, gesturing about with one upraised palm, the newspaper still suspended like a tropical plant over his head. 'Here? In the rain?'

'Well,' I began, not really thinking things through before I gave voice to them, which I admit has ever been my own most grievous fault, but being rather too eager to get out of the rain, 'well then, you'd better come back with me to my office.'

If I'd given this any proper consideration I would have seen how inappropriate this suggestion of mine was, to say nothing of the possible danger to my person. After all, I didn't know this fellow from Cain. On the other hand, I'm rumoured to be a man of God, so what evil need I fear?

We were silent as we returned, and I sneaked him in through the rear gate as if we were neither one of us up to any good. It did cross my mind as we passed into the inner courtyard that he'd already twice gained entry without any such help, including as it would appear as far as the upper corridor, and this was not as it should be. Not, as I've said, where there are children. But to my eternal shame I was perhaps more worried at that moment by the possibility we might encounter one of my superiors. I'd ruffled a few feathers over the years within the inner hencoop. If anyone dreams that an institution might be above power politics by virtue of being religious, all I can assume is that they've never set foot inside a seminary!

I suppose I'd long been tolerated as a harmless enough character, given to eccentricities and unorthodox opinions, but it would not do to have one of the politburo question my sense of responsibility. Not that! Not when the protection of the innocent had been my single preoccupation over the years, and my sole reason for putting up with their nonsense. I wouldn't care to conjecture what it was that made them put up with my nonsense!

After an eternity, I closed the door of my office behind us, turned the key, twice, and then pulled the bolt. I remember feeling, as I turned about, that this really was a most foolish position to find oneself in. I mean, suppose he really was a lunatic? I had no grounds to believe anything to the contrary! But on the other hand, there was something so vaguely comical about the whole set up, and about his every gesture, that really it felt at times like we were acting out a rather second rate farce. So to gain a little more time, and indeed because it really was a most dismal evening, I began to fiddle with the electric fire.

'Please, take off your coat. You must be soaked to the skin.'

He stood where I'd left him, his eyes nervously flitting from lock to window, but stock still besides, and arms hanging helplessly by his thighs. The dangling newspaper was dribbling water in a puddle at his foot, for all the world as though he'd wet his pants. I laughed, I'm afraid. I suppose when one is nervous, one is very often moved to laugh.

'Please,' I repeated, 'your coat?'

'My coat? Oh yes, of course.' I immediately stepped nearer to take from him the water-heavy overcoat, but also to examine him at close quarters. Anything more than three feet away and my eyesight is quite hopeless. So it was true, then, he really was about an inch shorter than I, though admittedly given to stooping. He had neither hat nor shawl, and the hair was matted to the scalp. But it was so wet that I wasn't quite sure whether it leaned towards straw or grey. One feature was striking, however. The pair of eyebrows! They stood up in wisps and twitched like two antennae, giving him for all the world the appearance of a beetle. The coat, incidentally, was of an old-fashioned design, with beaver fur on its collar.

'Now, perhaps you'd like to tell me, to what do I owe the pleasure?'

He shuffled about, most beetle-like, and began to patter in a voice whose pitch was throttled high by his state of anxiety.

'You're Br Martin. I knew at once you must be Br Martin. The glasses, you see. It was the first thing he'd said about you. Big, thick glasses. Ha ha! So that's that. I knew immediately it must be you.'

'For God's sake,' I said, 'calm down. Really, you're not making the blindest bit of sense. Who said to you I was Br Martin?'

'The boy.'

'The boy? What boy.'

'I...,' he began, and then he wavered. It was not merely his voice. He quite literally teetered on his feet, and had to put his fingers on the corner of my desk to regain his balance. 'I don't know his name!' he gasped. He appeared to be in despair. There were tears, I'd swear it, when he squeezed the bridge of his nose. 'I've never known his name!'

I mentioned I'd had something of a presentiment upon first seeing this character. It now returned with a vengeance to rifle through my innards.

'Please,' I said, 'won't you sit down? Perhaps a glass of water…?' Martin Ffrench you old fool, I thought as I left him, here's this man like a drowned rat and all you can think to do is to offer him a glass of water! On the other hand, my temporary absence from the room gave him time to compose himself. When I returned from the washroom he was seated at the desk and had set out before him a cutting from a newspaper. Evidently he had carried this concealed on his inner body, because it was warm and dry, no companion to the sodden sheets that had served him for an umbrella. I set down the glass and lifted up the page, as his gesture invited me to do. I read it through, twice, and shook my head, not quite understanding. It was the story of a criminal investigation. A murder investigation, to be precise. I looked at him, waiting for some sort of explanation, and all the while the sense of foreboding grew heavier in my gut.

The next hour was one of the heaviest and most painful of my life, certainly since the breakdown. Of course I'd been vaguely aware of the story: a vagrant who'd been brutally bludgeoned to death; the difficulties in establishing his identity and the suspicions that he was ex-British army; then some time later the Garda breakthrough and the arrest of the minor, who was by all accounts mentally disturbed. From within my lair I do try to keep abreast of current affairs. I knew vaguely that the trial was pending. But because, in this case, the suspect was underage, the press were under a stricture not to reveal his identity and referred to him only as 'the youth'. For legal reasons, as the parlance has it.

Examining the evidence before me, it didn't take me more than a moment to realise who this youth was, and my heart sank through the floorboards, I needn't tell you. But as for the bizarre individual that at present sat at my desk, this half-drowned bringer of dreadful tidings, it took me quite a deal longer to see how he fitted into the scheme of things. Unwilling to give me a direct answer whenever I approached the subject, unwilling even to tell me his name, he merely said, with a characteristic sense of the theatrical, that he was the most despised of God's creatures. I noticed there was an ill-disguised look of cunning about his face whenever he mentioned God's name, as if he were calculating the effect such a pious invocation might have on a religious man. He also told me, base flattery this, how the boy had constantly sung my praises. He even went so far as to claim that he had told him that, in the event of a disaster, I was the only one to be trusted within St Luke's! This sounded doubtful in the extreme. I felt I knew the boy better than this.

What he was slightly more forthcoming about was the role of a character by the name of Fergal Bates.

'Let us say,' he muttered, 'that he is my nephew,' peeping at me conspiratorially from under lowered eyebrows. Now, it seemed that this Fergal fellow had been picked up by the authorities some months since, though as to the precise nature of his misdemeanour, I was left in the dark. He told me, in a low aside, that he had entrusted the boy to his care, but that his trust had been betrayed. 'Betrayed!' he sobbed. As to the arrest, all that was vouchsafed to me was that it involved the Vice Squad. I could draw my own conclusions, he went on, and when he had added this last remark, his head sunk into his hands, and his mouth fell open. I waited, a very model of patience.

'Catastrophe!' he howled at length. 'Absolute catastrophe!'

'What do you mean?' I demanded.

'The arrest, it was a disaster!'

'I don't follow you.'

'Fergal,' he said, prodding his own heart with his fingers, 'whom I had been like an uncle to, all his life... Fergal betrayed me.'

'You?'

'Me! Yes! Me, who had even been like a father to him. Well, let that rest. Perhaps for that I could be brought to forgive him. As God is my witness, I believe I could!' he added, peering at me to gauge the effect of the deity's unspoken testimony. 'But what is far worse, what I simply cannot forgive him for, and will never forgive him for, is that he turned state's evidence… against the boy!'

'But see here,' I said, more than a little exasperated by the man's histrionics, and by his infuriatingly elliptical manner, 'what sort of evidence can this Fergal chap have had?'

'That's just the point!' he cried, and then in genuine despair, 'I don't know!' He banged his fist on the desk. 'But you're absolutely correct, Father. I ask you,' he went on, now gesturing about the room as though there were a metaphysical jury ranged about the four walls, 'what sort of evidence can he have had?'

'Well,' I tried, 'surely if you say he's your nephew, you might ask him?'

He stared at me with a look of absolute horror. 'Ask him? But don't you realise, Father…'

'I'm no longer a priest,' I interrupted.

'But don't you see, he would never listen to *me*. And besides, I can't go.' He had lowered his head again, in the manner of a guilty child. 'I am,' he whispered, 'a wanted man.'

He'd begun to fiddle about at his inside pocket, and I had the bizarre idea that he was an overgrown schoolboy searching for an excusatory note. At length he extended a small piece of paper, folded. This contained nothing more than the address of a flat, executed in the same childish hand as the note that had been thrust under the library door.

'You must go and talk to him. You! You must make him retract his evidence.' He put his two hands together and raised them towards me. 'For the love of God.'

'But look here,' I said, turning away, exasperated at last by his constant iterations, 'I don't see why you've come to me about all this.'

'Because,' he pronounced, magnificently, 'I have no-one else to turn to.' Then he tapped the newspaper article, which I had replaced on the desk, and laid what he considered to be his trump card. 'Because *we* have no-one else to turn to.'

Now that he had delivered himself of his so-called nephew's address, he was suddenly in a dreadful hurry to leave. He shuffled past me to the door and he shot back the bolt. His face was a construction of the most absolute relief.

'When you see him,' he paused, perhaps genuinely unsure how to acquit himself, 'when you speak to him, you might tell him that "Uncle" sent you.' He nodded, satisfied, shook my hand, nodded once again, found that the door was still locked, turned the key, twice, nodded to me for a final time and then scuttled away down the corridor, leaving me standing dumbfounded in the centre of my office, the small piece of paper held limply between thumb and finger. He had been in such a hurry to take his leave that, to one side, his overcoat still hung gloomily from the hat-stand, an ominous circle of rainwater darkening the carpet beneath it. With my weak eyesight, I momentarily mistook its bulk for an eavesdropper.

'Here!' I called after him, 'I say!' But he had quite gone. How precisely he managed to negotiate the unlit labyrinth of corridors with such unerring celerity, and find his way out unnoticed into the night, I have never fathomed.

•••

All through the next day I was in the most excruciating state of indecision. At times, I wondered if the visit of this beetle-man hadn't been an invention of an overheated brain, too used to the quaint machinations of literature. But I held the tiny scrap of paper in my pocket, and in my office, a coat, far too broad for my meagre shoulders, dangled to the left of the door.

It bothered me immensely that 'the youth' should be in such a grave position. I'll follow legal precedence and decline to name him. And yet, bizarrely perhaps, I was absolutely certain of his innocence. I had not the slightest grounds to be able to decide the matter either way, but it remained an article of faith with me. The boy had committed no murder! Was incapable of committing murder, in point of fact. So that it must needs follow, if I was in a position to influence the matter in any degree, even if this entailed what the law would term interfering with a witness, then it behoved me to act without scruple or hesitation.

All day I prayed silently for guidance and in the end, as I retired for the night, I decided, like the wilful child, to take the Lord's silence on the subject for acquiescence.

The following day, which was a Sunday, I made my way by train down to Dun Laoghaire. I hadn't been out there in donkey's years. One becomes immured in a termites' nest like St Luke's, and it's as if it's a world sufficient unto itself. The cloistered life! You might even say that within the *Refuge of St Luke the Evangelist*, my library realm was a cloister within a cloister! The changes that now met me were astonishing, even down to the electric green caterpillar that had carried me around the bay. If I might use the term, the transformations I noticed were nothing short of generational. On the dim horizon of my sight, a huge ferry that seemed more jet than boat was churning great cascades of white foam behind it as it sped away to England. I shivered to think how many years I had willingly cocooned myself away from the evolving city.

It took me perhaps a half-hour to track down the address; a small basement flat buried deep in a cul-de-sac that was itself tucked some three or four roads in from the coast. The place had a neglected look about it. The several steps down were uneven, the door was a shabbily painted yellow that was discoloured with lichen, and the electric buzzer gave no signs whatsoever of being wired up when I pressed it. I banged at the door with my fist and waited. But there was not the slightest indication of life within. Undecided as to what to do, I checked for the umpteenth time the little slip of paper and then repeated the tattoo on the door with redoubled force. It balked, mute as the door to a tomb.

It was a clear enough morning, and I decided to pass a pleasant hour down on the pier before returning to try the door for a third time. Then, as I climbed level with the street, a large figure, carrying aloft a brown paper grocery bag, bore down and all but collided with me. Seeing me emerge from what in more elegant times they used to call the area of the house, the man appeared to hesitate, and then pushed on past me towards the bottom of the cul-de-sac. There was something in his new motion that was altogether unconvincing, as though his feet no longer had a purpose to their journey.

This doubt was enough to fill me with renewed confidence. 'Fergal,' I called, and I saw his back visibly flinch, though he continued to slink towards the dead end of the street. 'Fergal Bates!' I called again, bold as the prelate in Kafka's *Trial*. "Joseph K.!" ha ha! Seeing that the game was up, he paused and turned slowly to face me.

'Who are you? What do you want?'

'I've come out here to speak with you,' I said, and then added in a no-nonsense tone I must have picked up from the classroom floor, 'it's a very serious business, Mr Bates.'

'But who are you?' Then he squinted. 'Has Mahood sent you?'

I stepped closer and looked to his eyes, piggy and suspicious. I considered how I might best set him at his ease, gain access to his flat.

'I'm… a man of *God*,' I said, somewhat embarrassingly. And then I added, 'it was "Uncle" who sent me.'

'Un-kill?' he exclaimed in utter disbelief, stepping backwards and cleaving the two syllables as though to make separate words of them. As luck or fate or indeed God would have it, at this ejaculation the bottom of the paper bag split open and groceries cascaded severally to the pavement. He at once disclosed such fluency in expletives as would bring a blush to a beggar.

I crouched down, ostensibly to help round up the rebellious cans and packages, but also to register him into my field of vision. Against my better judgment, I've always put a certain amount of stock in first impressions. Now, one tries not to be unkind, but in this instance I was immediately impressed both by his bulk and his breathlessness. Simultaneously, I felt that he couldn't but notice my relative frailty.

'So, aren't you going to invite me in?' I tried, with a suggestion of coyness that surprised my own ears. He was looking beyond me towards the main street, his hands all the while searching blindly for the fallen groceries.

'Listen, I don't know what the fuck you think you're doing out here, but I've absolutely nothing to say to you. *Rien*! So why don't you just piss off back where you came from.'

'Haven't you indeed?' I retorted, emboldened by the *soupçon* of anxiety I noted on his face. 'Well, Uncle seems to think the contrary. He tells me, in fact, that you've a great deal to say to me.' I was at this moment, I remember, tendering towards him a packet of Jacob's Cream Puffs. I've no idea why such a detail remains embedded in my memory so long after the encounter.

He nodded four times, colouring furiously. 'Then let's get the hell off the street!'

The room into which he led me was of as little cheer as its exterior had suggested. It was a gloomy den which, at a modest reckoning, hadn't been cleaned in a calendar month. There was a smell of sour milk. Moreover, it was cold. He indicated a place on the sofa where, if I moved some less than salutary magazines, I might sit down. He made no move to offer tea or coffee or to light the electric heater, but sat heavily into a decrepit armchair not two feet in front of me.

'You're a priest.' He stated this. He did not ask it.

'I was,' I corrected, 'at one time. Many years ago.'

He grunted.

'I suppose you know why I've come to you?'

'Because Malcolm Little sent you,' he jeered.

'Malcolm? Is that his name?'

'I thought you told me you knew the bastard!' For the briefest moment he looked alarmed.

'It was he gave me your address, that's certainly true. But I wouldn't say that I know him.'

Once more I saw, through glasses darkly, his eyes narrow and peer suspiciously about.

'Wait a minute! Who did you say gave you my address?'

'I just told you. This Malcolm chap. The one who calls himself "Uncle".'

'You're a dirty liar is what you are!' His eyes blossomed open. 'It was Mahood sent you! Or else, no, I've got it! You're a free-lance porker, snooping about for truffles for the gutter-press. You know how I know? Malcolm doesn't know my new address!' Ludicrously, he now mimicked a lisping girl. 'So how do you explain that, mister, hunh?'

'I can't explain it. See here, as God is my witness...,' I began, but he cut me off.

'You're no priest!'

'No,' I said, 'I'm not. At one time I was ordained, but not any longer.'

'I'll tell you what I think.' Here he leaned forward until his elbows all but touched my knees. No accent, this time, but the pitch dropped menacingly into a Dublin growl. 'I think you're a fucking chancer, that's what I think.'

'Look,' I said, beginning to wonder if I wasn't just a little out of my depth, 'I'm not a man to beat about the bush. I think you know the affair that brought me out here.'

There had been some sort of sly calculus going on behind his piggy eyes, and whatever secret conclusion its iterations had come to, he sat back, as though relieved. I say as though, because he was patently trying on mask after mask.

'You told me who brought you,' he declared, 'but you have not told me *what* brought you. You want me to guess.' He tapped fingers on either side of his nose, playing a man who was deep in thought. Then he mimicked an accent out of J. M. Synge.

'Sure maybe you'll be telling me, mister honey, and save me having to phone a friend.'

I answered slowly, to counter his malicious facetiousness, but also because I was beginning to wonder what precisely I was doing out here with such an oddball.

'It's my understanding that you're to give evidence at the Raymond Fowler murder trial.'

'And it was "Uncle" who told you that?'

'Yes.'

'What was he like?'

I hesitated. 'You wish me to describe him?'

'Oh, I dare say you'd be able to make a stab at describing his appearance. It's always... *de trop*. But I was rather more curious as to his character. Did he seem to you in good spirits?'

'Good God, no! He's in altogether a miserable plight. Really, he's a most miserable wretch. If you want to know, he holds you responsible for his present plight.'

'Ha ha! Does he now? And what of my plight? Did he mention that?' He gestured around the room as though it were the vilest dungeon in the world. 'Do you think I'd choose to live in a kip like this? I've my own place, you know. And now, I can never return to it. Malcolm *fucking* Little!'

And then he raised two fingers, as though intoning a chant: '*There is no misery in this world as lofty as mine own. Book of Fergal, chapter one, verse five. Let us pray.*'

'And the trial?' I asked.

He sat back, as though deflated. Perhaps he'd been hoping for applause. 'Well Father, or whatever it is you call an ex-Father, maybe you have it wrong. Maybe I won't be giving any evidence at all at all.'

'Oh?' I said. One tries to be Christian, but this individual really was making the most unsavoury impression on me. Compared to his carry-on, the beetle-man had been helpfulness itself.

'Because maybe,' he went on in his mocking, desultory fashion, ill-disguised by the range of assumed voices, 'just maybe, the defendant is going to plead guilty. Now, what do you think of that?'

'Guilty!' I cried. 'But..., how can he?' I didn't know what to say. This had quite taken the wind out of my sails. He leaned back as far as the chair's complaints would permit and stared straight at me, a supercilious list to his brow. Then he waited. At length his expression teased the question out of me.

'But can he really be guilty?'

'Ah-ha!' he cried, and stood up. Then he smiled, and all ugliness appeared to have melted from his tone. 'Will you have a cup of tea, Father?'

I had set out for Dun Laoghaire that Sunday morning with hope burning brightly inside me. I returned a far more gloomy individual. I think, indeed, that I was as near to despair as at any time since the breakdown of thirty years before. From what this Bates character had told me, and I'd little reason to doubt his word, counsel for the defence was prepared to enter a guilty plea, albeit on the basis of diminished responsibility. It only remained to be seen what sort of a plea bargain the prosecution was prepared to countenance before the whole case was wrapped up.

Naturally, when I'd recovered from the nasty shock, I'd protested that although prone to fits, the boy I knew would never have deliberately hurt someone, much less have committed a murder.

'You knew him back in the kip he was in before he ran away?'

I realised I'd not as yet properly introduced myself, and, remembering that it had meant something to Malcolm, his erstwhile friend, I told him I was Br Martin Ffrench. For all the reaction that he showed I might just as well have said Friar Tuck.

'And this precious boy of yours, I suppose he's not the same raving psychopath that left Malcolm Little on a life-support machine?'

'When was this?' I cried, not knowing whether to believe him.

'Oh, a year ago. Maybe a tad more.'

'And this attack was… unprovoked?'

'Not quite.' He grinned. 'I wouldn't quite say it was unprovoked.' His grin doubled. 'Oh, your protégé went on and robbed the place, too.'

I was truly shocked. I remember thinking soon after I'd taken my leave that this latest revelation must be the absolute nadir of our fortunes, sent perhaps by the Lord to try our faith in His providence. And I must confess, at that moment my faith was being sorely tried.

One other needle was nagging at me as I sat on the green, electric train that wended slowly north-side. Before I left, I'd asked this Bates character how Malcolm Little had come to know the boy. In place of an answer, he gave out a low, ugly guffaw that sent shivers up my spine.

'I think now, Father, you'd better ask him that one yourself!'

VIII | Doyler

The split goes back to the time the brother scored the real bad stuff. Had to shoot it in at the back of the knee so he did. By that stage Joey had to shoot into the veins of his legs because his arms was already that fucked up he couldn't use them any more. That's how far gone he was.

Of course he'd had bad trips before, but this was something else entirely. This was the real bad shit. Pure poison, man. Three days in agony in Tallaght Hospital so he was. There was no saving him then.

I wasn't allowed in to see him on account of I was too small but from what the ma tells me Joey was writhing and thrashing about for three days, like as if something was trying to escape out of inside of him. His muscles was all tensed up, like he was being stretched on the rack or something. She said his backbone was arched so far back she was afraid it was going to snap in two at any moment. Three days man! Can you imagine? Three fucking days.

It was Jacko Corrigan who first said to the ma that the stuff Joey took must've been cut with strychnine. Later on, the papers said the same thing, because it wasn't only Joey was affected by it. There was a couple of junkies oh-deed down in Bray the same week. Later on again, Jacko told me it most probably come out of the same batch that Anto McSorley had been passing off around the estates as pure. He didn't say that bit to the ma, but he told me so he did. After things began to go sour between the two of them.

Anyway, Joey's death was just the start of it.

You see Jacko and the brother had always been thick as thieves together. Ever since we moved out to Shankill from the flats, back in the 80s. They'd always been in the same class in school, even when we were in the city centre, though Jacko must've been nine or ten months older than the brother. Of course I was too small to have gone to school back in Sheriff Street. I can barely remember the flats. But anyway, the ma says it was like living in a ghetto so it was. The smell of piss everywhere and graffiti and every other kind of shite all over the walls and needles in the stairwells.

She said she couldn't wait for us to get the hell out of it.

And then after that the pair of lads was enrolled out here together, in the same school and everything. Though to begin with they tried to separate them by putting them into different classes. Fat chance of that working! Mr Parr the PE teacher who taught karate used to call them Joey-Jack and Jacky-Joe. Like Jackie Chan or something. He was always messing so he was. And then Jacko Corrigan was always big for his age and he was great at the GAA so he was in Parr's good books right from day one.

The two lads even got suspended on the same day so they did. That was after McNeil's tyres was slashed, right there in the schoolyard in front of his office window. Ha ha! Right under his fucking nose, man! It wasn't them that done it. It couldn't've been them. And what's more McNeil knew it couldn't've been them because they were supposed to be on this biology field trip to the Sealife Centre in Bray on the day it happened. But McNeil knew well enough, all the same, that they must've known it was Anto's gang done it. But there again, there was no way on this earth they were going to grass up the likes of Anto McSorley. Are you joking me?

And not just because he was Anto either. You didn't grass up anyone. Ever. It's that simple.

Anto and his gang was bad news, even in those days. He'd been expelled the year before so he had, after he got caught pushing drugs in the jacks. So he had it in for McNeil ever since. Swore out loud to the cop sergeant himself that he'd get even with him one day. So then he'd been up in St Pat's off of the North Circular doing six months juvie, but now he was back on the estates. So there was no prizes for guessing who it was done over McNeil's car for him! Every one of us knew it had to be Anto.

So then the next thing, when McNeil tries to sit on the pair of lads and make them point the finger, that's when Joey tells him he can fuck right off for himself. Right to his face, just like that! Jacko told me so afterwards, when we're walking home after school. He makes Rozzer pretend to be McNeil, and himself pretends to be the brother. You know what you can do, Mr McNeil, sir? You can go and fuck right off for yourself! Ha ha! So that's how come Jacko and Joey got suspended. They'd've most probably got expelled if it hadn't have been for Fr Houghton, putting in the good word and everything.

Of course, word soon got around to Anto McSorley about how the two boys had got suspended for not grassing him up. Now he already knew Joey to see, on account of Joey had the hell of a habit to support. Even in those days, and he barely fourteen years of age! Fourteen, man! The ma knew all about it, too. You should've seen the state of the arms on him! Suffering Jaysus! It made me sick so it did. The inside of the elbow all bruised up yellow and purple like an apple that's gone bad, and more holes in it than a pincushion. Myself and Rozzer used to look at it anytime he went asleep, or if he was spaced out of it or something. That's when the two of us swore a solemn oath we'd never touch the stuff, not with a ten foot pole. It's pure poison, man.

The ma of course used to shout at Joey and to belt him about the kitchen with the back of her hand, and then she'd scream and call him every name under the sun until the neighbours started banging on the walls. He got so bad in the end he even went through her purse a couple of times. I'm not telling you a word of a lie. Took every penny, and the baby upstairs screaming with the hunger on account of sometimes we had to water down the milk we gave her. So then one day she told him he could get the hell out of the house if he didn't kick the habit, and she belting him about the head as she said it.

Joey never fought back. He never even defended himself. Not once. He just sort of used to cower down and took what was coming to him. But then seeing his face the next minute the ma'd be all tears and begging him down on her knees, saying how he was only fourteen years of age and how the drugs would be the death of him. She was right too. He was already more like a walking skeleton than the brother I knew. All he ever ate by that stage was the odd spoonful of vanilla ice-cream, anything else he'd just push across the plate a couple of times with his fork and say he wasn't hungry.

But sure you know yourself. She might as well have been talking to that wall over there for all the heed Joey ever paid her. I swear to you, when you're that far gone, there's no power on this earth can get you back off the powder.

There was no reason for me and Rozzer to have ever crossed paths with the likes of Anto McSorley and his gang. The Shankill Pitbulls. I mean, we were never going to be part of the drug scene. After what happened to Joey and everything it was hardly likely I was going to start shooting that shit into my veins. In fact I wouldn't even do solvents anytime that Rozzer and the O'Shays was sniffing them, getting high and everything. The eyes glazed over and talking pure shite, you call that a high? Fuck off!

But anyway at that time he wouldn't've been seen dead hanging around with anyone our age either.

I guess the same would've generally been true for Jacko and Joey, too. It wasn't so obvious where Jacko was concerned, but Anto was the best part of two year older than the brother. But then it was Joey that had the habit, and I suppose Anto must've known him to see from pushing so much H onto him. And then of course like I say, he must've heard about the two of them sticking up for him in front of McNeil, so that was that. They were in.

I couldn't tell you exactly what they did or didn't do inside of the gang, all I can tell you is that by the time that Joey oh-deed a couple of years later, Jacko Corrigan was already risen to Anto's right hand man inside of the Pitbulls. So he must've known if it was Anto was after cutting the stuff with strychnine.

So anyway, to cut a long story short, the next big thing that came between the two of them was on account of Judith Ross. She's Rozzer's big sister. They do say there's always a mot involved if you look hard enough into anything.

Now to be fair, Judith is what you'd call an absolute kitten. In school everyone always used to be teasing Rozzer that there was no way the pair of them could've had the same parents and all. He might be strong as an ox, but he's no fucking picture, Rozzer. Whereas Judith, Jaysus Christ man! To be totally honest with you, I bet you anything one reason that Jacko Corrigan used to hang around a bit with me and Rozzer was on the off-chance of getting to speak with Judith. He wouldn't've been the first, either.

The only problem was of course that Judith was after getting herself involved with Anto McSorley. Why or how that ever began I could not tell you. It doesn't make any sense, a bird with her looks. A real decent skin, too. Always laughing and messing. She could've had anyone she wanted so she could. I must've asked Rozzer about it a hundred times, but he knows no more about it than I do.

Maybe it's just that Anto was such a big shot around the estates. The big fish in the small pond, as Jacko used to say later on. I mean, he was no Monk or Tony Felloni, but still sometimes something like that can impress a girl, seeing everyone nodding to him and paying their respects. She was young enough when it started, like. Not even Junior Cert, or just. And of course he had a bike, a 750cc, and could take her anywhere she wanted to go. Anyway, maybe she didn't have a lot of choice in the matter. From what Rozzer says Anto was always bothering her, calling her up on the phone at all hours of the night and sending around presents and all sorts of other stuff, most of it that had fell off of the back of a lorry.

I know Jacko Corrigan wasn't altogether happy with the way Anto carried on where Judith was concerned. It wasn't that he mistreated her or anything. Not as such. But he was like a fucking antichrist if he seen anyone joking with her. Honest to God, he was psychopathically jealous of her so he was. And of course Jacko had always been sweet on her, that much was obvious to a blind man.

It must've been about this time that the whole bit happened with your man up near Dalkey, the young fella that was bunking in the shacks down on the beach. Again, I don't know the ins and outs of it. I do know he was supposed to have been seeing Judith on the sly. I believe Jacko seen them together up on Killiney Hill or something and then he went and told Anto. It's like I say, whatever he might've thought about it, he was still number two in the Pitbulls, and anyway, he most probably wanted to get the spotlight off of himself where Judith was concerned. I don't know how true it is, but Rozzer says that Jacko and Anto nearly had a fist fight the previous summer when Anto found the pair of them drinking cider together down by the harbour wall in Bray.

For one reason or another best known to himself, Anto decided to take care of the young fella up in Killiney without involving the Pitbulls. I suppose maybe he wanted to keep what was a domestic strictly that. A domestic. But there again, he needed to have enough muscle behind him to make sure the lad wouldn't get away on him. So that's how come he told myself and Rozzer to come along that night. Of course it wouldn't've been the first time he'd called on Rozzer, especially since he started doing a line with Judith Ross. And at that stage Rozzer had already got a reputation around the estates for being a hard man. Very handy with a bicycle chain, when it came to a scrap. Jacko himself was to be number four, partly on account of he knew where the young lad was supposed to be hiding out, but partly if you ask me because Anto wanted to leave him in no doubt as to what'd happen to anyone else who was ever caught doing the business with Judith Ross. D'you see what I'm saying? It was meant to be like a demonstration for the benefit of one Jacko Corrigan.

Everyone knows the story of what happened that night. We held him down, and Anto carved his face up with a Stanley knife and told him he'd cut the bollox off of him if he ever saw him round the place again. After that we torched the place. Anto had been bragging about how he was going to douse him with petrol and throw a match, but I don't know how much of that was just to put the frighteners on Jacko. It's one thing cutting someone's face up, I mean they're hardly likely to go to the pigs to complain about it. But murder's a different league entirely. And all on account of a girl? Myself and Rozzer talked him out of it as we made our way along the shore. Though Jacko didn't say a word. It's funny. But anyway, like I say, I get the distinct impression Anto was just mouthing off at the time about the petrol.

Word soon got back to Judith about what had happened. I couldn't tell you who it was told her. It wasn't me or Rozzer, that's for sure, and I have my doubts it would've been Anto. He'd've been more likely to have let her figure it out for herself, once she'd seen how the young fella had skidaddled and the kip burned down to the ground. So that leaves Jacko Corrigan. If it was Jacko, I'm not exactly sure what he was thinking of. Maybe he figured it'd help to turn Judith again you know who, seeing what a brutal fucker he was and everything. It'd depend on how far gone she was on your man. Of course, any number of other people could've seen the state of his face and told her afterwards, it's not as if she doesn't have her own set of friends. Your guess is as good as mine boss.

But I can tell you one thing for free, if that's what Jacko's plan was, it worked a treat so it did. A couple of nights after the scarring I was around at Rozzer's gaff, up in his room on the play-station, when we heard one God Almighty row coming from downstairs. Shouting and screaming they were, raising such a racket that you'd swear it was *her* face he was trying to cut up. She kept screaming get away from me, and then get your fucking hands off of me. You couldn't make out what he was saying, but. Just these muffled growls every now and then coming up through the floorboards. A low sort of a sound, like an animal growling. And then she'd start screaming again, you're a fucking animal Anto and get the hell away from me. It got so bad that a couple of times Rozzer went as far as the top of the stairs. If Anto had actually laid a finger on his sister I don't know what he'd've done. He wouldn't've just stood by. And then fuck knows what would've become of Rozzer, if he'd laid into Anto McSorley. Jaysus Christ, it doesn't bear thinking! All I can tell you is first she stormed out, and then he trashed the kitchen so he did. It's the mercy of God that Rozzer's da was doing time in the 'Joy for aggravated assault, or there would've been a right mill. Paddy Ross is a bouncer down in the Porterhouse in Bray and he's a hell of a left hook so he has. He was a pretty handy middle-weight in his day, I believe.

So then the next thing you heard was Anto's bike revving up outside, a big bastard of a Kawasaki, and that was the last we ever seen him around at Rozzer's gaff. He mightn't've thought he was done with Judith, but she'd made up her mind that she was done with him. It was only a matter of waiting for the right opportunity. Or so she thought, anyway.

But the other thing about it was it was obvious there was no love lost between Anto and Jacko Corrigan over it. It wasn't so much that he was exactly able to blame Jacko for the fact that she wanted shot of him. What it come down to was prestige. There was plenty of rumours doing the rounds about how Jacko Corrigan had been sweet on Judith, and there was no way a man like Anto was going to be prepared to lose face over a girl. So you can see how things had already begun to cool down between the two of them. And then there was the hen night at Hannifin's. But I don't want to get ahead of myself and anyway I don't know how much of that is actually true. But one way or another, the whole thing had already started to get very messy by that stage.

•••

A couple of months after the bust up in Rozzer's gaff, one night at about six in the morning, there was this almighty racket outside of our house, a car revving and racing and sounding off the horn like nobody's business. Woke up the baby and everything. So I pulled on my clothes and ran out to see what all the fuss was about. Who was it only Rozzer, and he after lifting a Beemer off of the Vico Rd. Come on, says he, we're going for a spin. There was another young fella in the back of the car that I knew to see. I'd seen him hanging around with the Pitbulls, Jason, I believe his name was.

It must've been him had hot-wired the car back up in Dalkey. Where we going? says I to Rozzer, already swinging in through the door. He was still racing around in circles, pulling these crazy hand-brake turns, so it was all I could do not to break my fucking neck. But by now I could see the ma's bedroom light was after going on and I wanted to get the hell out of there before she copped it was Rozzer outside. Wicklow! says he. Grand job! And off we shoot, doing a hundred and twenty down the dueller as far as Ashford and half way back up the other side through all the early morning traffic. Jaysus, it was mad so it was. I hadn't been out joy-riding since the previous summer, but wherever Rozzer had learned to drive since then, it was foot to the floor all the way like he was at Mondello fucking Park.

Anyway, to cut a long story short, we eventually torched the car outside Newtownmountkennedy, so the knackers'd get the blame for it. Then we began to make our way up over the hills along the back roads. So the next thing your man Jason disappears for about an hour and when he comes back he has a few naggins of whiskey on him, and it wasn't long before the three of us was well gone. And it still only nine in the morning what's worse.

We slept off the booze by the Vartry and then Rozzer says he has to go down to Delgany to see a girl. So he said anyway. It was the first I heard of any mot he was supposed to be seeing. If you ask me he was too bloody lazy to traipse back over the mountains, but he had to make up an excuse to save face. Like he had a mot down in Delgany that none of us had ever heard of. Yeah right! But however in any case that left myself and this Jason character to make our own way back through the hills on foot. It was getting a bit cold and we were quiet, with the effects of the booze worn off and everything, and anyway not really knowing one another from Adam. Then after about an hour we come across this campsite, one big tent and a smaller one beside it, and a clothesline with washing hanging out on it. There was all sorts of pots and pans around the place too, and the remains of a bonfire. Fucking knackers! says Jason, pulling open the door of the big tent and starting to rifle through whatever he found inside of it. Then he turns his attention on the little tent that had only supplies in it, and he firing out the boxes and bags like he was a poltergeist or something. But there was fuck all worth taking, just cans of food and rice and cooking oil and all that sort of crap. So Jason starts kicking it about the place, for a bit of a laugh like.

You know the way you have to act kind of tough, I mean when you don't know someone? So anyway I started in at the same lark, playing football with a head of cabbage and then pulling down the clothesline and dragging the washing after me over the dirty ground like it was a bullfighter's cape with your man Jason chasing after me holding these tent pegs to his head as if they was the horns of a bull. There was this little stream running down from where the trees were thicker, and I was just about to take a lep over it to escape him when this wild man appears out of the woods with a dog tearing after him.

Jaysus, before I knew where I was he had me upended with his shoulder and once he had me down he clattered the side of me head so hard I seen stars for a week so I did. That's what it felt like anyway. The next thing I did actually see was the dog pulling out of Jason's arm and he trying to swing a belt himself, and wherever he'd come out of it was the same young fella he was trying to connect with, the one that'd been seen hanging around with Judith months before. Your man with the scar across his face.

Jaysus, between the pair of them and the bloody old dog biting and yapping and pulling they give us one hell of a beating that day. I swear to you I was sore for a week so I was. I'd one side of the jaw swelled up the size of a football, and I'd more bruises on me than a fucking punch-bag. And Jason come off even worse so he did. He broke two fingers trying to punch the first fella, he'd a couple of dog bites on his arm and his lip was split open so bad they'd to give him a tetanus jab and a dozen stitches so they did. It was the mercy of God he didn't lose any of his teeth. But it's a crying shame that Rozzer wasn't there with us. If Rozzer had've been there, it would've been a different story entirely.

But the beating was only the start of it.

By the time the two of us had limped back to Shankill, word was already out that Rozzer had been lifted by the guards and he trying to thumb a lift on the N11. Then a couple of mornings after that they came for Jason. Know what the pair of them had done? They'd only pulled into a fucking garage to fill up the tank immediately after they'd hot-wired the Beemer! And then to add insult to injury the pair of fucking eejits done a runner without paying for any of it! So the pigs had both of their ugly mugs all over the closed-circuit. I suppose you look at it one way, it was a lucky break where I was concerned. It meant the pigs was happy with just the two of them. But did you ever in your life hear of anything as dense? A Jaysus self-service station, if you don't mind.

The following weekend, it was already late in the evening, Jacko Corrigan calls round to the gaff.

'Get your coat on, Doyler, you're wanted.'

'Wanted by who?' says I.

'Anto McSorley wants to have a word with you.' You could have floored me with a feather when I heard him say that. I was amazed for two reasons. Number one, on account of a summons to talk to Anto McSorley was about the last thing in the world I was expecting to hear, and number two, on account of Jacko Corrigan had never called me Doyler before. Doyler is what he used to call the brother. Before he died like. Joey Doyle. I looked at him when he said it to see if I'd heard him right and I'd swear I saw him look away real fast, like he was embarrassed or something.

Anto was waiting for us down behind the sewage treatment. He was on his Toblers, just himself and the bike. He nods to Jacko, and then says he wants me to describe the ins and outs of the beating. In particular, he says he wants me to describe who exactly we'd been up against. He'd only heard the barest bones of it from Jason, the two lads still being held in custody and everything after being charged with two counts of theft and reckless driving, and he not having any great wish to give the pigs a hint as to what he might be thinking about it.

I was surprised by the fact he seemed more interested in the wild man of the woods than by the young fella with the scar. I mean, I'd assumed, when I seen that Jacko Corrigan was involved, that he was interested on account of Judith Ross. But no. He was more interested in the other one. So I described the older guy in as much detail as I could, the army jacket and the baldy head with the string of long hair at the back.

'Did he have a funny accent?'

'What class of an accent?'

'I don't fucking know. Did he have an English accent?'

'I couldn't tell you, Anto. I never heard him say anything.'

'You mean to tell me that all this time he's beating the two of you, he doesn't even say one fucking word?'

I shook my head. I didn't see what he was driving at. He looks hard at Jacko, and then he looks back at me, sort of fierce like.

'How about a tattoo. Did he have a tattoo?'

'A tattoo? What kind of a tattoo?'

'A tattoo! Fuck sake!'

I racked my brains. Try as I might, I couldn't picture the man clearly. How he smelt, yes. The more I tried to picture exactly what he looked like, the more the smell off of him came back to me. Sort of smoke and wet and bad underarms. I shrugged my shoulders.

'Here on his arm!' Anto shouts right into me face. 'Did he have a fucking tattoo here on his arm or didn't he?' In a flash it come back to me. I swear to you it was that vivid I could see it as plain as if it was on my own arm.

'He did have, Anto. Right there where you say. It was like a picture of a knife or something, and some sort of a motto wrapped around it.'

Anto fired a knowing look at Jacko. 'That's our man!' says he, making an ugly grimace. Then he sort of nods in my direction. 'Tell him.'

So Jacko begins to explain to me how it's not the first time they've had a run-in with your man. The English cunt. How it all began a couple of year ago when the Pitbulls had a serious stash of crack hidden out in an old ruin of a farmhouse not too far above Aughrim. That was in the days when Matt Gillespie used to be number two in the Pitbulls, before he got done trying to bring gear over from Amsterdam. So one day when Matt goes down to pick up some of the stash, he finds every single one of the bags has been split open with a knife and the snow scattered all over the gaff, no use to anyone anymore. From what Anto chipped in, there must've been twenty thousand worth of powder in that stash, and it now being blown to the four corners of County Wicklow. Jacko says Anto literally went through the roof when he heard about it.

Anyway Matt has a good look around the place before he brings back the bad news, to see if there's any clues as to who might've done such a crazy thing. But the only clue he finds is a couple of rabbit snares made out of chicken wire, and wood-shavings where someone's been carving. Still, it's enough to give him an idea. So he explains to Anto how there's this vagrant he's come across in the vicinity when he was casing the place. Said he had a dog, and a tattoo on his arm and a funny accent, like something you'd hear out of Brookside.

'Go and find him, and find out if it was him,' says Anto, 'and if it was, he'll be sorry he ever set foot in this country, the limey cunt, I can promise you that.' But there was no sign of your man, and anyway, there was other more urgent matters at the time. The Pitbulls owed the half of that stash to some baron up in Tallaght you did not want to mess with. It was as he was trying to arrange to get some more gear in to replace it that Matt Gillespie got stung. Set up by the Dutch police so he was. So that sort of put your man on the back-burner.

Of course thinking about it, it was Matt Gillespie being behind bars that gave Jacko the chance to move up the ranks. It's an ill wind, as they say.

'Now show him what you've got in your pocket,' says Anto, still talking like he's biting on a lemon. So Jacko puts his hand into his pocket and pulls out a phone and puts it on the table.

'I don't get it,' says I.

'D'you know what that is?' says Jacko. 'Have a look.' I looked. 'What?'

'It's only state of the fucking art, that's all. Takes fucking pictures and videos and everything.' You must remember this was back when they were just bringing in the 3Gs. Third generation like. So then he sort of leers. 'You take one of these boys happy slapping with you and you could show the results in the Multiplex screen up in Tallaght so you could.'

I put the phone back down and stared at the pair of them. What the fuck has any of this got to do with me like? Anto looks that pissed off I thought he might actually lay into me. But that was all an act. It was left up to Jacko to explain yet again.

'We had an entire van full of the stuff got knocked off in Dun Laoghaire. It was hid out down by Vartry while we were looking to find a buyer.'

I examined him more closely. You could say I'd begun to put two and two together. 'So then, that's where Jason disappeared off to the other day?'

He nodded. 'Now,' says he, 'where did you say you ran into our friend? Where exactly?' So I tried to explain as best I could.

'You see,' says Jacko, 'a couple of days ago the guards was tipped off about that van. When Anto was bringing a client down on Tuesday to take a look at the merchandise, the place was crawling with the fuckers. It was just as well the bike can do cross-country.'

'How can you be sure it was your man tipped them off, but?'

'Why?' says Anto, real nasty like. 'Maybe it was you?'

I shook my head at Jacko as if it was himself had said that. If I'm honest with you, I was too scared stiff to look directly at Anto.

'This is the first I've heard of any mobile phones, Jacko. I swear to you.'

'It fucking better be,' says Anto, 'because if I find out it was you, you're a dead man, Joey Doyle or no Joey Doyle.'

It crossed my mind at that moment that if anyone had tipped off the guards it was just as likely to be your man Jason, trying to cut a deal or something, but I decided I was better off staying shtum about it.

'The point is,' says Jacko, reassuring like, 'can you find your way back to your man's campsite?'

I thought about it for a second. 'I can give it a lash,' I says to them.

'You better do a bit more than just give it a fucking lash,' says Anto, picking up his helmet and making to leave. Interview over!

A minute later I watched the red tail light bob across the dunes like it was a mad scrambler.

'What the fuck was that all about?' says I to Jacko, as soon as it was well out of sight. 'Well you might ask,' says he, spitting on the ground. 'Well you might ask, Doyler.'

•••

So the following evening Jacko calls around for me in the car, and we head off down the dueller in the direction of Newtownmountkennedy. This was the first time the two of us ever really talked. I mean, a good talk. It was during that drive that Jacko told me all about Joey. How he'd warned him to steer clear of the Pitbulls and find another supplier. He said he always suspected that if the last dose he'd scored had've been cut with strychnine, like the papers said it was, then it was almost definitely Anto who was responsible for it. That was the time he was having the trouble paying back our friend up in Tallaght over the lost crack and the twenty grand, and he didn't give a flying fuck who got hurt or stung in the process of clearing that particular debt. That was the real reason, so Jacko said, why he'd cosied up to him and joined the Pitbulls properly after Joey died. He wanted to be sure of his facts.

'So are you sure of the facts?' I ask him.

'Pretty much,' he goes, looking at my eyes in the mirror, 'and if he didn't do the cutting himself, he didn't fucking raise a finger to stop it being done. And that comes to the same thing.'

After he said that he looked at me again for a bit, and then eyes back on the road. Then we drove for a while without anyone saying anything. I was quiet because I wanted to let what he'd said sink in. It wasn't as if it came as any great shock. I'd always kind of known Joey'd scored the gear from the Pitbulls. But what I wanted to figure out was why Jacko Corrigan was saying this to me tonight, now. Nearly two years after the brother died like.

'So what's the plan?' I go, after a while, as much to break the silence as anything else.

'What plan?' He gawked at me when he asked that, like he was angry or like I was after insulting him or something. I'll always remember that.

'What does Anto want us for?'

Now he smirked. It was almost like he was relieved. 'Anto? He wants to give our friend a beating he won't soon forget, that's what he wants us for.'

I sat back in the seat. 'Which one of them?' I go. Now he laughs out loud. Not like a real laugh, as if he found what I said funny, but as much as to say 'you've hit the nail on the head there!' I laugh, too. I'd always suspected Anto wasn't prepared to let Judith Ross simply disappear out of his life. Neither was Jacko Corrigan, for that matter.

Anto was waiting for us in this lay-by on the back road to Roundwood. He was wearing leathers, which I suppose was natural enough, seeing as he was after riding there on his bike, but still I couldn't help but think it was as if he wanted to look like the young fella he'd had scarred, the one that Judith had been sweet on. It was still early enough, not quite dark, and the birds was kicking up a bit of a racket as if they were scared of the coming dark. You couldn't even hear any traffic from where we were. The sky in the west looked like it might've been steeped in blood so it did, I'll always remember thinking that.

I looked up and down the road, surprised to find him waiting there on his own.

'There's just the three of us?' I go. Anto and Jacko are both of them big men you wouldn't want to mess with, but still I'd been expecting a few of the heavies from the gang. Anyway, whatever he was thinking, he ignored my question.

'Just go and make sure the camp is still where you and Jason was beat up. Don't let yourself be seen, right? I want to surprise the fuckers. And don't fucking take all night about it either.'

I nodded, thinking he was finished, and hopped over the wall to get on with it.

'Where d'you think you're going?' he growls at me. 'Come back here you little runt.' He pulls this plastic bag from out of the inside of his jacket and hands it to me.

'What's that?' I go.

'That's to take care of the dog with. It eats that, it won't wake up for a week. Just leave it down where it can smell it.'

'We'll wait for you here, right? Now move!' put in Jacko, his voice a lot rougher than it had been in the car. So I moved.

It took me the best part of a half-hour to find the camp, so that by the time I got there it was pretty near dark and hard to see anything. There was a thin scratch of a moon, not much more than my thumbnail there, hanging just over where the sun had gone down. Still, there was light enough to put me on my guard. I lay down on my belly at the edge of the trees up above the camp, all needles and everything over the ground and smelling just like a Christmas tree. It was fucking uncomfortable too so it was, but I had to make sure they wouldn't see me.

I must've lain there a full ten minutes. There was no fire lit, and no sign of the dog. After a while, I don't know what got into me, but nothing would do me only to crawl down and take a closer look. The whole place seemed even more deserted than the day myself and your man Jason had stumbled across it, but still I wanted to be absolutely sure before I reported back to the boys. So to cut a long story short I crawled down the side of the hill on my belly, edging myself along on my elbows like I was in a war picture or something, and then when I got as far as the base of the clothesline I unwrapped the hunk of meat that Anto had doped and I laid it out flat, making sure to sprinkle dirt over it so it couldn't be seen, only smelled.

I took one more look around. The place was eerily quiet. The white light of the moon was making everything seem like it was cut out of tinfoil and black cardboard. Ever have that feeling, like when you're in a dream, that you've been there before like? I can't explain it, but that's how I felt now. Like I was in a dream. Like I'd seen this exact scene before. There wasn't even a breeze to make the branches move in the woods. And then, just as I was about to get up and go, I heard this moan coming out of the big tent, right next to where I was lying. Or it wasn't exactly a groan. I don't know how to describe it. Anyway it put the heart crossways in me so it did.

I lay there like I was dead. Every now and then, something like a wail would rise up out of the tent, but sort of muffled. It's hard to describe it to you. And once or twice the canvas shook, as if someone had just kicked it. Jaysus Christ, I thought, don't tell me one of them is murdering the other! I literally couldn't think of what else it could be.

Now here's the funny part. If the pair of them was having a go at one another, that was my perfect opportunity to make my escape, right? But still I don't make a move. It just goes to show you, I was more scared of getting back to Anto without being able to tell him exactly what was going on than I was of getting caught by the wild man that had gave me such a battering just the other week. So instead of trying to sneak away, like I should've, I actually edged up to the side of the tent, and I lifted up the corner of the canvas just enough to be able to peek inside.

What I seen was mad so it was. The young fella was inside on his own, lying stretched out with his face out towards me, and he thrashing about from side to side. Maybe it was on account of the moonlight but he was that pale it was as if he was made of chalk or stone or something, and there was this sort of a grimace on his face like he was in pain. In the moonlight the scar looked like it was glowing. His arms and legs were stuck out as stiff as pokers. It made me think of how the ma had described Joey lying in the Mater hospital. And as I ran back to tell the boys what I was after seeing, the thought actually crossed my mind that maybe he was after taking a hit laced with strychnine. I'd no other way to explain it.

I was poxed lucky, too. On the way back I nearly ran straight into the English cunt, making his way back to the camp with a rabbit hanging out of his hand and the dog bounding all about it like it was a puppy. It was the mercy of God they didn't see me.

Before I could get my breath back Anto literally jumped on me, pushed me up against the wall and clamped my jaw between his fingers.

'Where the fuck've you been, Doyle, you little runt?'

When I finally got him to ease his grip, it took me a while to make sense of exactly what I'd seen.

'And there was no sign of the limey cunt or his dog?'

'Not in the camp. I nearly run into them on my way back here.'

'You left down the meat?'

'I did, Anto.'

He was staring hard at his motorbike helmet.

'Describe your man again,' puts in Jacko. 'His fists was thrashing about?'

I thought carefully about what I'd seen. 'His arms were stiff, I didn't notice the fists. It was the head was thrashing about.'

'He must've been having a fit all the same,' says Jacko. 'Judith told me she once seen him having a fit.'

Jaysus, no sooner had he said the word Judith than Anto stares at him as if he was after insulting his mother. Jaysus you could've cut the atmosphere with a knife so you could. I thought at the time it was because Anto was beginning to realise how much time Judith must've spent with our friend with the scar, but thinking about it afterwards, I think what really got on his wick was that it meant Jacko and Judith must've been talking together about it, and that she'd told him more than she'd told Anto.

The two of them continued to stare like they was shaping up to one another and then Anto spat on the ground and went down to the shore of the lake.

'What's got into him?' I go.

'You shouldn't've said anything about Judith Ross.'

It wasn't me who'd said anything about Judith Ross, but I didn't let on.

'But I thought the two of them was finished,' says I, as much for mischief as anything else.

'You have your shite!' he goes, as much as to say she might be finished with him, but there's no way he's letting her get away that easy.

After that we both looked down to the shore, where Anto was skimming stones out towards the centre of the reservoir. You could only just make out the circles where the stones hopped, because the moon had already gone down by this stage. He must've kept up that lark for about twenty minutes.

When he came back he looked like he'd calmed down, but there was something else in his eye. I don't know how to describe it. It was as if he was about to make a sneaky move in chess or something.

'Right, here's what we're going to do,' says he. 'There's three of us, right? You,' he poked a finger into my chest, 'you're going to look after the mutt. D'you have a blade?' I shook my head, and he pulls one ugly mother of a knife out of the back of his jeans.

'What do I want a knife for?'

'In case,' he goes, as if he was talking to a prize tool, 'the fucking mutt hasn't eaten enough of the dope. If it so much as makes a whimper, cut open its throat. D'you hear me?'

I nod and take the knife off of him. It's much heavier than it looks, as if it has lead inside of the blade or something. A real ugly bastard.

'Now, you can look after Scarface,' he goes to Jacko, but with his back turned on him. He sort of spoke to him over his shoulder. 'How long did Judith Ross say his fits usually last?'

'Judith Ross didn't say. I got the impression from her it went on all night once it started.'

You would've had to have heard the tone of voice he used when he said the words 'all night'. He was staring at the back of Anto's head as if he wanted to bore a hole in it. There was no love lost between the two of them, that's for sure.

'Right, here's what I want you to do. If he's awake, take care of him. But if he's still knocked out, don't lay so much as a finger on him, right? I don't want him marked. You stand over him, that's all. Here.' He turns round and hands a tiny paper sachet to Jacko. 'That's the rest of the powder I give the dog. Mix it up with some water or something and force it in between his teeth. Make sure he swallows it. I don't want him waking up till we're well out of there.'

He begins to march away without looking at us, like someone who's used to having his instructions obeyed.

'Leave the limey fucker to me,' he growls.

The orders took me by surprise. Even besides what he told me about the phones, I'd figured mostly he wanted to vent his anger on the young fella, Scarface, on account of Judith Ross like. But from what I could make out now, the main score he wanted to settle was with the older guy. Jaysus, I thought, maybe the vanload of mobiles was worth a sight more than he's letting on.

There was a lot more signs of activity about the campsite by the time we got to the trees up above it. First off, there was a fire lit, fairly newly lit to judge by how the branches was crackling. I could see the rabbit hanging upside-down out of the clothesline and it skinned and shiny in the light. The older guy must have pulled Scarface outside of the tent so he could warm up a bit, because now you could make out the head and shoulders lying just behind the flap. He was still out of it, though. But meanwhile the other guy was busy bending over the mutt, who was lying at the foot of the clothesline, panting and whimpering. So it was obvious he was after swallowing a good chunk of the poisoned meat when his master wasn't looking.

'What is it, Keaton? What's the matter boy?' he kept on going, fingering the dog's jaws between his hands, and true enough now you mention it, his accent was kind of Brookside.

I felt Anto's hand squeezing my leg, and he nodded for the three of us to slide back out of earshot.

'Ok, listen to me. Here's what we're going to do.' He was staring hard, whispering, but the night was so still I was afraid the whispers might carry over the top of the hill. 'Youse two go back up to where you were, and when you see me wave, start pelting him with stones, right? I'll be laying in wait for him over there by the hollow.'

So we began to search around for stones to stuff into our pockets and as we did, I seen him prise a rock the size of a baby's head out of the ground.

A big fucker, that size I swear to you. Then I seen him slip it into something that looked like a sock. I'm not sure if Jacko seen it. I don't think he did.

'Now, as soon as I've clocked him, get down there as fast as you can to make sure the other two are well out of it. Right?'

We nodded, and we began to sneak back up to the top of the hill. Have to tell you, boss, I felt my guts do a somersault when I seen the size of the rock he'd slipped into that sock. But there was no turning back now.

We'd no sooner got back up to the crest of the hill when Anto waves his arm, and the pair of us begin to let fly with the stones. 'Who the hell is that? Who's there, damn you?' shouts your man, with the limey accent on him, and then one of my stones gets him on the elbow. Jacko was by this time standing up and openly taunting him. So of course he grabs up a stick from under the clothesline and charges up the hill after us, but he's in such a hurry that he loses his footing when he's about half way up.

I don't know what class of devil had got into Anto McSorley that night, but before your man has even the chance to get back on his feet he breaks from his cover and lays straight into him, swinging the sock over his head like something out of Braveheart. Then he crashes it into the side of his head with such force that you literally felt the crack from where the two of us was standing.

'Get fucking down to the others! Now!' he screams, standing up astride over your man's body, with the sock hanging down from one hand.

Jaysus Christ, he's after killen him, I thought. Or maybe I even said it out loud as I ran down the hill to where the dog still lay, whimpering and panting like the life was about to go out of it.

I knelt down and took the dog's head between my hands and then I patted it. I don't know why I done that. Maybe it was the only way I could stay sane at that minute. When I looked up again Jacko had edged the young fella a bit more outside the tent, and he seemed to be messing with something in his hands. It was too big to be the sachet of powder, though. It was only when the LCD come on for a second that I realised it was a mobile. One of the batch of 3G numbers they'd knocked off, most probably. Turns out later they'd already stashed the half of them before ever the guards got tipped off, which makes me sort of wonder about things. Like maybe it was all a set up. Jaysus, you'll be doing well to get any coverage up here, I can remember thinking. It just goes to show you how your mind can have the most common or garden thoughts, even when your heart is racing twenty to the dozen.

I could hear grunts and heavy breathing from up behind me, and when I turn around I can see Anto, his back turned towards us, dragging our friend by the legs down towards the campsite. The jacket had folded back under him like a cloak but still his head bumped and banged at every dip and tree root. Jacko was still messing about with the phone, and didn't make any move to help him.

He dragged him in until he was at the far side of the fire and now he was lit up in orange and red flickers, but the head was turned so I couldn't make out how bad the skull had been cracked. One thing I can tell you, there was no sign of life in his arms nor legs.

'Is he dead?' I go.

'Shut the fuck up, you! Did you give Scarface the rest of the dope?' 'I did,' said Jacko, stepping towards him. No sign of the phone now, whoever he was texting.

'Right,' says Anto, unrolling the sock and letting the rock drop out of it onto the ground. 'Let's get this over with and get the fuck out of here.'

I stand up. My legs is shaking, not with fear, but more with adrenaline. As if someone's shaping up to me. How much of this whole scenario Anto had planned or foreseen, to this day I couldn't tell you. I mean, to a certain extent it had to have been pure chance, the boy having the fit and everything. But now he was acting as if he'd planned the whole thing. Maybe that's what he was thinking about all the while he was hopping stones across the lake.

So anyway he picks up the rock again, this time using the sock like it's a glove, and he pushes it against the side of your man's head, wiping it about like it's a sponge. As he does this the head rolls about towards me and I can see by the light of the fire that the eyes is half opened and like they were made out of beads. That's when I knew for certain he was dead. When he pulls the stone away, one half of it is black with blood.

'Here', he goes, reaching it out towards me, but turning the sock so I'd be able to take it without getting my prints all over it. At least, that's what I reckon he was about.

'What?'

'What? Put the fucking thing in the young fella's hand, that's what.'

I'm still staring at the corpse's eyes, twinkling like a dummy in the firelight, and I must've stopped a bit too long, because the next thing he took a hold of my hand and slapped the rock into it, sock and all.

'You're already an apprentice so you are, if that's what you're thinking.' Then he fires a sneering look at Jacko. 'The both of yiz are.'

What he meant to say was accomplice. It just goes to show that even he wasn't thinking quite as clearly as he thought he was.

'They'll know you fucking hit him up there on the side of the hill,' taunts Jacko. 'There'll be traces of blood all over the grass. And you know what else? There's probably microscopic fibres of cloth stuck into that wound so there is.'

'Who are you, Miami fucking Vice?' He looked like he was about to blow a fuse, but took control of himself just in time. 'Anyway, who's to say, smart arse, that the boy couldn't have pulled the body down here himself?' He takes a couple of steps away from the fire until he's as dark as a shadow.

'I'm heading on first. It's safer that way.'

So to cut a long story short it was left to myself and Jacko to arrange it as best we could that it was the young fella had cracked our friend's skull open.

We're nearly all the way back to the car without having spoken so much as a word. I suppose each of us is lost in his own thoughts. I mean, it's not every day you suddenly find yourself an accomplice to first-degree murder.

Or an apprentice, as Anto put it. It made me wonder all the same if Jacko was as shocked by what had just happened as I was.

When we were just short of the car, I turned around to him to break the silence like. So I asked him what he'd been doing on the mobile. Jaysus Christ Almighty! I'd no sooner said it but he fetched me such a belt to the ear that I was deafened for a week so I was. I swear to Christ it could've burst my eardrum.

'What the fuck you do that for?' I shouted at him. I'm not telling you a word of a lie, the whole side of my face around my ear felt like it was gone numb, and my skull was ringing like a bell that's just been struck. Jacko grabs my jaw between his fingers like Anto had done earlier and he pins me against the door of his car.

'Did you love your brother Joey? Did you? Or were you just letting on to?' he hisses.

'What the fuck has Joey got to do with it?' My words sound like they're out of a cartoon or something he has my jaw clamped that tight. He shakes his head and relaxes his grip ever so slightly. He looks like he's well pissed off.

'D'you realise what's going on? Have you any idea what's going on here?'

Then he let me go. I was still rubbing my ear and staring straight at him, as if I was thinking of starting on him or something. But that was really because, to be honest with you, I didn't have the first idea of what was going on.

'Listen to me Doyler,' he says. 'That fucker is after getting us involved in a first-degree murder. D'you not realise that? He had that whole thing planned all along so he did.'

'But I don't get it. Why would he want to do something like that?'

'Because that's the why! That's the way Anto fuck-face works. That's why he'd do something like that.' He looked livid. But I could see he was just trying to find the right words to say what was on his mind. 'Now he has a sort of a hold over us. D'you get me?'

'But he's the one done the murder, Jacko. He's the one split your man's head open.'

'Yeah, in your eyes maybe. But in the eyes of the law we're just as guilty as he is. Because we were there, and we done nothing to stop him. D'you get me? Not only that, you could argue we helped him do it. And that means that you and me is as guilty of murder as he is. Do you know nothing about the law?'

I must've been still in a state of shock, because nothing he was saying to me seemed to be going in.

'But the young fella, Scarface. He's going to take the rap for it. Isn't that the plan?'

'That's the plan all right. But we'll see that when we see it. In the meantime, the three of us is bound together as thick as thieves. That's the way he's figured it.'

I shook my head and spat at the ground. To tell you the truth, my jaw was still aching and my eardrum was still ringing. And I did not like one bit what Jacko was after saying to me. But still I was in too much of a state to think things through.

'But there's one thing he didn't figure on,' he said after a bit, tapping the side of my face where his fingers had just recently been pressing, 'and that's that I was up to him all along. Oh, I had his measure right enough!'

'What're you talking about, Jacko?'

He put a threatening finger under my nose. 'You ever say a word to anyone about that phone, and I swear to fucking Christ I'll kill you.'

'The phone?' I must've been the right eighteen-carat eejit that night, and that's for sure. He nods at me like the two of us know exactly what he's talking about, and so I smile back, not knowing what else to do.

'He can think again if he thinks he can outsmart Jacko Corrigan.' And as he tapped the top pocket where he kept the phone, he whispered 'insurance', winking at me. But it was only when we were half way back to Dublin that I realised that what he'd been doing earlier on wasn't texting.

He'd only been taking a video of Anto McSorley, dragging the corpse down the hill to the campsite! That was his insurance, like.

•••

Sometimes you only begin to figure something out properly when you've to explain it to someone else. Know what I mean? A couple of days later Rozzer was back out of juvie on bail so I had to explain to him what had happened while he was gone. Not a squeak about the phone, though, or what Jacko'd said after.

If I thought he was going to be shocked, I'd another thing coming. He shrugged. Then he shook his head and grunted. As if you killed a bum every day of the week, like. It pissed me all the way off so it did, seeing him taking it in so natural and everything.

But then a bit later on when we're drinking cider down by the sewage treatment, Rozzer says to me, 'I still don't get it, but. How come youse didn't just do the pair of them in, instead of messing around with downers? Youse could just as easy have killen the young fella while he slept.'

'Why'd we want to do in the two of them?' I go, playing dumb like. I wanted to see what sort of hole he was going to dig for himself.

'You ask me, it'd've been the easiest way. And what's more, that way you could be one hundred percent sure there was no witnesses.'

'Yeah,' says I, 'you've a point. But that way, there wouldn't be no main suspect, either. Whereas our way, when the guards finally do come across Scarface, they'll call off the investigation. Case dismissed!'

I should've mentioned the young fella had long since disappeared. In fact they didn't come across your man for a couple of days, and he died in hospital without ever regaining consciousness. So he'd plenty of time to make his getaway. For all his bossing us about, that was one part of the show that Anto McSorley hadn't factored into the equation.

So that was all right. The Pitbulls had got rid of one enemy for good and what's more, Anto had put Scarface out of the picture for good without

Judith Ross having got wind of any of it. And then, if what Jacko Corrigan said had any truth in it, now the three of us was bound together by the fact that if one of us went under, we all went under.

Of course, he knew nothing about the phone, but then there was no way of knowing what way things would pan out if that ever came to light. Whatever way you looked at it, if push came to shove, there was no getting away from the fact that we were all three of us accomplices.

So that was all very well. A few months went past, and at the hearing Rozzer ended up just having to do a few hundred hours community service. But he got handed six months suspended too, that was the point. So from now on, he'd to be on his best behaviour. No more fighting or joy-riding for Rozzer Ross.

That's another thing. That Jason guy sort of disappeared from view, which leads me to think that maybe I was right about him all along. Maybe it was him tipped off the guards about the mobiles. From what Rozzer said, he already had a suspended sentence for breaking and entering, so it was pretty fucking suspicious they didn't slap him back into juvie straight away. Instead of which he got the same deal as Rozzer. And then like I say, he disappears from view. It makes you think. Why would anyone disappear except he had something to hide, right?

But then the other side of the coin is, if it was Jason tipped the pigs off, that meant there was no reason at all for us to have killed the English fucker. For Anto McSorley to have killen him, I should've said. And then, to make matters even more confused, two months after the guards found the van, a good batch of the phones starts appearing around the estates. So maybe the guards wasn't the only ones was tipped off, if you follow me.

In the meantime, things on the surface seemed to have blown over between Anto and Judith Ross. At least, he was never seen around Rozzer's place any more, and she was starting to get on with her life. She even got kept on in the hairdressers down in Bray where she'd been working part-time the previous year. So everything was looking pretty rosy there.

Jacko Corrigan had eased off too. Word was he'd parted company with the Pitbulls. Or the Pitfalls, as he began to call them. He's a gas man!

Whether he jumped or he was pushed is another story. But one way or another he was hardly to be seen in his usual haunts around Shankill. I've an idea he was involved in some sort of a scam up in Dun Laoghaire involving skimming credit cards, but I couldn't tell you for sure. One way or another, he wasn't to be seen much about the estates. All of which goes to show you how much I knew! I found out later on he was seeing Judith Ross on the sly all along. But there again, the pair of them was so careful that not even Rozzer knew anything about it. So it's hardly surprising.

It all got to be like the whole episode down in Wicklow had never even happened. I swear to you, there was times it seemed more like a bad dream than something that had actually took place. And then one day, out of the blue, Jacko Corrigan calls me up on the mobile to say the guards has finally caught up with Scarface. Asked me was I on my own, which I was, and then told me to shut up and listen. Not to say a word over the phone.

This changes nothing, he warned, after he'd explained about the arrest. Absolutely nothing. He's only a suspect for now, and for all we know, the whole thing might be a trick they're pulling to make the real killers let down their guard, d'you get me? So you say nothing to no-one, right? Not even to Rozzer. Especially not to Rozzer! D'you hear me? But then he hung up before I'd the chance to reply.

Later on, just for the crack, I checked the call register to see what number he'd rung from, but the number was unknown. For all I know it might've been from the very mobile he'd had with him down in Wicklow that night.

So that was all right. The pigs had their suspect, Jacko wasn't around much and Anto McSorley was back strutting around the estates like he ruled the roost. Just like old times, as they say. But then one night all hell breaks loose. There was to be a bonfire down on the strand, and from early on you could see a good crowd of shadows moving around it, even from a distance. I wasn't particularly thinking of heading down. You could hear the motorbikes scrambling over the scrubs from early on, and I'd no great ambition to run into any of the Pitbulls. Pitfalls is right! Fact I was just heading to the video store when Rozzer runs into me, all out of breath and the eyes sticking out of his head.

'C'mon Doyler. Quick!' says he. 'Anto and Jacko Corrigan is shaping up to one another.'

'Jacko Corrigan is down there?'

'I'm after telling you,' he goes, already starting back in the direction of the seafront for fear he might miss something. 'C'mon to fuck!' He's not exactly what you'd call fast, Rozzer, all sixteen stone of him, so pretty soon I'd caught up with him, and as we jogged down I kept on asking him questions as they occurred to me.

'What's he doing down there?'

'I don't fucking know. Why shouldn't he be there?'

'Is he there long?'

'He's been down all evening, rolling spliffs.'

'On his own?'

'No. The Kelly twins is with him.'

These were a couple of tough characters he knew from the Gaelic football. I doubt they had but two front teeth between them.

'And c'mere,' says I, 'hold on for a second.' It suddenly struck me that if the two of them were having it out, it might be about you know what. And then it was definitely my business. 'C'mere, what are they scrapping about? Did you find out?'

Rozzer stops for a minute and leans his hands on his knees to get his breath back. 'Judith,' he gasps. 'They're fighting over Judith.'

Judith! We ran on, but by the time we got down as far as the bonfire, the place was crawling with the guards. There was two squad cars pulled over to one side, with the blue lights flickering and walkie-talkies going. And everyone was sort of standing around the place in little groups, not wanting to move away just yet. But of Anto and Jacko, there was not so much as a sniff.

We got some of the details later on from Dónal Kelly. He said at first himself and the brother Seán was trying to calm everyone down because they could see how they were outnumbered by the Pitbulls. But then it was Anto himself told his lackeys to back off. This was between himself and Jacko Corrigan.

'A real sneaky fucker, aren't you?' he shouts, throwing bits of shingle at Jacko, to make sure he can't ignore him. 'You think I wouldn't find out? You and Judith Ross? Yeah? But I'll tell you one thing, I'll fix you so your own mother will puke at the sight of you.'

Jacko wasn't one bit afraid of him. Not even after he pulls a real ugly mother of a knife, and starts passing it from hand to hand. It wasn't as if Jacko didn't carry his own blade on him.

That was when Rozzer ran off to find me. It must've been the ma told him I was gone to get a DVD. But from the way Dónal Kelly described things, the two lads went down as far as the shoreline to have it out. Maybe they figured it'd be quieter down there. Fat chance of that! There was a couple more of the Gaelic team knocking around, and between them and the Pitbulls and whoever else had been hanging around the fire, they made like a semi-circle against the sea. Like it was an arena out of Mad Max or something.

But from what I can make out, there was a lot more circling and threatening than actual fighting. A couple of times they got close enough to grapple or to pull at one another's clothes, and once they went down in the water, but besides a few scrapes and scratches, and a single cut to Jacko's hand that wanted stitches, there was no real damage done again the sirens broke up the circle and sent everyone scarpering.

By the following Monday, word was out that Jacko better not show his face around Shankill any more if he wanted to keep it. There was some pretty ugly graffiti sprayed across the front door of his house, and all over the jacks in the GAA club. From what Rozzer said, it was the same story down around Bray, near the salon where Judith was working. But I couldn't get nothing out of him as to how she was taking any of this. Where herself and Jacko were concerned, Rozzer had been just as much in the dark as I was.

But then the following Friday, about two in the morning, I got the fright of my life so I did. I woke up to find Jacko Corrigan leaning over the bed, and as soon as I opened my eyes he clamped his hand down hard over my mouth. It was dark in the room, but I could see his eyes lit up like there was batteries in them.

'Where's me phone?' he hissed.

'What?'

Then with his other hand, the one with the stitches and all, he shakes my jaw like he's trying to tear it loose. 'Where's me fucking phone?'

'I swear to you Jacko...,' I mumbled out as best I could, being as I was hardly able to move my cheeks or lips. This was getting to be a fucking pattern with them!

'The mobile, for fuck's sake!'

'I swear to you Jacko...'

'You're the only one who knew anything about it. So you better fucking tell me what you done with it.' He loosens the grip and instead makes a fist, a huge, meaty fist, not two inches under my nose.

'I swear to God, Jacko. I know nothing about your phone!'

A light went on in the landing. 'What is it, Stevie? Who's there with you?'

'It's no-one, ma. Go back to bed.'

Jacko was clenching both fists now, but it was more like he was about to turn them on himself than on me. They were clenched that tight you could see they was hurting him, especially the one had been cut. Then he let out a long yell like there was a head of steam building up inside of him.

'Stevie!'

'It's all right ma. It's nothing. Go back to bed.'

Jacko puts his face so close to mine I can literally smell his next words.

'Who the fuck did you tell about that phone? Think real careful before you answer me.'

'I swear to you Jacko. No-one.'

'Not even Rozzer?'

'Not even Rozzer, I swear.'

He gets up from the bed and starts to pace about the room. I got the impression he sort of knew all along it hadn't been me took his Jaysus phone.

'Jesus Christ!' he kept saying, 'Jesus Christ!'

'Keep it down Jacko. The baby.'

'Have you any idea what this means?' I'd swear his two eyes were literally glowing in the dark, they were. 'Have you any fucking idea, Doyler?'

And then he walked out of the room. It was the last I ever saw of him.

IX | Br Martin

For the next three days I was reduced to a state of utter helplessness. The problem was, I had absolutely no-one to turn to. Of course I turned to the Lord, as one does at such times, and spent long hours in prayer and contemplation. But I expect you're familiar with the saying that God helps those who help themselves? I believe it profoundly. But I was exasperated by the fact that, in this case, I had not the least idea of how to go about helping myself. It was a state of helplessness, or paralysis, that I'd been reduced to once before, and it terrified me. A second trip out to Dun Laoghaire seemed pointless, and as for Malcolm Little, my beetle-man, I'd neither phone number nor address to place myself in contact with him. My only hope was that he'd return to pick up the old coat with the beaver collar that still hung in my office, like a corpse from a gibbet. As time went by it began to appear that he scarcely felt its loss. Besides, from what he'd hinted, I deduced that he too was in some sort of trouble with the law.

This left the possibility of trying to get in touch with the boy. Looking back, I'm not sure what it was that held me from taking this step. Of course, it was by no means certain that I'd be allowed to speak to him. He was, after all, the defendant in an impending murder trial. Then, to complicate the affair, if it came to the summoning of character witnesses, it seemed to me most desirable that I should be subpoenaed. I might lay claim to know the boy far better than anyone else. It would be foolhardy indeed to put such a resource in jeopardy.

As I look back, however, with the advantage of objective distance, I've come to believe that the real reason I held off from seeing the boy was simply this. I was scared stiff of what I might find out from him. His innocence must remain an article of faith, and I dared not put it at risk. And so, with the exception of trawling the back-copies of newspapers for anything that related to the case, I was reduced to a state of nervous paralysis. And with it, there came just a hint of the old paranoia.

I was struck to the quick by the indifference that reigned all around me. Everyone, it seemed to me, was content to go about his or her daily routine as though nothing had happened. And yet, one of our own charges was to face a murder trial quite alone! True, for legal reasons the boy had not been named. But that Br Giraldus should not have been informed by the authorities, that seemed quite beyond the pale of probability. It was therefore a source of both chagrin and mortification that no-one had seen fit to inform old Martin Ffrench! Frankly, I thought it was abominable carry-on on their part, to say nothing of the loss to counsel for the defence. I was silently furious.

For my part, I kept my own counsel, and took care that no-one should see anything out of the normal orbit in the old man's movements. Outside of the library, when not waiting by the phone in my office, I prayed fervently for guidance. In the oratory there reigned the most profound silence. But that's the Lord's way. To deduce from it indifference is not merely mistaken, it is to misunderstand the majesty of His concern for us. You're smiling? Well, something, some inexplicable caprice, led me out of St Luke's on the third evening. I see the Lord's hand in it. But I'm quite content that you call it Providence if you prefer. In any event, the vigil in my office was taking its strain on my nerves, and I felt I needed to escape from what I imagined were prying eyes.

Providence directed my steps to the small park where I'd previously encountered my beetle-man. I paced about it, methodically, from corner to corner and about the perimeter, as though executing some geometrical problem. When I'd exhausted all the permutations, I repeated the figure. I daresay, if an alien in space had been observing my movements at that time, he would have concluded that man is really the most absurd animal in all of creation and that the planet Earth was bereft of intelligent life!

It was already dusk, and I can clearly remember how bright the evening star had begun to shine. I began to feel it would be imprudent to stay out any longer, and was just taking leave of the square when I saw the familiar figure step out from a phone-kiosk diagonally opposite to the entrance.

I immediately rushed across, without so much as pausing to look up and down the road. It was the mercy of God that there was no traffic or I would've been killed outright.

'I say!' I called after him, still running, and at first he picked up his pace without turning about. 'I say!' I called again, and this time he turned to meet me. I was quite out of breath. He took me by the forearm, glanced about the street, and then ushered me hurriedly into a nearby public house.

He told me later on that it was the first time he'd ever set foot inside the establishment. If so, then he must have the most acute nose, for we'd no sooner pushed through the door than he unerringly scented out a snug that was quite hidden from view. He also nodded to the barman as though he knew him of old, summoning by some imperceptible gesture two double gins with bitters. I objected that I was quite unaccustomed to spirits, but he would have none of it.

'You spoke to Fergal?' he inquired once we were seated, trying, as it seemed to me, to give the impression that he was jaunty. To my eye he looked fagged out.

'I did,' I retorted, 'three days since. I had expected to hear from you far earlier than this!'

'As a matter of fact,' he said, eyebrows twitching merrily, 'when you found me just now, I'd been trying to get through to St. Luke's on the phone! Ha ha! How's that for a happy coincidence!'

I didn't reply to this, merely continued my examination of him. 'So!' he exclaimed. 'How did you two get on?'

'Not at all well.'

'Oh?'

'It seems,' I continued, unmoved to smile, 'from what your "nephew" had to say for himself, that the boy has been prevailed upon to plead guilty.'

'Guilty!?' His face drained of all colour and became immobile. 'Nonsense!' he exclaimed at last, shaking his head emphatically. 'He's lying to you!'

'I don't believe he is,' I replied, calmly. I felt that by observing his reactions I was coming to know the man and, as I watched him, I raised the glass and took a sip from it. To my untrained tongue the concoction tasted as palatable as after-shave! I slapped it back down onto the table between us. He leaned forwards.

'But see here,' he whispered, in a vexed tone, as though it were I who'd been counsel for the defence. 'There's no reason on this earth for him to plead guilty! What you're saying is absurd!' He sat back. 'I won't believe it!' And as he sat back he looked away, and pursed his mouth like a petulant child. I should very likely have laughed, if the business were not so serious.

'Your nephew told me,' I began, when it became clear he'd quite made up his mind not to speak further on the matter, 'that you were once set upon by the boy. Is there any truth in that?'

In place of replying to this he shrugged, all but imperceptibly. There may have been a tiny snort, as of dismissal, to accompany the gesture. Then he raised the glass to his lips, which were the thick lips of a sensualist, and tossed off the gin, still without deigning to look at me. Instead, he made eye contact with the barman and signalled that he wished to be served another double.

As we waited for this next libation to arrive, I leaned forwards and peered straight at him. He pretended to be unaware of, or uninterested in, this scrutiny. In spite of his poise and air of shabby gentility, he really was rather the worse for wear. His clothes were creased, even down to the cravat, his eyes, which were heavy and protruding, bore the red tracery of insomnia, and there was a growth of silver stubble upon his jowl which glistered when the light struck it. Made one think of a winter's field touched with hoar-frost.

'You really are going to have to trust me, you know. I can't very well be of any help if I'm to be kept in total ignorance.'

When he'd received and, with some difficulty, paid for the second glass he again looked at me, considering what I'd said, or at least, giving the appearance that he might be doing so.

'What about you, Father? Do you think he did it?' he asked, at great length.

'No, of course not.'

He nodded, as if weighing up this reply. He really had missed a calling for the stage.

'How can you be so sure?'

'And you?' I asked. 'If you had even the slightest suspicion, would you have come to see me?'

He considered this. 'Yes. Yes, I believe I would.' He leaned forward until his face was so close to mine that I could smell the gin and bitters on his breath. I have heard it said that gin has no smell. It's patently untrue.

'Do you want to know something?' he asked. 'If I thought it would do any good, if I thought there was even the slightest possibility that I might be believed, I'd make a formal declaration that it was I who killed their precious vagrant.'

I'm not sure what precise noise I made in reply to this, but I have the impression he took it for a snigger. Nothing can have been farther from my mind.

'You don't believe me?' There was a new catch in his breath. 'You think I'm making it up? Fetch a pen! I mean it. Right now, right this minute, fetch pen and paper! You shall have your declaration. I shall dictate it to you, and then I shall sign it!' But he'd begun to shake his head, as though to add 'if only it would be believed.'

I began to form the impression that he was rather drunk. Perhaps he'd been in this very pub earlier, looking for the courage to venture as far as the public phone.

'It's a very… Christian thought,' I affirmed, having no wish to alienate the man.

'Love!' he declared. This word, coming from his lips, made me queasy. Inadvertently, he had lifted my glass and, as though offering a toast to love, he now polished off its contest. 'No greater love a man can have,' he quoted, looking about the snug for a gallery, 'than that he lay down his life for his friend. Isn't that it?'

'But the point here is surely that it wouldn't do the blindest bit of good for you to try to do anything of the sort!'

'Alas!' he cried. 'You're right, of course. But you must know, I have considered going to the authorities. They only arrested the boy on Fergal's word, you see. I think he was… jealous of him.'

'Jealous?' I repeated. None of this was making the blindest bit of sense to me.

'Jealous,' he insisted. The barman had materialised to remove the empty glasses, and Mr Little petitioned the same again.

'Not for me!' I interrupted.

'A sherry then, or a glass of wine? You'll have something!'

'Perhaps a wine,' I acquiesced, impatient to get back to our conversation.

'Do you know the full extent of Fergal's evidence, so-called? Hearsay! Nothing but hearsay!' He'd leaned forward so close that once again I got the sweet waft on his breath. 'He told the police that he'd overheard Bluebottle talking in his sleep about the murder!'

'Bluebottle?'

'The boy,' he exhaled. 'It was my name for him.'

'But you can't mean that's it?'

He nodded, as if words were beneath contempt.

'That's the full extent of their evidence? He heard him talking in his sleep?'

He nodded again, his eyes hooded with heavy lids.

'But that simply can't be the whole story! They'd never have arrested him unless they had something more solid to go on. Have you…'

At this point, most inconveniently, the barman returned and set down the drinks on the table. This Malcolm character drew out his wallet and after a moment found, to his evident horror, that it contained no more credit.

'Would you… do the honours?'

I was acutely embarrassed. It's not my wont to carry money on me, certainly no more than a few coins. Within St Luke's the practice is generally discouraged.

'I'm rather afraid,' I said, blushing to the roots of my hair, 'that I can't!'

'Could you give us a moment?' he said to the barman, smiling effusively.

'I'm rather afraid we don't carry about any money. Not unless a specific occasion demands it.'

'But you'll be able to get some?'

'I'd really rather not,' I replied. He scowled at this, wilfully misunderstanding me. As though money were the issue! So I spelled it out for him. 'See here. I'd have to give a reason to the powers that be. As it is, no-one in Luke's knows I'm out here with you. I think we'd both prefer if it remained that way.' He shifted, and ran a finger about the inside of his shirt-collar.

'Ah!' He continued to grin like an oversized Cheshire cat. 'But the thing of it is,' he added, 'I can't get any money either.'

'Don't you have one of those bank cards?'

'Now that's just the point, you see. The police!' he looked about, to be sure that the barman remained out of earshot, then leaned close in to me. 'The police are capable of tracing ATM receipts. It's not a chance I can afford to take.'

'Well then it's perfectly simple. We'll just have to tell the barman to take the drinks back.'

'Ah! But they're already opened, you see.' And then his body language relaxed as though he'd just made the move to clinch a game of chess. 'I'm afraid there's nothing for it Father. You'll simply have to squeeze more funds out of your superiors!'

So there was nothing for it. I made my way back towards St Luke's reluctantly, to say the least, leaving his grin poised like the Cheshire cat over the drinks. The cold air slapped me. Perhaps it was the little I had imbibed, being entirely unused to spirits, but I began to feel quite agitated. It wasn't so much the question of money, inconvenient as that was. It was the two words he'd spoken: 'love' and 'jealousy'. On that scoundrel's lips the words were profanation. But this was not a territory I was prepared to let myself return to for even a minute! And so I shivered and hurried along the street. Well, the thought came to me as I approached the gate, one blessing at least. Now that I've run into him again, I'll be able to get shot of that blessed coat with the beaver collar!

It was by now quite dark in the courtyard, and when I saw the rubbish bags piled up beside the outside toilets, I knew that Br Malachi had cleared up after the evening meal. This meant that Br Giraldus would likely be retired to his room. My eyes moved up to the yellow glow of his window and, despite my dreadful eyesight, I could swear that I saw a silhouette standing at it. Damn your luck Martin Ffrench, he's up there watching out for you! Pure fancy, of course, but the image had me so flustered that I quite literally collided with Br Malachi, coming out of the refectory with a final sack of rubbish.

'Ho! Steady!'

He has a great, booming, bass voice, Br Malachi. Really, quite the medieval monk! He was forever singing. Usually you'd hear him coming a mile off.

'What has you out in this inclement evening, *mon frère*?'

He calls me 'mon frère' because of my name. Ffrench, you see. Pressed against his barrel chest, I was suddenly mortified. What if he should smell the spirits off my breath?

'Nothing, I…'

'A happy coincidence! I've been meaning to say to you all day. That cobbler you sent me to…'

'Cobbler?'

'The shoe repair merchant you advised me to see!' I stood back from him and watched him extend a leg from under his habit. 'Wonderful, *mon frère*! Truly,' he quipped in his great bass voice, 'truly, a mender of soles!'

The cobbler! A thought struck me. Providence again, you see.

'By any chance, Malachi… you paid him in cash, I expect?' Now the point is, in St Luke's we don't really carry money. Part of the vows, you see. But of course when repairs are to be done outside, it's a different issue. Simple matter of approaching the bursar. 'What I'm trying to get at…'

His face, jolly and round, was really rather comical as he looked down on me. I couldn't help but smile back. 'If you haven't already returned it, I don't suppose you could see your way to letting me have the change?'

He wagged a rakish finger at me. 'You've found another second-hand bookshop, haven't you! We all must control our secret passions, *mon frère*!'

'In point of fact… there's a beggar I want to help out.' Well, I thought, a white lie will do no great harm. Now here's the point. The upshot of this 'happy coincidence', as he'd put it, was that I returned at once to the public house with a pocket full of change, sufficient in any event to cover the cost of our embarrassment. But not with the coat. Call it what you will, but I see the hand of God in that, too. Like a body in a gibbet, that blessed coat still hung in the corner of my room. But for the moment, I was blissfully ignorant of its testimony.

By the time I'd returned to our hideout in the pub, any feelings of giddiness had begun to subside. Almost from the moment I re-entered, it was patently clear that whatever signs of drunkenness my interlocutor had earlier displayed had been little more than play-acting. Why he should have done this was less clear. I could think of nothing that he might have been trying to hide. Surely it hadn't been a pretext to wheedle some funds out of the orphanage?

I paid for the drinks, then waited for him to resume where our conversation had let off. But he remained silent, smiling facetiously. With so much at stake, it was not an attitude that I was prepared to tolerate.

'Now look here, this Bates, your nephew. What precisely has he done?'

'Fergal? Ah, I see! You mean why was he arrested?' He nodded, as though he'd been expecting the question. 'From what I can make out, since it's never entirely come out in the wash, the damned fool was arrested for distributing a particularly nasty species of video. The snuff movie, I believe they term it on the street. You know what those fellows are, I expect?'

'I have an idea.' A shiver of disgust ran through me.

'You'll tell me it's a particularly western vice. On the contrary!' He was a picture of complaisance now. I let him talk on, eager to make him out. 'It seems to me that the obsession with watching is fundamental to being human. I defy you, Father, to find a single culture that isn't fascinated by the spectacle of violence. Or sex, its baby sister. No. What differentiates the western world is technological, nothing more.' He'd raised his glass to his lips but, finding it drained, he pretended instead it was a camera lens.

'We are living,' he pronounced, 'in a supervisual age. D'you know, for years my life was made hell by the attentions of a prying neighbour? But let that rest. A stroke got her.'

He was no longer drunk, but here in the snug, it appeared the talking bug had bit him. I tried hard to look pleasant. 'Surveillance,' he said, waving a hand grandly, 'is fast becoming the rule rather than the exception. Nothing, it seems to me, goes unrecorded anymore. Behold the CCTV, mighty guardian angel of the body politic! It has more eyes than Argos himself! Did you know that the attack on the Twin Towers was the most recorded event in history?'

'No, I didn't,' I replied, having little appetite for his newfound enthusiasm. I could not see how any of it related to my concerns. Or his, for that matter. 'But the boy,' I said. 'It's not at all clear to me how precisely you want me to help him.'

Mention of the boy returned him to the sober present. In an instant he'd aged ten years.

'I've been giving that some thought,' he affirmed, setting down the glass. 'While you've been away. It's absolutely essential you talk to his lawyer.' He passed over the table a folded piece of paper. 'This is the address.'

I looked at the name of the law firm. 'And what do you intend that I should say to him?'

'Her!' he corrected, delighted with my error. 'Joe Conlon is a woman. Josephine, I daresay.' I shrugged, and he appeared to grow impatient. 'Well it's obvious what you have to do! You must convince her to drop this nonsense about a plea bargain!'

'I think perhaps you overestimate my powers of persuasion. If they've made up their mind about the plea…'

'But coming from a man of God,' he interrupted.

'A man of God is scarcely likely to have much sway in a court of law.'

'But at least you'll try,' he declared, and he was already rising. Indeed, he appeared to be in a great hurry to take his leave. 'You see, you must. He has no-one else to turn to.'

He was backing away, as though afraid of my every movement. He had delivered the address of the lawyer, and was scared stiff that I might return it to him. I stood, and put the paper in my pocket.

As we stepped out onto the street he offered me his hand, and the Cheshire cat grin betrayed his sense of relief.

'One minute,' I said. 'There was one other thing I wanted to ask you.'

'Oh?' he said, the eyebrows twitching facetiously. Evidently he felt that he had survived our encounter.

'You haven't thought to approach Ms Conlon off your own bat?'

'But I can't!' he positively sang. 'I'm afraid, you see, I'm a wanted man.'

'That's just what I wanted to ask you about. Tell me, what was it that Fergal Bates said to the police about you?'

'Ah!' he went on, but I could sense that he was nervous. And so was I. Then he said something that, dear Christ, I thought, and hoped, never to have heard again, so long as I lived.

'I will tell you, if you insist. If you really want to know. I promise you that Father. But only if you'll hear my confession.'

•••

I won't try to set down the kaleidoscope of impressions this singular individual, from the very first, had elicited in me. One is reluctant to give in to prejudices. One struggles not to draw too hasty conclusions from a person's dress, from the pitch of a voice or the tilt of its intonations. Nevertheless, there had been something barefaced about Malcolm Little's performances, as though he were defying one *not* to pigeon-hole him. And, of course, his friend Bates' cryptic hints had been grist to that particular mill.

Without any doubt, it had been a deliberate, if not entirely conscious, choice on my part not to consider his character, or how it might bear on his relationship with the boy. It was incidental to the absolute imperative of helping in every possible way his present distress. But if Malcolm Little had wanted to incite me, if he had intended to raise the hairs at the back of my neck and make my soul recoil from the insinuation, he could scarcely have chosen a more injurious parting shot. After all, I'd told him umpteen times that I was no priest.

Had he been so cynical as to drag up the buried past? It was absurd to think so. How can he possibly have come to such knowledge? But the sand walls that cupped my certainties had abruptly collapsed.

It was in a state of absolute turmoil that I retraced my steps to Luke's. One thinks, because of the accumulation of years, that one has rid oneself of one's phantoms. That time, and force of habit, have finally quietened them, until you come to hope that they've finally been exorcised. You think never to see them rise again from the forgotten grave, to torment and to tyrannise. How vain the hope! A single sentence had swept away the years, wrenched open the tomb. The turmoil inside me was every bit as fresh and as pitiless as that of thirty years before. I was so nervous, so disoriented, that I actually walked straight past the main gate and had to turn back.

I've no wish to revisit that time. I'll provide the barest outline, no more. Dear God, it all but destroyed me.

At that time, I was the junior cleric in a parish of three. Never mind where. I'd already been appointed there for about a year and, together with Fr John,

I was encouraged by the PP to become actively involved with the youth of the parish. Fr John is not his real name. But let that rest.

In those days I was Fr Thomas Ffrench. Dear God!

In particular, the PP was very keen that I learn from Fr John's energetic engagement with the under fifteens' football team and the senior boy scouts, who were raising funds for a new youth club. Between the various drives, quiz nights, jamborees and speeches, Fr John's week would have needed to have contained eight days, and each day to have thirty hours. But he seemed to be a man whose enthusiasm was matched by a boundless energy, and he was as likely to tog out and join into a soccer game as to stand by the sidelines and simply coach the team.

And yet there was something reserved about him. Not only that, but after the PP had asked me to muck in so as to ease his commitment load, his behaviour towards me indicated that he profoundly resented these incursions into his domain. He seemed to go out of his way to marginalize my involvement, and would answer my queries reluctantly, and in such a way as to make it quite impossible that I should carry out my duties effectively.

I took this very much as a matter of course. You're soon disabused, in the seminary hothouse, of any notion that the religious vocation is in some way incompatible with the jealousies and vanities that man has ever been prey to. If anything, the seminary seems to bring them out!

But then events took a far more sinister turn. One evening, after soccer practice, I overheard a number of the boys horsing about as they waited for the bus. In the course of their foolery, a couple of them made some high-pitched allusions in which Fr John was implicated. Showers, scoldings, that sort of thing. It was all dressed up as high jinks. And besides, he'd be a fool indeed who would put any great stock in schoolboy humour. But it was enough to put me on my guard.

After that episode I became more alert. At every opportunity, I placed myself within earshot of their groups, particularly at such times as they thought the adults had left. A disturbing pattern began to emerge. It was far too early to talk of proof. There's little quite as contagious among schoolboys as their own imaginings, and these can be notoriously cruel, coarse and irrational. But I was lacking in experience. Rather than biding my time, I approached the PP rather too early and laid before him my fears.

Now, I've no wish to blame the man. He was somewhat elderly, and, if I may say so, more than a little vague. I think, too, that there was a reluctance on his part to believe that the sort of perversions I was touching on could possibly surface in a small parish, rural and Irish. You must take into account the decade I'm talking about. A more innocent age, or at least, so we all thought. Everyone thought it. The PP absorbed my suspicions, nodded, but also shook his head with a wry smile, as though I were describing the foibles of a harmless eccentric. Or at the very worst, the dodges of a secret drinker. The carry-on I was hinting at could scarcely be imagined in his country of the Riordans, and the Kennedys of Castleross. Yet he was no fool. I thought at the time, and continue to believe, that when he first assigned me to assist Fr John in his extramural duties, it was in part so that I could keep an eye on the man.

I was dismayed by his disinclination to pursue the matter further. But to be fair, when I insisted on the point, he at last gave his consent that I could approach the bishop directly. Although he may well have felt it, he did not suggest that I should first place myself on more certain grounds. And as it turned out, this was a pity. It emerged later that one mother in particular had expressed her doubts to him about Fr John's 'enthusiasms', and when he smiled her off, she'd pulled her boy out of the scouts. I think, all in all, the old man was mightily relieved to put the discomfiting interview to an end and to be able to return to his study.

A week went by. An excruciating week. I could barely stand to look at Fr John, and it seemed to me that he eyed me with renewed distaste and suspicion. At last Monday morning arrived, the occasion of my audience. It was an interview upon which the career of my entire life has hinged.

'Tom, I hope I find you well?' The bishop himself met me at the door, effusive, making a point of using first names. It made me wonder if he'd been forewarned as to the purpose of my visit. But he had a reputation for being a charismatic. As we entered, he placed one of his oddly elongated arms about my shoulder. He steered me into his study and, smiling, gestured towards a line of three chairs. 'Please, take a pew.' I could not bring myself to return his smile, and declined his offer of coffee, although my tongue was pitilessly dry.

Our interview was to last, I know, precisely twenty-four minutes, for its every turn and nuance became rutted in my memory over the months to follow. I had thought never to have had to revisit this dreadful… I had hoped, when at long last I was reborn as Br Martin, that this… that these minutes had finally been washed from my memory.

The bishop temporarily left me alone in his study. He was an energetic man in his middle forties. If he'd not actually lived in the United States, he certainly affected an American drawl! I could scarcely imagine an interlocutor more diametrically distinct from our PP. His charismatic views, as was well known throughout the see, were tinted with the latest fashionable terms from California, and I noticed that a large percentage of the books that graced his shelves had likewise migrated across the Atlantic. My eye was drawn to the table, where there stood an imposing crucifix upon which the Christ was missing both arms. A legend ran around the base: *He has no hands but ours*.

'I see, Tom, you're taken with my Cross of Ypres.'

I hadn't heard the man re-enter, and the brusque, nasal voice went through me, setting me shuddering like a bell.

'The original was found, so the story goes, in a bombed-out church at Passchendale, some time toward the end of the Great War. Once the armistice had restored the general peace, the local clergy had a parley about how best to restore the work to its former glory. As the story was told to me, it was a humble Sister of Mercy, a sometime mystic, who first suggested the statue should instead be left exactly as it had been found. It was she who proposed the legend, too. It had come to her in a dream, or a vision as we would have put it in an age less sceptical than ours.'

While he was speaking he had stood to one side, and had laid his hand once more upon my shoulder. 'But like everything else, Tom, it expresses, in its simplicity, a profound truth.'

Now he moved into view, perched himself jauntily on the side of the desk, and looked directly at me as though awaiting a reply.

'A profound *responsibility*,' I proposed.

'Indeed!' he applauded. 'You've hit the nail on the head! There can be no more awesome responsibility. Sometimes, Tom, I wake at night and, with no exaggeration, that responsibility weighs so heavily on me that I wish I was anything but a priest. A musician, maybe. Did you know, when I was a younger man, I rather fancied myself as a musician? The jazz trumpet, that was my thing. Ha ha! I guess you've God to thank for saving the world from that prospect!' He smiled broadly, but it was a smile whose enthusiasm I couldn't bring myself to return.

I saw him frown. 'Look, Tom. I've a good idea what all this is about.' He lifted a letter that bore the livery of our presbytery, and went through the motions of perusing it. 'It seems you've expressed a number of rather serious concerns. Things in the parish aren't quite the way you expected them to be.'

'With respect,' I began, a little dazed, 'it's not about the parish…' He forestalled me with an open palm.

'Don't get me wrong, Tom. They're legitimate, these concerns of yours. I'd be worried if a young priest arriving fresh from the seminary didn't have a number of concerns! The real world never quite matches up to our ideals! And when these ideals have become tainted, there's nothing quite so invigorating as the criticism of an idealist.'

'This isn't about idealism!' I cried, rather too excitedly. It would've been far better to have remained calm. 'With the greatest respect,' I continued, 'this isn't about ideals. This is child abuse!'

'Now wait…'

'How can a man like Fr John be permitted…'

'Now hold on!' He had coloured and his mouth had grown rigid, but now he restored the smile to his face. His voice, nasal once more, resumed its drawl. 'Hold on, Tom. Steady, cowboy! So far, it seems to me that all you've got to go on is hearsay. Am I right?'

I shook my head, feeling how my skin burned. My heart was thumping inside my ribs, but I couldn't muster the words to form a reply.

'Hearsay,' he went on. 'Stories, told by boys, and for their own amusement. Schoolboys. For God's sake, Tom, schoolboys!' Then he squeezed my arm. 'I've been reliably informed that, behind my back, they call me Dicky Rock! Ha ha! How do you like that?'

And the rest of it, I thought. There was no shortage of nicknames doing the rounds.

'You've been a boy, Tom! You must know the mixture of garbage and fantasies that schoolboy humour feeds on!'

I was speechless. Literally, no words came to me. My breathing, it seemed to me, was inordinately loud. He must notice it, too.

'But let's allow, just for a moment, that there is a *grain* of truth in what you've... been privy to. I don't believe it. John's a good guy. But let's imagine, just for a moment, that one of the shepherds has temporarily strayed. It's not beyond the realms of possibility. We're all of us human.'

He paused, but I got the impression he had not finished. Not by a long chalk. I got the impression, too, perhaps unfairly, that he had prepared in advance a counter for every possible argument I might put to him.

'What's our first duty, Tom? As pastors, I mean.'

'As pastors, our first duty is to protect and guide the flock.'

'To protect and guide the flock. It's well said. And you'll remember, of course, that we have been told that there is more joy in heaven over the one lost sheep that's found than over the ninety-nine that are safe and sound and righteous. Now consider this, Tom. Suppose that it's a shepherd who is wandering. Where does our duty lie now?'

I remained silent. I could feel my cheeks still burning like firebrands, and my breath panting in and out as though I were an asthmatic.

'Every one of us is subject to temptation, Tom. J.C. himself was tempted, and not merely once. Three times! Let's not lose sight of that! But there's no temptation so great that we're not allowed the grace sufficient to resist it. Sometimes, and it's lamentable, we are called on as priests to stay the pace with the sinner as he flounders about for this grace. Sometimes we see him wilfully ignore this grace. But it's not ours to condemn, when time and again a sinner lapses. Seventy times seven, Tom! If the Lord God forgives our offences, how much more it behoves His anointed, every one of us a sinner, to forgive.'

He paused, for effect. How odious his American voice was to me at that minute!

'Now,' he tapped the PP's letter, 'your concerns are commendable. I greatly applaud your decision to come to me with them. It shows a keen sense of your responsibilities. It also argues a keen sense of what is meant by the apostolic succession. The mother church is no democracy, Tom. She's not a free-for-all. Her structure is hierarchical, necessarily so. She demands absolute obedience. A vow of unquestioned obedience. I, for my many sins, am a bishop, a shepherd of the shepherds, if you will. And I, in my place, must defer to the archbishop, and he to the cardinal. It's how J.C. himself ordained things when He was among us, and it's the very meaning of Catholicism. We might not like it. As western liberals, it must offend our sensibilities. But no-one said the chosen path is easy, and that is how we serve Him on this earth. That, Tom, is how we become His hands.'

A second time he paused. He was nodding in the direction of the crucifix. My eyesight is poor at the best of times. At that time, I might as well have been blind.

'And if one of the fingers is gangrenous?' I whispered, deliberately pacing my words. 'If, within this church, there is a criminal, abusing his position of trust? Even taking advantage of it? A wolf dressed in sheep's clothing, to use your image.'

'With respect, Father, you're talking about God's chosen,' he said, in a low voice.

'I doubt that.'

'Now you've gone quite beyond the pale!' His palm came down hard on the table. 'How dare you presume to know God's will?' For a second, the Americanisms had abandoned him. So he made an effort, hoisted a smile.

'Tom! Tom! J.C. called Matthew, a tax-collector and collaborator! And Mary Magdalene. And Saul, for God's sake, who in his time was the foremost assassin and murderer of Christians!' He picked up the cross and held it out before him like a talisman. 'Look at this crucifix! Consider it well! "He has no hands but ours." And now, look at the hands that He himself chose, look at the instruments that were made to perform God's will on earth.' The cold smile slipped from his mouth. 'And you have the temerity to say *I doubt it*!'

He was suddenly aware that he was mimicking my voice. Then he seemed to become conscious of how ugly the atmosphere in the room had become, and he shook his head slowly.

'Tom! Tom!'

The piper's son, I thought.

'You did the right thing in coming to me. As your bishop, it is incumbent upon me to take this responsibility, this heavy cross, from your shoulders.' Standing from the desk, he smiled deliberately and nodded. 'You won't need to lose any more sleep over this matter. That'll be my privilege.'

He began to shepherd me towards the door, and as we reached it, he again looped one of his long arms about my shoulder.

'I hope that helps set your mind at ease.'

'What will you do?' I asked.

'What would you have me do?'

'Well,' I began, in no way feeling the weight lift, 'you'll need to talk directly to Fr John.'

'On hearsay? On the strength of schoolboy high jinks? Come on, Tom! As the bard said, I would have grounds more relative. But I will say this. If it ever comes to it, I'm a great believer in what's called UPR. *Unconditional* positive regard, Tom. Are you familiar with the writings of Carl Rogers?'

'I've heard the name,' I said, without enthusiasm.

'He's a very great psychotherapist. Most innovative. Now, in his therapy, he proposes a general praxis based upon three things'. He began to count out on his fingers. 'Number one: empathy. Number two: congruence. Number three: UPR. Unconditional positive regard. Unconditional, Tom. That's the way to true therapy. I think, in humility, we as priests and as pastors have much to learn from the likes of Carl Rogers.'

'And in the meantime?'

'I'm not following you.'

'Do I gather more proof?'

'No!' His fingers squeezed my shoulder sharply. 'No! I think the best thing you can do, Tom, the best thing that any one of us can do in a situation like this, is to pray for patience and for guidance. Pray to the Holy Spirit. I often feel he's the forgotten man of the Trinity! Within the fortnight, it'll be my privilege to once again confirm the young Christians of your parish. Think of the gifts that the Spirit will confer on them. *Right* judgment. Understanding. Fear *of the Lord*. We could all use a second instalment of those particular gifts.'

If only I'd left it there. If only I'd been content to hold my counsel. But instead I pressed on.

'But what if some direct evidence were to come to light?'

He wasn't impressed. 'Such as what, *exactly*?'

'I don't know, *exactly*. But suppose it was absolutely beyond doubt that minors are being interfered with. What then?'

'Then you'll keep me informed, of course.'

'And the police?' I insisted. I should have let it rest.

He grimaced. Any residual warmth had left his eyes. 'Your hypothetical problem, Father,' he pronounced, in a tone that would brook no argument, 'would be a matter for the church. And for the church alone.'

He didn't actually add 'I hope we understand one another', but in his glacial eyes I read the expression. Twenty-four minutes had elapsed, and my audience was at an end.

Now, it happened that the following Thursday I was to hear confessions. A number of schools were preparing for the sacrament of confirmation. Confessions were part and parcel of the preparation.

It had crossed my mind that, one day, I might be faced inside the confessional with a child who'd been abused. From the tutorials at the seminary, it's one of several excruciating possibilities that one is made aware of. But in my recent imaginings, I'd associated Fr John's activities exclusively with the older boys, with the under fifteens football team and the senior scouts. He had little commerce with the primary schools. If I was feeling any trepidation as I entered the confession box, it was a residue of the bad taste that the bishop's forbidding expression had left in my gut as I took my leave of him. Dear God!

The first pews…

The first pews, filled with children, were already drawn up inside the church. I nodded to the teacher as I entered the box. A minute went by. None appeared to be moving to enter, and I remember I drew the shutter back. It was uncanny, but I thought I could hear shuffling inside the booth beside me, as though there were already someone waiting. 'Yes?' I prompted. Then a voice began, low and contrite.

'Bless me Father, for I have sinned.'

I started and jumped back from the grill as though it had been electrically charged. It was him.

I should've walked out there and then. I would to God I had walked out. Because what he divulged to me that day in low and tortured whispers confirmed the very worst of my fears.

I hadn't any intention of dwelling upon this time. Dear Christ! It's painful for me to remember it. I'll be brief. In the weeks that followed, Fr John came to my room, twice, to have me again take his confession. But on both occasions, I'm afraid to say that I refused to hear him. I turned him away. What made the situation appalling is that I'd come to believe in my heart that it had been the bishop himself who'd suggested he take me as his confessor. I think in retrospect I've been unfair to the man. But at the time I was convinced of it. And this suspicion devastated me.

All I can say is how I reacted to these developments. I won't pretend to have any knowledge of what drove the others who were involved. Perhaps they were acting in good faith after all. Only God can know that. Three years later, Fr John was quietly packed off to Stroud. What I can state with absolute certainty is that I became convinced that I'd been gagged, quite deliberately and, if I may express it so, quite cynically. And in consequence, I felt a most absolute helplessness. I was uniquely aware of what precisely was going on in the parish. And yet, because of the seal of the confessional, I was the one person who was helpless to protect the most vulnerable within that parish. It was an intolerable situation, and it had to end. Perhaps now you can begin to appreciate how a casual reference to confession made by a man like Malcolm Little had abolished thirty years at a stroke and thrown me once more into turmoil.

The remainder can be said very simply. My world fell apart. First my faith in the church went, then my faith in humankind. Finally, I fell apart. It's curious, for a while you hold it together. For several weeks, you continue to function, as though you're operating on autopilot. I'd asked for leave, and was granted it. The bishop himself inquired after my health and my morale. Perhaps if I were to be assigned other duties, elsewhere? And then, of all things, one morning I slipped while crossing Capel St Bridge. I fractured my arm. I think my organism must have been stretched to breaking point, because a single blow to the system, a physical mishap, was enough to push me over the edge. I'm mixing my metaphors!

I suffered a complete breakdown. I became clinically depressed. If you don't know what that means, I'll try to give an idea of my experience of it. Imagine you're lost at sea, floundering about, miles from any shore. That is the image of your circumstances. They seem quite hopeless, but as yet you have your mental health. You stay afloat. Now, imagine you swim by mistake into a great ocean of seaweed. Every stroke becomes impossibly laborious, every movement, an enormous strain, and still there is no shore. That is depression.

Depression is a medical condition. It has its biochemical explanations. It's as though the cylinders in your brain are no longer firing. They put me on lithium for it. But what was far more serious, I fell into despair. I despaired of this world, and I despaired of myself. If the truth be known, I despaired of God. And I had thought of nothing but the priesthood, ever since I'd turned thirteen! I'd had an early vocation, you see.

To cut a long story short, for I've no wish to dwell on myself, the Almighty took pity on his wretched servant. After what might have been a year and what might have been five, a most unlikely encounter led me to inquire into the position of librarian at St Luke's. Two years later, I became a Brother. As is the custom here, I took a new name. I became, as they say, born again. And I'd found a way to serve God, with no hierarchies, no absolute obedience, and no sacraments. What was better still – what was my true salvation and my path out of despair – I'd found a new vocation. I was being called to be a guardian of the young, to watch, from the vantage of my library, over all the young lives that passed so vulnerably through this institution.

This brings us back to the present, in the way a dropped wire shorts out a circuit. From the first I had, I say again, endeavoured to suspend any prejudices I might have felt towards this figure, this beetle-man. He declared that the boy was in trouble and in need of my imminent help, and he showed a great concern for him. I had no desire to press his character further. Admittedly, it was more difficult to relegate the matter to the back of my mind after the trip to Dun Laoghaire. The Bates individual had left a very unpleasant taste in my mouth, and his insinuating smirk was a lash that I flinched from. But now, with the casual jibe about confession, it was all I could do to fight down a surge of nausea. I stumbled back in the direction of St Luke's and, as I've said, I missed my turn and had to double back.

I had thought to find sanctuary in my office, a quiet haven where I might calm my passions and review the events with a less turbulent eye. I was gravely mistaken. I had no sooner closed the door behind me and shaken the drops from my hat when the hulking figure of the coat caught my eye.

Seeing its weight brooding there in the corner, I felt a shiver run through me. And of course, what made it all the worse was, I'd just missed the opportunity to get rid of the blessed thing! He'd disappeared, once again, leaving me with neither address nor contact number.

You're a terrible fool, Thomas Ffrench! How is it it never dawned on you to have a look in the pockets to see if there's any sort of an address book, or even an envelope itself? The thought made me giddy. I remember I turned the key in the door, as though it was a shameful act I was about to perform. But I was determined to see it through. I don't believe I felt a presentiment, exactly. A sense of revulsion, certainly, or at the least a queasy feeling as I touched the fur that lined each pocket. I noticed, too, a faint scent, curiously akin to hairspray, emanating from its vicinity. The two outer pockets were empty, except for a pair of kid-leather gloves, a handkerchief and a couple of matches. I glanced to the door. Nothing for it then, I'd have to try the inside pocket.

There was a package of kinds, wrapped in paper, and what felt like slides of cardboard inside it. I pulled out the package and made for my desk. The paper was held around the items by an elastic band, and I easily slipped this off. A number of photos slipped out and across the desk, the old kind, like you used to get from a Polaroid. It took a moment for the images to swim into focus in the pools of my glasses.

I gasped aloud. They were disgusting. Three naked, wanton images. And they were of the boy.

I quite literally collapsed into the chair by my desk, my right hand wiping the photos to the floor. The paper in which they'd been folded dangled limply between the fingers of my left. When I'd recovered my wits sufficiently, and calmed my breathing, I opened this paper out and glanced at it.

It was a sketch, or several sketches to be accurate, passably executed in charcoals. The figure it repeatedly showed was evidently that of they boy. And he was quite naked, his genitals erect and grossly enlarged.

A week passed.

God forgive me, I disposed of that coat. I tied it up in rope the very next night and stuffed it to the bottom of one of Malachi's skips. God forgive me, I had a right maybe to give it to one of the charity shops. It was an expensive coat. Warm. God knows our city has never lacked for the unfortunate or the homeless. But I couldn't bring myself to do it. It was as if the blessed coat itself was contaminated. I buried it deep in that skip as if that horrible dissolute had been bound up inside it!

The sense of betrayal, of cynical, barefaced duplicity, had quite literally stunned my will. I felt a deep, deep anger. I'm tempted to say a righteous anger, but if it was, it was paralysed by something that was even more insidious than the disgust that filled my mouth. During the time of my previous breakdown, I'd suffered from rushes of paranoia. Now, I had the sense that I was being laughed at. I don't merely mean the certainty that this Malcolm character had taken advantage of me. How can I put it? It was a metaphysical laughter. I felt that the shape of my whole life in St Luke's was in danger. Some malevolent force from outside the walls had taken away that which was most pure and had trampled it into the mud before my eyes.

This malicious laughter was still echoing about the corridors when, on the following Sunday, I was informed that there was a visitor awaiting me in the meeting room. I was so confused by the message that I quite forgot to ask who it might be. But I'd not had an outside visitor in years, and it seemed clear that it could only be this devil incarnate, this odious pervert who was bent on corrupting my ward.

I was almost glad that I would meet him again in the flesh. I foresaw my indignation explode into a ferocious tirade that would drive him from the building, and with his departure, I foresaw the exorcism of the demons that had returned to torment me. Needless to say, I'd burned the horrible images.

But I pulled open the door, and his beetle-like agitation was nowhere in the room. Instead, an old woman who was unknown to me stood severely before me.

PART IV

X | Gwendolyn

He was about the last person I was expecting to find at the door. Scarcely seen hide nor hair of him since the affair with the cats. He was too *disturbed*, he informed me.

Then, later, after I'd arranged to have the youth taken into care, I got the distinct impression someone must have informed against me. I may have been a little premature in this, but I had my certain suspicions as to who the informant would be. In any event, he'd quite disappeared from view, that's the point. Must have thought I was the wicked witch who'd banished summer. I might've told him it was all done for his own good. But really, where was the point?

Far too much work to be getting on with to be greatly bothered by his figairees. There was an upcoming commission with Dun Laoghaire-Rathdown that I was particularly interested in tendering for. Had entire reams filled with preparatory sketches. But as yet, the clay remained recalcitrant.

Normally wouldn't have answered the door for love nor money. One hates to make one's inspiration dance attendance on the casual caller. But I'd had a frustrating morning, you see. Every pinch I'd added or taken away had muted the piece, in place of revitalising it.

'Well,' I said, 'look what the cat dragged in!'

He stood in that infuriatingly indecisive manner of his, neither coming in nor going on. He really was, for all the world, a fifty-year old adolescent. 'Well for God's sake don't just stand there gawping!'

He followed me into the kitchen, head bowed and eyes sly. I could see his mind was up to something. His posture had acquired that louche aspect I was long familiar with. His clothes, I noticed, were considerably more creased and ill-matched than was his custom. But he was wearing the cashmere tartan scarf I'd bought him when I'd visited him in France, thrown jauntily over one shoulder. An attempt to soften me, no doubt. I'd certainly never seen him wear it prior to this.

'Well?' I asked, eyeing him from top to toe. Really, he had the appearance of having just crawled out of bed. 'Cat got your tongue?'

He shifted about. Wouldn't look me in the eye. For the first time, examining at greater length his bedraggled clothes and lifeless complexion, one got the feeling he wasn't simply playing a part. I went over to him, took his forearms. 'What is it?'

His eyes still avoided all contact, and I'd to strain to make out the croak that broke frog-like from his mouth.

'I beg your pardon?' I said.

'They've arrested him,' he replied, and freeing himself from me with the exhortation 'Gwen!', he paced over to the window, where he repeated, in six carefully enunciated syllables, 'they have arrested him!'

'Whom?' I asked, not amused. If it's that corner-boy, I thought, it's good enough for him.

'Fergal!' he cried to the courtyard, and then turned to fix blood-rimmed eyes upon me. 'Fergal!' he repeated, more softly.

'Oh, nonsense! What on earth would interest the police in a toad like that?'

'Gwen, they've arrested him. That's all I can tell you about it.' He took a pace towards the interior of the room, eyes blood-shot and wild, and, as I could now see, on the brink of tears. 'They picked him up yesterday evening, at his own flat. At his own flat! He's being detained at Store Street even as we speak!'

'On what charge?'

'I don't know! I don't *know*!'

'Well,' I said, 'what of it? It's his own lookout, surely.' He was making no sense.

'Don't you see?' he stammered. 'He'll tell… *everything*!'

'Oh for God's sake! Tell what, exactly?' I was becoming quite cross with him. 'What tale can Fergal Bates possibly have to tell to the police?'

He shook his head, bitterly, as if I were in the process of denying him. Hot tears were making him squinny at me.

'Gwen,' he snivelled, '*please*!' Then he added, in a whisper, 'for God's sake!' He'd begun to extend two stubby hands towards me. At any moment, I fully expected to hear a cockcrow.

'Go home, Mal. Go to bed.' I'd turned away from him, signalling my disapproval as one imagines a Victorian mother might have. And, when I failed to hear any movement behind me, I aimed a dart at his vanity. 'You look… dreadful, you know.' I remained stationary for perhaps ten minutes, considering. It seemed to me that he was too fantastic, too highly strung, for it to have been of the slightest benefit to either one of us to have continued the conversation there and then. When at length I turned about, he had gone.

I daresay I could've been more patient with him. If I'd known the full extent of his difficulties, I daresay I would've been. But there you are. Life provides us with ample opportunities to bewail our past impatience.

I spent most of the afternoon working furiously on the *maquette*. If it had done nothing else, the encounter with Malcolm Little had energised me. Now, entire contours rose and were pruned back until the clay began to assume some sort of definition. I became so engrossed in the process that before I knew it, it had grown dark.

I determined the next morning to call in on Mal on my way to see Victoria Campbell. I'd made use of Victoria twice before in casting a piece into bronze and I'd found her approach refreshingly open to interference. When it comes to casts, the finish is everything, you see. A hint of *verdigris* can be every bit as eloquent as lines on a face. My work was not at a stage where I was ready to do anything but talk to the girl in the most general terms. But then her studio is in Ringsend, and it suited me to have a pretext for my journey to Mal's place.

A general gloom had hung over the house for quite some time. I turned into the Mews, and as I was fiddling in my purse for I know not what, I was all but run off the footpath by an electric bath-chair. It was his neighbour, the same insufferable Ms Ramsay who for many years had pried into my every coming and going.

Serve you bloody well right! I whispered, staring hard after the waggle of the contraption's slow posterior. That'll cheer old Mal up, when I tell him how I was nearly run over by that puritanical old bitch!

But the doors to the house were sealed as tight as her lips had been. I peered in through a murky windowpane. The interior had that dank and lifeless aura you get in an aquarium from which the water has been drained. Most disquieting. Course, there wasn't a cat to be seen about the place. But this was something far more sinister.

Over the next few days, I found that the fool had absconded! Quite literally! Taken fright, and now he'd gone into hiding, God alone knew where. At his age! And with his character! You'd think he'd have had more sense.

I began to regret not having paid the daft bugger more heed when he'd come out to see me.

From a few discreet inquiries, I found out that no additional money had been withdrawn from his bank account. At least, none from the one and only bank account of which I was aware. I also found out that Fergal Bates had been released without charge within twenty-four hours of his arrest. So that appeared to put paid to any notion that the roof was about to come crashing down upon poor Mal's head.

The silly fool, I thought, it won't be long before he returns cap in hand, like the arrant schoolboy he always was.

But I'd underrated not merely his determination. It soon came to light that I'd also underestimated the dangers that Fergal Bates' indiscretions had placed him in. On the morning of the twenty-third – I clearly remember the date because it coincides with my birthday – a letter arrived, postmarked, of all places, Westport, Co. Mayo.

My Dearest Friend,

For although I begin to discover with what dogged determination and incalculable secrecies you have conspired against my happiness, I must imagine you to have considered you were acting in my best interests, and therefore, I will continue to call you "friend".

You will be aware, I think, of the dismal turn that my affairs have taken since F's disclosures to the Garda. You will know, too, that Bluebottle has been taken in for questioning. From what I've learned of the measures you've taken behind my back, I have little doubt but that this must be a source of no small satisfaction to you.

For me, however, it is a source of nothing but the most acute misery. I think, Gwen, that you have at all times, and perhaps disingenuously, chosen to misconstrue the feelings that have been aroused in me by this boy, this, my own Bluebottle. Certain it is that in my past, I've done very little to recommend my better nature to you when it has come to the preferences I feel for my "rough diamonds". I've never been entirely frank with you, and for that, I would beg you to accept the sincere expression of my regret. But you have never felt yourself to be bound by the common morality, Gwen, and in this I think, we can both be said to have encountered a kindred soul. Society has other views, alas, and now I find I am no better than a common outlaw, forced to leave home and to go into hiding.

I suspected that one day things might come to this pass. To an extent, perhaps, I have even deserved it. But that is not what is at issue, dear friend. What is at issue is the fate of an innocent boy. And intimately tied to his fate, my own sanity. I say innocent. I state it again. You look at him, and you see at once a common rent-boy, and worse, the dangerous psychopath who put me into intensive care. When you do so, you see him, my dear Gwen, with the same eyes as society. Yes, he did put me into intensive care. Yes, he killed my cats, an act of the most atrocious and gratuitous cruelty. I will not deny it.

But neither will I deny him. My Bluebottle has been wrongly accused, Gwen. I know he has! You've read the newspapers, so you'll know about that vagabond who, some time ago, they found clubbed to death in the Wicklow Mountains. Now they want to pin his death on the boy! But he didn't do it. Don't ask me how I know. I know it with my entire soul. That is enough.

Now, I've taken the liberty of writing a long letter to Joe Conlon, the barrister. I think you've heard of her? I realise it's a little out of her sphere, but I've asked her to act with counsel for the defence. The lawyer they saw fit to provide the boy is utterly hopeless! I know you'll probably be cross with me. But Gwendolyn, it's absolutely essential in a matter like this that we have someone in whom we can place an absolute trust. If he were left to the provisions of the court, I ask you, what chance would the lad stand?

I spoke to Joe on the phone yesterday, and while it's not exactly written in stone as yet, it would seem that, in principle, she might be interested. But the crux is, at this particular juncture I am in no position to meet her costs. It's not that I don't have the money, there's the irony of it. God knows I have the money! You know how much the house must be worth, Gwen. It would only be a matter of taking out a second mortgage. I have the money! But I ask you, how do I dare to access it? The police, at this very moment, will have placed a wire on every one of my resources.

Dear friend, do not abandon me in my hour of need! I'm asking you, too, to act as a go-between and confidant. Who else have I to turn to?

Yours, in hope, in expectation,

Malcolm Little

P.S. Don't imagine, Gwen, that I want justice to prevail purely so that I can have my Bluebottle back again. If we pull this off, I swear to you, if you so wish, I will undertake never to set eyes on the boy. It shall be as you decide.

You sly old codger! Well, happy birthday Gwendolyn! My first reaction was to screw up the letter and dispatch it into the nearest waste-paper basket. But on second thought, I read it through, twice. And I had to laugh. I laughed long and hard at it. There could be no doubting that it was a cry from the heart, for in Mal's case, what is that maudlin organ if not a vaudeville theatre?

Next, I re-examined the postmark. Westport, Co. Mayo. Then he can only have been staying at the Hamiltons. To leap from a postmark to a particular guesthouse might appear, I daresay, precipitate. But I knew Mal like the back of my hand, that archetypal creature of habit. Once, when he feared an immanent blackmail at the hands of one of his 'rough diamonds', I'd spirited him away to that very guesthouse. The change of ocean had greatly revivified him. If I knew my quarry, that would be where he'd presently gone to ground.

I looked inside the envelope to be sure that it contained no other secrets. I wouldn't have put it past him to have enclosed some token of his infatuation; an earlobe, perhaps! But the letter was the sum total of his communication.

Of course, it was quite out of the question that I should bankroll his latest piece of foolery. Besides everything else, I knew Joe of old, before ever she was a barrister, and it seemed unlikely that such a case could interest her. In fact, now I thought about it, it was I who'd introduced her to Mal. '*I think you've heard of her*' indeed! If I knew anything, she'd be far more likely to get involved in the case if it had the relish of becoming a feminist *cause célèbre*, and fat chance of that!

It wasn't the money, either. I had little doubt that Mal would honour any and every pledge he might make in the course of his present crusade. No. If

I determined to refuse him, it was quite simply because I knew he was no longer well off, and I absolutely refused to help him flush good money down the toilet. Besides, if the boy really was innocent, which I have to say I very much doubted, I daresay there are plenty of safeguards for that eventuality built into the Irish legal system.

So that was all very well. A few weeks went by, and I thought nothing more of the whole affair. I was moderately surprised that he had not re-emerged, tail between the legs, but a discreet inquiry to the Hamiltons informed me that as yet he was in funds. The only unpleasant shock I received was on the morning I read that 'fearless women's libber, Josephine Conlon' was to take up the case. Was she really going to devil for that hopeless Higgins character whom free legal aid had seen fit to provide? More fool you, I thought. It'll hardly enhance your reputation, and as for your bank account, well! *On verra*!

The first intimation I got that the sly old devil had slipped back to Dublin came not from Vera Hamilton, as I'd expected, but from Dan Maguire. Evidently, he'd given poor Vera the slip by concocting some cock and bull story about needing to meet such and such an acquaintance up in Sligo town. To allay suspicions it seems he'd left an empty suitcase, containing an entire fortnight's unpaid bills, behind him on the bed!

Dan rang me to say that, during the afternoon, a call had come in from a branch in Drumcondra, of all places. Said that one Malcolm Little was requesting an overdraft, in cash if you don't mind. Of course Dan instructed the manager to fob him off. He knew too well about my concerns, particularly when the full nine thousand had been withdrawn by his lordship not three months since. And so he passed me on the message.

Drumcondra! Here was a fine conundrum. Now, what power on earth would draw the likes of Malcolm Little up to Drumcondra? To the best of my knowledge, he'd only ever ventured north of the Liffey when Fergal Bates lived in that dreadful little flat off Berkeley Road. The self-same den Manus Bates had bought to hide his mistresses, in point of fact. Well, I was drawing complete blanks! In the end, I decided to give Joe Conlon a call. It was about time to have a good old chin-wag and get to the bottom of the whole sorry affair.

We met the next morning over coffee at an unassuming place I know in Ranelagh, where it was unlikely we'd be overheard. But I was greatly disappointed in Joe. Course, hadn't seen her since she began to devil for Sherry & Sherry. The bar had evidently changed her. There was no other explanation for it. The "fearless women's libber" seemed almost embarrassed to be sitting next to this old dyke, and as to sharing gossip *à propos* of the case, nothing doing! She did relent when it came to the very small matter of Mal's finances, but only to the extent that he'd paid a considerable amount up front by money order. I smiled at this. If she'd been more forthcoming, I might've warned her. He'd scarcely be in a position to pay by cheque, not when there wasn't so much as a red cent left in his account.

But she did drop one tantalising hint. I've never been able to satisfy myself as to whether this indiscretion was deliberate. At one point her phone rang, and although she stepped outside to take the call, from a wince at the corner of the mouth and a rapid eye movement, I knew perfectly well who was on the other end. She had no very great intention of disguising the fact. When the call was ended and I was getting up to pay, she informed me that Mal was constantly pestering her to for God's sake assemble a team of character witnesses. Then, almost under her breath, although not entirely, she added: *as if, in this day and age, they'd pay the slightest attention to what a priest might have to say...*

Now, this *was* interesting. I began to put two and two together. A character witness who was also a priest. A bank in Drumcondra. I trawled my memory, and from one of its recesses I dragged up an intimation that the boy had been raised in some kind of charitable institution. No doubt it was on the north side. From here, it was but a short step to pinning the orphanage down. The Refuge of St Luke the Evangelist. A little detective work and I'd soon have the priest in question, too!

But the name wasn't quite so forthcoming as I'd imagined. Course, it would have been a great help to have known the boy's name. In my disappointment at seeing how conservative Josephine the firebrand had become, it had quite slipped my mind to clarify this small matter. But I'd be damned before I'd call her up again with such a ridiculous question. Papers couldn't carry the name, of course. To make matters worse, the deadline for the tender at Dun Laoghaire-Rathdown was beginning to loom large. There was nothing for it. I'm afraid the business of looking out for Mal would simply have to be placed on the back burner until that was out of the way.

Daresay you think that sounds selfish. Daresay it is! I'm a selfish old woman.

I needn't have bothered. Eventually, Patricia Hyland HRHA won the commission. *Quelle surprise*! Her winning sculpture, what irony, is entitled *the man who loved cats*! But I wasn't to know which piece would be chosen until the following May, so it was all systems go right up to ten minutes to five on the day of the deadline, and then a hectic taxi-ride through Dublin's impossible traffic.

Saturday I took off, exhausted; on Sunday I began my search in earnest and by Tuesday I'd whittled the list down to three candidates. There was a Giraldus Lazzari, who was principal of the institution; there was a second-level teacher with the baroque name of Columbanus Maolruaidh; and there was a librarian called Martin Ffrench. Two Fs, Galway name. Decided to go with a hunch it would be him. I'd frequently seen the lad curled around a book, and besides, it seemed the point of least semantic resistance. In the course of the taxi ride, as Clonliffe College and then the Refuge of St Luke the Evangelist drew steadily nearer, my hackles began to rise. I'd been raised in a Hertfordshire public school, you see. Over there, the odd Anglicanism was as innocuous a ritual as topiary or afternoon tea. The Irish Catholic church, with its murder of crows, excites in me the most profound loathing.

A bespectacled woman met me at reception. She had no need of veil or crucifix to mark her for a nun. Some essence of sterile devotion had seeped into her limp hair and her narrow-faced complexion.

'I wish to speak to Martin Ffrench.' I refused to call him Father, or Brother, or whatever else these imbeciles might choose to dub one another.

'Is he expecting you?'

'He is not.'

The woman conducted me into a large, ill-lit room filled with a cloying sweetness. I was left waiting for little more than a minute or two, but it was time sufficient for me to dislike the place intensely. Easter was to be early this year, and a bunch of cut lilies lay criss-cross on the table, overpowering the air with waxy perfume. It's a flower I detest at the best of times. In the present surroundings, it put one in mind of funeral parlours. Quotations from the scriptures were ranged in black frames about the walls, but these I imagine I could have endured. Far more nauseating were the slogans picked up, one would have to assume, off the floor of an American advertising salon: '*CH—CH: U R missing*'; '*Give God what's right, not what's left*'; that sort of glib rubbish.

The door groaned open and a skinny figure skipped in, a diminutive old man though deceptively taller than you'd expect, with a scrawny neck and eyes that wobbled at the bottom of two great jam-jars. An image from a hundred years ago came to me, quite unbidden, out of that era when I'd been a boarder in Hertfordshire. He seemed, to my fancy, the very incarnation of one of the pilgrims from the *Canterbury Tales*. White, and bony, and concealing, I was sure, an unbridled misogyny under the religious habit. By the same token, I must've appeared to him a hybrid of the Wife of Bath and Lady Bracknell.

I was surprised to observe he had coloured to the gills, as though he were embarrassed rather than merely dismayed to see me there. Can't imagine why. For my part, I was so predisposed against his sort that I took it to be a sign of guilt.

'I've no great love of the clergy,' I stated, before he had so much as opened his beak.

He cleared his throat, and, eyeing me coyly but at the same time calculatingly, he made an open gesture with his two palms.

'I've spent the better part of my life,' I went on, dryly, 'in battle with your church.'

'My church?' Now he was squinnying across the table into my face, myopic as a mole.

'The Roman Catholic Church,' I specified, no doubt unwisely, 'has been an unmitigated disaster for this country, ever since they established their precious Free State. Indeed, for quite a number of centuries before that! I had the good sense to be educated in Hertfordshire, and so I've always been able to see it for what it is.'

'I must protest,' he smiled, feigning he was appalled. But behind the glasses the enlarged eyes were trying to take my measure. 'The Catholic Church and I took leave of one another many years ago.'

I was not to be pacified.

'You are a religious man,' I declared. 'You've devoted your life to the propagation of faith. So let me tell you, just so that we understand one another, that I consider all religions to be equally objectionable.'

'Well,' he laughed, or tried to, 'I expect they are objectionable! They've certainly never lacked for those who've persecuted them, which means, I suppose, there must be something to object to within them.' He held back from approaching me, by which I mean he seemed to be taking advantage of the fact of the table, with its bier of heady blooms. It impeded him from the etiquette of approach. Daresay I must have appeared quite the Medusa.

'I don't believe….?' he intoned, leaving the question dangling. It is a quirk I dislike as I dislike a damp handshake.

'Gwendolyn,' I said, brusquely. 'Gwendolyn Furlong.'

He shook his head, intimating that he did not know me by reputation. This scarcely came as a surprise. It would have been difficult to imagine anything as scandalous as a Matisse or a Modigliani had ever found its way within these walls, much less one of my works.

I decided to cut to the chase. 'He's come here to see you, hasn't he? I know,' I stated, 'he's come here to see you.'

At once I saw him colour, and I was certain I'd not been mistaken. This was my man all right.

'Then you're a friend of Malcolm Little?' he twittered.

'A *friend*?' It seemed peculiar to hear, at that moment, the very term from Malcolm's letter. 'Yes, a friend.' He coloured, blanched, coloured again. Really, his complexion blazed like the periodic beacon of a lighthouse. Or it was a face drawn up beside an unsteady campfire. 'You don't think much of him,' I declared.

'Did that man send you here to find me?' he put to me after quite a time, more with the nuance of an accusation than a question. I'd come here prepared for battle. I wasn't in the least put out by the way our interview was shaping up.

'Not in the least,' I declared. 'Indeed, I think he'd be entirely mortified if he was ever to find out I'd come here.'

'And why did you come?' He'd begun to fidget at his sleeve. What can he be trying to hide, I wondered.

'You tell me!'

He picked up one of the lilies, a languorous bell, and examined it with eyes rheumy and greatly enlarged by the lenses. 'I haven't the foggiest idea,' he said, mildly, still holding the flower. I had the fantasy it was the pollen that had enflamed his eyes.

'Perhaps you *will* be able to tell me,' I waited for him to put down the lily before I went on, 'why you despise him?'

I expected him to quibble with the word. He did no so such thing. 'Why? Because he's a constant danger to children!' He stared straight at me, challenging with his cleric's avian anger. 'Because he and his type are a vicious threat to God's innocents!'

'This isn't about *children*!' I leaned across the table until my face was within three feet of his. 'With respect, this is about one pubescent youth.' And, I played my trump card, 'you can hardly call *him* one of God's innocents.'

His face was quite puce as he retorted, and was straining equally towards me on his pullet's neck. 'Your friend is a *danger*, that's what he is. A pervert, a corrupter of youth.' Then he drew his head back and added, almost sadly, 'a sick man.'

'That is outrageous!' I narrowed my eyes. 'I suppose you've proof of this do you?'

'When he was last here,' he shut his eyes, 'he left some photographs on the floor of my office.' His lips were so rigid he could articulate only with the greatest difficulty, 'and with them, a *disgusting* sketch.' From the face he pulled, he might have been describing excrement. He went on to outline the charcoal he'd found in the pocket of Mal's coat. I had to laugh, and I did so. Well, the old rascal! Months before, I'd done a number of preparatory sketches of the boy. My idea was to work them into a sort of response to Manet's *Olympia*. The male plaything. Came to nothing, of course. But one morning, I'd noticed that one of the papers had gone missing. Hadn't thought much about it. In the chaos of the studio I'm constantly losing things. So the old rascal had lifted it! Ha ha!

'You find this funny?' he gasped, horrified.

'No,' I said, wiping a tear from my eye. 'No, it's not funny. Lamentable. Ludicrous. But not funny.'

'Kindly explain to me,' he exhaled, panting as though we'd just been wrestling, 'what all this is about. Why did you come here?'

'Very well. I'm deeply worried, that's the why and the wherefore. I'm worried that my friend, as you call him, is very like to do something entirely foolish.' I looked for a reaction. He seemed too exhausted to be able to give one. At that moment, he looked more lifeless, more waxen, than the flowers strewn liberally across the table.

'I think I can safely say that neither one of us wants to see the two ever come together again. You take the boy's part. That's understandable. He was raised under your wing. He's like one of those orchids, about to come into bloom in time for your Easter service, and you'd be horrified to see him blighted before that happens. For my part, I'll be honest. I couldn't care a hoot about the boy.' I stopped, to see how he was receiving my speech. He was gawping at me as one imagines a capon must stare at the snout of a vixen that's poking into the chicken-coup.

I walked over to the window and gazed at the inner court. 'I'm greatly afraid,' I crowed, 'that dear, deluded Mal is about to do something foolish. Has a dreadful martyr complex you see. Now! There's something at last that you can understand!'

I turned about. He was motionless.

I spelled it out for him. 'He's likely to try to sacrifice himself for his great passion. He fancies himself in love with your delinquent. Perhaps he even is. It really doesn't make the blindest bit of difference, one way or another. The point is, in his present plight, Malcolm Little has finally found the melodrama that all his life he's been waiting for. I think, if anything, the matter of the scar adds a touch of noble piquancy to his project.'

'The scar?'

I examined him. 'You didn't know?' I was taken aback. It had been in all the tabloids. But one could see he wasn't playacting. Daresay *The Messenger* is the only publication to penetrate this sanctum. 'They… disfigured him.'

I watched his Adam's apple oscillate up and down. 'Who?' he squawked.

'Who scarred your boy? I don't know. Ruffians.'

'And is he…?'

I began to feel for the first time a twinge. Not of conscience. Not quite of pity, either. A twinge. Let it rest at that. 'They ran a knife along one cheek. Here. You see?' He was moved to manoeuvre round the table that had hitherto separated us.

He began to examine my cheek as if it, too, had been scarred. 'Oh Dear God!'

'Rough city out there, you know. Wouldn't be the first young man to have got into a scrape.'

'When did this… happen?'

'Oh, many months ago, now. Long before that chap Fowler was murdered.'

'Dear God!' he repeated.

'It's not so bad as all that. He's young.' I squinted archly at him. 'He won't lack for girlfriends.' The old rooster was now looking at me as if, at last, I was beginning to make sense. Perhaps I wasn't such a vixen after all. Perhaps he saw the means by which to protect his clutch of chicks. 'Malcolm Little wants to sacrifice himself for this *beau*. Throw himself upon the mercy of the court and take the blame for how he turned out. I will not stand idly by and watch him do it.'

'And what do you want of me?' he asked. 'Where do I fit into any of this?'

'You?' I fixed my eye on him as if I were about to pin a specimen to a wall. 'You are going to help me.'

XI | Fergal

Rat-at! Rat-at! Nails, driven in through the ear. There ought to be laws against raping a hangover in this manner.

Kindly be so good as to fuck off please.

Rat-at-at! Christ, would you have some patience!

The narrator must have fallen asleep on the sofa, again. His pants, when at last he lays hands on them, are turned nine parts inside out and ten parts unwilling to cooperate.

Giving up the unequal struggle, I swaddled my naked loins in the duvet and, hobbled and teetering, I shuffled to the door and inched it the merest sliver ajar. I was afraid it was about to detonate, again. 'What do you want?'

It took a moment before the blob resolved itself into a vaguely humanoid form. A black coat. Glasses. And a hiss: *you lied to me!* I snapped the door to.

Oh God! I wept. Why me? Why today?

'I'm not going to go away, you know.' The voice was muffled, but through the door I could feel the vibrations tickle my forehead. I was tilting forwards, gingerly, against its reassuring timbers. Why *now*?

'I'm not going to go away!'

With supreme lassitude, with my headache wincing like a fluorescent bulb, I opened the door fully onto the morning. Correction. Onto the afternoon.

'You *lied* to me!'

I walked away, who wouldn't have, and re-entered the inner sanctum. It was invitation enough for him to follow. Without any direction from my will, my body listed against the nearest wall to hand. From this temporary haven I peeped at the intruder.

'You lied to me.' I shut my eyes. If I slap the side of his head, I thought, perhaps I'll dislodge the needle and the record will stop repeating.

'You lied! I spoke to Joe Conlon this morning on the phone. She has most certainly *not* decided to plead guilty.'

I returned a diluted smile in his general direction, and pinched the bridge of my nose. Will no-one rid me of this meddlesome priest?

'In fact,' he went on, with the persistence of a dribbling faucet, 'it seems the case for the prosecution is anything but straight forward. There's a great deal of forensic evidence that, quite simply, cannot be made to fit in.' The tap hesitated. I could sense a drop quivering upon its lip. 'Why? Why did you lie to me?'

I opened my eyes onto eyes made huge by glasses. Too much of Venus doth dim the sight. He was standing as red-faced, rigid and unwelcome as a morning erection when one wishes only to drain the bladder.

'If I tell you,' I said, meekly, 'will you promise to go away?'

Cut to the window. The light fades, twice, and is seen to rally, twice. This indicates the passage of a period of not less than thirty-six hours.

Return to same scene, but with evidence of a defeated effort to tidy the dive. A third person has joined the party, and is balancing prudishly on the maw of a treacherous armchair. An elderly crone.

Tea has been served. Decidedly not Earl Grey. But all terribly, terribly civil. *A single string, pizzicato.* The level of mutual trust is that of the triangular gunfight that climaxes Leone's *The Good, the Bad and the Ugly*. Close-up on the three sets of shifting eyes.

The only purgative I'd found, to rid my hangover of the cleric, had been to agree to see these intruders together on the next day but one. I'd no idea, when he'd mentioned an older woman, that he was referring to Uncle's antique hag. The Sapphic sculptress. He didn't seem quite to know himself who she was. Perhaps if I'd known, I wouldn't have bothered to stack away the knickers and porn mags with quite so much zeal.

Spurred on by the threat of a glowering migraine, I'd prematurely agreed I'd share with them everything I knew that pertained to the hobo's death. I've little doubt that this was bad form. I'm no legal expert, but the DPP was preparing a case which would, necessarily, draw on my testimony. So this unhappy couple were, technically, to be legal about it, interfering with a witness. But there you are. We all can't arrange our lives by the letter of the law.

'He didn't *say* that he'd killed the bugger.' This was our narrator speaking. 'He didn't state, in so many words, that he'd bashed in the old boy's skull. Shall I tell you again?' I looked from one to the other. Think Sergio Leone. 'I saw him act out the murder in his sleep. He brought down his hand,' I explained, 'thus.'

They weren't happy. But they were too suspicious, each of the other, for either one to be the first to contradict or query. 'You're a tough audience,' I exclaimed. I stood up, rather casually, and strolled to the window. It was a dull day outside.

'There is, when all is said and done,' I went on, turning my back to them, but in such a way that their frames were just visible in the corner of my eye, 'only the one actual witness.'

The reaction was gratifying. The priest, or monk, or whatever nuance of cleric he was, strained his neck around through one hundred and eighty degrees, while the sculptress all but fell into the gaping armchair.

'There was a *witness*?' they cried, united as the chorus in a Greek tragedy.

'There was,' I said, suddenly panting. 'Keaton, by name.' My hands became ears, erect. 'A dog.' I could have milked the moment, I suppose. I'd had precious little sport over the previous weeks.

The woman stood up. Her mouth looked like it might be chewing on a lemon coated in Prussic acid.

'You are *not* telling us everything.'

'About the murder?' I clarified.

'You're not telling us everything you know.' She paced in front of the padre, about-faced, then stopped still and turned a Gorgon's stare on me. 'There's more to it,' she declared. 'What,' she demanded, 'do you know about his scarring?'

'The Judas kiss?' The felicitous phrase seemed to take them both by surprise. The male, who I remember styled himself Brother, had pivoted about so much that the silver screens of his spectacles were directly examining me, even as his chest faced towards the female. But the female was oblivious to his contortionist display. Basking in their expectation, I was gripped by a thought that took me entirely by surprise.

'I *do* have some little snippets of information,' I exclaimed. 'And do you know what? So far, neither the Old Bill nor the Right Honourable Josephine Conlon LL.B. has thought to ask me about this. So here's the deal...'

I returned to my rightful position at the centre of the room and took again my place on the sofa beside the friar. Even the old lady must've been impressed by the conspiratorial, forward leaning posture I now adopted, because she resumed her precarious perch on the mouth of the armchair.

'Here's the deal,' I repeated, rubbing my palms as though I carried an unrolled spliff between them. 'I really have been having rather a sterile time of it since I've relocated out here. But you chaps have given me an idea.'

I looked from one to the other. They weren't at all sure what to make of this development. 'What do you say we do a bit of sleuthing together? I mean, the three of us.' I poured out the remaining dribble of Tesco Value tea, more leaf than liquid, into the triad of mismatched cups. 'Don't you think that would be a giggle?'

The truth of the matter is, our hero wasn't entirely play-acting. Having abandoned my town flat as fast as a rat from a wreck, I'd had to lay low in this hovel for fear that Mahood would catch up with me. I'd spilled the beans on him and his sorry outfit almost before they'd had time to drag me into Store Street. I'd even helped with a photo-fit of Anto, I mean the

Anto that inhabited my circle. He'd made such a pretty picture in squares and triangles!

To begin with, there was a faint whiff of romance in playing the desperado, quivering at every revving engine, sneaking out to the corner shop once it got dark like a truant schoolboy. But within three days I was sick to death of it. I had neither company nor entertainment. Funds were becoming desperate. Nevertheless, I hadn't once mustered the courage to venture back to Nelson St, to pick up telly or laptop or to raid the cupboard. If Mahood was bent on vengeance, which I didn't doubt for a minute, the flat was sure to be watched.

I was mad for diversion. And besides, I smelled an opportunity for a free lunch. I was also, let's be honest, curious. Call a spade a spade! A murder, a scarring, and now three sleuths who disliked one another intensely? It had all the antagonistic muscle to kick-start the old, sclerotic dream that saw F.D. Bateman a screenwriter. What I proposed to my two new buddies was the inspiration of a split-second in which all the above considerations flashed through my mind. I verily believe I was as surprised and delighted with the proposal as they were.

They, by which I meant principally the old virago, would bankroll a weeklong stint for me at the Pier Hotel in Bray. A room with a sea-view was bound to recharge the batteries of recall and hone the faculties of inquiry. I would follow up such leads as came to memory, track down such persons as I'd overheard Mr Bluebottle allude to, and I'd even visit all the sordid scenarios of his steamy little saga. They would meanwhile pursue such trails as they saw fit, and, as these fell cold, they might pester Josephine for warmer ones. Thrice during the week would we meet up, to compare notes, as they say in the sleuthing business. To my astonishment, they agreed at once.

One thing intrigued me. I mentioned, *en passant*, the desirability of contacting dear old Mal, to discover such scraps and titbits as the old bugger might have hoarded. I may just as well have said Beelzebub. She coiled herself erect and magnificent, and insisted I would do no such thing, while he spluttered and gaped from teacup to floor, his face an apoplectic violet. What could it mean?

•••

Within the week I'd packed a festive holdall and set off for jolly Bray. What larks! The Pier Hotel was known to me of old. Once, as a child, Manus had brought me there on one of his business trips. It was the Easter recess, I remember. I think mother had the quaint idea that I might act the role of chaperone, a temporary curb on Daddy's desires. My presence would remind him that, while he rollicked, she repined in the Hospice for the Dying at Harold's Cross.

Twenty years on I was delighted to see how little the place had changed. The carpets were still shabby and asthmatic, the windows rattled in their casements and the corridors were irregular, ill-lit, and meandered like Alzheimer patients into doorless corners. It had been a world of infinite adventure for an eight year old.

As I unpacked the holdall I surveyed my draughty view. For a hotel that styles itself the Pier, it has precious little perspective onto the harbour. There is an esplanade, true, an Edwardian leftover against whose grey stones the geriatric wave that crosses from England expends its garrulous foam (Mentally, I was already composing my epic film script. Nothing short of a *palme d'or* for F.D. Bateman!). The hint of a harbour could be glimpsed. But a pier? It appeared not.

Sprawling on the quilt, I took the time to review the several leads I had to go on. They were scarcely more honest or encouraging. There was a villain whose name was Anto, and who lived, in all likelihood, in Shankill. He might be distinguished by a nose-ring. There was a second in command, a Diarmuid figure, an amorous youth whose name had escaped me. And to complete the triangle there was the inevitable female, whose hair was unevenly dyed, and whose name was Judy, or Julie, something of that ilk.

Damn it, I thought some time later as I lay soaking in the tub, Uncle is bound to know something. The problem here, needless to say, had nothing to do with the discomfiture that contacting him directly might cause my confederates. It was as ticklish as a Rubik's cube, and as I moved one facet into place, another fell out of alignment. On the uppermost tier, Mal was no longer staying at Martello Mews. Like our nomadic narrator, he'd gone into hiding, and had ditched his mobile, or at least, was immune to answering it. Nevertheless, I reasoned, he had evidently been able to track yours truly down. How else did the cloistered Brother find my dive in Dun Laoghaire? Now it was likely, on balance, that the sculptress knew Mal's present whereabouts. But how to tickle her to disclosure, without arousing her suspicions?

The second dimension of the cube involved the possibility of approaching Josephine Conlon directly. I hadn't entirely lied with regard to the guilty plea. To lie is to tell a deliberate untruth, whereas I'd been given to believe by the DPP that a plea bargain was by far the most likely outcome. Perhaps the prosecution wanted to put my mind at ease *qua* the inconvenience of being called as star witness in their trial while I was still caught up in my own unlawful and unequal trial of wits with Mahood. But what might induce Joe Conlon to trust me with Malcolm's new address, and how might I keep the manoeuvre secret?

The third axis of this exquisite puzzle was the altogether more profound problem of what to say to the old bugger if I did catch up with him. He was scarcely likely to feel any warmth towards sincerely yours, not now that the Garda Síochána were informed of his elective affinities. Only an appeal to the boy's predicament might move him on that score. But would he take my word that that was what I was concerned with, without my appealing to the testimony of one Br Martin Ffrench? And how could I do that without scrambling the top tier of the cube.

Ticklish indeed.

I dined magnificently on toast and kippers and then gravitated by instinct towards a bar called Clancy's, a pleasant dive just short of the High Street.

It was scarcely three in the afternoon. By five, I already had the name of one Anthony McSorley, the Westy of the deep South, and a good idea of where I might find him. Birds of a feather, I'd thought, sifting through the bar's motley precipitate, and, to mix zoological metaphors, selecting the most dissolute of the bottom feeders upon whom to fasten my curiosity and charity. His tongue was loosened before the first pint had been drained. I further learned that the said Anto was the head of a gang he called, rather picturesquely, the Shankill Pitbulls, and that narcotics was their caper. There'd been some sort of a turf war with a Bray gang a couple of years before, the viciousness of which had brought him a good share of local notoriety if not affection. Using the excuse of the toilet, I scribbled the information I'd gleaned into my brand new spiral-bound pocket-sized sleuthing notebook before returning briefly to the counter to take my leave. One more thought, did this street pharmacist have a lady friend? Unfortunately, my new pal couldn't tell me.

I went back to the hotel, very pleased with myself on account of my day's work. There was a message waiting for me at the front desk. It was brief, and to the point. *The girl's name is Judith Ross – Br Martin.* I found out later that he'd been out to see the defendant that same morning, at the psychiatric wing of I know not what prison or hospital. Will it be believed that the idea had never so much as crossed my mind? I could see the tiles crumble from the facets of my Rubik's cube. I slinked back to my room, lay down heavily on the bed, made a paper plane of the page from my spiral notebook, and, launching it towards the waste-paper basket, I trumpeted a Wagnerian fart into the giggling bedsprings.

The following morning, at eleven, we had the first of our merry meetings. The monk filled in a few more details of the interview. He had been, apparently at his own request, at no time left alone with the boy. He'd arranged the visit under a purely pastoral guise, as he had no wish to arouse the suspicions of the custodian at the very first hurdle. It would be useful to be allowed unfettered access to the defendant as further points arose. The latter had spoken as if he were mentally slow, or heavily sedated.

'He's not at all sure what he can remember. They have him so confused with their questions and medication, he doesn't know what's up and what's down. And dear Lord, his speech is so slow.' Then he sighed, and looked at his own palm as if it had offended him. 'At one point, he talked of feeling the weight of a rock in his hand.'

'So he does remember, then?' I prodded, and mimed the motion of clubbing. Instinct had held the detail of the blood smudged lettering on the mirror from my confederates. Murder most foul. 'No! Not in the least!' I could see that he was eyeing Gwendolyn as though her verdict meant more to him than mine. 'What he meant was, he could feel the weight of the rock there and then, as he sat beside his bed!'

'And no memory of Fowler?' Ms Furlong inquired, not amused.

He reddened, a trait he was prone to. 'When it comes to Fowler, he seems to have become fixated on a single detail. Every time I tried to approach that subject, he mentioned only a rat's tail. Apparently, that's how the hair was gathered at the back of this man Fowler's head.'

'Did he recognise you?' I asked, suddenly.

'Oh,' he smiled, 'he had no difficulty in recognising me.'

'Not altogether fool, then,' commented Gweny, in a dry aside.

There was a silence, and taking advantage of it, I informed them in a blasé manner that, since I'd arrived yesterday afternoon, I'd discovered the full name of the individual who'd scarred the lad, the name of his gang, and even the racket they were involved in. It was fully my intention to pay a visit to Shankill on the morrow. Gwendolyn nodded severely, and then said, if that was all, she really had quite a number of things to do. She got up to take care of the bill.

Once she was out of earshot, Cadfael leaned forwards over the table and touched me on the forearm.

'I didn't want to mention the name of the girl,' he whispered, tipping his forehead towards the cash register as if to intimate before whom. 'I'd prefer if we keep it to ourselves for the moment.'

I smiled complacently, patted the hand that was touching my forearm, and half closed one eye. He could count on Fergal Bates' discretion.

Feeling a bit at a loose end, I thought I'd wander down to the harbour and look at the boats. I was not in luck. Evidently, the year was still too young to trust the sea's temper. There was an infestation of swans gathered about where the Dargle dribbles its beery waters into the harbour-mouth. I was surprised at their abundance. It threw my mind unexpectedly back to my last sojourn in Bray, when they were tall and plump enough to ride, and hissed most serpent-like at my boyish attempts to do so. It was the year that mother passed on.

'Fergal!' I was ripped untimely from my reverie by the weird sister in the tweed coat. 'I wanted to have a word,' she continued.

'Oh?'

'How do you find the Pier?' I was surprised at the question. It was not my experience of her manner that she should make small talk. 'A disappointed bridge!' I beamed. It was lost on her. 'I suppose it's comfortable enough. Why do you ask?'

She shook her head. If it wasn't patently obvious, she wasn't the sort to spell it out to me.

'I wanted to have a word,' she began again, 'in private.'

I looked at the March waves being chased headlong across the water. 'You won't get much more private than this, unless of course the swans are eavesdropping.'

'What did Martin Ffrench say to you? I saw you two whispering when I went up to pay.'

'Br Martin? Nothing. He asked me what I thought of your sculpture.'

She wasn't moved to reward my witticism with a smile.

'He had nothing of any account to say,' I assured her.

'The point is, I don't trust him. You shouldn't either. He's an idealist.' She began to fuss about inside her handbag. 'I want you,' she went on, even as the search continued, 'to deal directly with me. You're to tell him only the basics. Here.' She'd pulled out a couple of envelopes and was extending them directly towards me. For a moment I thought they must contain money. But they were nothing more than SAEs. I looked at her as if I didn't understand. 'If anything important comes to light,' she explained, and then specified, 'I don't mean trivia such as Anthony McSorley, I mean something really substantial, then you are to deal directly with me. You will communicate it at once using these pre-paid envelopes. When it comes to our regular meetings, you will in no way allude to this. Do you understand?'

'Perfectly,' I replied. 'The padre to be kept in the dark.'

'He's a fool,' she said. 'He's a holy fool, and they're always dangerous. He believes that boy capable of no wrong.'

Whereas you…, I mused, but I thought better of interrupting her departure with an impertinent postulate. She was bankrolling this entire gravy train, and boy did she know it.

Back at the Pier, the disappointed bridge, I began to reassemble the facets onto my Rubik's cube. He didn't trust her, and didn't want her to know the girl's name. She didn't trust him, and wanted anything substantial reserved for her eyes only. Neither one of them trusted Uncle, but I could see no reason to keep him out of the picture. But they would never trust me if they found I was approaching him behind their backs. Whereas he wouldn't trust me, unless one of them would vouch for me. And then there was Josephine Conlon, who certainly wouldn't trust any one of us if she knew what we were up to.

As I fiddled with the newly configured puzzle, I determined to adopt that priceless colonial maxim: *divide and rule*.

I began to run the bath.

•••

When I returned from Shankill the next day, I prepared to write my first epistle. It hadn't been an entirely fruitful journey, but neither had it been entirely wasted. For one thing, I'd picked up a pretty fancy mobile for next to nothing. Off the back of a lorry, as the fellow says. Gweny could hardly raise an objection to that little expense, the which I had driven down as zealously as though the money had been mine own. I could hardly be expected to be a private eye if I didn't have the means to be contacted. Besides, as I spelt out in the postscript to my letter, with this sort of technology to replace our snail mail, I could even send her images if the need arose. And then, haggling over its price had given me the perfect cover to ask a few pertinent questions.

So it turns out Judith Ross is very well known as the gangster's moll. Or his ex-moll. I didn't want to make the hawker suspicious, and so I had to let on I already knew everything the old dear was telling me.

Were you not there at the fight last Friday? I was away, I winked, you know how it is. Oh I do, son. Jaysus, you should've seen the way the pair of them went for one another. The mercy of God one of them wasn't kilt. I'm not telling you a word of a lie, that Anto had a knife that length. Ah go on! He did! That length! And the other fella? Well Jacko'd a knife too. Sure he had to defend himself, son, didn't he? Of course he did! Drugs, was it? No, son! Amn't I after telling you, they were fighting over Judith so they were. Women, says I, ah now! Sure everyone knows that Judith Ross's always been sweet on Jacko Corrigan. And isn't she right? He's a gentleman, not like that other gurrier. Ah now, says I.

I didn't want to push my luck, but as I was about to set off on my way, a 100W light bulb lit up over my skull.

Listen love, I said to the hawker, waving my new purchase jovially, I thought I might give old Judith a call. You wouldn't happen to have her number on you? Are you mad? She looked at me as if I'd two heads, and I thought for a moment I'd blown it. Why don't you drop in and see her? And she gave just sufficient a nod to indicate the corner on which the Ross house could be presumed to stand. She's never in Bray of a Tuesday afternoon. Bray? Bray! That's where the hair salon is. She done a lovely job on me sister last week. Bray, of course she works there! What am I thinking? I swear missus, if my head wasn't screwed on… Go on over and see her, son, that's my advice to you.

I opened my mouth wide in an expression of delight and, rotating my phone-arm like the sail in a Donegal wind farm, I put as much distance as I decently could between us. I will, I cried back into the breeze. I just need to blah blah blah first.

I sat before a latte in the dining room, my pen dawdling over a complementary stationary pad which graced the hotel's business address with an image of a fanciful pier. How much information to impart? And how much to reserve for Martin Ffrench? It was a pleasant dilemma.

Dear Gwen,

It's been an interesting day. I find that, as with rye grass, the more one pulls at one root, the more other roots unexpectedly break the surface. I now have a number of definite names to follow up.

You remember that second individual we talked about? His name is Jack, and last week he was willing to fight a duel with our friend Anthony, all for the love of a girl. Can you guess who? I have a lead to follow her up, too, and will look to it tomorrow. Naturally, I won't mention any of this before our clerical friend.

Incidentally, I thought it wise to invest in a phone. If you'll give me your number I'll send a text, and that way you'll have mine. It might be a more convenient way to stay in touch on the QT. I'm quite certain our friend the monk won't have a mobile.

By the way, I thought I'd ask you. What's between him and Uncle? Every time either one of us mentions Malcolm, he blushes like a schoolgirl!

Talk soon, yours etc.

F

I looked at the bare initial and nodded approvingly. A cipher was quite *de rigueur* in this sort of affair.

I drank the latte – it had gone cold – and set out to find a post-box. As I did so I was humming. I don't believe I'd caught myself humming a tune since before the days of Mahood! As I walked the village streets, I made a mental note of all the hairdressers and beauty salons I came across. But that would be another afternoon's work. Sufficient unto the day was the letter that I carried in my arse pocket.

Bray is a quaint resort, scarcely changed since the days when Edwardian ladies with great perambulators and protruding bustles ambled its fustian walks. Such an air of genteel decay! A main thoroughfare with a memorial to the Great War still flaunted the name Prince of Wales Terrace, the McDonalds was disguised as a mock Tudor town hall, and every letter-box I came to bore the initials of a dead sovereign, daubed over in thick emerald gloss: VR, ER, GR. Post colonial. Have I cracked that gag before?

And Fowler, the ex-hobo, was ex-British Army. They'd made that great forensic leap when they'd read his tattoo. More imperial graffiti! By God, the new film-script that F.D. Bateman was hatching would be nothing if not damnably clever.

I wondered was there any great point in dropping back into Clancy's. The pin money the old woman had advanced me wasn't going to last for ever, but on the other hand, I had a magnificent thirst. I entered and, adjusting my eyes, I saw that my bottom feeder had not moved from his stool in two days. I hailed him, slightly dismayed that nothing but suds graced the pint glass before him. There was nothing for it but to have it refilled.

'Terrible,' I tut-tutted.

'What?'

'That case in the papers.'

'What case?'

'Oh, that oul' tramp they found clubbed to death, down there in the mountains. They say it was a young fella done it.'

'D'you want to know something?' He leaned towards me, prodded me on the side of my arm, and contorted his mouth so that he was speaking entirely out of one side of it. 'That was no tramp,' he growled, and then inclined even closer. 'That fella was SAS.'

'No!'

He winked. It was a delivery which he adjudged worthy of half the pint in a single swallow. He wiped his mouth with the back of his hand, and belched.

'And do you know what else?' I simply smiled at him and shook my head in admiration. 'It wasn't the young fella done it at all. That's just a cover-up.'

'Is it? Do you tell me so?'

'That's right,' he said. He leaned closer, his mouth as one-sided as Fred Flintstone's. 'They have forensic evidence, so they do, to say there was more than one of them involved.'

'Was there indeed?'

'There was.'

'But tell us, boss. How do you come to know all this?' I didn't allow the slightest suspicion of doubt to blacken the pitch of the question. He again poked my arm, as though it were a doorbell. 'The wife's brother-in-law is in the guards.' Then he winked. 'Harcourt Street!'

The next morning, being again a red-letter day, I set off for the usual café with a spring in my step. I was humming symphonically. I'd begun to realise that if I played Penelope and teased out the threads of this correctly, I'd have enough yarn to stay on at the Pier for a month.

Gwendolyn was evidently delayed, for the good Brother was sitting on his lonesome by the window, peering like the White Rabbit up and down the street. Not having a private income, he had not ventured to order. I motioned two regular coffees.

'Tell me,' I asked, taking advantage of the hiatus, 'there was something I've been meaning to ask you. What is it with you and old Gwen?'

'What do you mean?'

'You know she calls you the holy fool?'

He appeared to savour the epithet. 'I daresay she's right. A holy fool!' Then he paused to look at me. 'You're not a believer, I think.'

'There is no God,' I wagged a clever finger, 'and Dawkins is His prophet.'

My bon mot was rewarded by nothing more gratifying than a puzzled 'Dawkins?'

I rose to the challenge with a riposte that, I admit, I'd been toting in my breast for some time. 'Decades of crossing Darwin and Hawking is bound to throw up at least one Dawkins in the end.'

He shook his head. I was getting nowhere.

'But old Gwen and you. What's going on, eh?'

'I still don't see...'

'I mean, ok. Every time I mention Malcolm Little, it's as if I've…' There it was! It was like ringing Pavlov's bell. He flushed the colour of a sunburned radish, and his eyes became huge, as though he were marvelling at the world through a pair of magnifying glasses. I wondered if I might winkle a means of contacting Mal from beneath his myopic scrutiny.

'You don't have any time at all for him, do you?'

He didn't reply. 'Is that Christian? I mean, aren't you guys supposed to forgive? And it's hardly as if he's an Arnold Friedman or…'

'I'm sorry?'

'Forget Arnold. What I mean to say is, Mal's a pretty harmless character, when you take him in the round.'

'Is he?' He was fidgeting and looking away. I had him on the ropes, and no mistake.

'I'll tell you. Let me talk to him,' I said, in a consoling voice. 'I'm sure, for all his weaknesses, his heart is in the right place.' He was staring out at the street, suddenly impatient for the old girl to show up. His impatience goaded me into further motion. 'I'll tell you what I'll do. If you let me know how I can contact Uncle, I'll tell you a couple of things before Gwen gets here. For our ears only. What d'you say, do we have a deal?'

He was still looking away, still russet hued. I felt I had to keep striking while the colour still glowed. While we were still alone.

'I heard a rumour,' I said in a low murmur, 'that Raymond Fowler might have been SAS.'

'SAS,' he repeated, mechanically. Mal's name had knocked him off his perch, and he was still flapping about to regain his equilibrium. 'He's about as much SAS as your granny,' I scoffed. I'd decided, on a whim, to offer a morsel more substantial. 'What I did find out, and this I think we might keep between ourselves, is that they think there might've been more than one attacker.'

He turned to me and his eyes bloomed as wide and pale as narcissi. At that moment there was a tinkle at the door, and Gwen blustered in. Saved by the bell!

'DART,' she snapped, lips pursed tight as a miser's sporran. 'You simply cannot depend on public transport in this country.'

She stood, dominating the table, ran a cold eye up and down the bill of fare, and then demanded of Nadya, the pretty Polish waitress, a camomile tea.

'Please be so good as to ensure it comes in a separate pot,' she specified. 'I cannot abide when it's served in a mug, like a drowned mouse with the string trailing outside.'

Like a floral tampon, I smirked to myself, but my receptive mind was distracted by a cylinder which, beneath the table, poked my thigh. I looked to the padre. He frowned at me, twice, with eyes which never quite looked away from Gwendolyn. It was charming to watch. I accepted the thin tube and slipped it into my side-pocket.

Suddenly I was impatient to be away. The ritual of our mutual dissimulations had never seemed so pointless or so drawn out. I shared a few spoils, as did my buddies, each more eager to keep an eye on what the other was up to than to advance the investigation. After an eternity, I became so impatient to be away that I paid the bill myself.

I hurried back along Prince of Wales Terrace and pulled the paper cylinder from my pocket. It unfurled into a brown envelope, addressed in unjoined letters to: *Br Martin Ffrench, The Refuge of St Luke the Evangelist, Lower Drumcondra, Dublin 9*. Its mouth was already torn open, and I lost no time in extracting a page that looked in any case as if it had been ripped in haste from a child's exercise book.

I know you despise me. I will not try to justify myself. I might say that I am as God made me, but let that rest. Whether for good or ill, we find ourselves on the same side in this beastly case. I would implore you, then, to make use of me. I don't ask that you like me, just that you keep me informed, and if there is any way at all in which I can serve, no matter how desperate, that you tell me at once.

M

So he was at the single initial lark too, the old bugger! The note did include a gem, all the same. An 085 number. This was clearly new. I would swear Mal's old number had been part of the 087 network.

Brother, I cried, we have a deal!

The following morning the hotel telephone detonated into my eardrum at three minutes to ten. It was Gwen. I *never* told you to get a mobile phone. I don't have a mobile phone, and I see no reason for you to have a mobile phone. If I wanted you to buy a mobile phone, I would have told you to buy a mobile phone. I have no intention of picking up the tab for your mobile phone, you may be quite sure of that. Are you still there? Yes, I'm still... Another thing. I want you to know that I'm not at all happy with your letter. What do you mean by a 'duel'?

I explained. Silence. I went on to mention that, immediately after breakfast, I intended to track down the girl. Silence.

'Are *you* still there Gwen?' Silence.

'I want you to know,' resumed a voice as sweet as Prussic acid, 'that late next week I intend to go to France, where I will be staying with my dear friend Valerie Yates. I would expect, therefore, that you will have completed everything you're *supposed* to be doing in Bray before I leave. Before I leave, mind. I've informed reception that the room will no longer be paid for once I leave.'

To the dialling tone, I replied that I'd see what I could do, but was she aware that she was a right royal pain in my hairy hole?

The exchange quite spoiled my breakfast. I dislike any form of compulsion. It does not aid digestion. The Pier, with its irresolute corridors and fustian smells, had really begun to grow on me. Her indigestible refusal to pick up my outlay on the mobile, which for her benefit I had whittled down to a risible thirty euro, had also stuck in my craw.

I was loath to call into any of the hair salons that morning, if only because the crone had practically demanded that I do so. Instead, I made for the harbour wall to weigh my options. So the old bird intended to fly to France? This appeared at first glance to put paid to the author's intention of staying on indefinitely at the Pier.

It seemed that the crux came down to two things. In the first place, was there any truth whatsoever in what Fred Flintstone had told me in Clancy's? If there was, and if the barfly's wife's brother-in-law could be trusted to exist, it would change the entire complexion of the case. One cannot be many. But why had there been no mention of such a doubt in the papers?

Of more immediate interest, how would I be able to string Gwendolyn the Grey along beyond her supposed departure date? Here, it was apparent to my calculus that the more oblique the threads of information, the longer they might be made to serve. It would be premature to disclose to her what I'd mentioned to Br Martin. What was required, for her portion, was that I weave Jack and Jude more squarely into the tapestry. After lunch would do for that. In the meanwhile, I looked forward to having a good old natter with Uncle over the phone. The trick here would be to pre-empt his hanging up on me immediately I spoke. I hit upon a stratagem.

'Hello?'

'Br Martin Ffrench asked me to…'

'Who is this?'

'…call you about Bluebottle. He…'

He hung up. Too soon, I thought. He needs more time, bless him.

A gull veered past me. My eyes were drawn by it south along the shoreline as far as Bray's skulking headland. Three summits, and a diminutive cross. An epiphanous moment! When I come to pen the film-script based upon all of this, for my opening shot… I made a rectangular frame of my two hands.

The aesthetic was interrupted by the bicker of the mobile. 'Private number', flashed the LCD. I took the call, which hissed accusingly. Then, a long, grand, thespian and condescending sigh announced: 'I am returning your call.'

'Uncle?' Silence, dignified. 'Is that you?'

'You said that Br Martin had a message for me?'

'Uncle!' I really was delighted to hear from him. His histrionics had quite literally brought a tear to my eye! 'Yeah, listen. He asked me to ring you…' I was interpreting the Brother's gesture somewhat liberally. 'He says he thinks you might be able to help us with the case.'

There was a persistent if unenthusiastic sea breeze blowing, and it intensified the sounds of static that rustled from the receiver. 'Uncle?'

'I'm listening.'

'I'm down in Bray. The sea!' I held the receiver toward the sea. 'I'm here, Mal, to help the Bro and your friend the sculptress find evidence that might get Bluebottle off the hook!' The receiver made a number of noises, as though at the other end Mal were busy unwrapping his from cellophane.

'Here's the thing, Uncle. When would it be possible to meet up?'

Beep, beep, beep. I attempted to dial his mobile number, but with no success. Still, I thought, mission pretty much accomplished. Now the old bitch has a bone to chew over. He's bound to ring me, sooner or later.

I went for lunch in the usual café, where I was disappointed to find that Nadya was on her day off. I sat over an insipid lasagne, and as I turned its lukewarm entrails with a fork, I considered my next move. Based on the snippets that I'd already garnered, it would be child's play to track down Judith Ross. The point was, what use to make of the interview I was about to have with her. I slapped my forehead, painfully. It had never entered my head to ask the good padre what Bluebottle's real name was. The lapse astonished me so much that there was nothing for it but to laugh aloud. You're some bloody sleuth, Fergal Bates! You're already five days into your mission to find out everything you can about a common housefly!

I decided to postpone meeting the girl until that matter was cleared up.

Instead, I thought, I'd have another dip into Clancy's aquarium to see what bauble I'd find in the murk. On the way there, as I was about to pass by the *Cut Above the Rest Unisex Hair & Beauty Salon*, a rather exquisite girl, very tall, with purple, dread-locked hair breezed out of the doorway. It seemed churlish to pass up the opportunity to exchange the time of day with her.

'Excuse me, Miss.'

'Yes? What you want?' From her accent, I guessed Eastern European. Her eyes had the blue of the Baltic in them.

'Do you happen to work in the hairdressers?'

'Yes, I work here.'

'I don't suppose you'd know a Judith Ross?'

She coloured. I wondered why. 'Judith not in today.'

'I see. That's a shame. Do you know when she will be in, love?'

She shrugged, a gesture which in Riga or Vilnius means 'I don't, and if I did I wouldn't tell you, creep, so get lost and leave me alone.' Seeing that I was still standing in front of her, she turned and showed a quite magnificent profile while she lit up a Lucky Strike. Superb, sculpted cheekbones were deepened while she sucked. I stood, enthralled.

'She has not been in for many day,' she exhaled upwards in a smoke ring, and then, turning, intensified her expression into 'scram, or my boyfriend punch your face in.'

I made to leave, and decided to toss off a happy, parting shot. 'She's in trouble, isn't she?'

My Baltic beauty didn't react, and I resumed my downward progress towards Clancy's. Before I got to the corner, however, I was overtaken by the plosive consonants of high-heels ricocheting off concrete.

'Are you police?' she asked. For someone whose make-up was so eloquent, her voice was disappointingly inexpressive.

'No. Not police.' Then I beamed. 'I am a Private Investigator.' I watched her brows puzzling out the expression with knitting needles. When it was clear they'd teased out the meaning of the term, I went on. 'I know Judith is in trouble. But I'm here to help. I'm on her side. Look… I'm sorry, I didn't catch your name?'

'Nadya.'

Two Nadyas, within so brief a span! They were the two angels to whom the brace of Antos were fiendish counterparts.

'Look, Nadya. Can you tell Judith that she can reach me at the Pier Hotel? My name is Bates. Ferguson Bates. Here, I'll write it down for you.'

I skipped all the way back to the hotel. It's astonishing, the revivifying effect that a pair of ultramarine eyes touched off by mascara can have on one's flagging spirits. I felt instinctively I'd now enough material to fire off a second epistle to the old lady, one that might just winkle a few more days at the seaside. Surely I'd have to stay on here, if only to give the girl a chance to contact a private eye.

When I got back into my room, I found on inspection that a voicemail had been left on my mobile. Uncle, the sly bitch, had figured out how to do this without having the ring-tone make so much as a tinkle.

Fergal! Don't expect me to forgive you! You have wounded me far too grievously for that. Your behaviour has been quite abominable, and well you know it! You have destroyed any possibility of my happiness, you have turned me into a common criminal, and you have driven me from my home. However, that is not what I have to say to you. I want you to listen carefully. You tell me that, after everything you've done, now you wish to help Bluebottle. I have no reason to trust you about this. And yet I will trust you. I will choose to trust you for the sake of your late father. In Manus, at least, I knew I'd found a man who could be depended upon when push came to shove. Now, you tell me that you're not acting alone in your search for evidence. There are three of you. Fergal, I want you to listen very carefully. Don't trust Gwendolyn! Do you understand? Martin Ffrench you can trust. But I'm sorry to say that the only thing that is driving Gwendolyn in all this...

And that was it! The voicemail was cut off! I could guess the rest. *The only thing that is driving Gwendolyn is an overweening desire to see your lover, Bluebottle, squarely behind bars!*

From what I'd seen of the old harridan, she was more than capable of carrying off such a measure without so much as blinking.

My next thought was, wouldn't it be a lark to include the bones of Uncle's message in my letter to Gweny!

I didn't do it.

I'd like to say it was compunction that held me back, but perhaps in the end it was just laziness. It would require far too much effort and invention to explain how Uncle had attained my number.

The next day was uneventful. Rain from across the Irish Sea drove in periods against the rattling pane, and I was not moved to venture outside. March is such a female month. On the following morning, interrupting a full Irish breakfast, I received my reply from Gwendolyn. She was to fly to Nice earlier than expected, in fact, as early as first thing Tuesday morning. She would not, under any circumstance, extend my stay beyond that date. I would have to find the means of contacting this girl myself if she failed to contact me before then. She had already arranged with the manager the account for the room. Any additional expenses were my own concern. She had also cancelled our usual meeting at the café on account of a migraine, and had informed Br Martin accordingly.

Migraine your granny!

I went back up to my bedroom in a mood of black melancholy. For a while, I stared at the rivulets of water that made the grey sea shimmer like a desert mirage.

It's pointless, I thought. Sooner or later, Master Bates, you'll have to go back to the dismal basement five streets behind Dun Laoghaire, and resume a troglodyte's existence. I would have counted out what remained of my resources if I thought they might stretch to one last glorious drunk, but I knew too well they would not. Then, as I was about to give in to despair, *de profundis clamavit* the bedside phone.

'Mr Bates?'

'Yes.'

'There's a visitor from Poland here to see you.'

'Nadya!' I cried aloud. As I capered down the stairwell, my mind oscillated between visions of the two eastern beauties I knew to bear that enchanted name.

At the desk was a tall man with a spherical head. It was close shaven, a Polish head. 'You come with me,' it said.

'Nadya?' I whimpered.

'Judith! She want see you.'

We got into a box-shaped car, left-hand drive, and sped off into the mountains. I was nervous at being tendered out over the thin white line that so flippantly divides Irish country roads. If that wasn't bad enough, as the scenery became filled with lakes and pine trees, my ears began to fill with banjo chords out of *Deliverance*. At heart, I am a city boy.

Make small talk, damn it Bateman!

'So, uhm… what part of Poland are you from?'

'Bratislava. I'm Slovak.'

'Ah!'

An Irish mile went by.

'I thought you were Polish.'

'Everyone here think I'm Polack. No. Slovak. Slovakia.'

My reservoir of small talk had run dry. His too. Soon, mercifully soon, we pulled into a laneway in Delganey.

He led me up to a small flat that was set above a real-estate agents. Inside, a huge figure with black hair and blacker eyebrows was hulking beside the door, while a girl sat on a futon that was draped in a quilt.

'It's ok, Peewee. You can leave us.'

The giant grunted and left the room, accompanied by Chatterbox the Chauffeur.

'My baby brother,' said the girl, meaning the giant. 'He looks after me, he does. Any time he's not doing community service!'

She was pretty, right enough. She was no Nadya, but she had an understated, Irish kind of beauty. Marvellous complexion, clear as a rock-pool. And eyes! Eyes like the lights on a Garda car.

'You're a private detective?'

'I am.'

The eyes eyed me with a flash of suspicion. Glorious! 'Jacko didn't put you up to this, did he?'

'No.' Then I thought I'd throw out one of my few sprats to see what shark it might hook. 'Neither did Anto McSorley.'

'Anto! Anto doesn't fucking know I'm here, does he?'

'No,' I said. 'Not yet.'

'Listen,' she said, looking down at her toes which, earlier, she'd been nail-polishing. 'I don't know who you are, mister. But I love Jack. I'm not going to do nothing that might get him into trouble.'

'No,' I repeated. 'Where is Jack?'

'He's gone.' The magnificent eyes flashed directly at me. 'He left the country. On the boat.'

'When?'

'Last night.'

'You didn't go with him?'

'How could I go with him? We're through!' She made an involuntary jerk when she said this, eyes turning from me, and I could see they were hot and moist. I didn't want to violate her emotion, as they say. Besides, it would've been a disaster to push her over the edge into tears. I've a horror of female tears. But I couldn't very well remain silent.

'It's on account of the fight he left?'

'The fight?' Her eyes, bright as searchlights, fixed on mine once more. 'How d'you know about the fight?'

'I know they had a go at each other.'

I can't quite explain what changes shifted across her face during this last exchange. But it was enough to tell me that there had been another fight besides the knife-play between Jack and Anthony. I pounced. 'What did *you two* fight about?'

She shook her head. Then, with a catch in her voice, she decided to come clean.

'After the business with Anto, like when he found out and everything, we both of us knew that Jacko'd have to clear out of Shankill. I told him he could come down here and stay with Nadya and Dimitri. Just for a while, like. Anto doesn't know nothing about this place. We figured the two of us could move away, probably over to England.

'So that was all right. But then, while I was helping him to pack and everything, he insisted on going down to the bonfire. Said he wasn't going to be run out of his own home without saying goodbye to everyone first. That was the night the two of them had a go at one another. I knew nothing about it. I was still in the house, helping Mrs Corrigan to help him pack. And that's when I found it.'

'Found...?' I bit my tongue. She hadn't heard, mercifully, or if she had, it hadn't registered. At all costs, I had to be sure not to interrupt her flow.

'At first I didn't know what it was, like. I didn't know what to make of it. Mrs Corrigan had been called out by one of the neighbours to see what the guards was doing down by the shore, so I was on my own in the house. That's when it began to dawn on me what it was. It was obviously Anto, but for fuck's sake, what was Stevie Doyle doing there?'

She stalled. She was staring hard at her toenails. Ten scarlet piggies.

'And that's when you had the fight with Jack Corrigan?'

'That wasn't till later. I never let on I knew anything about it. I needed time to think. So I began to find out a lot of things. I had a good long talk with Peewee, and anyone else that might know something. And I began to find out some things. Like that Jack was there on the night they'd cut Bluebottle. He'd always told me it was Anto done it.'

Bluebottle! So, even here, the nickname would serve…

'I tell you, I was sick so I was. And now there was this, too, to say they were setting him up? I'd only just realised now it was Bluebottle was being charged with murdering the tramp. But I still didn't know what to do. So when Jack wasn't looking, I took it away on him and hid it.' Her eyes flicked to me from her toenails in momentary doubt. 'I love Jack! I really do!' Her voice was fracturing. She stared at me as if to be sure I wasn't laughing at her, and pulled the back of her hand rapidly across her eyes.

'When he found out it was gone he went absolutely spare, so he did. He didn't think it was me at first. But there was no-one else it could've been, like. I hadn't told anyone about it. I didn't know who to trust.'

I could have said, you can trust me. I was on the cusp of it. Mercifully, I did not. Instead my words surprised and delighted me.

'Would you trust a priest?'

'A priest!'

'I can put you in touch with a priest. He's the old guy knew Bluebottle from the time he was in the orphanage. You must've heard tell of him. I mean, when the pair of you used to… you know.'

Suddenly, she seemed to become aware she'd been talking to a total stranger. 'Get out!' she screamed. 'Get the fuck out of here!'

The door swung open, and the huge youth with the single eyebrow bumbled in. You'd think I'd been about to assault her virtue.

'It's ok, Peewee. The man is just leaving.'

'You know where to contact me,' I said, and skirted around him, quick time.

Monday night arrived with indecent haste. God, I thought, I really have to see this through to the end.

There was no moving the old Gorgon, though. She remained steadfast. Not a penny more would she squander. My story must have made some sort of impression, though. She gave me an 0033 number and informed me that, if any concrete evidence did come of what I'd said, I should get in touch with her through Valerie Yates. Concrete! she repeated, as though it were a partition wall we were talking about. So help me God, I thought, that concrete will cost you more, ounce for ounce, than crack cocaine. But what precisely was this concrete? And how could I wheedle it out of Judith Ross? And most ticklish of all, what was I to do with it then?

On Tuesday morning, I told the receptionist, blithely, that I intended to stay on at the hotel another night. I then rang Uncle, and informed him he could bloody-well bankroll me! When I'd explained how finely poised my investigations were, he declaimed, with hoarfrost on his voice, that he would find a way.

It would turn out to be a magnificent decision on my part. That very evening, I found a package waiting for Mr Ferguson Bates in the pigeonhole behind the front desk. It had been delivered by hand.

Back in my room, I unwrapped it with mutinous fingers. Have I used the trope before? I found, inside the bubble-wrap, a mobile phone and a neatly folded letter.

I don't know who I can turn to. I only know I'm going to go mad if I don't do something. I swear, though, if anything happens to Jack over this, I'll kill myself so I will. Please give the phone to that priest you were talking about. He'll know what to do with it. I can't take resposibility [sic] for it any more. But I know if Jack ever finds out, he'll kill me. I only hope I'm doing the right thing.

It was unsigned. I lifted the phone as though it were a religious artefact and marvelled at it. It must have been from the same batch as the one I'd latterly picked up in Shankill. Now, how to unravel its secrets?

I'd suspected a voicemail, or a text message. At the very best, a photo. Instead, the grainy home-movie that animated the screen was nothing short of extraordinary! Then the boy was not only innocent, he was being framed. And in my palm, squat as a grenade, sat the incontrovertible proof.

Fergal Bates hardly slept a wink that night as he fondled the three possibilities that lay before him.

Bear with me now. Firstly, he could use the phone to patch up his frayed relationship with Uncle. He had done him grievous wrong, it is true. Surely such a peace offering would go quite a way to patching up the breach. A second possibility was to comply with the girl's instructions. That course certainly seemed to have the most probity. To pass the ball on to Uncle was to invite a fumble, and in any case, how was he to approach the powers that be?

The third possibility was the most tantalising. I'd rung the French number, and after an interminable delay, I'd been put through to Valerie Yates. A half-hour later, the black and midnight hag returned my call in person. I outlined for dear old Gwen the very valuable piece of concrete that I cradled in my hand. Then we began to haggle. She might have had its brother for a mere thirty euro, but the present one must be worth thirty times that sum at the least. I named a round sum. A thousand! she spluttered, and so on, back and forth for ten minutes. It was my turn to hold firm. At long last, the consignor held out for nine hundred glorious euro.

Wednesday must have been dole day at Bray Post Office. A long, impoverished queue snaked back on itself seven times, nationals and non-nationals caught up equally in its coils. Note to self: social welfare was something to sort out the minute I got back to the parish of Dun Laoghaire-Rathdown. The weekly bundle of notes, though scarcely adequate to the dignity of a screen-writer, can help make even the dankest basement palatable. The queue wound slowly towards the counters, and as it did, I reviewed with pleasure the happenings of the previous fortnight. What a turn around in my affairs! *Counter two please!* Really, there'd been times when I was worried I might tip over into depression. Now, I might reasonably consider making a start on that blessed script. *Counter five please! Counter three please!* After all, I had no shortage of raw material. And as for funds…

Environmentally aware, I'd recycled the bubble-wrap. Then, as I'd fondled the phone before entombing it in the as yet unaddressed package, and was gazing admiringly at the advancing tide, my two familiars had reappeared. By my right ear, a habit-clad monk in thick glasses ceased thrumming a harp to wag a disapproving finger. The boy is innocent, rose his chant, address that package hither and we can prove it. By my left, an ogre in red prodded with goad and glee and lucre. Her music was far less uplifting, but she had all the best lines.

There were now only two people left between myself and the counter. The smell of poverty has so much of hopelessness in it. As if the will has been sapped, and the body odours must declare it. I fixed my eyes on the hair-oil of the small man who alone remained in front of me. *Counter three please!*

I made my way to the small window. The woman examined me, indifferently. But I wasn't here to look for welfare. I placed the parcel lovingly on the counter and beamed at her.

'Registered mail,' I said, 'to France, please.'

XII | Bluebottle

The air is heady with linseed oil. It's like a legion of Sunday painters is hidden out among the gorse. I look back at the old man, short of breath but still sprightly.

'Know what Fowler used to say about this time of year, Bro? Said it's like as if Nature has hatched out and trailed egg yolk all down the side of the Head. What d'you think of that?' I breathe in another lungful of air sweet as coconut, with just a bit of the sea on it. 'Used to call it 'Fledgling Spring,' so he did.'

I've to stoop over to catch his words on the wind.

'I should've very much liked to have met your Raymond Fowler. He sounds a most remarkable man.'

'He was that,' I laugh. 'Remarkable is exactly the word for him. Now you have it! He was one of the few true blue friends I've ever had.' And then I wink at him, 'present company excluded, of course.'

The old man has stopped temporarily, and he's leaning his hands on his knees. I look away as far as the horizon, feeling pure fucking wonderful. They'd warned me in the clinic about soaring too high. Could be a prelude to another crash, they said. Fuck them, on a day like this? What do they know, with their white coats and their stethoscopes?

'You never told me Bro, when we were back in Luke's and all. I never knew you'd been a depressive.'

'Well, it's not the sort of thing one likes to have published abroad, is it?'

'I suppose.'

'Besides, think of how young you were. It'd hardly have been responsible of me to have laid such a load on young shoulders.'

'Young. Aye. Whereas I believe you've been in that library since before the printing press was invented!'

'But not any more, it seems.'

'What?' I'm floored. 'Why not?'

'There's a Miss Ward, whom I've been asked to train in. Soon enough, Miss Ward is to become Sr Agatha. Then, bit by bit, Sr Agatha will begin to take over my duties at the library.'

'What'll you do?'

'Oh, there'll be plenty of things for me to potter about at in an institution like Luke's. A tattered coat upon a stick will still serve as a scarecrow, you know. I don't think my work is quite done there yet.'

A couple of minutes on, we've reached the summit. Once again, I survey the great curve of the horizon, and the headlands rising out of the mist to the far end of the bay. The Bro's made his way over to the foot of the concrete cross, and now he's poking and squinting as if he's searching it for fossils.

'1950!' he calls out, having presumably found one.

'You wouldn't have had this story back in 1950!' I call back to him, letting on to hold a mobile phone to my ear.

He stays quiet. Seems almost stung to silence by the remark. His eyes is wandering from the foot to the top of the giant cross, but he must've been made dizzy from craning his neck so much because he stumbles back a couple of steps before steadying himself.

'I bet you anything, Bro. *You* want to find His hand at work behind all this.'

'Well,' he goes, shaking his head the way he does when he's thought about something a long time, 'it has all worked out rather for the best.'

'Has it! Jaysus, how d'you make that out?'

He shakes his head, all smiles.

'Ok Bro. We'll do the sums. Right?' And I begin to count out the questions on my fingers for him.

'A real decent skin, clubbed to death? Myself, scarred for life? Down there,' I point to the housing estates, set out in pretty patterns like they're still part of the architect's model, 'there's a couple is on the run even as we speak, scared stiff to go back to their own homes so they are. And there's a couple of other characters is scared to go back to their homes too, but the less said there, what? And now to put the cherry on it you even tell me you're being dumped from the library?' I shake my head. 'In all fairness, that's hardly what you'd call the best of all possible worlds, Bro!'

His hand is still on the rough concrete of the cross. 'But it could've turned out a great deal worse.'

'Could've! Said like a true Christian! Tell us, Bro, d'you never get tired of turning the other cheek?' I'm looking at him leaning there, his hand on the cross and the pair of us hundreds of feet up above the ocean, like something out of the temptation of Christ. I'm really feeling giddy now. Pure fucking wonderful, like I haven't felt in weeks. The sea air is blowing all the cobwebs and dregs of lithium clean out of my brain.

'Being Christian isn't always easy,' says he. Is he colouring from the effort of climbing or from what he's trying to say, as much to himself as to me, like? Hard to say. 'But then no-one said it was meant to be easy. Oh, did I tell you? I spoke to your friend Malcolm Little yesterday, for the first time in many weeks. From what he gave me to understand, he'll soon allow himself to be back on talking terms with his nephew. There!'

'What?'

'Don't you see it?' And he holds up his hand like it's meant to be the hand of God. 'If it hadn't been for his initiative, I'd never have been moved to call on Fergal Bates. And if he, in turn, hadn't taken up the gauntlet…'

'You're predisposed to find God's plan in everything, Bro, that's your problem.'

'Well, what of it?'

And then I think, maybe he's right. What of it? 'D'you remember, Bro, you once told me that the galaxies is like the thumbprints left by the creator?'

'Well? I daresay I may have said that.'

'You daresay! Go away with you!'

'The cosmos is full of patterns. Scientists are continually finding patterns, all throughout creation. Historians, too. It doesn't take a priest to find patterns.'

'Then I'd say to you, that's on account of the pattern is already to be found printed into their retinas.'

'Well, maybe you're right.'

'Meaning maybe I'm not.'

Then I feel like a bit of mischief. 'Anyway,' says I, 'aren't they meant to have proved there is no God? What's this his name is, that Fergal Bates was on about? Dawking or something.'

'Richard Dawkins.' The Bro nods his head, as much as to say, ok, you've asked for it. 'A story is told,' he smiles, 'of a great oasis in the middle of a desert. Every night, for miles round, the nomads used to gather about that oasis and look at the stars that were reflected in it. And they'd listen to the musicians and elders and holy men recite tales of the star gods. Now, one night, a man came from a foreign land. A scientist. He listened to the myths these holy men wove out of the reflected constellations, and he grew steadily more exasperated at their inventions. Ok, he said to the council of elders. Allow me two weeks. The request, though unusual, was granted. And for the next two weeks, the scientist examined the great oasis from shore to shore. He sounded it; he dredged it; he used sonar and radar and every class of gadget you could think of on it. And at the end of the two weeks, he called another meeting of the council. He showed them the results of his study. You see, he declared in triumph, I have shown beyond any doubt that there are no stars in your oasis.'

I grin back to him, the codger. 'That's a sleight of hand, Bro. You won't get me that easy. Everyone knows that there's stars!'

'But the point is, for all his science, the man was looking in the wrong place, and with the wrong equipment. You won't ever admit it, I suppose, but it *was* a singularly strange sequence that led to your acquittal.'

I have to look away from him. I know by the look of him that he knows something I don't. 'Ach, I bet you anything you want the DPP's case would have collapsed, one way or another.'

'Do you really think so?'

Too many contradictions, Bro. What about the trace of fibres they found in the wound? I was supposed to have used a rock, is all. How were they going to explain that?'

'Yes, I daresay you may be right.'

'Go on,' I says, 'but what? You've medals for your ifs and buts.'

'But, if it hadn't been for that camera-phone showing up when it did, they'd scarcely have gone looking in Anto McSorley's wardrobe. After all, there was nothing to say *you* couldn't have disposed of a bloody sock.'

He has me. I look back at him, the sly old hen. 'That's something I still don't get, but. How exactly did that phone come to be in your possession?'

He stands up straight and lets go of the cross. Obviously he's chuffed to bits at the question. Like he's been waiting for me to ask it.

'It seems that your friend Fergal…'

'Don't call him that, Bro! He's no friend of mine.'

'Well, in any case, this Fergal chap pulled rather a dirty trick on Gwen Furlong, the sculptress. By all accounts, she'd refused to pay up until such time as she had the artefact squarely in her hands. So he copied the film onto his own mobile, the rascal, and then sent her that instead. I shouldn't like to speculate on how much he conned her out of!'

I whistle. Fuck me! And she'd probably wiped that video the minute she got it. So, then…

It's too much to think about. Way too much. There's a steady breeze streaming up from the shore, and I spread out my arms as if I'm about to take flight. Poking just out of the sea mist, Howth Head is shimmering like a vision of Hy Brasil.

'What'll you do now?' goes the Bro.

'Me? Don't know. England, maybe. I haven't given it a whole lot of thought.' I look at him. He's sitting now, eyes closed, with his back to the base of the cross. It suddenly comes to me how old he'd got.

'D'you want to know something odd? All the time I was in the funny farm, it's as if they were wiping memories from my mind. I can't remember a single fucking line out of Rilke, would you believe that?'

'*Night*,' he goes, after a moment, eyes still closed, '*when a wind full of infinite space gnaws at our faces...*'

I'm literally gob-smacked. I mean, what's the chances, right? 'That's real fucking spooky, Bro! That's the very line I wrote up on the wall when I was staying in the hut, down on Killiney beach! How weird is that?'

'It was the line we were arguing over the night before you ran away from Luke's. I'd come across a different translation, and we were arguing over which was the more accurate.'

'I've no memory of that. I'm telling you, those feckers in the nut house is after wiping out half of my memories, Bro.'

The cold wind is making the scar smart, and I begin to knead it with the tips of my fingers.

'It's not so bad, you know.' His eyes are open now and his boggledy glasses are looking at me, as concerned and baffled as any father or mother looking at their adolescent kid. 'You won't lack for girlfriends!' says he.

What in the name of Jaysus would you know about girlfriends? I mean, please! Of course, I say nothing.

The sky is enormous, like a huge blue dome sitting on top of the horizon, and not a cloud in it. There's a tiny plane high over the Kish Lighthouse. As Raymo would've put it, in his limey accent, stretched out with the two hands behind his head and gazing to the blue yonder: 'see that nib of a plane, dragging a white line across the ozone, and already the high winds of the stratosphere is wiping away all trace of it? The sky doesn't scar.' And then he'd go on, 'from up there, we look just like child's toys in a dollhouse world, untroubled by passions or jealousies.' Raymond Fowler. R.I.P.

And up here, above it all, above all of their passions or jealousies on the crown of Bray Head, stands two miniature men. Bipolar depressives, the both of them! Only, one is near the start of his life, and the other, much nearer to the end.

And that, Bro, is pattern enough for me.